A ROLL OF THE BONES

THE CUPIDS TRILOGY
BOOK ONE

A Roll Of The Bones

TRUDY J. MORGAN-COLE

Breakwater Books
P.O. Box 2188, St. John's, NL, Canada, A1C 6E6
www.breakwaterbooks.com

Copyright © 2019 Trudy J. Morgan-Cole
ISBN 978-1-55081-798-0

Cover painting: detail of *Girl Chopping Onions*, oil on panel, 20.8 x 16.9 cm, 1646, by Gerrit Dou. Royal Collection Trust, UK.

A CIP catalogue record for this book is available
from Library and Archives Canada.

We acknowledge the support of the Canada Council for the Arts, which last year invested $153 million to bring the arts to Canadians throughout the country. We acknowledge the financial support of the Government of Canada and the Government of Newfoundland and Labrador through the Department of Tourism, Culture, Industry and Innovation for our publishing activities.

Printed and bound in Canada.

Breakwater Books is committed to choosing papers and materials for our books that help to protect our environment. To this end, this book is printed on a recycled paper that is certified by the Forest Stewardship Council®.

Canada Council Conseil des Arts
for the Arts   du Canada

Newfoundland
Labrador

Canadä

Author's Note

THIS BOOK IS A WORK OF FICTION, BUILT UPON THE REAL HISTORY of the Cupids Cove colony (also known as Cuper's Cove, or simply Cupids) planted in Newfoundland in 1610 by John Guy. Readers who are curious to know where I have altered or invented pieces of the story that deviate from recorded history may wish to check the Afterword for more information.

Throughout the novel, I have modernized dating, with the new year beginning in January, as ours does, rather than in March, as English people at that time would have reckoned it.

The epigraph for the book, and those at the head of each chapter, are taken from Robert Hayman's *Quodlibets,* published in 1628—the first book written in Newfoundland.

The Air, in Newfound-Land is wholesome, good;
The Fire, as sweet as any made of wood;
The Waters, very rich, both salt and fresh;
The Earth more rich, you know it is no less.
Where all are good, Fire, Water, Earth, and Air,
What man made of these four would not live there?

—from *Quodlibets: Lately Come Over from New Britaniola,*
Old Newfoundland, Robert Hayman, 1628

A Match is Contracted

*First grows the Tree,
and then the Leaves do grow;
These two must spring
before the fruit can show.*

BRISTOL
SUMMER 1609

O N THE DAY IT BEGAN—THE DAY THAT PICKED UP THEIR
three lives like a child picking up stones from the path, shook
them hard, and laid them down in an entirely different road—
Nancy was the first of the three to wake. And since Nancy's journey
was, of the three of them, to be the longest and strangest, you might
reckon it was Fate's touch that wakened her at the same time dawn was
streaking through the shutters, just before St. Stephen's bell chimed
five of the clock.

In truth, she woke early because she needed to use the chamber pot.

Rolling out of the bed she shared with her mistress Kathryn, Nancy
pulled the pot from underneath the bed. After squatting over it, she took
her russet kirtle from a peg on the wall and dived back inside the warmth
of the bed curtains where Kathryn was gently snoring. Nancy stripped
off her nightdress, put on a clean shift, kirtle, and apron, braided her
hair and tucked it up under her coif, before getting out of bed to take
the chamber pot downstairs.

The large upstairs chamber held two beds—one for the children, and one that Kathryn and Nancy shared. The master and mistress's bed, in the inner chamber, was already empty at this hour. From the children's bed, Nancy heard Lily talking to herself in a high-pitched singsong; little Edward must still be asleep. The oldest boy, John, slept downstairs with the apprentices. Also downstairs, to keep an eye on the boys and the fire, was Tibby, the maid.

So while the room upstairs was still quiet but for Lily's song, the hall downstairs already stirred with life. The fire was crackling after being banked for the night; Master Gale and the boys broke their fast at the table, and Aunt Tibby kneaded the morning's bread loaves while Mistress Gale cut slices of cheese from a big wheel in the centre of the table.

"All right, lads, Ned's gone for water, and we need wood brought in before you start work, so step lively," Mistress Gale called to the apprentices as they finished their pottage. The lads headed towards the door just as Aunt Tib said, "Ah, good morning, love, you're up," to Nancy, and Mistress Gale added, "Get yourself something to eat now, Nancy, and then go haul my daughter out of the sheets—she cannot sleep late, today of all days. Johnny, take that pot from Nan and go dump it in the privy."

"No, I'll go." Nancy slipped through the door out into the cool morning and crossed to the privy at the back of the yard. All around, from other houses, she heard the same sounds of waking as she heard in her own: householders, servants, and apprentices rising to chop wood and haul water, empty slop buckets, and begin cooking the day's food, as the craftsmen and housewives of St. Stephen's parish began another day.

A busy day, for the Gale household. Master Gale and his wife were entertaining guests to supper, which meant a larger and finer meal than usual. Nicholas Guy, the shoemaker, was coming to dine, and bringing his father and sister with him. Like as not he would make an offer today for Mistress Kathryn's hand in marriage, and everything about the house and on the table must be at its best. Nancy and Kathryn were to go to the fishmonger's, while Mistress Gale and Aunt Tib dressed and cooked the capons and goose.

Busy with plans for the day, Nancy did not see Ned Perry coming into the yard with two water buckets until he nearly ran into her. "Have a care, you great oaf," she said, sweeping past him. "You could have had my kirtle soaked through."

"Oh, fine words from a woman who's carrying a chamber pot and not looking where she's going! I'd have been the worse off in that encounter," the rascal shot back. In faith, the apprentices were a nuisance, and Ned was the worst of them, Nancy thought. He and she were of an age; he'd come to his apprenticeship at fourteen. He was learning the stonemason's trade when she had been learning to brew ale and do fine needlework and make simple remedies from herbs. Since the day he came into the house, he had made it his mission to torment and tease her.

Nancy had lived in the Gale household since she was four years old, when the plague had taken both her father and mother in a single week. She remembered neither of them: the only family she knew was Aunt Tib, her mother's sister. Master and Mistress Gale had not turned away their serving girl's orphaned niece, but had shown her the rare kindness of keeping the child and letting Nancy grow up as a companion to their daughter Kathryn, training her so she could find her own place in service someday.

At eighteen, Nancy ought to have found that place by now. A household like the Gales', with four children and as many apprentices, neither needed nor could afford two servants. But Nancy and Kathryn had grown up as close as sisters, and every time the subject of Nancy going to service in another house had been raised, her young mistress had refused to hear of it.

Now, with an offer of marriage from Master Guy, that would all change. When Kathryn went to a household of her own, there would be less need than ever for Nancy here at the Gale house. Whatever Kathryn Gale's future might hold after today, Nancy's world was bound to be turned head over heels.

But there was nothing to be done about that—nothing Nancy could do by fretting, at any rate. Finished with the privy, she went back into the kitchen, laid down the empty chamber pot by the door, and helped herself to breakfast.

ANOTHER CHILLY SPRING MORNING, ANOTHER TRIP DOWN TO THE water pipe on the quay, and another day of Nancy Ellis being a saucy minx. Nothing new under Ned Perry's sun.

Back in the kitchen with the buckets of water, he stole a piece of cheese off Nancy's plate. "Get your own breakfast and keep your hands off of mine, you knave," she said, slapping his fingers away.

"Mistress Tibby, Nancy hit me!" he cried. He had already eaten a bowl of pottage, but now put a couple more slices of cheese—not Nancy's—on top of a slab of yesterday's rye bread.

The maid laughed but did not look up from the dough she was kneading. "As if I've not got my hands full with the youngsters, the two of you behaving like children again."

"'Tis not the two of us, only Ned. I've bigger fish to fry than quarrelling with the likes of him," Nancy told her aunt.

For a moment all three of them—Ned, Nancy, and Mistress Tibby—shared a smile. It seemed long years ago when Ned was a new apprentice, when teasing the girls sometimes earned him a cuff on the ear. Mistress Tibby made no favourite of her niece; she was as quick to chide Nancy as she was one of the boys. Tibby's main concern was always to keep everyone in their proper place: she would let Ned away with saying things to Nancy that, if he said them to Kathryn Gale, would earn him a slap. Inseparable as the two girls were, he was quickly taught the difference in their stations and the things he might say to one but not to the other.

"Right then, no time for dallying," said Mistress Gale, pulling on her cloak. "I'm off to the butcher's for mutton. Nancy, you and Kathryn go to the fishmonger's as soon as ever you can, and Tibby, we will have everything here well before noon so we can begin cooking. Supper will be at five."

"And we'd best get to work, lads," said Master Gale, rounding up the apprentices and his son John. They were laying stone and carving a frieze for Sir John Young's banqueting hall up on the hill.

Ned bent his head close to Nancy's. "So, will Master Guy make his offer today, do you think?"

"'Tis no business of yours, is it? You will go on cutting and laying stone whether Mistress Kathryn is married or no." She stood up from the table, brushing crumbs off her apron and putting cheese, bread, and a slice of cold pork pie on a trencher for Kathryn, then headed towards the narrow staircase that led up to the sleeping chamber.

Ned quickly banished from his mind an image of the young mistress sitting up in bed, her curls no doubt loose and tumbled about her rosy face, her nightdress a little agape at the neck—. No. Hardly the thought to be entertaining on the day when a man was coming round to make an offer for Mistress Kathryn's hand in marriage.

———————

BEHIND THE BED CURTAINS, KATHRYN GALE LAY HALF-AWAKE, listening to the household stir around her. Nancy's side of the bed was still warm; she was always out of bed at least an hour before Kathryn.

I ought to be up and about. There was a deal of work to do today, and while her chief concern was what to wear and how to dress her hair so she would look well for Master Guy, her mother had other expectations. There was food to be cooked, the house to be cleaned, everything to be put in readiness for the grandest supper the stonemason's household could produce.

Now she heard her younger brother and sister rolling out of their bed and complaining about the cold. Now their small feet thundering across the floor. Kathryn listened to it all drowsily, the weave and shift of their voices, the rise and fall of her family's noises from the big room below. Everyone down in the hall to break their fast, and one set of steps, light and sure, coming the other way.

Nan twitched the bed curtains open. "Oh good, you are awake. Here." She laid the tray down beside Kathryn without ceremony. Every morning for—how many years? *Anyone would think you were a lord's daughter with your own lady's maid*, Kathryn's mother said. But she did not order Nan to stop bringing Kathryn's breakfast to her. Kathryn's mother could have ordered Nancy to do any number of things; she could have sent her away, years ago, to serve in another household. A household where she would know her place, where she would cook and scrub and not have the cheek to say to her mistress, "Eat that now, and get dressed; of all days you can't slug abed today."

"I know," Kathryn said, tucking into the pie. "I have been thinking on my gown. Are you quite sure—"

"That your old blue kersey shows your bosom to better advantage than the new green one? I am, and what's more, you know in your heart that I'm right." Nancy sat down on the edge of the bed. "Hair, gown— everything is decided, and there'll be nothing gained by changing any of it now. Your mother wants us to go and buy fish."

"Mama said the blue gown was more becoming, but only you would tell me it makes my bosom look better."

"'Tis naught but the truth, my Kat."

"What would I do without you, my Nan?"

Nancy—who would never have dared call Kathryn her pet name in front of any of the rest of the household—stood up quite suddenly and busied herself with the bedclothes, although she could hardly make the bed with Kathryn still sitting up in it. "Well, mayhap you'll find out, when you marry Master Guy."

"Never! I'll not go to any man's house without my Nan—you know that. I've always said."

"What you say may not matter, once you have a husband."

"I'll tell him before I ever accept his offer. I'll say, 'Master Guy, my father will talk to you about my marriage portion, but I have one request that may as well be chiselled in stone. My Nancy comes with me, or I come not at all.' How think you he'll like that?"

"He will think you a bold minx, to be making such demands."

Dressed and heading out into the bustling streets with Nancy by her side, Kathryn turned that phrase over in her mind. *A bold minx.* Not, perhaps, what she should aspire to as she prepared to receive an offer of marriage. *A virtuous maid. A good wife.* But perhaps it would not hurt if she had a little of the bold minx about her. Some men liked a little boldness in a wife.

Passing an innyard on the way to the market, the girls saw a stage being hammered into place beneath a brightly coloured tent. "Oh look, Nan! The players have come to town! I wonder what play they'll do."

Nancy took hold of Kathryn's elbow, steering her past the inn. "Whatever it may be, you'll have no time to go seeing plays tonight."

"Indeed not. Tonight I shall be the heroine of my own romance."

"You and your romances!" In truth, both girls enjoyed going to see the players when they came to Bristol, or listening to tales Kathryn's mother told by the fire at night. But Nancy always kept her feet firmly planted on the ground. Kathryn, for her part, liked to imagine herself as Helen of Troy or some other famous beauty men would fight and die for.

"You needn't remind me that life is no romance," she said now, following Nancy's lead past the stage and towards the fish market. "But I dare to hope at least that I will like him and…well, that he will be fond of me. Papa won't make me marry a man I don't like—he's always promised that—but how am I to know until we're wedded?"

"I doubt you can know. That is why I intend to steer clear of the whole business."

Kathryn laughed. She'd given up long ago trying to change Nancy's mind about marriage. Nancy had a good example before her in her aunt. They had all thought, once, that when Tibby left to marry, Nancy could step into her place, but Tibby had turned down the few offers she had had. She had kept company with a carpenter's journeyman for a time, but in the end she had sent him packing and given no reason save that she was better off as she was.

"I'm no fool," Kathryn insisted. "It will be good enough if he is kind to me."

"Like as not he will be. Who could be unkind to you?" As they passed a stall displaying the hanging carcasses of freshly killed pigs, Nancy leaned closer and whispered, "And if you've doubts, I've heard the butcher's wife is sickly, so you may want to bide your time to see if he's a widower soon. You may not like the smell, but think of the pies!"

"Oh, you are wicked. Anyway I don't fancy a widowed husband—he'd forever be comparing you to the first wife, and there would be children to look after." Children were all very well in their place, but

Kathryn was quite looking forward to getting away from her younger sister and brothers. She would have her own someday, of course, but she had no interest in taking on another woman's brats. No, a successful shoemaker from a good, fast-rising family would make a fine husband. Master Guy's cousins were merchants, and he might well go into trade himself someday. And not bad-looking into the bargain, though he must be nearly thirty.

They were almost at the fish market. She took Nancy's hand and gripped it tight. "Wish me luck, Nan."

LUCK HAS LITTLE ENOUGH TO DO WITH IT, NANCY THOUGHT. SHE had a busy afternoon of it—they all did, scrubbing down the stone floor, boiling the capons, roasting the goose, making mutton pies and fish pies. Aunt Tibby made a quince tart as well, and Mistress Gale baked ginger-cakes, while Kathryn made a trifle before luring Nancy away to help her dress and fix her hair.

Master Gale and the lads returned from work late in the afternoon, and not long afterwards came the guests: Master Nicholas Guy with his father and his unmarried sister, Mistress Joanna. Nancy and Tib were kept busy bringing dishes back and forth from the hearth to the table, where family, guests, children, and apprentices all crowded around the board. It was a far more elaborate meal than the Gale family customarily ate, and rather than the usual family chatter, the conversation centred on the guests. Talk turned from the Guys' shoemaking business to their cousin John, the wealthy merchant.

"Is this a serious business, this plan of Master John's to go to the New Found Land?" Master Gale wanted to know. His wife added, "'Tis a most dangerous venture, is it not?"

"There is danger in it, yet the opportunity for profit is great," said Nicholas Guy. "John and his brother Philip are petitioning the king for a royal charter, and are full of preparations. John has chosen a fair site for a settlement, and means to gather a company of men to go with him next summer, if the funds can be raised."

"And if they find settlers willing to take on the risk," put in his father.

Aunt Tib thrust two fish pies into Nancy's hands. They had been keeping warm on the hearth and the pans were still a little too hot. "Don't dare drop those," she said, as if Nancy were still eight years old. "When you've put them out, fetch some more wine." She rolled her eyes and darted a glance at Joanna Guy as she said *more*; it was clear she was troubled at how quickly the guests were going through the food and drink. It had seemed like such a bountiful feast when it was being prepared earlier in the day.

When the last of the ginger-cakes was eaten and the dishes cleared from the table, Nancy looked forward to having time to sit down by the hearth with Aunt Tib and enjoy her own meal; she had eaten little and was half-starved. Master Gale and Nicholas Guy went outside, walking in the work yard. Nancy brought wine to Kathryn and her mother, Joanna Guy and the elder Master Guy, who all sat near the fire talking. The apprentices and the younger Gale children had been pressed into service to clean the pots and platters, a job that was being accomplished with a good deal of squealing and splashing.

Nancy met Kathryn's eyes as she filled her cup. Outside, Kathryn's father and her future husband were negotiating the terms of her marriage, while she sat here making idle chat about embroidery patterns with Joanna Guy. *And 'tis not her future alone they are deciding*, Nancy thought. She hoped, of course, that her young mistress, her dearest companion, would be happy in wedded life. But she could not think beyond that wedding day, to imagine what might become of herself.

Kathryn's promises to bring Nancy into her new household were all very well, but the decision would not rest with Kathryn. If there were no place for her either in Nicholas Guy's household or here in the house where she had grown up, Nancy well knew she would be in service in some stranger's house. Any future she tried to imagine seemed cold compared to the warmth of this house, the life she had always known.

Master Gale stepped back into the room and called Kathryn out to talk with him and Master Guy. The rest of the little group around the fire grew quiet then, until the men came back in with Kathryn between them, her hand tucked into the crook of Nicholas Guy's arm, and stood by the hearth. Master Gale clapped his hands for attention and announced he had accepted Nicholas Guy's offer for his daughter's hand, and they would marry at Christmas.

Nancy could count on her fingers the number of times Kathryn had talked to Nicholas Guy before today. The shoemaker had made excuses to strike up conversation when Kathryn and Nancy went into his shop to be fitted for new boots, had spoken a few passing words to her in the market. But, little as she knew the man, Kathryn looked happy, holding onto his arm as the betrothal was announced. *For tonight I will think only of that, of her happiness*, Nancy promised herself.

When everyone had drunk more wine, and cheered and congratulated the couple, the guests went home and the last remnants of the feast were cleared away. Tibby lit rushlights around the hall as the sun slipped towards the horizon and shadows filled the room. Mistress Gale hurried the little ones up the steps to the sleeping chamber, and Nancy went out with a pail of slops to empty in the yard. Ned Perry stood by the woodpile splitting logs, and moved closer when she pulled the door closed behind her.

"So 'tis all settled, then," he said. "Mistress Kathryn and Master Guy."

"It seems so." Nancy could feel all the things she had vowed not to think of tonight rolling back in, like fog settling over the river.

"That's good, then. Good for Mistress Kathryn, I mean." Ned dragged his toe through the dirt, turning over a few small stones.

"Good for everyone," said Nancy. "The Guys are a rising family. Did you not hear him going on tonight about his cousins and their trading charter to the New World? They'll be among the city's foremost merchants soon, and I doubt Master Nicholas himself will stop at making shoes. 'Tis an excellent match for the Gales."

"Aye, and that's all that matters, is it not?"

"What do you mean?"

There was a sullen set to Ned's mouth, which was usually quirked up in a foolish grin. "Marriage. Making a good match, bettering one's family, rising in the world. That's all the reason anyone gets wedded."

"Why else should they? Are we living in a romance?"

"Of course not." He bent to gather up an armload of wood. "You'll think me a fool, I know."

"I already think you a fool, so whatever is nattering at you, it won't lower my opinion."

Now he did grin, the crooked half smile she was used to seeing on him. "'Tis only that—well, my brother Dickon, he apprenticed with the baker in our street, and it ended with him marrying the baker's daughter, and now he's in a fair way to inherit a bakeshop when her father dies, d'you see?"

"Ned." She did see, all too well. He was a feckless lad, but she had never thought him entirely brainless. "You've not been apprentice here four years with the fool idea in your head that you might marry the master's daughter?"

"No, of course not!" He looked full at her now, and she saw that he was sorry he'd spoken at all. She was not used to having to look up at him: they two had always been of a height, and as Nancy was tall for a girl, she'd stayed at eye level with him till last year, when suddenly he'd shot up by a hand-span. Now his green eyes looked down at her, glittering with something that might be shame. "Only—why not? I know 'twould be reaching too high for me, but—why?"

"Lord, you silly knave, a dozen reasons. None of the apprentices is going to marry into this shop. Peele the baker had no sons living. Master Gale has John and Edward to inherit it all. He has always meant for Mistress Kathryn, and Lily too, when her time comes, to marry well. Kathryn's beauty is the best coin he has to bargain with. He'd never give either of his girls to an apprentice. Never mind the fact that you can't take a wife till you've served your time as a journeyman, and that will be years from now. You couldn't have been such a goose as to think —"

"Of course I wasn't! You needn't chide me. I've been told all my life that any man with ideas above his station is a fool. It was—a dream, only. And if you ever speak a word of it to—well, to anyone, but especially—to anyone, I'll..." He looked down at the bundle of wood he carried and his grip tightened on it. Nancy remembered that she had pulled the tail of his hair and given him a good punch on the jaw when they were both fourteen, and when Ned pushed her away he was the one got beaten, for hitting a girl. Now they were no longer children, and he was at a loss. Nancy saw his shame; no childish threats would change that.

She saw, too, that there was more to this than the hope of marrying into Master Gale's trade: it was Kathryn herself Ned had dreamed of, and who could blame him? Kathryn was beautiful and merry and sweet-natured, and she was kind to him. She was kind to everyone. And all this time Ned had cherished foolish romantic notions about her. His misery was stamped plain on his face.

"I wouldn't say a word of it—not to her, nor to anyone," Nancy promised. And to show she had not guessed what truly troubled him, she added, "You'll be a journeyman and then a master mason in your own right in a few years, I don't doubt—Master Gale says you've a great gift for the work. You need not marry into a shop in order to succeed. I am sorry for calling you a fool—anyone may have dreams."

"Can they?" She had already started to walk down to the end of the yard, wanting to hurry away from the strange intimacy of this moment. She was embarrassed both by him and for him. "Do you?" she heard him ask as she walked away, but she did not turn to answer him.

A Marriage is Solemnized

Thou talk'st of men of Judgement. Who are they?
Those, whose conceits success doth still obey.
Wise men's wise counsel is but their conceits;
If they speed ill, they are sad wise deceits.

BRISTOL
DECEMBER 1609

S HE STOOD AT THE FRONT OF THE CHURCH IN A GOWN THE
colour of wine, made of some rich-looking stuff and trimmed
with a white ruff that stood out against the gown and the black
curls of her hair. He wasn't one to notice women's clothing; couldn't
have told what any of the women of the house was wearing at the end
of dinner, but this was different. Kathryn Gale was up there on display,
like a ruby in a polished silver setting. Standing up in church pledging to
love, honour, and obey Nicholas Guy. Ned Perry sat in the pew with the
rest of the apprentices and servants and a good few of the neighbours,
and felt his heart like a stone inside him.

He could not remember a time when he was not in love with Kathryn
Gale. He had known her even before he took up his apprenticeship
with her father; the pretty little girl with the black curls was half the
reason he was eager to leave home and start his apprenticeship. He had
been a child then, had fancied himself in love because she was pretty
and lively and mischievous. He had known nothing of desire, but in a

year or two, when he had learned about it as all boys do, Kathryn was there, her young body budding and desirable, ready-made to step into his dreams at night.

He had never breathed a word or given a careless glance that might betray his feelings—until, in a moment of folly, he'd spoken to Nancy Ellis on the night Mistress Kathryn's betrothal was announced. And Nancy had laughed in his face. Thank God she only thought he had dreamed of inheriting Master Gale's business, not that he fancied himself in love with Kathryn. Then, truly, he would have deserved her mockery.

In his worst moments he had looked at the two young lads, John and Edward Gale, and remembered that Mistress Gale had already lost two babies to childhood fevers. *They could yet be left childless, in need of an heir,* he had caught himself thinking. Then was immediately horrified. Had he really—not wished, exactly, but imagined the deaths of two children as his own stepping stones to becoming a master mason and marrying a beautiful girl?

Regardless of what murky stuff lurked in the depths of Ned Perry's mind, all the members of the Gale family continued healthy, and preparations for Mistress Kathryn's marriage to Nicholas Guy went forward. Now they were all gathered in St. Stephen's church on St. Stephen's Day—doubly auspicious, as the older men said Stephen was the patron saint of stonemasons, though nobody prayed to saints nowadays. After their troth was plighted, everyone went to Small Street, to the house of Nicholas Guy's cousin John, for the wedding feast.

John Guy's home was grand enough that the family and guests dined in the hall while servants and apprentices ate at a separate table in the kitchen, rather than all at the one board. While tucking into a roast of beef, Ned made conversation with one of John Guy's manservants, George Whittington, a hearty fellow a few years older than Ned himself. It was another mark of John Guy's standing in the town that he could afford to employ two manservants, and this Whittington basked in the glory of his master's station. He had a loud voice and rollicking laugh, and he flirted shamelessly with all the maids.

"So you'll be nearly finished your apprenticeship, then?" George asked Ned as they ate.

"No, I've three years yet to go."

"And will you go on working for Mason Gale, when you finish?"

"I doubt it. Walter there," Ned nodded across the table at his fellow apprentice, "is finished next year, and will serve as journeyman, for Master Gale has none now. There's not enough work for two journeymen, so I'll likely go farther afield to seek work. Master Gale says 'tis not as it used to be in his father's time, before the monasteries were broken up. Back then the great churches and abbeys were always hiring stonemasons. But there's still work to be had on rich men's estates, and the guild will likely help me to find a place."

"Aye, the rich will always be building palaces for themselves. 'Tis a grand thing to have a trade, and you might well be master yourself someday." A serving maid passed with a pitcher of ale, and Whittington pinched her bottom as she filled his mug.

It *was* a fine thing to be apprenticed in a trade, and Ned knew he was more fortunate than the young man beside him. For all his good looks and easy charm, and the fine house he served in, Whittington was likely the son of a servant and could never aspire to more than a life in service. The random chance of his birth meant he would never be his own master, while Ned had at least some small chance of becoming a master mason. So narrow were the paths of life, and so high the walls around you, keeping you on that path.

"I hope I will be," he said aloud. "'Tis not easy to change one's lot in life."

"Not here in Bristol, at any rate. Not in England at all, maybe. But there's more to the world than Bristol."

"As your master is keen to remind us." Since the match between the Gale and Guy households had been announced, everyone in the Gale family had been aware of the business dealings of John Guy and his Newfoundland Company. "You don't mean to go with him to the New Found Land, do you?"

"That I do," said George, wiping his mouth on his sleeve. "'Twill be a grand adventure, and where's a man to see the likes of that if he stays his whole life in Bristol? Sure, if I like it, I might well live out my life over there."

"Marry a native woman and live in a tent made of animal skins?" Ned laughed.

"I'd not say no to rolling around in a tent with a fair brown maiden. Think how wild those women must be, living as free as the beasts of the field." He paused as if fixing the awesome spectacle in his mind. Then he shook his head. "But as to finding a wife, Master Guy says there will be folks settling down there permanent. He wants to build a proper settlement like James Fort in Virginia. Cultivate the land as well as fish the seas—Master Guy wants adventurers, men who'll build a new world."

"And you truly would go?"

"If he'll have me. He is looking for skilled men mostly, not servants, but I've been with the family since I was eleven, and I'm a hard worker. I mean to bring my younger brother as well—we both want the chance. You ought to think of it, for he'll be looking for stonemasons."

"Do you have family, besides the one brother?" Ned asked. "What would they make of you going over there?"

"I've an older brother who's been fishing off the New Found Land every summer since he was fifteen. He says 'tis a grand place over there. Not just the sea teeming with codfish, but miles of land for anyone who wants to clear it and plant it."

Ned didn't press the question of whether George had any family beyond the two brothers—a mother, perhaps, who might weep at the thought of her sons going off to a land beyond the edge of the world, never to return? A fishing voyage was one thing; fishermen returned home in autumn with coin in their pockets. Ships might be lost at sea, but the voyage back and forth across the ocean to the cod-fishing grounds was a familiar one for many men. The idea of actually living, wintering over in that wild and alien place, was another thing altogether. The tale of the lost settlers on Roanoke, though they'd disappeared before Ned was born, was still told whenever men spoke about settling new lands. And the Englishmen now in Virginia were having a hard time of it, according to the tales told on the Bristol docks.

With the wedding feast done, Ned went back to his work. His days went on much as they always had, though the household was not the same without Mistress Kathryn's pretty face at the table. He was surprised, too, by how much he missed Nancy's keen glance and sharp tongue. Mistress Gale, though as busy as ever, sighed a great deal and fussed over the younger children more than was common.

On Sundays after church, Ned did not go back to the Gale house, but walked the few streets over to his parents' home in Tower Lane to dine with his own family. The table was crowded for dinner: Ned's parents, the younger children who lived at home, two sisters out in service, and two of his married brothers with their wives and babes.

Ned knew his parents were proud of how well they had done by their family. His father was a journeyman carpenter who earned enough to rent this small house. Ned's mother had borne twelve children, of whom eight had lived, the oldest ones married and giving her grandchildren already. All the older boys had been apprenticed to good trades. By any standards, the Perry family was a success for people of their station.

On the Sunday following Mistress Kathryn's wedding, after Ned had described the bride's dress as best he could for his mother and sisters, talk turned to John Guy's New World venture. "'Tis a mad scheme," said his brother Francis, but Dickon said, "I don't know that I'd call it mad. Everyone swears 'tis good country over there. A man can live and die in Bristol and never own the house he sleeps in. Over there, anyone who goes with Master Guy might live like a prince."

"Live like a prince, or die like a savage," Francis countered. "I've talked to many a fisherman who's summered over there. Even the summers can be bleak and cold, bound in by fogs and lashed by rain. None can imagine what the winter is like. 'Tis not a land like Jamaica or Virginia, endless sunshine and balmy breezes."

"As long as the soil is good and there are forests full of trees, and plenty of fish in the ocean, what harm if the winters are cold?" Dickon replied. "'Tis no colder than Scotland, and the Scots flourish even in the Highlands."

"The Scots may flourish up there, but they're keen enough to come flooding down here on the king's coattails and seek land and honours for themselves in England," Francis said sharply. "Even the Scots won't live in Scotland if they've any other choice."

"You're aping complaints you've heard your betters make," Dickon countered. "We are not talking of Scotland, but of the New Found Land. You'd build yourself a sturdy dwelling to keep out the cold there, plant your garden and catch fish in the summer, and have enough food to keep you through the winter. Trap for furs in the winter, I suppose—good money in fur if you can ship and sell it back here."

"Well, 'tis not likely you'll find out," Dickon's wife, Bess, said. She seemed alarmed by her husband's interest in the New World. "Master Guy's hardly going to be looking for bakers to found his new colony."

"No, a trade like Dickon's needs a town around it to thrive," said the elder Master Perry. "John Guy is looking for carpenters and masons, though. 'Twill be hard work, but what a grand thing—to make a town sprout from the ground up, where there's naught but open land now. No one who lived out his life in England would ever have such an opportunity."

His wife clicked her tongue in disapproval. "Faith, Michael, you sound almost as if you'd go yourself, were you a younger man."

"I can't promise I would not, though I'd have to think long and hard if I had a wife and family already." His eyes met Ned's across the table. "A young fellow like yourself, Ned, with a mason's skills and no ties, and a connection already to the Guy family—you'd be well set up to go with him."

"Don't say such a thing!" Ned's mother protested. "We'd never see the lad again, and he might be drowned at sea or eaten by wild beasts!"

Ned himself had remained quiet throughout the conversation. "Not all who go over there will live out their lives and die there," he said now. "Some will go for a season or two, then come back home wealthy men."

"Things are different, for men of means," said Francis. "I'm sure rich merchants like the Guys will spend a few seasons over there and then come home with gold in their pockets. But 'tis not so for poor folks. A working man who goes across the ocean to settle in a colony will likely only make that journey once in his life."

"But for such an opportunity—" Ned's father began, and let his words trail off.

Walking home from his parents' house, Ned took a long way around. He went by way of the quay, where the river was filled with ships. On any day other than a Sunday the docks would be busy with men unloading silks and oranges, wine and salt cod—cargo from every part of the globe. Today, the docks were quiet; the ships moored with their sails furled. When he turned from the river back into the cobbled lanes, lined with houses and shops so close their upper stories almost touched overhead, he thought again of the image that had come to him when he first talked with George Whittington. Narrow lanes, narrow paths for a man's feet to follow.

His parents had done the best they could with the cards dealt them in life. All his mother wanted was for their sons and daughters to do just as well. Francis thought the same way: most of the family did. But his father saw something else, something Ned and Dickon glimpsed too. And only Ned was in a position to take advantage of it.

For most men, in most times and places, there was little chance, if any, to change that path, break out of those narrow lanes. But here in Bristol, in the year of our Lord 1610, there would be such a chance—for any man brave enough to throw over a good apprenticeship and a safe path. Shuffle the cards, cast the dice, roll the bones: take a chance. A chance that might end, as his mother warned, in a lonely death far from home. But it could end otherwise. A man might change his fortune, if all things fell in his favour.

THREE

A Journey is Purposed

Great Sheba's wise Queen travelled far to see,
Whether the truth did with report agree.
You, by report persuaded, laid out much,
Then wisely came to see, if it were such.

BRISTOL
MARCH 1610

KATHRYN CAME DOWNSTAIRS AS DAWN LIGHT SPILLED through the diamond-shaped windowpanes, to find Jenny Piper sweeping the floor, Nancy stirring pottage over the fire, and Joanna Guy kneading loaves of bread; all busy at work already. In the other room, she heard her husband and his workmen setting out their tools. Try as she might, Kathryn had not, in three months of marriage, rid herself of the habit of being the last one in the household to wake.

How different it was, waking up here than in her parents' house! The two houses were similar, except that the large main floor of Nicholas Guy's house was divided into two rooms: a hall and a workroom. The upstairs was like her father's house: one sleeping chamber she shared with her husband, and a larger one where the rest of the household slept. It still felt odd to wake in the morning next to this man who was still half a stranger to her, instead of beside Nancy.

After the marriage, Nancy had tried, for a few days, to continue her practice of bringing breakfast to Kathryn in bed. But the scorn that had drawn from Joanna Guy and her servant Jenny had quickly ended the habit. Kathryn knew by now she would never earn the respect of her sister-in-law or of Jenny, who had helped Joanna run the household for years. But she was learning to avoid things that would make Joanna's contempt any worse.

Now, as Kathryn came into the kitchen and took a bowl to the hearth to fill with pottage, Jenny took the bowl from her hands. "No, you sit down, Mistress. Let me serve you," she said, every word sharp as a knife.

"Thank you, I'll serve myself. Don't let me keep you from your work." Kathryn took the bowl back, filled it, and sat at the table. "Nancy, I want you to come with me to market today. I've a mind to look for a goodly chine of beef for to-morrow's dinner, along with a few other things. We could look to find some greens for sallats, and such, if any are about."

"Ah, yes—as to to-morrow's dinner." Joanna drew herself up to her full height—she was a tall woman—and folded her hands at her waist. "I've already made arrangements with the butcher for some venison— Jenny and I will make a stew of it, along with the capons for pie and the goose. With all that, I hardly think we'll have need of beef as well, will we?"

Fighting down the slow burn of rage in her stomach, Kathryn kept her voice as pleasant as she could. "I had thought we had agreed to a chine of beef with the other dishes. We spoke of it only yesterday morning."

"We did, but the price of the venison was so good, I thought it would make a nice change. We rarely get game this time of year."

"Well, best to be up and doing. There's a deal of work to be done if we're to have a stew and pies and a roast goose all prepared." Kathryn abandoned her plans for the beef. The next day was Sunday, and Master Nicholas's cousins and their wives were coming to dine after church. Nicholas was anxious to make a good showing for his more prosperous kinsmen.

"Oh, sister, you need not trouble yourself—Jenny and I have all well to hand. You and Nan might go out to look for greens for sallats, as you proposed—though 'tis hardly likely there'll be much, this time of year. We can as well do without. You'll need do nothing but play the hostess to-morrow."

Kathryn caught Nancy's glance, and the slight shake of her head. "We'll go to market, indeed," she said. "It's you who need not trouble yourself. If you need anything, only tell me, and we'll bring it home." She picked up her bowl and spoon, but Jenny was there almost before she had risen to take them away to scrub.

"Of course they have it all well in hand, as ever they do," Kathryn fumed a half-hour later, when she and Nancy made their way down to the market through the chill of the March morning. "What can I do, when neither of them ever says a word I can fault them for, yet they cross me at every turn? If I complain to my husband I'll only look petty."

"Joanna has been mistress in that house since her mother died, and she has no intention of moving aside for her brother's wife," Nancy said. It was a conversation that already felt old between them. In the first weeks after the wedding, Kathryn had been all for making a scene—putting her sister-in-law in her place, asserting her rights as mistress of the house. She had even thought to dismiss Jenny Piper and leave Nancy as the sole woman servant.

But Jenny had been with them for years, and was married to Robin Piper, the journeyman cobbler who worked with Master Nicholas and his father. It was a tight-knit little crew until the new bride and her maid had arrived.

By now, she and Nancy had given up trying to solve the problem: they only cared to escape the house when they could. "It will all change when I have a child," Kathryn said now. "Surely nobody can deny, then, that I am mistress—and you can be the nursemaid, with no need for Jenny to think you are taking her job."

"She and Mistress Joanna will think you've ideas above your station if you have a nursemaid for your baby," Nancy pointed out. "It is true, though, your own status will be clearer when the babe is born. As for mine...I'm afraid 'tis not so simple. Would it not be better if—."

"No! I'll hear no talk of you leaving me. Not alone with the two of them all day! 'Tis not to be thought of." Kathryn threaded her arm through Nancy's and pulled her friend closer. She had said it so lightly, so many times: *No one will ever separate us.* Yet she had not truly thought through how much more difficult it would make her already-difficult position, to bring along her own maid, another mouth for her husband's household to feed. But lacking her dearest friend and only ally, how could she survive?

Her husband, of course, ought to be her ally. But she would not draw him into the fray. *We must all put on polite faces,* Kathryn thought, *so the master thinks everything is running smoothly.*

The thought of putting on a polite face reminded her of when she had accompanied her father, years ago, to the big house of Sir John Young, to collect payment for work Master Gale had done there. The walls were adorned with paintings—Kathryn had never seen the like. She had been awed by the beauty of the pictures, even more than the grandeur of the house in which they were hung. She had stood a long time staring at a portrait of a plump, dark-haired lady in a shining blue gown, wishing she could be that woman in that dress. Kathryn knew she would never be a noble lady and wear such a gown, but she felt, sometimes, as if she were sitting for her portrait now. *Mistress Guy, Wife of Nicholas Guy.* Sit still and compose herself, and try to look the part. If she sat long enough, the picture might come to life.

"At any rate, if we wait for me to bear a child before I can be mistress, we will wait awhile yet, for my flowers have come again," she said. "And Joanna will know that, of course, with Jenny taking the linens out to the washer woman."

"You've been wed but three months. Your mother was married a year before she quickened with child."

"As she is fond of telling me." They had reached the market, back in the old neighbourhood. Her husband's house was near the almshouse above Christmas Street, outside the old city walls that had been the boundary of her world in childhood.

Joanna had been right, of course, about finding few greens for sale at the end of winter. But regardless of what they bought, Kathryn enjoyed a visit to the market, which bustled with housewives and servants doing their shopping. Blood from the butchers' stalls mingled with the dung in the streets to create a foul-smelling slurry at their feet as Kathryn lifted her petticoat and overskirt clear of the ground, but the pleasant aroma of cakes and savoury pies from the bakers' stalls almost balanced it out.

On a busy day such as this, it might be mid-day before Kathryn had any chance to talk to her husband. Which was as well: she was still a little unsure what to say to him when they were alone together. He was kind enough, and never harsh, but his mind was filled up with business. At noon she brought him a slice of pork pie and a mug of ale and asked him to tell her all about the gentleman he had just served.

"'Twill be a grand order, if I can get it—if he's satisfied with the first pair, he means to order for his whole household. Ladies' shoes for his wife and daughters—the finest calfskin. With an order like that I should be able to take on another apprentice."

Kathryn perched on a stool near his worktable as he ate; the other men had gone into the hall to get their noon meal, so the steady tap-tap of hammers was quiet for once. She admired her husband's ambition. She knew already that his real love was not shoe leather itself; he did not take pleasure in it the way her father did with stone, for its own sake. Rather, he aspired to his cousins' station in life: to be a merchant; to have a fine new house; to feel the clink of coins in his hands instead of hammers.

"All is well for to-morrow, is it?" he asked. "You women folk seem busy in the kitchen."

"Everything is well in hand."

"Good, good. Now, what do you have planned for the banqueting course—a pudding, a trifle?"

Kathryn had thought a trifle, something she had a good bit of practice making at home, would be nice, but, to no one's surprise, Joanna had already started cherry and plum tarts. Kathryn told her husband as much, wondering at his sudden interest in the details of the menu.

"I need you to help me with a little matter," he said. "I went to Peele the baker last week to order something special. 'Twill cost a bit, for it is a marchpane subtlety. I thought to celebrate the plans for the New World voyage in fine style. You must tell no one of this, but go and get the subtlety from him to-morrow before church, and store it somewhere where none will see it before dinner is over. I wish to surprise everyone, even our own household."

She was pleased beyond measure that he had chosen her, rather than his sister, to help him plan this. Pleased, too, to see this small trace of whimsy in him. For if she had found a fault in her husband, it was only that she sometimes thought him a little dull—kind and hard-working, to be sure, but a little lacking in both imagination and humour. She did not think he would like to go see the players with her, and it was hard to make him laugh at a jest. That he had thought of something as frivolous as a confectionary to celebrate his cousins' venture made him seem a bit less serious and remote. She went to the bakeshop as promised and locked the confection away in a chest before the family went to church the next day.

When they sat around the table after church, Kathryn took pride in her place as mistress. What did it matter, after all, that Joanna and Jenny had done all the cooking and planning? Joanna was relegated to sitting by her elderly father's side; Kathryn sat at the head of the table with Nicholas and greeted his lofty cousins, while Jenny and Nancy glided back and forth silently, putting one dish after another on the table.

The talk was all of the New World; no one in the Guy family spoke of much else these days. John had recently returned from London; Philip had engaged a ship, the *Fleming*, to carry them across the ocean. "We hope to be ready to set sail sometime in June," he announced.

"Only three months! Surely there is a great deal to be done before then," said old Master Guy.

"More than you might guess. We are working all hours of the day to draw up our lists of stores we will need and find the best suppliers. We want enough in store to keep forty men for a year, for there will be little we can grow or raise ourselves in the first year, though we will catch and salt codfish for our own provisions, as well as to ship back to England for sale."

As the maids cleared away the trenchers, Nicholas Guy rose, a cup in his hand. Kathryn stood too, and quietly slipped from the table. Nancy, her only confidante, had already taken the confectionary from its chest and had it on a platter, ready for Kathryn to bring to the table.

"It is a great honour, my kinsmen," Nicholas Guy said, "for my wife and I to host you here in our own house, and indeed I am honoured to have so good and honest a help-mate as my Kathryn to welcome you to our table. Our hearts are full of joy tonight at the news that Cousin John's great endeavour is about to go forward." On the word *forward* Kathryn moved to the table, holding aloft the platter for everyone to see. "Gentlemen, in celebration of this great new venture, we drink to your success, and I give you—the New Found Land!"

It could not have been timed better: Kathryn laid the pewter plate with the subtlety on the table before them just as he said *the New Found Land*, and everyone applauded. The moment was all they had planned for, and Kathryn exchanged a quick glance and smile with Nancy before turning all her attention to her husband and guests.

The sculpture itself was a cunning thing, though a little smaller than she had imagined it. Somehow in her mind, despite knowing what they had paid for—more than they could afford—Kathryn had pictured a giant sailing ship made all of pure sugar, taking up half the table, evoking gasps of wonder from the guests. That sort of thing might appear on a nobleman's table—she had heard tales of such. Marchpane was more affordable, if less magical in appearance. Peele the baker had produced a modest little marchpane barque about the size of a well-fed house cat, and the sails looked a little heavy—it must be hard to create from almond paste the illusion of canvas sheets filled with air. The figurehead on the prow, cunningly carved, was beginning to melt a little bit, drooping into the bow of the ship. But everyone clapped nonetheless and said how fine it was.

"A fitting tribute indeed, Nicholas!" John Guy said above the applause, and raised his glass to his cousin.

Nicholas Guy took his seat, and drank, and wiped his mouth on his sleeve. "And a fitting moment to tell you, cousins, that I have given much thought to the offers you have made, and decided that if you still want to add me to your number, I am ready to make one of your colonists when the *Fleming* sails in the summer."

Kathryn felt the shock like a blow to her stomach. John and Philip Guy and their wives were nodding as though this were news they had expected to hear; even old Master Guy gave a harrumph of approval. Kathryn met the eyes of her sister-in-law and saw that Joanna was the only person there who shared her surprise.

"But we have spoken of this!" Nicholas Guy insisted much later, when everyone had gone home. They were upstairs in their sleeping chamber, while below Joanna directed Nancy, the Pipers, and the apprentice boys in cleaning up the dinner. Even here in the bedchamber Kathryn would not burst out with the reproaches that sprang to her lips, but only say, "Why did you not tell me beforehand that you had made up your mind to this? Or that you would announce it tonight?"

Nicholas Guy sat heavily on the bed, rubbing a hand through his hair. "You knew I was thinking of going out to the colony."

"You talked of being interested in the venture—sometime in the future, you said! You assured me it would not be this year."

"I gave no assurances." He looked up at her, his narrow face serious. "I did not think myself that I would go this year, but speaking with John since he came back from London has convinced me this is the right time to go."

"And you announced it tonight before them all without even telling me first? Do you think Master John did not talk to Mistress Anne before deciding to go out to the New Found Land? Or Philip with Elizabeth?"

"I am sure my cousins have both discussed the plan with their wives many times," Nicholas admitted. He pulled off his doublet, standing before her in only his tunic and hose. "John and Anne have been married fifteen years; they have four children with another soon to come, and she manages his household when he is away on his ventures. Philip and Elizabeth, though they are younger, have likewise been long married and have sons already. At their time of life, a husband would naturally seek the counsel of a wife who is mature and has proven her worth."

"What are you saying—that I have not proven myself worthy of your confidence?" She could feel tears, just at the edge of her eyes. "Because we have been married only a few months? Because I am not with child yet? Or is it some other fault in me?"

He crossed the room to her, put his hands on her shoulders. "No fault in you at all, dear girl. But you *are* a girl—you are eighteen years old and know nothing of the world outside your father's house. You know I have great ambitions, and I plan for you to be at my side as I rise in the world. A season or two in the colonies will help me build my wealth and rise to a higher station. I do not intend to be a cobbler all my life, nor you to be a cobbler's wife, I can assure you."

"I—I know all this. But you never said—"

"Dear girl, even a man like my cousin John, whose wife is a matron of great wisdom and experience—even in such a case, this decision is the sort that a man makes in consultation with other men. Taming the New World is men's business, though in the end we will have to bring women out with us."

"And will they bundle the women off, without consulting them? Is that a decision men must make also?" She was trembling with the effort of fighting back tears and anger. And her husband was undoing the laces of her gown, pulling her shift off her shoulders, baring her skin to the chilly air. She wanted to pull away from him, shrug her sleeves back up over her arms and turn her back.

"I am sure those men who bring their wives out to the colonies will have long and tearful discussions with them first," he said with a smile. "There are women in Virginia already, and from what I hear, more of them eager to join the men over there. 'Tis a grand adventure, you know—yes, it is, don't shake your pretty head at me."

"But—you'd not expect me to go over there?"

He frowned for a moment, thinking, then said, "I doubt it. I do not think I would stay there so long myself. A year or two, to build my fortune. I will acquire land there, but I would have someone else to work the land and fish for me. I will go for a season with my cousins and hope to return to you a wealthier man, with a better name here in Bristol."

As he spoke, his fingers continued the business of undressing her, till her clothes lay on the floor in a heap and he drew her onto their bed, behind the hangings. It really was freezing in this room, even within the curtains of their marriage bed where he now drew her down beside him. His promise that he had no intention of staying long in the New World did a little to blunt the shock of his announcement that he was going at all, but Kathryn knew she must not fret him about it. No man would be anxious to rush home from the colonies to a nagging shrew of a wife.

"Then I suppose it is best that you go," she said, letting him pull her into an embrace. "Only...it seems so soon...I wish I could be sure I was carrying a son for you, before you go."

"Ah well, we know the remedy for that," he chuckled. Then he rolled over on top of her, and Kathryn closed her eyes. She had gotten used to this business now, and it was not unpleasant, though it was hard to believe that what Master Nicholas did in bed was the same kind of passion that caused people to abandon fortunes and overthrow kingdoms. But, she reminded herself, those kind of things only happened in stories. Nobody expected great passion from a tradesman's virtuous wife.

She thought again of the serene and beautiful woman in the painting and composed herself to lie quietly beneath her husband's touch.

A Judgement is Carried Out

Diverse well-minded men, wise, rich, and able,
Did undertake a plot inestimable,
The hopefullest, easiest, healthiest, just plantation,
That e'er was undertaken by our Nation.

CUPIDS COVE
AUTUMN-WINTER 1610

"PERRY! OVER HERE!" CALLED NICHOLAS GUY AS NED pushed the wheeled barrow up the slope.

"On my way!" Master Nicholas sometimes called him by name and other times, if they had anything to do with stone, he called Ned "stonemason," though Ned had not even completed his apprenticeship. Of the thirty-nine men in Cupids Cove, Ned was the only one with skill in masonry. He saw that in the colony he might become a master mason simply for lack of anyone more skilled to fill that role, but in these first months they were building little in stone. There simply was not enough time before winter closed in, so the palisade wall around the settlement, as well as all the buildings, were being built of the wood that grew abundantly all around.

The rutted and stony ground under the barrow's wheels had no softness left to it; the first frosts had come a fortnight ago and the temperature had stayed cold. It had been a long, mild, sunny autumn, the trees holding their leaves till late October, but now the men felt the teeth of winter in the air.

Those first months, the expedition had felt as if it were charmed. The crossing had been rough—but not spectacularly rough, Ned now understood from talking to the more experienced sailors. Only his own inexperience at sea had made him think he was like to die when the ship pitched and rolled in the waves. He was sick enough that he swore he'd never cross the ocean again, which was as good reason as any to make himself a life in this new world.

Once they were on land they had fair weather, and their work proceeded quickly in the long days of late summer and autumn. They had toiled hard to get the dwelling-house and storehouse closed in and to finish the palisade wall. The frosty nights were not too cold to bear now that they no longer had to sleep in pits dug into the ground and covered with canvas, as they had done during the first weeks.

Many fishing ships had been in the bay when Guy's ship arrived, and the fishermen had come back and forth to the colony from their fishing stations up the shore to share news and trade supplies. The fishermen had sailed home at the beginning of autumn, as had the *Fleming* that brought the colonists over, laden with timber from the forest and salt fish from the seas. Since the ships had gone, the settlers had seen no other humans but themselves. Neither natives nor pirates, despite their fears.

Yesterday had seen two firsts: the first snowfall, a light dusting of white across the frozen ground, and also the first serious accident. John Morris had crushed his leg while chopping down a tree, resulting in a dark, ugly wound that left him unable to walk. The surgeon who had come over with them, Reynolds, had ordered Morris to rest, along with James Stone, who was suffering stiffness in his knees and had taken to his bed. That left them short two men as they worked to complete the buildings before snow came.

As they gathered for supper last night, Master John Guy had spoken about Morris's accident, giving the wounded man an extra ration of spirits. He also gave the men a warning. "We must carry on and be more vigilant than ever to avoid mishap. For what might be a small thing back in England could end a man's life here."

Ned felt no envy for Morris and Stone, left behind in the dwelling-house while the rest worked. The New Found Land was not a place where a man would choose to lie abed. Even under layers of wool blankets and fur coverings, the beds were as chilly as they were hard. Nothing warmed you up except work. Lying abed might produce far worse results: today, Morris was running a fever. Reynolds could do little more than sew up wounds and splint broken limbs; he had a cache of medicines, but he was no physician, and had little skill or experience in using those remedies. In a community of all men, you could not even hope for a cunning-woman who could heal with herbs and potions, as you might at home.

Ned unloaded his barrowful of wood at Master Nicholas's direction. "I'll get a start on that window frame now," he said. The colony's supplies had included not one, but two glass windows for the dwelling-house, a luxury that showed how serious Governor Guy was about planting a permanent colony.

"Good man," said Master Nicholas with a nod. He was a younger and more vigorous man than his two cousins John and Philip, and he was a fair master. Ned knew that any small burn of resentment he felt towards Nicholas Guy had less to do with the man's leadership than with the fact that he had Kathryn Gale in his marriage bed, and had left her back in Bristol. *If she were mine*, Ned thought, *I'd not have sailed halfway across the world; you can count on that.*

But she was not his, and such thoughts were themselves better left on the other side of the sea. Master Nicholas strode on as Ned settled in beside Tom Percy and George Whittington, setting the window frame into the final wall of the dwelling-house. When Ned pointed out a fault in Whittington's work, the other man took the correction with a good enough spirit. "I never claimed any skill at building," he shrugged, pulling out the nails he had driven in. Despite the chill of the morning air and the skirl of snow still on the ground, he had peeled off his shirt and was working bare-chested.

"You must have a furnace inside of you," Ned said. "I'm warm enough when I'm working, but the chill of these mornings is enough to take the skin off a man."

George wiped sweat from his forehead with the back of his arm. "Aye, I've got the lusty humours—always hot inside, no matter how cold it is outside."

"I hope to God it is only your lusty humour and you're not brewing a fever. The last thing we need is an outbreak of plague." They had had a near thing of it with George's younger brother, Marmaduke, who had been sick with smallpox on the ship coming over. All but the surgeon had kept well clear of him till he recovered, and no other man had fallen ill, but the thought of plague or fever spreading among their little company was a frightening one.

"Sure, as far as plague goes, we're better off here than back in England," Tom Percy said. He was a dour, quiet young man, and he rarely joined in the talk and laughter while they worked. "The crowded houses and narrow streets, everyone pressed together—that's what breeds plague." Tom glanced beyond the building they were at work on, to the pale-blue sky and the shimmer of the water in the sheltered harbour beyond. "We're in the best place we could be here—far from cities where folk live crowded on top of one another."

"It may be so," Ned allowed, grunting as he lifted a large piece of timber into place. "But we eat and sleep in each other's pockets here. Sickness would spread damn fast in such a place."

"There's open space all around. I went into the woods the other day to cut firewood, and I wasn't ten minutes' walk from here when I could hear no sounds of voices, no hammers or axes or picks, nor them damned chickens and goats. Nothing but the wind and water and the cries of the birds."

"And the growl of a bear that might come out of the woods and tear you to shreds," George said. They had seen one of those huge beasts during their first days in the colony, and taken care to keep well clear of it.

"Well, I never saw no bear, and I'll tell you the truth, I was half wishing I could stay out in the woods, save that I knew you all needed the wood I was cutting."

"You'd have come into one of the native villages soon enough," Ned pointed out. "The fishermen have seen 'em."

"I want no village, savage or English. When this place is built up enough that we can spare one man's labour, I'm going to go off into the woods. I'll build myself a little cottage, and be free of the sound of other men's voices."

"Well, excuse me for talking then," said Ned. It was a long chat to have had with a contrary bastard like Percy.

George Whittington, driving in a new nail to replace the one he had removed, snorted. "Off in a tilt in the woods, is it, Percy? Wouldn't you be searching out that savage camp and hauling off one of their women, at least?"

"Ah, pay no mind to Percy, he's made up his mind to be crooked," Ned said. "I 'low you'll be off looking for a native maid in the woods if we're here without women much longer, George."

"If I don't find one of them, I might be coming after you or even Percy one of these nights," George grinned. He seemed a decent enough fellow, George, and most of what he said was pure foolishness. "I had a whore down on Bristol docks three hours before the ship left," George went on, "and I've been counting the minutes ever since. Four months is a bloody long time for a man to go without nowhere to put his cock except in his own hand, I'm telling you that. If Master Guy don't bring out some girls from England soon, you beardless young fellows are going to have to watch yourselves at night, is all I'm saying. 'Tis not natural."

"As long as you're not worried about what's natural, I'll tell the she-goats to watch out for you, George," bawled Matt Grigg, trundling past with another load of wood.

"Oh, you mock me, but there's no telling what a man will do if you make him go a year without so much as a poxy dockside whore around, never mind his own bonny sweetheart."

"Any sweetheart you got, Whittington, most likely *is* a poxy whore," Tom Percy said. He and George had gotten into a fistfight in their first weeks in Cupids Cove, and Governor Guy had had them both whipped. Now the two men confined themselves to sniping at one another.

Ned did not tell Percy or Whittington or anyone else that his own experience of sweethearts went no further than one of those same dockside whores, though, he hoped, not a pox-ridden one. She had been very young and seemed shy and sweet, which was probably not the best choice—he ought to have paid a few pennies more for an experienced older woman, who would show him what to do. But there he was, eighteen years old, and he'd never had a sweetheart—always thought there'd be time enough for such things when he was further along in his apprenticeship. And, if he was truthful with himself, his dreams about Kathryn Gale had kept him from having too much interest in other girls during the years he was an apprentice in her father's house.

When he had decided to join the expedition to New Found Land and knew they would be a year, at least, over there with no women in sight, he had made up his mind to have a woman in the same way he had approached packing his few possessions: this was a thing he had to get done. A man couldn't sail off on the ocean and risk dying a virgin over there. He had asked the eldest apprentice, Walter, where to go and who to ask for. Walter had taken Ned with him to a whorehouse with a decent reputation, and Ned had chosen that poor little doxy. Who, to be honest, he had probably picked not just because she was the cheapest but also because her dark hair, brown eyes, and rounded cheeks put him in mind a little bit of Kathryn.

It wasn't an hour of passion the poets would sing of. But Ned had got the business done, so that whatever happened after he wouldn't have to blush when fellows like George Whittington made jests about beardless virgin lads.

"That won't do," he said to George now, pointing his attention back to the wall. "You can see daylight in that space there—here, this will make it fit better." It gave him some ease, put his feet back on solid ground, to give instruction to the brash, confident Whittington. True, Ned had trained as a stonemason, but his father was a carpenter, and he knew more about any sort of building than did Whittington, who had spent his life waiting on Governor Guy.

They finished that last piece of wall and put in the window before the morning was over, broke for a meal at noon, and turned to other chores later in the afternoon. Ned hitched himself up to the wood sled and hauled a load of birch from the stand of trees to the fireplace in the dwelling-house. With no horses or donkeys yet, the men did all the dragging and hauling themselves. He made several trips back and forth, stacking the wood—it was fearsome, as the weather got colder, how much wood they went through. Last winter back in Bristol had been the coldest he could remember in his life, but this New Found Land winter promised to be even colder, and their shelter was hardly as sturdy as a row of city houses back home.

The men finishing the roof of the dwelling-house were fitting boards into place and hammering. Tom Percy was in the saw-pit with Frank Tipton all afternoon, preparing timber for the endless building projects. Other men filled other jobs: Marmaduke, a slight fellow even before his illness, was cooking over a stew pot, while another man took loaves of bread from an oven nestled in the coals of the newly built hearth. Still others were mending boots and clothes so they could still be used, or sharpening and repairing tools that were wearing out from overuse. All these tasks had to be done in the afternoon, for this time of year the dark of night dropped down early and there were too few candles to waste on trying to work after dark.

When night fell they ate the stew, sopping the bread in it, washing it all down with ale. The day's work done, the enormity of this vast, cold land seemed to press in on all the men, force them to sit closer together, talk louder, laugh at rowdier stories. The noise within might ward off the dangers outside.

Tonight the talk was bawdy, with further speculation on George Whittington's need for a woman and the various ways he might relieve his urges. Then the masters—John and Philip Guy, William Colston, and William Catchmaid—joined the labouring men around the hearth. That put an end to the loose talk. Now they spoke of practical things, of the boats they would build in the workhouse during the winter months.

A few of the men wrote letters home in the flickering firelight. No ship would cross to England now until spring, but some men were so devoted in writing to their wives or sweethearts that they penned a few lines every night. Others, who could not write, got the learned men to write down their letters for them. If everyone kept putting down messages at this rate, they would have the equivalent of a small library to send back to England by the time a ship went back that way. Or, more like, they would run through their small supply of paper before Christmas.

Ned could write a little, as much as a mason would ever need to. Not enough to attempt a letter. In spring he would send greetings by Nicholas Guy's letters to the Gale household, and ask that someone there tell his parents he was well. What more was there to say, other than to tell them he was alive and well, that despite the hardships of this life he liked the colony and was glad he had come?

He thought sometimes of Kathryn Gale's face, the face that had occupied his dreams for so many years. Without her daily presence, the picture in his mind was fading. He remembered other things, other people, more clearly than he remembered her. One of his mother's housecats, the friendly one that would curl up at his feet to sleep. Playing pranks at the Gale house with Walter and Billy. A particular pork pie Mistress Tibby baked, and the way she had of cross-hatching the pastry on top. Nancy Ellis's face when she mocked him, then how she would, almost against her will, burst into laughter at something he said.

He lingered on that last image, Nancy's face alight with mirth, before he fell to sleep. It seemed wrong to dwell too long on thoughts of Kathryn, now that she was another man's wife and that man was sleeping just a few snoring bodies away. But her tart-tongued maid, far away on the other side of the ocean—Ned dreamed of Nancy, more than once, in the long nights when fresh air and hard work dropped him into deep sleep.

He woke from that sleep to another day of hard work; one day led into another, and as the weeks passed, the crisp, cool autumn slipped towards a chilly winter. Cupids Cove took shape around them. A dwelling-house, a handful of outbuildings, thirty-nine men and their beasts contained within a palisade fence: it was not a town, nor even a village, yet Ned was beginning to think of it as his home.

Ned believed, generally, that every man should look to his own business and not trouble about what other men did or thought. Yet he found himself, a few nights before the feast of Christmas, drawing Governor Guy aside after the evening meal to say, "Sir, I'm not easy in my mind about Tom Percy."

John Guy gave him a sharp look. He was a good master; he knew all the men under him, even if he might hesitate over the names of some, and he treated them all fairly. "What's the trouble with your friend Percy?"

"'Tis not that we're friends, sir—I don't know that he has a friend. He talks of going off into the forest alone, to live apart from the rest of us. He says he can't be with the rest of mankind." Tom had mentioned this several more times in Ned's hearing, after that first occasion. "I'm afraid the hardship of the journey, or maybe just the change from England, is turning his mind."

Guy nodded slowly. "They say it can happen, though we've been fortunate so far in the whole lot of you—men of sound mind. Has he a sweetheart back home he's pining over, something like that?"

"No, sir, he's spoken of no woman. I know every man has his private troubles, sir. But his talk about living alone in the woods—well, it don't seem right to me."

"You're quite right—we can't have men getting on like that. The success of the colony depends on everyone keeping in good spirits and working together." John Guy looked out over the harbour of Cupids Cove, where the sky was already darkening, barely four hours past noon.

"We have a long stretch ahead of us till spring," Guy said aloud. "From all I've heard tell of this New World, the weather only gets harsher after midwinter and stays cold for months on end. We cannot have men taking leave of their senses. Keep an eye to Percy; tell me if his spirits take a turn for the worse." He frowned. "I wish I had found a minister able to come out with us. There's a heaviness that comes over men's spirits in a place like this."

Ned doubted that Tom Percy was a man to find comfort in talking to a minister or reciting prayers. The man's gloomy mood had noticeably darkened as the long winter nights drew in and the snow thickened. When the other men spoke of things they longed for back home—wives and sweethearts, familiar meals, pubs and shops and friends—Percy huddled into himself and said nothing.

On Christmas Day, the men feasted on one of their goats, sacrificed for the occasion. They made the best of the holy day, laughing and telling stories of Christmases past, speculating on what their families were doing. Back home, there would have been division between those who thought, in the old papist way, that Christmas was a day of feasting and celebration, and the more reformed folk who believed a holy day was best spent entirely on your knees. But here in the colony, such differences mattered little. They would have their church service in the morning and feast as best they could for dinner, wringing whatever pleasure they might out of the day.

"They all want to go home, but this country is the only bloody place for a man like me," muttered Tom Percy, creeping up behind Ned.

"'Tis a fine place indeed," Ned said, trying for hearty good spirits. "A man can make a grand life for himself here."

"Not this place, not Cupids Cove." Percy looked around at his fellow colonists, huddled in twos and threes around the hearth. "I told you, I must get away. Build a little tilt where I can fish and hunt. I'm not fit to be around my fellow man."

"Now that's no way to talk at Christmas-tide. Peace on earth, to men goodwill."

"No man here would have goodwill towards me if he knew the truth."

"Come now, have a drink and put your troubles behind you. The governor has given us all an extra ration of aquavit for the holy day." Another of the shortcomings of a settler's life was that Guy had brought just enough liquor to keep forty men going till supplies arrived from England in the spring, but no more. They had built a brewhouse down by the saltwater pond and brewed their own small ale, but it was weak stuff, and there was little chance of the men getting good and drunk even on a feast day—which, no doubt, suited the governor's ideas of an orderly colony just fine.

No salvation for Percy in spirits, then, any more than there was in prayer. Heavy snow fell on St. Stephen's Day, the first real howling storm they had seen in the New Found Land. Gusts of icy wind battered at the shutters of the dwelling-house as the swirling fingers of snow reached in through tiny gaps in the window frames and walls. It had been cold for weeks, but this kind of cold was another creature altogether. Wind shook the building that had seemed so secure just days ago. The fire was a pathetic attempt to warm the place, and men and livestock alike huddled as near to it as they could, the men wrapped in layers of blankets and furs. They gave up sleeping in their ice-rimed beds in the sleeping loft, and slept beside the fire, though in that hollow cold the flames gave off no more heat than a candle.

The storm went on all day and into the night. Most of the men lay sleepless in the howling wind. There was talk and storytelling again, but they were far less cheerful than they had been on Christmas Day. The Bristol men had rarely seen such storms as this, but a few of those who had lived in the north of England told tales of wind and snow fierce enough to freeze a man to death.

"Come men, we must keep our spirits up, we must not be daunted!" bawled Master Philip. In the absence of a clergyman, either Philip or John Guy led Sunday worship, reading the service from the prayer book and then a sermon from the Book of Homilies. Philip Guy relished this duty more than his brother did; he was often the one heard chiding the men, but to give him credit, he was just as likely to use divine authority to encourage, as he was doing now. "Let us sing a psalm tune, and commend our safety to God above!"

The men joined Master Philip in a weak version of the hundredth psalm, though it could not be said they were exactly singing to the Lord with cheerful voice. Turning the musical efforts towards drinking songs, as George did soon afterwards, helped a little. Eventually most of the men managed some kind of sleep. Ned rolled himself as tight in his blanket as he could and slept next to two of the goats, enjoying the warmth of their animal bodies despite the smell. They didn't complain, as men did. Surely somewhere deep in their dumb beast nature they must have wondered why they were in this cold place, so unlike the Bristol farmyards they had been born in. But lacking words to utter their complaint, they gave a fair imitation of being content.

It was the lack of wind that woke Ned, the strange silence after twenty-four hours of howling gale and cracking timbers. He lay still, needing to get up for a piss but not wanting to move from the warmth of his blanket huddle. Though the storm had stilled, the bitter cold air stung his face. The fire had died to embers. He heard one man, then another, get up and use the buckets they had set aside for pisspots.

Finally he heard Nicholas Guy's voice. "What a sight!" He was standing at one of the windows, having scraped the frost clear of a small circle of glass that allowed him to peer out between the shutters.

The scene outside, once a larger square of window was cleared, looked both eerie and enchanting. Everything lay cold and still under heavy drifts of white snow. "I doubt we'll be able to get the door open," said Master Nicholas, looking at the mounds of snow piled against it. "Perhaps some of you smaller lads can squeeze out if we take out one of the windows. Then you can clear it away from the door with spades."

In the end, that was what they did—the glass window was taken out and the shutters removed so that Ned and Duke Whittington, the two youngest and slenderest of the men, climbed out through a window and tossed piles of the snow away from the door until they were able to push it open. Then all the men spilled out, and the animals too, marvelling at the transformed world the snow had left behind. The drifts piled nearly to the top of the palisade wall.

The snow lifted the men's moods. They were almost playful as they shovelled paths through it. Everyone save the two sick men, Morris and Stone—the one still feverish and uneasy since his injury, the other complaining of the pain in his joints—spent the better part of the day out of doors. They let the goats and pigs out, hauled in more firewood, brought buckets of snow to melt for drinking water. More than once Ned was slapped in the side of the head by a snowball hurled by one of his comrades. Their clothing was wet and everyone was tired by late afternoon, when they again gathered around the fire as daylight died.

After helping to clear the snow from the door, Duke Whittington had taken little part in the afternoon's work and play; he was huddled by the fire shivering as if the effort of shovelling had worn him out. Ned thought again how frail and young Duke seemed, how different from his bluff and hearty older brother. "Eat up, Duke," he encouraged the boy.

It was while they ate that Ned noticed Tom Percy was missing. He asked Frank Tipton if he'd seen Percy, but Frank only said, "I never noticed him gone. He's an odd fish, that one. This winter would get anyone's spirits down, but he don't even seem to try to keep his up."

After they ate, Ned was charged with the task of refilling the flour bucket and bringing a wheel of cheese from the storehouse. He found Tom Percy perched on a stack of bundles and barrels, staring off into space, fiddling aimlessly with a stick he held in his hands.

"What are you at, man? Come in by the fire, you'll freeze here. You might as well be outside; 'tis cold as the grave."

"Yes, I might as well be outside," echoed Percy.

"Aye, I know, your hermitage in the woods. Well, you'll have to wait till the weather breaks to build it. Till spring you'll have to put up with the rest of us or freeze to death. Come on back in."

"I can't put it out of my mind, Perry. 'Tis before me all the time, in my mind's eye."

"What is?"

"Hell. The flames of Hell."

Oh, Lord. Was the man some kind of puritan fanatic? "Marry, I'd say flames of any kind sound all right just now," Ned said, filling his bucket from a barrel of barley flour. "Here, make yourself useful and hand me down that cheese, there."

He gestured at the shelf but Percy, still turning the stick in his hands, did not move. "Don't mock Hell's flames, Ned. They're real enough. The pain of burning but no warmth, no comfort. I see them over and over, and his face in the middle of them."

"Who—the Devil?" Ned spoke lightly, suppressing a shudder. He hated this kind of talk.

"No, Dick Hanlon."

"Who on God's earth is Dick Hanlon, and what is he doing in Hell?"

"Ah, that's just it." Tom Percy's hollow laugh reminded Ned of last night's storm winds. "He's not on God's earth. He may well be in Hell. But I've no doubts about where I'm going. None at all."

Ned laid down the flour bucket. "Look man, I've had about enough of your hints and riddles. Something's on your mind: you're not fit to live among us, and now you say you're going to Hell because of a man called Dick Hanlon." The thought of buggery flitted through his brain, but it failed to alight. The pieces were falling into place, and the real answer was so much starker than unnatural vice. "Oh, Lord in Heaven, Percy. Did you murder this fellow Hanlon?"

Tom Percy closed his eyes, leaned his head back against the wall. He flipped the stick in his hands, and as the light glinted, Ned realized it was not a stick; it was a knife. The kind of knife every man in the settlement carried, for doing all kinds of odd jobs. Ned had one, but not with him at the moment. "I did. That I did. I killed him outside a pub in Rochester, on the fourteenth of April. Then I fled and came to Bristol, and signed myself on with Master Guy. As far as I could get from England and the king's justice." He looked up, opened his eyes for a moment. "I hardly need to tell you Tom Percy is not my real name."

"No...no, I suppose 'tis not." Ned eased down onto a chest of tools, not taking his eyes from Percy. He wasn't easy in his mind about sitting down side by side with a murderer, especially one who was armed. But then, if the story were true, he'd been sitting down next to a murderer, working alongside him, even sleeping next to him, since they left Bristol.

"Were you defending yourself?" He chose his words with care. "Did this Hanlon attack you? There's no sin in striking a man who's bent on killing you."

"I started it. I was drinking, yes, but not so drunk I didn't know my own mind. It was a quarrel over a woman—a faithless jade who promised herself to me and then ran around with Hanlon behind my back. When I found out, I beat her, and then I went looking for Hanlon. Found him in a pub, pretended friendship over a few pints of ale, and then I drew him outside and stuck my knife in between his ribs."

"Do you know for certain he died? You might have only wounded him."

"I heard later that night, people saying he was dead. I sent a friend to find out for sure. I killed the man, and I deserved the hangman's noose, but instead I ran away. I thought I could leave guilt behind in England with justice, but it follows me like a dog at my heels."

"You need to tell one of the masters. Governor Guy must know you signed on under a false name and that there are charges against you in England. But Master Philip might be the more sympathetic to tell your tale to first."

"Are you mad? I can't tell them. I don't even know why I told you—you'll run to them as soon as we're out of here, and then every man in the colony will know I'm a murderer." Percy, who had looked half asleep for most of the conversation, now hopped off the barrel where he perched and stood on his feet, holding the knife out before him like a warning. "What are we, Ned Perry? Two score men in the wilderness with not another Christian soul around on this whole island. We're here with no magistrate, no lord over us but John Guy. If the masters know what I am, they won't suffer me to live among them. They'll string me up."

A wildfire burned in the eyes of the man whose name was not Tom Percy. How long before he worked out that if he killed Ned here and now, the story need never get out? Ned began backing up slowly, step by step.

"You think I won't let you go," Percy said. "You're afraid I'm going to kill you, too."

"The thought did cross my mind."

"I never want to kill a man again," Percy said. Then he looked around at the storehouse, at Ned, at the door. "But I won't have you tattling to the governor. I can't have it known. If you want to live, and spare me from being a murderer twice over, you have to swear to keep my secret."

"I do. I swear."

"On your life?"

"On my life, my family's lives, in the eyes of God—get Master Guy's Bible and I'll swear on it if you please. Your secret is safe with me."

Tom Percy's tense body eased, and he let the knife loosen in his grip. "Fine then. Go your way. I thought I could come to this land and no one would ever need to know what I'd done, but in a way I am glad someone knows. You share a part of my burden now."

It was a burden Ned wanted no share of, and he lay awake for a second night, this time troubled not by storm outside but by conscience within. Somehow, he had to let John Guy know the truth, but what would Percy do if Ned broke his vow? Did a vow to a madman count in the eyes of God?

The king had named John Guy governor of the Cupids Cove colony, and if there was justice to be dispensed, the governor must do it. Tom Percy would have to hang. If Ned broke his vow and told Guy, he would have the weight of a man's death on his conscience.

And what if he kept the vow? Said nothing? If the man who called himself Tom Percy quarrelled with one of the other settlers and killed again, Ned would have *that* death on his conscience.

The next day, as the men tried to get back to what work they could do with the heavy snow outside, Tom Percy skulked near the edges of every group, speaking to no one but occasionally shooting dark glances at Ned. The two men passed each other that night on the path to the privy, and Percy grabbed Ned's shoulder. "You've told no one?" he said in Ned's ear.

"I have not. I gave my word." Ned wondered if Percy still had the knife on him.

"Maybe 'tis better if you do tell. So Master Guy can go ahead and hang me."

"If that's what you think, 'tis best you do it yourself," Ned said.

"You think so?" Percy looked almost eager.

"Yes. Make your confession to the governor, if you think he ought to know."

"Oh—that. No. I'll not confess again—not to any man." And with those words Tom Percy trudged back towards the dwelling-house.

Ned wished he could put the whole business from his mind and have nothing more serious to worry about than how to go to the privy in this icy cold without fearing his cock would freeze and break off in his hand.

As the final days of December melted away, so did the snow. The temperature rose, and the pure white drifts turned to a muddy slush under the men's boots as they trudged through it. Six days after Christmas, another fall of snow made everything white again, but this one came more gently, falling softly through the morning hours. The men shovelled away the snow from the palisade; work continued on the boats being built in the large workhouse they had enclosed for the purpose. Back home in England, there might be twelve days of feasting, but the colonists could ill afford so many days of celebration. Nevertheless, those charged with the task of cooking dipped into the stores for extra lard and spices to make the familiar stews and pies taste richer, and John Guy increased every man's ration of ale and spirits until Twelfth Night.

After a day's work in the new-fallen snow they ate pork pies: one of the pigs had been slaughtered just after Christmas. As the men were enjoying the meal, Master Philip struck up a carol tune and several voices joined in. Looking around the room, Ned noticed that Tom Percy was missing yet again.

He was inclined to ignore the man's absence. But Percy's secret and his own promise weighed on Ned's spirits. He still had not decided whether to tell John Guy about Percy's crime. By the time the men rolled into their sleeping bundles that night, Percy had still not reappeared, though no one but Ned seemed to have noticed.

John Guy was not yet abed; he often met with the rest of the masters for a few moments at the end of the day. Other times, he sat up writing letters. Ned waited until he saw the governor make his way back towards the sleeping quarters. Then he quietly got up, picking his way through the bodies of the other men and the sleeping animals, to intercept the governor.

"What is it, Perry?"

"You'll remember I spoke to you about Tom Percy?"

Guy's brow wrinkled. "I recall something of it, yes. You said the man was in low spirits."

"That's right sir. His troubles have seemed...worse, not better, since we began celebrating Christmas-tide. I've not seen him tonight."

"You're sure he's not here somewhere about the fire?"

"He is not, sir. I've looked."

Guy's eyes travelled up from the sleeping area around the fire to the rest of the large room. Some men had gone back to sleeping in their beds. Others, more troubled by the cold, stayed near the fire. "We will have to search for him, I suppose. Do you think he might really have gone off into the woods? Has he confided further in you?"

Ned opened his mouth to speak, then hesitated. "I...I do not know what might be in his mind, sir. He is greatly troubled. I found him alone in the storehouse one day, brooding. He might have gone there again."

Without further discussion John Guy turned towards the storehouse. Ned followed him, thinking of Percy with a knife in his hand, Percy desperate and ready to lash out. *I ought to have told Master Guy the whole truth at once,* he thought. *Better he knows that he's going to confront a murderer.*

But there was no hurry, no need to prepare for attack. When they opened the door of the storehouse they blinked for a moment, taking in the shapes that appeared in the dim glow of Guy's rushlight. John Guy moved his hand as if to cross himself in the papist way, then laid the hand on his breast instead. "God preserve us!" His voice cracked as if he were choking.

Ned remembered his last conversation with Tom Percy. *'Tis better you do it yourself.* Confess your crime to John Guy, Ned had meant. But Tom Percy had meant something else.

He had done it hours ago, from the look of the body that swayed and dangled from the storehouse rafter. Tom Percy, whatever his true name was, had found his hangman's noose.

CHAPTER FIVE

A Small Flame is Extinguished

Poor little I, that from earth have my birth,
Am but a clod, compared to the Earth.
How little now, how great shall I be then,
When I in Heaven, like to a Star shall shine?

BRISTOL
FEBRUARY — MARCH, 1611

WITH NICHOLAS GUY FAR ACROSS THE SEA, NANCY was back to sleeping in her old spot next to Kathryn. These days, with Kathryn's belly big with child, it was well-nigh impossible to sleep soundly beside her. She tossed and turned, got up half a dozen times to use the pot, snored and moaned in her sleep. Nancy found herself thinking wistfully of the narrow pallet bed where she had, for those few short months, slept alone.

"This might be the day," Kathryn said. Nancy hadn't even realized she was awake. "I hope it is. I don't know if I can go through another night like this one."

"No more can I, with your tossing and moaning."

"Just be glad 'tis I've got this beast in my belly, and not you."

"It never will be me, if I've got any say in it. Here, turn on your side and I'll rub your back a bit. I know 'tis hurting you."

"Like someone's been kicking it all night," Kathryn agreed, heaving over onto her left side. "As I suppose they have been, only from the inside not the outside."

Little feet inside, kicking at the walls of their prison. It was hard to imagine. Nancy had lived in the Gale house while all of the younger children were born, but she and Kathryn had been only children themselves. Too young, then, to be initiated into the mysteries of the birthing bed. Now, the more Nancy saw of pregnancy, the less she wanted to do with it.

Helping Kathryn dress was a fussy business these days as well. Months ago, Nancy had sewn extra panels into Kathryn's gowns and petticoats to make them roomier. Both girls had laughed while she did it, and laughed again when Kathryn first put the billowy gowns on, never imagining her belly would swell to the point where she'd need such a vast garment. But in these last weeks she found even those expanded gowns tight and uncomfortable, and Nancy had had to alter them yet again. "Everything looks terrible," Kathryn pouted when Nancy finally had the gown draped over her body. "I'm swollen up like a great ugly sow."

"Nonsense. A sow's got eight or nine farrow inside her, easy, and you've only got the one as far as we know. Here, put on this white collar—'twill draw attention to your face."

"That looks dreadful too," said Kathryn, peering in the mirror. Her cheeks were a little rounded from the extra weight she carried, but, as always, she looked anything but dreadful. Nancy was about to tell her so, but she had spent so much of her life cosseting Kathryn's vanity that the thought of doing it again suddenly made her peevish.

"Do you think you can eat now?" she said instead. "I'll bring you something if you feel you can." Sickness in the morning had made it nearly impossible for Kathryn to eat at all in the early months of her pregnancy. After she'd passed what they reckoned was the six-month mark, she had been able to eat again, but only lightly in the mornings. She was ravenous later in the evening, and Nancy often had to search the larder before bed to bring up some fruit and cheese. With Kathryn carrying Nicholas Guy's child in her belly, even Mistress Joanna dared not pass any comment about these late night meals in bed. Joanna still did not allow her sister-in-law to take any real hand in the running of the household, but now it was because she must sit and be waited on, never lift a hand, lest she do damage to the baby.

"I will try to eat something," Kathryn said with little enthusiasm. "Pass me my work bag, will you—what a cow I am, I can't even get up to cross the room and pick it up. Ugh. And I am so sick of sewing baby clothes—is that terrible of me? 'Tis not that I don't want to have a baby, or to have clothes for it—only I care not right now if I never see another tiny white shift again as long as I live."

Nancy, too, had done her fair share of sewing for the upcoming child, and she was thoroughly tired of it as well, but of course she could not say so. "You'll enjoy the change of scene today, anyway," she said, in a cajoling tone. Perhaps all the caprices and whims of childbearing women were the Almighty's way of preparing those around them to deal with the coming child. Surely no infant could be harder to appease than Kathryn herself was these days.

They were off to the Gale household after breakfast, with a trunk packed so they could stay until the child was born and a few months thereafter. Mistress Gale had wanted Kathryn to come back home last summer, as soon as her husband sailed for the New Found Land. Kathryn had refused, but only a few weeks later she had announced she was expecting a child—news she had not yet known when her husband left Bristol. Then her mother began pleading again for Kathryn to move back home.

Kathryn had agreed she would come home before the baby was due to arrive, so that she might give birth with her mother nearby and have her help for those first months of motherhood. The midwife thought the child likely to be born in March. With Candlemas gone a fortnight ago, it was high time, Nancy thought, to make the move back to the Gale household. Babies often came early, and the midwife's guess that it would be "sometime before Lady Day" was the vaguest of estimates.

So it was with relief that she stepped over the threshold of the house she had grown up in, carrying Kathryn's bag of clothes. Kathryn's brother John had come with them to carry the larger trunk, and as they came into the house, Mistress Gale bustled forward, Lily and Edward at her skirts, to collect Kathryn, while Aunt Tib came to help Nancy bring in the bundles. Behind the two women came Master Gale and the apprentices, all welcoming Kathryn home as if she were the prodigal son in the parable.

"What a sight you are for sore eyes!" Aunt Tib said to Nancy later, when Kathryn was settled up in the bedchamber with her mother and everyone else gone about their chores. Aunt Tib was laying out clothes to dry on the bushes in the yard, and Nancy fell to work beside her, glad to be doing familiar jobs in the place she had done them for so long, with no need to prove herself to supercilious strangers. "We miss yourself and the young mistress sorely about this place, let me tell you. With her and you gone, and now young Ned gone, sure 'tis like the life has gone out of the house."

The house still seemed to Nancy to have plenty of life in it—there were the three younger Gale children, Walter the journeyman, and the 'prentice boys. But she nodded and said, "No doubt we'll hear some word of Ned now, once the ships can cross. I know Mistress Kathryn is anxious for news of her husband."

John Guy's ship had left Bristol last summer, and for long months the folks back home had known nothing of their fate. Sailors newly arrived in port spread rumours of storms at sea, and everyone who had a man on board Guy's ship lived in fear that she might have sunk. Kathryn had sent a letter on a ship later in the summer telling her husband she was expecting his child, but they had no way of knowing if Nicholas Guy had received it. Finally, when the fishing vessels returned in autumn, the *Fleming* had brought back news that John Guy and his men had landed safely in the place Guy had called Cupids Cove.

Along with those tidings came, finally, some letters. One for Kathryn from her husband, which she had read out first to Nancy, then to Mistress Joanna, old Master Guy, and the rest of her husband's household, and finally to her own family back home. It said that the cooler weather of autumn found them all hard at work on a storehouse and dwelling-house for the winter, that their supplies were good, and that he missed his wife greatly. He spoke in grand terms of the beauty of the land and how abundant all its resources were.

Anyone could see that Nicholas Guy was laying the ground to ask, when he was able to write again in spring, if she would consider coming out there. For surely, if it was meant to be a permanent settlement, the very next thing would be to get the wives and maidservants to cross the sea. But Kathryn persisted in believing that an up-and-coming young craftsman with a good Bristol business, such as Nicholas Guy had, would not choose to stay permanently in the colonies. "Once he's lived through a winter there, surely he'll want to return home," Nancy said now, hashing it all out again with Aunt Tib.

"I'd say our Ned is wondering what he's got himself into," Aunt Tib said.

"That's who will never come back—fellows like Ned," Nancy said. "Rich merchants like Master John and Philip Guy can cross the oceans—sure, they can sail over and back as often as they want, supposing only they're not lost at sea. But I'd allow we'll never see Ned Perry on this side of the sea again. He'll live out his days in that Cupids Cove place."

"Well, that's a shame, a fine young man like that," Aunt Tib said. "Master Gale thought he had the makings of a good stonemason."

Nancy laughed. "'Tis not as if he's dead over there! He may never finish his apprenticeship, but I'm sure he can do a stonemason's work in the colony as well as here in Bristol."

"Oh, I suppose, but—'tis no life, is it? Savages and wild beasts, no town and no people about—what kind of life would that be for a fine fellow like our Ned, who always liked company and a good laugh?"

"Ned will do fine." Nancy could not really imagine the kind of life he must be living in that strange land, but Ned Perry had always seemed to her like the cat that would land on its feet no matter how far it fell. Nancy was concerned with more practical thoughts. She sorted through all Kathryn's baby clothes, helped wash the cradle and its linens, which had been sitting unused since Edward was a baby. All that in addition to caring for Kathryn herself, who grew harder to please as the days passed.

"'Twas wrong of him," Kathryn said clearly in the middle of one night, when Nancy was almost asleep and thought Kathryn had been so long since.

"What? What was wrong? Who?"

"Nicholas. My husband."

"Wrong of him to go away?"

"To leave me, yes. Me and his child."

"He didn't know the child was on the way, when he left."

"He knew there was a chance. Any time after we were married, I might have been carrying his child."

"By that reckoning, he should never have gone away. He would have had to stay in Bristol forever, on the off-chance you might be with child."

"Don't be unkind, Nan. Once we'd had a babe, our first, then, very well. He could go out to the colonies if he had to. But I don't want a husband who is far from home when our first child is born."

"And you've no wish to go out to the colony with him?"

Nancy expected an instant response. She was surprised at the little well of silence. "You wouldn't, would you?" she pressed. "Any woman would have to be mad to go out there."

"I'd not *wish* to," Kathryn said. "But what if...what if he says he wants to stay out there? What if Master John goes away and names my Nicholas the governor in his place? How could a man who wants to advance himself turn down a chance like that?"

Now Nancy was silent. She had always believed that Kathryn found the idea of the New Found Land as mad as she herself did—a foolish venture that had lured good Bristol men away from their homes. "So... if he were to stay, and ask you to come out with him, you would go?"

"I would have to consider it, at least. He is my husband, after all. *Whither thou goest, I will go,* as Scripture says."

"Ruth said that to her mother-in-law, not to her husband," said Nancy, who knew the story and liked it. Ruth the outsider, the foreign woman taken into the fold of Israel.

"Well, perhaps she did, but 'tis all in the marriage vows, and I've made those, so I would have to go if he insisted."

"Most women would not. Plenty of men go over to the colonies and their wives stay behind in England."

Kathryn sighed. "I'm tired. I need to sleep, only I can't find any position that doesn't make my back ache. Rub it for me again, will you? And don't worry about us being dragged off to Cupids Cove. 'Twill never happen. Master Nicholas will come home and see his son, and we will all be together. The only thing that keeps my spirits up is seeing it all in my mind like a painting—myself with the babe, and my husband by our side—and then he will never want to go over the sea again."

Nancy drifted off to sleep feeling that conversation had gone oddly wrong: it ought to have been she who was comforting Kathryn, reassuring her that Nicholas would come back. Instead, it had somehow become Kathryn's job to reassure Nancy.

She was woken by hysterical sobbing. "Nancy! Nan! Get up, help me! Something's amiss with the baby!"

Nancy woke to see Kathryn sitting up in the bed. From the adjoining chamber, Mistress Gale was already out of bed, rushing to her daughter's side. The sheets were wet all around Kathryn, but as near as Nancy could tell in the faint glow of moonlight through the shutters, they were not bloody. The midwife had said that, when a woman's time was near, something called the "bag of waters" in her womb would burst, and it might seem as if she had pissed the bed. "Nothing is wrong," she soothed Kathryn. "All is well; I think the babe is on his way."

When Kathryn's mother pulled aside the bed curtains, she confirmed Nancy's guess and sent her husband for the midwife. Aunt Tib came upstairs and bundled the younger children, who were still half-asleep, down to finish the night by the fire. She sent Nancy for clean linen and warm water.

"'Twill be an easy birth, I allow," Aunt Tibby said as Nancy returned with the linens. "She's built for birthing, our young miss. Good broad hips and all."

"She's built like me," Mistress Gale said, "but I can't say I had an easy time of it—you remember, don't you, Tibby? When I bore our Kathryn, how the midwife near lost both of us? And the little boy after that, the one who died in the womb?"

Nancy looked up sharply at her mistress's mother. She knew of Mistress Gale's trouble in childbearing—Kathryn's difficult birth, and the dead baby that followed a year later. Not to mention the two little ones who died before they were a year old. But these were no fit stories to recount at her daughter's lying-in.

"Have you a draught made up, to ease her pains once they start to come?" Nancy asked. That was enough to distract Mistress Gale, who was very proud of her store of herbs and simples, and had things in the storeroom even the midwife could not boast of. She went off downstairs to see what she had to offer her daughter.

"Are you in pain, love? Feeling the birth pangs yet?" Nancy asked, rubbing Kathryn's back as she had done so many times these last few months. Beside her, Aunt Tib, who was a great one for charms and blessings, muttered something under her breath. Nancy put little faith in charms, but anything that might ease Kathryn's labours could not hurt.

"No, nothing yet. It is too soon for the birth pains, if the waters have only just broken, isn't it?"

Aunt Tib broke off her incantation to say, "I've heard tell—," but was interrupted by the midwife, Granny Hayward, coming up the stairs.

"Pains can start before the waters break, or afterwards, or during— there's no rule to it at all," Granny Hayward said. "I've known a mother be labouring half a day and finally have to reach in and break the caul myself. But if 'tis broken already, that's a good start. Now, lay back and let me have a look at you, young mistress."

The other women withdrew while the midwife performed her examination, putting her hand right up into Kathryn's privy parts as if she could haul the baby out of there. But when Nancy moved towards the stairs, thinking she might help Mistress Gale with the brewing of a healing draught, Kathryn called out, "Stay by me, Nan!"

The midwife looked up. "If she wants her maid by her, then you ought to stay, girl."

Nancy went back to sit beside the bed. "Stay by me, keep rubbing my back or at least hold my hand," Kathryn insisted.

She regretted her promise to stay by Kat's side before the day was over. She would have done anything to flee that room, to be far away from the smell of blood and Kathryn's moans and screams as the pains rolled over her body.

At first, the midwife was pleased at how things were going. The waters had broken, the pains begun and had come about the right time apart. "Will it all be well?" Mistress Gale asked, fluttering around in the background with a posset in a mug of ale. "Is the baby strong and well? Will she be all right?"

"Only God can say, Mistress," said the midwife, but she hummed and smiled as she wrung out the cloths and handed them to Nancy to wipe Kathryn's sweating brow.

Nancy could feel the moment the midwife's mood changed. The older woman's brow furrowed as she ran her hands over the great mound of Kathryn's belly. "The babe should be moving down now. I'm going to rub her belly, try to force him down. He's loath to come out, needs a bit of coaxing."

"Ooohhhhh!" A moan burst out of Kathryn's lips. "Make it stop! Tear this thing out of me! I can't do this! I don't want to!"

"Well, you've little choice about that, my love," said her mother, coming to the other side of the bed to help cradle her daughter. "There's no going back. When I was having our Lily, now..."

"What is it?" Nancy asked as she heard the midwife take in a little gasp of air. "Is something wrong?"

It was a long time before the midwife would say it out loud, hours of Kathryn groaning and screaming and even cursing—curses Nancy wouldn't have even thought her young mistress knew, much less would speak in front of her mother. Nancy tried to keep her eyes on Kathryn's tear-stained, weary face, her mat of tangled dark hair—anything to avoid the terrifying sight of the midwife with her hand up between Kathryn's legs, reaching in, coming away bloody up to the wrist.

Granny Hayward sent Tibby down to the kitchen, rhyming off a list of instructions for a simple to make that sometimes hastened the birth. "Mugwort, motherwort, mint," Tibby recited under her breath, mixing the words with what sounded like another charm. She lacked Mistress Gale's gift for brewing remedies; even Nancy was better at it, but neither Mistress Gale nor Nancy would leave Kathryn's side.

"There's mugwort and motherwort on the shelf above the preserves, and mint in a pot lower down," Mistress Gale said, and Aunt Tib came back half an hour later with another posset that Nancy held to Kathryn's lips. Kathryn gagged over and over but finally choked some down, then threw up all over herself within a few minutes.

"She's been pushing for hours," Mistress Gale said. "How can the baby live through this?" Granny Hayward looked up and met Mistress Gale's eyes, and that was when Nancy understood that the baby's survival was no longer what the midwife was fighting for.

All day, all night. Whenever Nancy thought those nightmare hours had to end, time doubled back, twisted upon itself. It had been predawn darkness when Kathryn first woke, then daylight had flooded the room, and then it was dark. Now the sky was lightening again: a full day, almost.

Mistress Gale was crying, praying under her breath. "Merciful God, spare my poor baby, my poor girl. Your own virgin mother went through this, Lord. Have mercy, have mercy."

Kathryn's face was white. *She could die*, Nancy allowed herself to think for the first time. She had bled so much, laboured so hard, and all for nothing.

But Kathryn did not die. Weak, exhausted, pale, she had given up trying to birth the child, but her body had not. In the end, it seemed to have little to do with her—she had gone beyond anything but cries of pain, no longer answering her mother or Nancy, only whimpering in between the spasms. The midwife almost seemed to pull the slimy white thing out of her, when it came. It was no longer a triumphant burst of energy, bringing a child into the world, but the last exhausted writhing that expelled something no longer wanted, no longer needed.

"There, there, it's done. You're done. It's all over, you can rest." Mistress Gale leaned Kathryn back onto the pillows. Looking at the still white bundle as the midwife wrapped it to take away, Nancy hoped Kathryn was unconscious. But her eyelids fluttered, and it was at Nancy, not at her mother, that she looked when she said, "What... what was it? The babe...was it...?"

"Hush now. Hush. All will be—you will be well," Nancy said, and prayed Kathryn would not ask again.

"But the baby...?"

"Do not fret about the babe, now. You need to sleep. You've had a long, hard day."

Her eyelashes fell shut again, and she seemed to have fallen asleep. The other women all breathed sighs of relief. "Show it to me," Mistress Gale said to Granny Hayward. "Before you take it away, let me see it."

"Best not to, Mistress."

"No, I want to see. 'Tis better to know—that would have been my grandchild, if it had been born live. Kathryn need not see it, but I must."

"Very well then, come here, Mistress."

Nancy had no desire to see the thing that was supposed to have been Kathryn's baby. She sat by Kathryn's side, stroking her hair, trying to piece together the words to tell her about the baby. She sat there and waited, while Aunt Tibby came back to clean the room and change the sheets, and came back again with trays of food, while Mistress Gale paid the midwife and wiped away her own tears, while the midwife took away the blanket-wrapped bundle.

The room was restored to order. While she slept, Kathryn was washed and changed; she stirred and moaned but did not wake. After a time everyone had gone, even Mistress Gale, to see to things down in the hall. No one was left in the sleeping chamber but Nancy, sitting beside her sleeping mistress.

When Kathryn woke again she stretched and yawned like a kitten, and looked, for a moment, like her old self. Nancy had the wild thought that she might not remember, that the whole agony of childbirth might have been erased from her mind. They might go back to the time before, when none of this had happened.

Instead, Kathryn said, in a voice as clear as St. Stephen's bell, "Where is my babe? Is it a boy or a girl?"

"It was—" Nancy realized she did not know. "The child did not live. I'm sorry. I'm so sorry, Kat."

Kathryn gave a strangled little gasp, then was silent. After a moment, in a small, choked voice, she said, "Was it—can I see?"

"The midwife took it away. Your mother can tell you more; she looked on the babe, she'll know if it was a boy or a girl. Shall I go get her?"

"In—in a minute." Kathryn closed her eyes again. "It hurt so much—so much, Nan! And all for nothing. Oh God, for nothing."

CHAPTER SIX

The Winter is Ended and Spring Has Come

Wise men, wise Sir, do not the fire abhor,
For once being singed, more wary grow therefore.
Shall one disaster breed in you a terror?
With honest, meet, wise men mend your first error.

CUPIDS COVE
APRIL 1611

IN BRISTOL, NANCY SAT BY KATHRYN'S BEDSIDE. AN OCEAN away, Ned Perry also sat by a bedside, watching a sick boy burn with fever.

"Fortune has smiled upon us here," Governor John Guy was fond of saying. "The poor wretches out in Virginia—half of them were dead of disease or starvation after the first year. And look at us, men—look how well we have come through. God has blessed us, and the worst of the winter is over now."

He had said it in February, when John Morris succumbed to the fever and ravings he had suffered ever since he was wounded. He said it again in March when James Stone died after weeks abed, unable to walk on his sore and swollen legs. Governor Guy had urged Stone to get up, move about, even when the man protested he could not. When he was found dead in bed one cold morning, Guy had insisted the man had brought it upon himself—sheer laziness, till his limbs became paralyzed and his heart ceased to beat.

Three deaths, then, over the winter: Tom Percy, whose guilt had driven him to self-murder; then Morris and Stone whose illnesses had lingered since autumn. But the food held out; there was no outbreak of plague; the dead were buried in a clearing a little away from the dwelling-house and the living held on, hoping spring would come soon.

Then Marmaduke Whittington, the youngest of them, fell ill. George argued with Governor Guy, insisting his brother's ration of food and ale be increased. "He only wants building up! Trying to get by on short rations has taken the good out of him!"

"He was ever too frail to have come out to the colony," Governor Guy said. "We were lucky we all 'scaped getting the smallpox when he had it aboard ship, but 'tis clear he never recovered fully."

"If anything happens to Duke, I'll blame myself for bringing him out here," George told Ned, once Governor Guy had gone back to work. "He was never strong, and when he fell sick on the boat I should have known this life would be too hard for him. I thought I could look after him."

"And you are doing," Ned assured him. He liked the gentle, soft-spoken Duke far better than his braggart elder brother, but he felt some pity now for George. "Look here, today is my day for kitchen duty—I'll keep an eye to him while I work. You can go on down to work at the boatbuilding."

The governor was determined to keep the men busy over the winter months, even when there was no planting or fishing to do. Idleness was deadly, and so apart from the round of domestic tasks that included feeding the animals and themselves, everyone took turns in the enclosed work space, building the barque that Governor Guy hoped to launch in the spring to explore the coast, as well as some smaller boats for fishing. Most of the men knew nothing of shipbuilding, but they learned by doing, and Ned found he enjoyed learning this new skill.

But for now he was scrubbing out pots, baking bread, and roasting several small wildfowls on a spit over the hearth for the next meal. Those duties left a little time for him to look to Duke, who tossed and turned in his narrow bed, crying out in his sleep but never fully waking. For five days now, the lad had had a fever that seemed impossible to break. The surgeon had bled him yesterday, but his condition had not improved.

The men came back in from their various tasks around the site late in the afternoon and gathered for the main meal of the day. "Tough little birds, these are," Matt Grigg said, gnawing at a leg of one of the fowl. "Or mayhap 'tis only that Perry here is no cook."

"I did the best I could with them—tended them all day as if I were the mother hen herself," Ned said. "These wild ducks are on the wing all the time, not like barnyard chickens. They've no time to grow plump."

"Between Tipton shooting them and you cooking them, we're lucky enough to have fresh meat at all," said Nicholas Guy, and other voices chimed in agreement. They were all heartily sick of the salted fish that had been preserved back in the autumn, and there were too few of their own livestock to slaughter for any but the most special occasions. Anytime wild game was hunted or snared, it proved a welcome addition to the men's diets. Throughout the winter they had trapped small animals, both for furs to sell back in England and for meat to feed themselves. They had hunted, too, for larger game, including a huge antlered stag, bigger and stranger than any deer they had ever seen in England. It would have made good eating if they had been able to shoot it, but even with the help of their eager hunting dog, the hunters had had no luck in bringing it down.

In the middle of March they had seen seals on the harbour ice offshore. Going out onto the ice after them was a risky business and Ned was glad to be one of those who stayed on shore, skinning and gutting the beasts as the more daring men brought them in. The strong-tasting, fishy flesh had been grand while it lasted, but the seal meat was all gone now.

"Truth be told, I am growing proud of my cookery," Ned said now. He had rarely done more than put his own bread and meat on a trencher back home, but along with several of the other men in the colony he had now learned to bake bread, roast and stew various meats, as well as cook the ever-present pottage that fueled every morning's work. "If I were back in England, I could give up stonemasonry and take a post as a cook at some big house."

"Nay, I'd not give up masonry if I were you—I could repair yon wall out there with this bread," Jem Holworthy said, gnawing away at a hunk. When Ned pretended to throw a crust at him, Jem cowered in mock fear.

"Outside of the big houses, cooking be housewives' work," Frank Tipton said, "and 'twill be a good thing, Governor, when you bring us over some women to do it."

A chorus of voices joined in, wanting to know when the long-promised women would arrive. "I have made plans to return to Bristol in the summer," the governor announced. "I expect to be there over next winter, raising more funds and supplies, but also recruiting new colonists to join us the following year. And yes, there will be women among them, I do promise you that."

"But that's another year to wait!" grumbled Tipton, and several other voices around the hearth took up his complaint.

"Can you bring my missus?" Sam Butler asked, and another man said, "Can you leave mine behind, and bring the tavern keeper's wife from over the road instead?" Much laughter and bawdy talk, as well as a few sincere requests. Matthew Grigg had been betrothed to marry a girl back in Bristol, a dairymaid on one of the big estates, who had agreed she would come and join him in the New World if the prospects seemed favourable. "I will find her," John Guy promised Grigg, "when I am back in England, and if she be still willing, I'll bring her over. Perchance she has friends who would make the journey—a few comely dairymaids would not go astray among the unmarried men here, I am sure."

"She has two sisters, sir, as pretty as herself," Grigg assured him. "If neither of them is married or promised yet, they might all come. The fellows can have their pick of the other two as long as I can have my Daisy."

"And for the married men among you," Nicholas Guy put in, raising his voice above the murmurs of the men, "if your wives wish to come out—and if you want them—the governor will provide passage for any of them, and your children as well, to join you here. My own wife has, God willing, given birth to our child a few months past. I may not be the only one here who has a child he has never yet seen, but I hope they will join us next year, and my son will take his first steps here on the soil of the New World."

Ned was struck by a sudden picture of Nicholas Guy standing on the wharf here in Cupids Cove, greeting Kathryn with a small child at her hip. It could happen within a year—she could be here, walking on these stony paths, taking her meals at the cooking-fire. She would once again be as close, and as inaccessible to Ned, as she had been all the years he worked in her father's house.

"God's teeth, will all of you cease your clatter!" George Whittington's voice came sharply from the hatch that led up to the sleeping quarters. "We've a sick man here, in case you've all forgotten."

Governor Guy frowned and looked about to speak, but his brother Philip interrupted. "Is there any improvement to his condition, Whittington?"

"I see none." George came down the ladder and joined the men by the fire. "The fever rages as ever."

"I might try bleeding him again," offered Reynolds, "but I do not know if he be strong enough to stand it."

George shook his head and fixed his gaze on the governor. "When you go back to England, Master, are any of us who want to leave this place free to go with you? We're not indentured servants, to be bound over for a term of years, are we? I never signed no such articles when I came over."

"Now, steady lad," William Colston said. "We know you're concerned for your brother—"

"Damned right I am concerned, and if he survives this fever I mean to take him back to England. This country's too harsh for a lad in delicate health. Are we bringing folks over, only to die here?"

"That is hardly fair, Whittington," said Governor Guy. He had been sitting on a bench alongside the other men, but now he stood up. "You men all came of your own free will, and anyone who wishes to return may sail back when I do. Indeed, I mean to send back any who have proved unprofitable, not fit for this life."

"Unprofitable! You'd dare shame my brother for falling ill, and me for tending to him?" Whittington lunged forward at the same moment as Ned moved to one side and Matt Grigg to the other. Each grabbed an arm to restrain him.

"Do I need to remind you who is governor of this colony, Whittington?" Governor Guy asked. After a moment's silence, George said, "No, sir. That you do not," in a voice as cold and hard as iron. Shaking loose the grip of the men on either arm, he turned back towards the sleeping loft.

"What insolence, sirrah!" fumed the governor after George's retreating back, and lifted his hand as if he were about to order him to return. But this time it was he who was restrained, by Master Philip.

"Let the lad go, John. He is sore afeared for his brother's life and would not have spoken so if he were not deeply troubled."

"I doubt that," Governor Guy said, subsiding back onto the bench. "He has ever been too pert and forward for a man of his station. But now is not the time to call him to account."

The brief encounter broke up the easy mood that the men had enjoyed by the hearth, and they began moving away in twos and threes to prepare their evening tasks and make ready for sleep as the late-winter sunset drew on. In his own bed, a few hours later, Ned tried to banish thoughts of Kathryn Gale—or Kathryn Guy, as she now was. It was hard to imagine her here. She was a creature of Bristol, of streets and shops, of that civilized world they had all left behind. But so were all women—pretty girls like Kathryn, and hard-working maids like her girl Nancy, plump motherly housewives like Mistress Gale and his own mother. In a land where no Englishwoman had ever set foot, it was hard to picture one as part of the landscape.

Ned tried the experiment as he fell into a fitful sleep: Kathryn weeding the young plants in the garden at Cupids Cove. His sisters feeding the chickens. Tibby ladling up stew around the fire. But the only picture that came really clear in his head was Nancy Ellis, her auburn hair tucked up sensibly under her coif, scrubbing out washing on the rocks by the stream as he himself had been doing a few days ago. His imagination moved seamlessly into dream; he was crossing the stream on rocks as she squatted there on the bank, scrubbing away like a washerwoman. "Watch your step, Ned Perry," she called to him. "Lose your footing and you'll be swept downstream and out to sea."

"I've survived worse," he told her in his dream, jumping from the last stepping stone to the bank. "I've lived a winter in this place. I'm tougher than you think."

"So am I," she said, and stood up to face him, her eyes nearly level with his. Then she leaned forward, brazen as a whore, and kissed him full on the lips, and he gathered her into his arms. She was not soft and yielding like her mistress, whom he'd kissed and tumbled in many a dream before. She was taught as a bowstring, vibrating with energy and passion. In the heat of their kiss she bit his lip and he tasted blood, and he was wild to have her out of her clothes and beneath him on the riverbank.

He awoke suddenly, his cock standing at attention, the snores of the other men filling the chilly air around him. Blinking in surprise at his own dream, Ned got up and quietly made his way outside in the darkness to take a piss. While they waited for women to arrive, men were bound to have dreams.

The night was bitterly cold; there were hours still till dawn. Ned hitched up his breeches and laced them again, and went back into the dwelling-house. With the fire smoored for the night, it was scarcely warmer inside than out.

Instead of returning to his own bed, he stopped to see Marmaduke and found George pressing a damp cloth to his brother's brow. "The fever's not broke, then?" Ned asked.

"He's no better. Mayhap a bit worse. I cannot tell."

"You're exhausted. Go to your own bed and get some rest. I'll sit by him—I'll not leave him alone."

Protesting, George stumbled off to his bed. Ned, still stirred and troubled by his dream, did not find it hard to stay awake, though it was hard to watch the boy shift and turn on his mattress, to hear him murmur in pain. He was relieved when the murmurs subsided and the troubled breathing stilled. It took him perhaps a quarter of an hour to realize that the stillness was too deep.

He pressed his hand against Duke's brow. Cooling, cooling at last. He ought to wake George, or perhaps the surgeon. But no, what good could any of them do now? His vigil continued; now it was a death-watch, till morning lightened the skies.

When Ned told him, George knelt by the body, stricken into unaccustomed silence. "I should never have brought him," he said at last. "And if that fool John Guy dares to say how well we are doing with only four men dead, I swear I'll strike him, Ned—governor or no, I will."

"Hush now, hush," Ned cautioned, as others began to gather by the bed. But even as the news spread through the chilly gray dawn, a shout went up from outside. "A ship! A ship!"

Poor Marmaduke Whittington: his death would be only the second most important thing to happen this day in Cupids Cove. For a ship was coming into the harbour, and if it were a Bristol ship it would bring supplies and letters from home. Spring had come, and the outside world had found them again.

CHAPTER SEVEN

A Letter is Read

*Sweet Creatures, did you truly understand
The pleasant life you'd live in New-found-land,
You would with tears desire to be brought thither.
I wish you, when you go, fair wind, fair weather.*

BRISTOL
AUTUMN 1611

"

NOW, THIS MIGHT ONLY BE GOSSIP, BUT I'VE HEARD there's good bread flour for sale at today's market, and if 'tis at any price we can afford, I intend to have it. You're the quickest on your feet, Nancy, so you take yourself to market and see if there's any to be found," Mistress Gale instructed, counting out coins. "Tibby, you and I will stay here and see to the wash. Perhaps you can convince Kathryn to go to the market with you, Nancy?"

"If you want me to be quick, I'll be faster going and coming on my own," Nancy said, and Mistress Gale nodded. She was always looking for ways to get her daughter out of the house, to rouse Kathryn from the low spirits that had gripped her ever since the loss of her child. But the possibility of being able to procure flour at the market took precedence even over the hope of Kathryn's recovery. With last year's drought continuing into this summer, harvests had been poor all around, and when any sort of flour was available, the prices were high and supplies quickly gone. Stews and jellies had become the preferred meals, with bread, cakes, and pastries reserved for those times when flour could be obtained.

"I feel sure if only I could make her some nice wheaten bread, it would tempt her appetite—it always used to do, when she was a little girl," Mistress Gale was saying to Aunt Tibby as Nancy left the house.

In Nancy's opinion, all the manchet bread in the world would not tempt Kathryn, for what ailed her could not be cured either with the most nourishing of food or the most cunning of possets. Her mother had tried plenty of those, too, and in the process of helping her prepare them Nancy had added a good deal to her own knowledge of herbals and medicines. Red sage and vinegar had worked to dry up Kathryn's milk, and poultice of violet leaves had eased the pain in her sore breasts, but the acedia and melancholy that weighed her down would not be cured by anything in her mother's chest of herbs and remedies. She was not a mother as she had expected to be; she was not a wife in any real sense while Master Nicholas was so far away; she was not mistress of his house nor did she manage his business.

Instead of returning to her husband's house, Kathryn had languished in her parents' house for the last several months. As spring had turned to summer and now summer to autumn, there had been no lifting of her mood. The only advice anyone could offer a woman who had lost a babe was to try for another, and there was no chance of that in Kathryn's case.

In July a ship had come into port with word of the colony. It carried a letter from Governor Guy listing the names of the men still with him— two or three had died over the winter, but no one Nancy knew—and saying that all these men sent greetings to their families. So Kathryn knew her husband had been alive and well in the early spring when the letter was written.

Nancy enjoyed the walk in the warm air and the chance to be free of her mistress's oppressive sadness. She was thwarted in her search for wheat flour, but she did find a little rye flour. Despite the shortages, there was still plenty of buying and selling going on in the busy stalls huddled near the High Cross. All around, housewives complained about the food they could not buy. It had recently rained for the first time in months, but it was October now, and the rain had come far too late to save this season's crops. It would be a long, hungry winter, especially for the poor. Already there seemed to be twice the usual number of beggars on the streets.

At the fishmonger's stall she met Jenny Piper, who was a trifle more courteous to her now that they were no longer living under the same roof. Jenny reported that Mistress Joanna was well, but old Master Guy was rheumy and tired easily. They, too, were eager for news from Master Nicholas.

Nancy parted company with Jenny and walked home by way of Broad Quay before returning to the house. She often went by the docks when she was out, hoping to see a ship that might have news from John Guy's colony. This day she was rewarded: a fishing vessel just back in port had brought word that a ship out of the New Found Land was coming not far behind them, with John Guy himself on board.

She hurried home to bring the news, first to Mistress Gale and Aunt Tib in the kitchen, then to Kathryn. "I got a little rye, and some lovely Somerset cheese, and there's going to be codfish for our dinner, but best of all, John Guy is on his way home! The word on the docks is that he may be back in port within a week."

Kathryn lifted dull eyes from her needlework. Her contribution to the household these long months had been to take over the sewing and mending, which she could do without having to be up and about much. "Do you think Nicholas will be with him?" she asked, something like hope brightening her face for a moment.

"There's no way to tell who might or might not come with him," Nancy said. "At least, for sure, he will bring letters and a bit more news than he sent in the spring."

When the *Comfort* docked in Bristol with John Guy and a handful of other colonists aboard, there was no sign of Nicholas Guy, but there were, as promised, letters. Though the governor's time was much taken up meeting with his company of merchants, he sent word that he had a letter for Nicholas Guy's wife, and wished to deliver it by his own hand.

So it was that John Guy, governor of the New Found Land colony, came to the house of John Gale the stonemason, and was seated in the best chair in the house, next to the hearth. "Your husband sends his kindest greetings, mistress," the governor said, and drew out a letter that Kathryn reached for hungrily, but did not open. Nancy waited by the hearth along with Mistress Gale; Tibby had taken the younger children out with her to get eggs from the farmer's stall, so as to allow for some peace and quiet in the house.

"How fares my husband? Is he well?"

"He is very well—or at least, he was when I left the colony a few weeks ago. Hard at work in tending crops and building boats. He has not had much occasion to pursue a shoemaker's trade in Cupids Cove, but you would be surprised how skilled your husband has become at boatbuilding. We have all had to learn many new skills—a man must be a bit of a jack-of-all-trades to survive in the New World."

"It is hard to imagine," Kathryn said, "but he knew he would not be making ladies' fine leather shoes over there."

"Still, his skills come in handy for such things as repairing boots and sewing up bags and such—we make do with everything, for until we send a ship back with more supplies, the colonists must get by on what they have."

"And when will such a ship go back? Can I write a letter in reply to this?" Kathryn looked almost eager.

John Guy frowned. "I hope that another ship will make the journey soon, and you may certainly write a letter to send on it. I myself will spend the winter here in England, raising further money for the colony. When I return next year, I hope to carry more than letters." He let the comment hang in the air, as if daring Kathryn to ask what else he intended to take.

"You mean to bring over more colonists?"

"I do indeed. Thirty-five men cannot people the New World by themselves. When I come back I will bring cattle, and more working men, but the most important thing I will bring is womenfolk. Without women, there can be no permanent settlement."

"Well, that is certainly true enough," Kathryn said with a tiny flare of her old spirit. "God did not put two men in the Garden of Eden, despite how much work he could have got from them. But will you find women willing to make such a treacherous journey?"

The room grew quiet. Mistress Gale let out a stifled gasp, and Nancy reached out to put a hand on the older woman's arm. After a moment John Guy said, "I'm sure there will be some young women of the servant class willing to try such an adventure, who will come out and marry our labourers and apprentices. But it is our great hope that some of the wives of the men who are already settled there will choose to join their husbands also."

Kathryn looked down at the unopened letter in her hand. "You think that...that women such as I should go out there?"

"It is very much our hope—not mine only, but the hope of many of the married men there—that their wives will do so."

Kathryn lifted her eyes. "Will your own wife go to Cupids Cove, Master Guy?"

John Guy cleared his throat. "Well, now. My Anne would be reluctant to undertake such a journey. We have young children, you know, of an age where their health and safety is most precarious. And of course, I have substantial business holdings here, that she must manage for me in my absence. Philip is hoping to persuade his wife Elizabeth to come back to the colony with him. We are thinking of...of young couples like yourself and my cousin Nicholas, who might begin their families in the New World."

"It is a terrible thing to ask of a woman!" Mistress Gale could keep silent no longer; the words burst out of her. But even as Kathryn said, "Mother—" in a tone of warning, John Guy cut her off.

"I know it is." He looked from daughter to mother and back again; his eyes slid past Nancy, presumably not even registering the presence of a servant. "It is a great deal to ask, and any of the women who do make the journey will have to have great courage. This past winter has not been easy, even for the menfolk; still less easy will winters be for the women who will come. But come they must, if England is to have a colony there."

Kathryn played with the letter, turning it over and over in her hands. "My husband meant to keep his home and business and wife here in Bristol, even as you are doing, and return after a season in the New World. 'Twas never intended to be a permanent move."

"But it must be permanent, if we are to have an English colony. And the women—not just servant girls—" here his eyes flickered, for the first time, in Nancy's direction, "but respectable married women, guildsmen's wives, must come with their husbands. I know women are unlike men; they are bred for home and hearth, not for the open seas and adventure. But in these times, when we are creating a whole New World across the sea, there must be women who are willing to move to new homes and new hearths." He stirred in his seat. "Mistress, I must excuse myself. I have meetings to attend and many people to visit. Read your husband's letter, and think over what I have said."

When John Guy was gone, Kathryn looked at her mother and Nancy. The letter still lay unopened in her lap. "Mother, can you leave me to myself to read this letter? I will read it to you afterwards, I promise—but leave me with just Nancy here while I look it over for the first time."

As Mistress Gale left and Nancy sat down on the bench, Kathryn broke the letter's seal. "Is it possible Governor John is entirely wrong about what is in this letter? I hoped Master Nicholas would send word he was coming home—even if not till next summer. But this...Nan, it seems as if he is talking about a lifetime."

"Read the letter. His words may be quite different from what his cousin represents."

Kathryn pulled out the letter and stared at it for a long time before starting to read aloud:

My deare Wife, I take my Quill in Hand on this, the first day of September, to write you this letter. Inclos'd with it you will find some letters I writ before, so that you will heare a little more of the storey of our Dayes here in Cupids Cove. I Praye you read thru them at your Leisuire for I would have you knowe the Truth of what it is like to live here, in my most fervent Hopes that when my cousin retournes again, you will come with him.

At present all the Men heere live in two large Dwelling-houses, and it is our Intention next year to begin upon the building of another House, so that when our Numbers have been swelt by the arrival of our Wives and sundry others, we will have places for all.

You will see in my earlier Letters, my great Grief And Sorrowe at the newes that our Childe was lost to you, and that I could not bee there to comfort you. Yett I have great Hopes our next Childe will be a son or daughter of the New Found Land, and that we will bee together again. For I have found this Land so riche and good, and so great the Opportunitys here, that I am minded to try it awhile longer, to see what Fortune can be made.

I finish this Letter with greetings to all my Household, and to my Sister and Father, and also to your Father and Mother and all in their Household. They will be Angrey, I know, at my plan to Steale their dearest Treasure, yet they should be Proude to have such a Daughter, that might be the Mother of a new English family in a New Land. To the household in your Father's house please send allso the greetings of his former Apprentyce, Ned Perry, who does well for himself here in Cupids Cove and wishes to be Remember'd to all at home in Bristol. He bade me say in especial a greeting to your dear Nancy, and to tell her the New Found Lande has need of Women with a sharp Tongue and witty Spirite such as her's.

And I will say the same for you, my good Wife, leaving aside the part of the Sharpe Tongue, for yours is not. But I dare say your spirit is as strong as Any, and would be a greate boone not only to Mee, but to all this colony.

Your loving Husbande,
Nicholas Guy

It took some time to read it. Kathryn had learned her letters at petty school when she was a child, and could even write a little, but she was no scholar. In the silence that followed, Nancy said, "So he truly means to stay over there."

"So it seems."

Nancy pulled her hand from Kathryn's and put an arm around her shoulders. Kathryn relaxed into her embrace, and after a few moments, Nancy felt her shoulders shake with sobs. Had it really been less than two years ago that they had sat in St. Stephen's church watching

Kathryn exchange vows with Nicholas Guy, her future laid out rosy and secure? How quickly everything had fallen apart. What became of a woman whose husband had crossed the ocean to a new country and did not return for years? She was not a widow, could not marry again. She was, quite simply, an abandoned wife.

The two women sat in silence for a long time. They were interrupted at last by the arrival home of the rest of the family. Kathryn excused herself and went up to the sleeping chamber with the rest of her husband's letters, meaning to read through them before nightfall.

She had finished them by the time Nancy brought her up a bowl of eel stew that the rest of the family had had for supper. "What else does he say?" Nancy asked.

"Much, and little. He does his best to make it sound as if it were a place I could be content."

"So, what will you do now?" *Stay here in my father's house*, Nancy hoped she would say. Though what she really wanted was the impossible: *Turn back the clock.* Go back to the way things had been before her marriage, before the child, before anyone thought of going to the New World. Make a different match, with a man who would not leave Bristol.

Kathryn sighed. "I suppose I will have to consider how it might be done. What will be involved in preparing. Governor John says he will not leave till next spring, so there will be plenty of time to plan."

Nancy stared at her, the meaning of her words taking a moment to sink in. "You mean...you are considering going over there?"

"Marry, what else can I do?"

A thousand things, Nancy wanted to say. "You could go back to his house, keep his household until he comes to his senses and returns. If he ever does. You could stay here with your parents, if you preferred."

"To what end? If he does not come back, what life is there for me here?"

"But—to go to the ends of the earth, to live where no English woman has ever lived? You said yourself, you cannot bear a child in a place without midwives or doctors. 'Tis all madness!"

"It is, for certain. But it is a madness to which my husband seems to have pledged his life. And as I am pledged to him, what else can I do but join him?" Kathryn had been staring down at her bowl as she picked at her food. Now she looked up. "I would dare to hope I would not go alone. You and I did vow to each other that we would never be apart. And that vow is as true to me as my vow to my husband. Could you abandon me, Nan, if you knew I was determined to join my husband in Cupids Cove?"

It was on Nancy's lips to say *No, of course not, I will never leave you.* She had always believed her life and Kathryn's were tied together, more truly than if they were joined by blood. But it seemed there might, after all, be a limit to their bond. There might be a place Kathryn was willing to go where Nancy could not, or would not, follow her.

CHAPTER EIGHT

Preparations are Made for a Journey

This holy hopeful work you have half done,
For best of any, you have well begun.
If you give over what hath so well sped,
Your solid wisdom will be questioned.

BRISTOL
SPRING 1612

"IS MY BLUE KERSEY GOWN HERE? IS'T PACKED ALREADY?"

"No, it must be downstairs."

"Well, go and fetch it! I refuse to wear nothing but blacks, browns, and greys for the rest of my natural life, even in the colony."

Kathryn paced the sleeping chamber in her father's house, looking into four trunks that stood open in various stages of packing. She put things in, pulled them out, tossed orders over her shoulder to Nancy. The lethargy that had fallen on her after the loss of her child, the fear that gripped her when her husband asked her to come to the New Found Land with him—all had melted like morning dew as soon as she made the decision to go. Kathryn's usual energy blazed again like the midday sun.

She had needed that energy, first and foremost for the confrontation with her parents. It was the outcome Mistress Gale had most devoutly feared ever since Nicholas Guy first went to his cousin's colony. Her son-in-law abandoning her daughter to go adventuring across the sea was bad enough. But luring Kathryn over there? That was unforgiveable.

Mistress Gale had raged, begged, and pleaded with her daughter to reconsider. Master Gale was, as ever, more temperate than his wife, but he had a long and serious talk warning Kathryn of the dangers of life in the New World. Wild beasts, unknown plagues, attacks by brutal savages or marauding pirates—anything might happen.

But there was no changing Kathryn's mind; every objection was mown down like grass before the sickle. Eventually even Mistress Gale had to accept the inevitable and turn her attention to helping her daughter prepare for the journey.

The few items Kathryn had left at her husband's house had been packed up and brought here to the Gale household. Nicholas Guy's business would remain in the hands of his father and sister, with Robin Piper managing the shoemaking shop. "The house will be cared for and the business thriving while we are in the colony," Kathryn told her parents. "When we make our fortune in the New World and come back to Bristol, Master Nicholas will be well set up to go into trade as a merchant."

Nancy joined her on visits to the shops: they bought fabric and sewed new petticoats, skirts, aprons, and gowns, stocked up on buttons and needles and thimbles and thread. Kathryn asked John Guy the names of the other women who were considering going out to Cupids Cove and met with them, discussing what they would need to bring to a land where there was no such thing as a shop or market. She took the pewter plates from her husband's house and sorted through them, deciding what was fit to take and then wrapping them carefully.

With everything discussed, from hairbrushes to chamber pots, there was only one subject rarely touched upon, and that was the vexing question of whether Kathryn would go alone. She would, of course, go on a ship commanded by Master John Guy in the company of at least a dozen other women. These women included Philip Guy's wife with her two small boys, and the wives of two other merchant colonists: Willian Colston and William Catchmaid. Colston's wife was bringing her unmarried sister. There was a dairymaid named Daisy who was promised to marry a man in Cupids Cove; she also had two unwed sisters coming with her. They were used to hard work and wanted to see the world, and said they would marry any man in the colony who'd have them, as long as he wasn't too old, too ugly, or too cruel.

What was not clear, as yet, was whether this tally of breeding stock that John Guy was importing to his colony would include Nancy Ellis. Kathryn brought it up almost daily, as she made her lists and plans. She spoke about "when *we* get to the New Found Land" and "when *we* are settled in Cupids Cove." Sometimes in bed at night, Kat would turn to her and say, "You will come with me, will you not?"

"I cannot do it," Nancy said. "I simply cannot."

And why not? That was the question, now. Once Kathryn's decision was made, it had gone from *How could you possibly consider going over there, Kathryn?* to *How could you let her go alone, Nancy?* Mistress Gale begged Nancy to go. "I can't bear to think of her all alone in that strange land, without any of us—without you! Why, you girls have never been separated!"

Nobody viewed Nancy's life as anything but a piece of Kathryn's, like an extra bit of fabric sewn into a gown to make it fit more comfortably. It was the life she had lived since she was four years old and had been put into Kathryn's bed to sleep with her at night, play with her by day, and eventually serve her. She tried to imagine standing on the quay waving goodbye to Kathryn, knowing she was going where Nancy would likely never see her again.

But the thought of standing on the ship's deck herself, sailing down the river towards the open sea, was even more terrifying.

Aunt Tib, plucking and gutting a capon for supper, listened when Nancy sought her out to confide in her. "'Tis a shocking thing, I've always said, this business of going off to them places. What do people want over there that they can't have right here in Bristol? A fine, well-set-up young man like young Master Guy, now—he got a good business, a house and a wife here. Or our Ned, poor little fellow, doing fine in his apprenticeship, best kind of prospects ahead of him. His poor mother, you know, she cries herself to sleep every night. And our mistress will be doing the same, no doubt, when young Mistress Kathryn goes."

"And what of me?" Nancy brushed up the feathers into a basket. "Who'll cry themselves to sleep at night if *I* go to the New World?"

Aunt Tib glanced up from her task. "If you're fishing for sympathy, I'll not give you the satisfaction of saying I would," she said firmly. "You know I'm not one to cry over what can't be helped. I hate to think of you over there. But one thing I will tell you—if you don't go with the young mistress, she's the one will be crying every night. She'll be lost without you."

"And that is all that matters." Nancy opened her palm and blew a little gust of breath at the feathers, and they drifted on the air for a moment. "What is good for Kathryn."

"What if you don't go with her? She will give you a good character, I suppose. Then you go to work in somebody else's house, do what I've done all my life. Help some other woman keep her house and cook her meals and raise her brats. Mayhap amid all that you'll find a husband of your own, and then you'll clean your own house, cook your own meals, raise your own brats." She looked up from the plucked chicken. "Either way, 'twill be a hard life—what woman's life is not?—but you'll turn your hand to the task at hand. Like I've taught you to do."

Turn your hand to the task at hand. Nancy turned the phrase—a favourite of Aunt Tib's—over in her mind all that day as she worked beside Tib and then helped Kathryn with her packing. She had not Kathryn's gift for making up pictures in her head of what might be, for imagining her life like a scene put on by players. Kathryn had a hundred images of what life in this New World might be like; Nancy could see only ships sailing away from the quay out to the ocean and off the edge of the world. It was a great void of nothingness in her mind. So was the life she would lead here in Bristol, if Kathryn went away without her. Neither was possible to imagine. But if she sailed off the end of the world, at least she and Kathryn would be together. In the end, what else had she to hold onto?

"Candles," Kathryn said later that afternoon, packing yet another box inside one of the large trunks. "I'll take six. I'm sure we'll be able to make tallow candles over there as well as we can here, but I doubt we'll have beeswax."

Tallow candles or rushlights, made at home, were for the few tasks that had to be done between dusk and bedtime; beeswax candles, purchased from the chandler, were saved for holidays and special guests. Would there be any such special occasions in Cupids Cove? Would the clean, pure light of the wax candles be a painful reminder of living in a civilized town?

Nancy gestured at the little pile of candles. "How long will half a dozen candles last? If we save them, perhaps, for a fine dinner when your husband entertains the governor, when you eat off your wedding plates and you wear the red mockado gown from your wedding-day—what then? Sooner or later, the last of the beeswax candles is burned. The gown is worn out and you can't buy another bolt of mockado. What then? No matter how we prepare for this journey, in the end everything we bring over will be gone, and we'll have to live off what we can grow or raise or kill. In five years, we will be living like beasts." She was horrified to realize her voice was breaking; when she said the words "five years" tears sprang to her eyes, and she pressed her hand against her mouth and bit it, hard, to stop from crying.

Kathryn turned from the candles, flew across the room and put her arm around Nancy. "My poor Nan! But—you said *we*. Have you decided?"

Wordless, Nancy nodded, still fighting not to break down in tears. When the urge to weep passed, she shrugged away from Kathryn's embrace. "I still think we'll likely die in the wilderness if we don't drown on the way there. But if you are going, I see no profit in staying behind. And I'm better at making candles than you are."

Now it was a joint enterprise: the two women planning together; Nancy often overruling Kathryn's opinion about what or how much to pack. Then John Guy came for a visit, briefly back in Bristol from his business in London, looked at their trunks, and said there would never be room for all four. He poked through the things they had packed, shook his head, told them what must be tossed aside. The beeswax candles could not make the crossing.

"We'll have beekeepers before long," he said, "and then someone will set themselves up as a chandler and make candles as good as any in England. The whole point of the place is that it must eventually be self-sufficient—we will have to trade with ships from England, of course, but we must learn to produce all we can. Buttons? Why need you so many buttons?"

"Spoken like a man," Kathryn said. "You've no idea how many buttons are needed to make and repair clothing, year in and year out. As well as all metal goods; knives and needles and kettles and such."

"We've a forge over there already where our smith can make most metal goods. Buttons, when you need them, you can buy from traders on the sack ships—we'll not be entirely cut off from the world, for ships come and go from England from spring to autumn. Only take as much as you and your husband and your maid will need—a plate, a bowl, a cup, a knife and spoon for each person. There's no need for a dining set for grand dinners. We must be thrifty, must reuse and repair and never, never let anything go to waste."

Master Guy limited them to a single trunk. He had recruited a total of sixteen women, he said, including Kathryn and Nancy. Half a dozen were already married or promised in marriage to men in the New Found Land. The rest were young, unmarried, and willing to consider wedding a colonist. "Women such as yourself, Nancy," he said, speaking directly to her for the first time. "I am glad you have decided to throw in your lot with us."

Nancy opened her mouth to say she had no intention of marrying anyone, least of all some poor fool who had signed his life away in the New World. But John Guy's attention had already moved on from her.

When they went to visit William Colston's wife and her sister, Mistress Tyler, the women talked about the difficulties they would face, the jobs they would have to learn to do, the things that would have to be made by hand. It was a daunting prospect, but they seemed to look forward to the challenge. Mistress Tyler clearly had hopes of finding a husband in Cupids Cove, where the selection of possible wives was so limited that she might look like an attractive choice. She was a thin, stringy woman in her early thirties, but drop her down in the barren fields of Cupids Cove and the men out there, who would have been without sight of a woman for two years, might view her very differently.

Nancy whispered these wicked thoughts to Kathryn in bed at night, when the curtains were drawn around them and no one could overhear.

Kathryn laughed as they plotted out various scenes that might unfold on the shores of Cupids Cove as the men there caught sight of Nora Tyler. "I imagine the dairymaids, Bess and Molly and Daisy, will be chosen sooner," Nancy said. "They seem like merry girls."

"'Twould be different men, though, would it not? The milkmaids will marry apprentices and labourers, while Mistress Tyler, if she does find a man out there, will likely wed a merchant or at least a guildsman."

"Do you think such differences will matter?" Nancy wondered aloud. "Will we all keep our station when everyone has to turn their hand to labour together?"

"*When Adam delved and Eve span, who was then the gentleman?*" Kathryn quoted with a giggle. "No, but surely people will still—I mean to say, we must have all sorts of people in the colony. And there will come a time when enough people have settled there that not everyone will have to delve and spin, but people can do the kind of work they are suited for."

And we shall all settle back into our proper roles, Nancy thought. Some things would never change. She folded her hands behind her head, looked up at the bed hangings, and said, "I wonder if Ned will fancy one of those dairymaids."

"Do you not think he's waiting for you?"

"For me? Why ever would he?"

Kathryn leaned up on her elbow. "Lord-a-mercy, Nan, he sent you a message saying you'd be suited to life over there. That seemed plain enough to me. You're of the same age and station, and you practically grew up together, here in this house. Would it not be natural, once you are both over there, for you to marry?"

"But you do not want me to marry, surely! The whole reason I am going is so I can continue to serve you. What good would I be to you if I go off and marry some 'prentice boy the moment we land?"

"Not the very moment, of course not. But someday...well, I'd love to have you by my side forever, darling Nan, but I've always thought you would marry at some point, even if we stayed here in Bristol."

"That was your plan. 'Twas never mine."

"But if you did, we'd still be close by each other. It might be that you and Ned could live in our household and—"

"Hush," Nancy said. "No more talk about me marrying Ned. Yes, he's a fine lad and all, but I would never marry him, especially when he ..." She broke off, collected her thoughts before her words, and finished, "...when he is almost like a brother to me. I think of Ned as part of the family."

"Then 'twill have to be one of the other colonists, unless you go off into the woods and take a red man for a husband. I wonder if they are like us—in all manner of ways?" And Kathryn was off on another trail of thought, making entirely improper speculations about the natives, and blessedly clear of the topic of Ned Perry. And what a good thing, Nancy thought. How terrible it would have been if she had blurted out *especially not when he has fancied himself in love with you since he came here as a 'prentice lad.*

She knew it was true: Ned's one careless confession had made sense of so many unguarded words and glances over the years they had grown up together. He had long cherished a fancy for Kathryn. Perhaps he dreamed of her still, but if she was in the New Found Land as Nicholas Guy's wife, Ned would have to bury those dreams deep again.

John Guy's ship was ready to leave Bristol in late May. Just as they had done on that day nearly two years earlier when the first ship left for Cupids Cove, crowds thronged the quay: those who were departing, loved ones who had come to say farewell, and dozens of curious onlookers coming to watch. The would-be colonists bustled their baggage to the docks along with the heifers, goats, and swine that were to be their travelling companions, rubbing shoulders along the way with dark-skinned Africans, swift-talking Italian merchants, busy Dutchmen unloading their cargoes. All the rich noises and smells and sights of the Bristol docks; Nancy suddenly thought how she had taken it all for granted, the background of her life, and now she would never see it again. Perhaps she had been wrong to turn her back on it all. She could have had a life here in Bristol without Kathryn—a hard life, as Aunt Tib had said, but an ordinary one.

Too late now. She would never know what her life might have been.

The whole of the Gale household was there: the master and mistress, the three younger children, Aunt Tibby, the apprentices. Neighbours and friends crowded nearby. There were tears and embraces and good wishes as the sailors finished stowing the last of the colonists' many crates and trunks on board.

Nancy had never been much of a one for tearful goodbyes, but she allowed Mistress Gale to take her in her arms as she said, "You dear, sweet girl, the only bit of peace I'll ever have is knowing our Kathryn has you by her side." Master Gale wished her every good fortune and told her they were trusting her to look after Kathryn. Only when Aunt Tib took both Nancy's hands in hers did Nancy feel a telltale burning behind her eyes.

"'Tis a hard thing, to have my only flesh and blood go off on the other side of the ocean," Aunt Tib said. "I'll think of you every day and say prayers for your safety."

"Say your prayers, and say a little charm or two in secret," Nancy laughed.

"Oh, you know I will, I've all the old blessings. Send word back to me, if ever you gets the chance."

My only flesh and blood. Nancy hugged Tibby's solid, muscular little body close to her own. The only family she had ever known. She wondered for a fleeting moment, as she had wondered before, about the mother and father who had perished with the plague. Had they ever been real, or only a respectable story for a maid with an unwanted baby to tell? *Are you my mother?* She had thought a dozen times that someday she would ask Tibby the question. Now, likely, she never would.

"I will send word. You know I will. Mistress Kathryn will write letters home and I'll add in all my own notes, with love for everybody but especially for you. I'll never forget all you've done for me."

"Aye, well, thank me by taking care for yourself," Aunt Tib said, wiping away tears with the edge of her apron. She was the only one to tell Nancy to take care of herself, not just of Kathryn, and Nancy cherished that farewell as she climbed the gangplank to the ship. She wondered if following that advice would prove impossible.

CHAPTER NINE

A Parcel of Females is Delivered

Clear-skinned, true coloured Wives, with exact features,
With wise, mild, chaste Souls, are the best of Creatures.
Clear-skinned, fair-coloured Wives, with exact features,
With shrewd, lewd, wild minds, are the worst of creatures.

CUPIDS COVE
JUNE 1612

THE FIRST ENGLISH VESSEL TO ANCHOR OFF CUPIDS COVE that spring was a Devon fishing ship whose men were surprised to find Guy's colonists still living in the cove. "We heard half of you died, and the other half went back to England," the ship's mate told Philip Guy, over the evening meal in the Cupids Cove dwelling-house.

"Not so! We have had only seven men die in two winters. Five went back to England last summer. There's a few of us gone down the shore to Renews to clear ground for a new settlement, but we still have two score men here, and the governor is bringing back more."

"And some women!" called George Whittington, to cheers and laughter.

"Well, I heard the lot of ye were turned pirate, thrown in your lot with Easton because he threatened to burn your settlement if you never paid him tribute," another of the Devon men said.

"No, not one of our men has turned pirate," Philip Guy said quickly, as if eager to dismiss the topic. "Not a one."

It was William Colston who added, "We did have dealings with one of Easton's captains. But they've left us alone now."

That was making short work of a long tale, Ned thought, but it was clear none of the masters wanted to discuss their dealings with Easton's men. Everyone who fished along this coast had to deal with pirates, and this Captain Easton sailed into Conception Bay with the greatest pirate fleet ever seen in these parts, according to the fishermen's tales. It was only to be expected that any attempt to plant a permanent settlement here would attract the pirates' attention.

One day back in the early spring, a tidy pinnace flying the pirate's black flag had sailed into Cupids Cove. The ship's guns were trained on the settlement, and the men of Cupids Cove manned their own three guns, ready to fire on command. It was Master Colston who decided to allow the captain of the pirate ship to row into the harbour under flag of truce.

The pirate captain wanted to meet with not just the masters but all the men; he knew Governor Guy was back in England and wanted to put forth the offer that any of the colonists who were weary of the venture could join one of Easton's crews.

"Rations are good aboard our ships, ye'll want for nothing. Any man who wants easy gold and good conditions on board is welcome to join with us, any time. I dare say ye'd do better under the black flag than under John Guy."

Ned remembered the clutch of fear in his belly, the terror that they would be pressed into the pirate's crew. He was ashamed, even now, to remember that what had frightened him most was not the prospect of being forced to rob and kill innocent people, but the possibility of spending most of his time for the next several years on board ship. If the dread of facing the ocean again had already convinced him to stay in the New Found Land instead of going back to England, how would he survive life on a pirate ship?

None of the men was anxious to take up his offer, but Captain Sly was untroubled. "Ye hear a great many stories about men captured by pirates, but the truth is, most of our crew came with us of their own free will, and the same is true for all Easton's ships." He waved a hand out at his own ship in the harbour. "'Tis not a bad life."

What Easton wanted, short of new recruits, was an agreement with the Cupids Cove colony. He would tell his ships to leave the settlement alone, even protect them from other pirates, if they in turn would agree to stay out of the coves and bays that Easton considered his territory along the coast. While Captain Sly sat down to negotiate with the masters, four pirates who had come ashore with him sat down for a meal with the colonists. They were all eager to assure the colonists that being a pirate was no bad life.

"Better than what ye got here, anyway," one of the men said, giving the dwelling-house a skeptical glance. Ned felt stung: he and the other colonists were proud of that building, and justly so, he thought. The settlement now had two completed dwelling-houses and a storehouse, several outbuildings, another dwelling-house framed out, three boats built and one larger ship under construction.

"Why are you so sure 'tis better?" he asked the pirate.

"You should see the grand house I'll build meself, once the time comes for me to give this up and retire back on land. I got a woman and two youngsters back in England, but tell the truth, I'm in no hurry. We're free to go with every breeze, to chase after gold or even just better weather. When the winter hits here and ye're all snowbound in this bloody great house, we'll be down in the Caribbean, enjoying the sunshine and the lovely native girls."

"Have you ever had dealings with the natives round here?" Frank Tipton asked. "We've been here near two years and not seen sign of one yet."

"They're not plentiful on this part of the island," the pirate said. "I never seen none meself at all, but Captain Sly says he talked to a fellow that saw some red men, over in Trinity Bay. They spend the winters inland, and come out to the coast when the seals come in. We don't trouble them and they don't trouble us."

By the time they met the pirates, the colonists had already made it through their second winter, harsher and colder than the one before. The crops had not prospered. Two men took chills and died not long after Christmas. By spring, the men were on short rations and growing discontented. Philip Guy sent Captain Sly packing with a promised truce, but Ned heard George Whittington and a few others wonder if they might not have been better off to throw in their lot with the pirates after all.

Waking on cold winter mornings in his blankets near the fire, Ned almost agreed. It was not only the toil and sometimes the hunger; it was the sense of being cut off from the world, especially when fishing ships went back to England in the autumn. Once winter closed in, it was as if they had fallen off the edge of the map. *Here be dragons*, he thought, remembering the inscription on a chart John Guy had shown them once.

Well, no dragons so far. Plenty of cold; a little hunger; lots of hard work. But worst of all was the knowledge that if he died here, it would be months before his family back in England even heard of his death. Their lives moved on without him. He did not know which of his brothers or sisters were married, what nieces or nephews had been born, even if both his parents were still alive and well.

He had thought of Bristol, of his parents' house and his master's house, more in his second winter in Cupids Cove than he had during the first. Home: a place where people bustled in the streets and goods were sold in the markets, where you could see the faces of women and children and old people instead of the monotonous sameness of the colony's men, who were by now all sick of the sight of each other.

When the snow had melted and the pans of ice disappeared from the harbour, when the pirate ship had sailed away, when the ground had thawed enough to begin planting again, the men looked every day for sails on the horizon. And though the first ship was from Devon, not Bristol, and brought no news of their home city, still they welcomed new faces eagerly and were happy to be able to tell the fishermen they were neither dead, nor given up, nor turned to piracy.

Not yet, Ned thought. The Devon fishermen also brought the news that Peter Easton's ships were gathering at Harbour Grace, where the pirates had built fortifications and were challenging the French and Portuguese fishermen who plied those waters. Every man in Cupids Cove fervently hoped the pirates would confine themselves to plundering and fighting foreigners, and not turn their guns against fellow Englishmen.

A Bristol ship came a fortnight later, and this one bore news. Governor Guy wrote to say he was returning in June. He was bringing with him twoscore new men, some for Cupids Cove and some to begin the new colony at Renews, as well as ten heifers, two bulls, and sixty goats. "And lastly, but by no means least," Master Philip Guy announced, "our governor has found sixteen women who have the courage to make this voyage and throw in their lot with us. Among these are my own wife, and the wives of Master Nicholas Guy, Master Colston, Master Catchmaid, and Sam Butler, as well as many unmarried women. He says that all are sturdy wenches of an age to marry and bear children, to which end I am sure you will welcome them."

Cheers went up around the room, and George dug Ned in the ribs with his elbow. "Those sturdy wenches won't hardly have their feet on the ground before they'll be on their backs, I don't doubt." George had regained much of his saucy humour in the year since his brother's death, and the prospect of the women's arrival seemed to reconcile him to the thought of staying in the New Found Land.

"'Twill be good to see women again," Ned agreed. "I doubt you'll be so quick to get any of them on their backs, though. Master Guy will want respectable marriages, not a slew of bastards. The women will no doubt be kept under close watch until proper offers of marriage have been made."

"I'll make any offer they like as long as I can get my hands on one of them."

Ned's own imagination had snagged on the news that Nicholas Guy's wife was to be one of the women colonists. Kathryn was, likely as not, even now on a ship crossing the ocean towards them. Coming to join her husband.

The third dwelling-house was already under construction. Now, as the news of the women's arrival spurred everyone to greater efforts in completing that house, Philip Guy determined how the settlers would be divided. He and his wife and children, along with the governor and the Colstons, would continue to live in the original dwelling. William Catchmaid and his wife, along with Sam Butler and his wife, would dwell in the second; Nicholas Guy and his wife would move into the newest house. The unmarried girls would be divided up into threes and fours under the watchful supervision of the married women, and the unmarried men also would be divided among the three dwelling-houses. Most of the new men were apprentices sent out by a noble-man named Sir Percival Willoughby, who had invested heavily in the New Found Land venture: these men were coming on another vessel and were bound for Renews. But all the women were coming to Cupids Cove.

A new energy thrummed through the cove. More male colonists, more cattle, and more grain were all good news, but it was talk of the women that kept the men entertained throughout the month of May as they worked at the boats and wharves and houses, planted their crops and built up the fortifications that protected the settlement from piracy.

"Will they be pretty lasses, d'ye reckon?" Frank Tipton wondered.

"I don't say Master Guy will have lined up all the women in Bristol and picked the handsomest—I'd say he'll have brought those who were willing, and healthy, and hard workers," Ned said. "But then, you're not so handsome yourself, are you?"

"There's not nearly enough of them to go around," George com-plained. "There's more than a score of single men here already, and how many of those new men coming over are unmarried? Those girls are going to be able to pick and choose. He should have brought enough for every man to have his own."

"Not likely there's so many women in Bristol eager to try this life," Ned said. He glanced back at the dwelling-house as he spoke, then out over the harbour. He had seen no other landscape but this for nigh on two years. He knew every path, every tree, every corner far better than he'd known the Bristol streets between his parents' house and Master Gale's house, even, during the years of his apprenticeship. Familiarity had made him proud of how they had made something out of nothing in Cupids Cove; he knew how settled it looked compared to the empty wilderness they had found on their arrival.

But it took no huge leap of imagination to think how it would look to the new colonists, especially to the women. How many of those wives and maidens, he wondered, were already on board that ship regretting their decision? Was Kathryn one of them? Did she look forward to the adventure? Or was she dreading life in the New World?

He thought of Nancy Ellis too, wondered if she would accompany her mistress. He had sent her that light-hearted message of welcome in Nicholas Guy's letter, urging her to come over, but he had not really thought she would. She might well be married herself now, though for some reason he found that hard to imagine.

Pictures of Kathryn—as she had looked on her wedding day in her velvet finery, as she looked at fourteen, tripping down over the steps of her father's house in a faded russet petticoat—kept popping into his head throughout the day, and sometimes at night too. And then, when she finally stepped onto the shores of Cupids Cove, he did not recognize her.

He stood with the others on the wharf, watching as the two boats from John Guy's ship pulled closer and closer to shore. Several of the new men had already been brought ashore; these boats were both bringing women.

"There's my Sal! Ah, she's here at last!" Samuel Butler shouted, and the men around him laughed and cheered as he took off his hat and waved it vigorously in the air. In response, one of the women in the boat took off her cap and waved it back at him.

"Is that Daisy?" Matt Grigg said. "I didn't even know she were coming! It is! 'Tis my Daisy!"

Nicholas Guy was also straining to see the faces of the women in the boat. "I believe that be my wife," Guy said, but when Ned looked back at the boat he saw not Kathryn Gale but Nancy Ellis, her thin face, sharp nose, and the straight line of her mouth clear to recognize even with the sheen of her copper hair covered by her coif.

Then, of course, he knew the girl next to her had to be Kathryn Guy, and the features resolved into familiar ones. By that time the boat was nearly at the dock, and men were throwing down lines to the rowers to catch, and offering hands to the women as they gathered their skirts and climbed the ladders.

The men whose wives or sweethearts were on board stepped forward first to greet them, while the other men hung back. Ned saw Kathryn clearly enough then, as she went straight to Nicholas Guy's arms. He turned from that sight to see that Nancy had just set foot on the ladder, and no one was offering a hand to help her. He reached down, and she looked up at the face beyond the offered hand.

"May the first face to greet you in the New Found Land be a familiar one!" he said, and she grabbed his hand, her face opening in a smile.

"Look at you, Ned Perry! All this way across the world and as foolish as ever, I allow." She kept her grip tight on his and let him take her other arm and help her up onto the wharf. Then she tried to move away, but he kept hold to her arm and pulled her in for an embrace.

"All the men with wives and sweethearts get a kiss when they arrive; shouldn't I get one from an old friend?"

"No kiss, but you can hold onto me for a moment. The ground is still swaying and I'm half afraid I'll fall," said Nancy, relaxing just for a moment in his arms before she stepped smartly back. "How long will I feel like I'm still at sea?"

"If your sea legs are anything like mine, you should be able to walk steadily in—oh, a month or two at the most," Ned said. "Lord-a-mercy, Nancy, 'tis good to see you. I never realized how desperate I was to see a face from home."

"I've no wish to flatter you, but truth be told, 'tis good to step off that ship and be greeted by a familiar face. Everything around is strange, but you seem the same as ever." She tilted her head and eyed him. "No, that's not so; you are a bit different. You do look...older, I suppose. There's more to your beard, anyway." She turned, reaching out her hand. "Mistress Kathryn! If you've done embracing your husband, come see our Ned—doesn't he look a fine, strapping fellow?"

And there she was. Kathryn's face dimpled into its usual smile when she saw him. "Dear Ned," she said, and enveloped him in an embrace. "'Tis like having a piece of our old home here in the New World, Nicholas," she called over her shoulder to Master Guy. "With my sweet Nancy, and dear Ned who was my father's apprentice since we were children—why, I'll hardly be homesick at all!"

Then everyone surged around, greeting and introducing the new-comers, and the men began carrying crates and trunks back to the dwelling-houses. Ned found himself near Nancy again, she carrying an armload of bundles and he with a trunk hoisted to his shoulder. He described what they were passing as they walked up the path from harbour—the stone walls they had built in the last year, the guns mounted on them, the plants in the garden. "But there'll be plenty of time to show you all that," he added as they reached the door of the small dwelling-house. "This is the newest of the houses, 'tis only just closed in, but Master Nicholas has a bed made for himself and Mistress Kathryn, and I'm sure she'll have you sleeping close by. You'll soon learn how much we value that fire on the cold nights here."

The new dwelling-house was much like a guildsman's house back in Bristol, save that a sleeping chamber for the master and mistress was built on the main floor rather than up above. This would allow them to keep a close eye on the unmarried girls, for whom beds had been made near the hearth, while several single men, himself included, slept in their narrow berths in the upper chamber. The main room had a table and benches in front of the large hearth, shelves for storage, and one glass window.

As Ned showed all this to Nancy, he studied her face, trying to cipher whether she was impressed or appalled at the place she had come to live. He caught himself doing that over and over during the women's first few days in the cove. He looked at them to see whether they saw it as a place a woman could settle, raise a family. For without the women, everything they were doing here was meaningless.

But much as he glanced at all the women to gauge their reactions, he looked most often at Nancy. Only now that she was here did he realize how much, back home, he had looked to her to reflect back his own feelings, or to set them straight. The wry quirk of her mouth told him that she found someone's pompous speech funny but dared not laugh aloud; the quick crease of her frown warned him when his own jest had gone too far. When there had been a job to be done back in the Gale house that had seemed impossible to tackle, he had waited to see Nancy roll up her sleeves and put her hands on her hips, then give that tiny, almost imperceptible nod that told him if all hands pitched in they'd tackle it. It was that nod he was looking for now.

Not that he was blind to the other women. His memory had been full of Kathryn, but he had not forgotten to daydream, as the other young men had, about the pleasure of feasting his eyes on so many female faces, so many softly curving forms. Matt's Daisy, a tiny blonde girl, had brought two sisters with her, Bess and Molly. They were younger than she, but both taller and broader, hearty farm girls who looked exactly alike: wide hips, curls the colour of honey, and broad faces that broke easily into smiles. There were two orphaned girls of sixteen, Jennet and Liza, close as sisters: they had grown up together in the workhouse. Two of the other married women, besides Kathryn, had brought maids with them: Mistress Colston had, besides her spinster sister, a serving girl named Hetty; Philip Guy's wife had brought over Elsie and Nell Bly, two daughters of a neighbour who had used to scrub and cook for her—both slender beauties with dark hair and dark eyes. Last of all was a thick-bodied lass called Maggie, a cousin to Sal Butler; she was neither clever nor a great beauty, but she was as strong as a man and a grand hand to work.

In the new dwelling-house where Nicholas and Kathryn Guy were master and mistress, George, Matt, Frank, Ned, and the other fellows lay in their beds in the sleeping chamber at night and discussed which girls were pretty, which looked strong enough to bear children, which were willing to allow a saucy word or a wandering hand without running at once to Master Guy with a complaint.

"Don't try anything with that one Nan," Ned overheard George tell Frank Tipton.

"You learned that the hard way?"

"I only meant to be friendly. She has a severe look, but she's a handsome lass. And I always did like red hair on a woman. So I said to her, ''tis lovely hair you've got there, Nan, I'd not mind giving that a stroke, if you'd let me.' Well, she whirled around on me fast as a spinning top, and quick as you like she said, 'That'll be Nancy to you, and you'll take no liberties with my name nor with my hair neither, George Whittington.'"

Ned stifled the urge to punch George in the jaw. "I could have told you that, George."

"You and her served in the same house, didn't you?"

"Yes, I've known her for years. She can be a right spitfire."

"Ah well, I won't make that mistake again. That one Nell, now—she looks like a gypsy or a Spaniard, and I wouldn't mind a taste of that. And then there's little Jennet: she's got the red hair too, but I'm sure she's not got such a high opinion of herself, being only an orphan from the workhouse."

"I wonder if they are doing the same with us," Ned mused. "Lying awake comparing which of us is the best looking?"

George seemed flummoxed at the idea. "Sure, they've come all this way, they ought to be glad to find a man willing to take care of them at all. None of them will want to stay a maid for long, I'm sure."

Perhaps so; from what Ned could see the women were overwhelmed simply with trying to settle into the colony. "What do you think of it all?" he asked Nancy a fortnight after her arrival, as the two of them carted sacks of rye down to the mill to grind into flour.

Nancy grunted as she pushed her wheelbarrow over a rock. "'Twill be hellish hard work, I can see. I admire the way everyone pitches in to get things built and done, but in faith, I never fancied myself doing farm work—caring for animals, or planting crops. I'm used to buying flour from the miller and making it into bread; 'tis a shock to learn there's no miller here, and we have to grind the flour ourselves. My back's sore already." She stretched out her long arms and tilted her head back to let the sun fall on her face as she set her barrow to rest by the little mill. "And 'tis not bad yet, is it? Warm enough, and sunny most days. But I can't imagine living in that house once it gets cold in the winter."

"Rain and snow and cold winds get through the windows, even when you do the best job you can of covering them. Betimes you'll be colder and wetter than you ever thought possible back in England."

She laughed. "Ah, that's the thing I missed about you, Ned Perry—your cheerful outlook. You do know how to put the best face on things!"

"What good would come of lying to you about it? If I try to hide the truth about how hard it will be, you'll be angry with me the first cold, stormy day." He looked out at the saltwater pond into which the little millstream flowed, and the deep harbour beyond, circled by its evergreen hills. "'Tis a beautiful country, though," he added.

"On a day like this, it is."

"Beautiful in winter, too, with snow on the evergreen trees and the pond in there frozen over. The frost on the bare branches looks like lace, sometimes. You'll see. 'Tis not all bad."

"You wouldn't go back to Bristol?" She made it sound almost like an accusation.

Ned shrugged. "The governor took a few men back with him last summer. They were not going home in triumph. They were either fellows who had asked to go back, or who he had decided were not cut out for this life. I don't intend to be one such."

Nancy shook her head. "Men and their pride. And see where it gets us?"

Ned shouldered a sack of grain and opened the door to the mill for her. "It got us across the ocean to the New World. Do you think ships full of women explorers would ever have taken us so far?"

The ring of her laughter made the air of Cupids Cove sound better than anything had sounded to him in a long time. "Not likely! A ship full of women would have turned around, gone back to port, and done something sensible, like making sure there was dinner on the table for everyone."

"And in faith, that is why men and women need each other," Ned concluded. "Men to explore new lands, and women to make sure dinner is on the table. Now that Cupids Cove has both, the colony will surely flourish."

Why men and women need each other. His own words flickered at the back of Ned's mind all the rest of that day. They ground the flour and brought it back, and, tired as they were from that morning's work, he went back to boatbuilding while Nancy and Kathryn made bread and cakes with the flour. At suppertime they all gathered around the board in their dwelling-house, Mistress Kathryn and Master Nicholas at the head of the table like lord and lady of the manor.

As the Scripture said, 'twas not good for man to be alone. A sensible young man thinking of his own prospects might stop brooding over another man's wife and look to someone nearer at hand, someone with a clear laugh like a steeple bell, auburn hair that shone like a polished penny, and steady brown eyes that looked unblinking at the world. Someone with a quick tongue in her head who would put a fool like George Whittington in his place. Might she not have a different answer for an old friend?

Only he had better make his intentions plain quickly. With twelve single women and nearly two score single men, it would not be long before she had another offer.

CHAPTER TEN

An Attack is Anticipated

'Tis said, wise Socrates looked like an Ass;
Yet he with wondrous sapience filled was;
So though our Newfound-Land look wild, savage,
She hath much wealth penned in her rusty Cage.

CUPIDS COVE
JULY 1612

"REMEMBER HOW I CHAFED TO BE ALLOWED TO MANAGE THE household back in Bristol?" Kathryn said as Nancy helped her into her petticoat. "How angry I was at Joanna for doing all the work! There's many a day now I'd be glad for the idleness that troubled me then."

"Go on now! If we started rhyming off things we miss about home, I doubt Mistress Joanna would be first on your list." As Kathryn pulled on a green fustian overskirt, Nancy moved around it, briskly brushing off the bits of dust, dirt, and twigs that seemed to cling to every garment in Cupids Cove.

Kathryn was mistress of a greater household here than she ever would have been back in Bristol, for under their roof in the dwelling-house lived four maids and six young men. Meals had to be cooked, clothes washed and mended for their household of twelve people, as well as everyone taking their share in the work of the colony. She was busy from dawn till dusk, and sometimes she and Nancy and the other women sat up by the firelight sewing and mending even after the sun had left the sky. In Cupids Cove, no one complained of idleness or boredom. It was, as they had been warned, a hard life, but she relished the role of mistress. Though she had no jingling ring of keys at her waist, it was possible to imagine herself as the chatelaine of a great estate.

Today, once the morning meal was eaten and the table cleared, animals had to be fed and the garden weeded: these were everyday chores. There was also ale to be brewed and candles to be made. As Kathryn and Nancy went from the bedchamber to the hearth fire, they saw the maids already hard at work. Daisy, Bess, and Molly More had all been dairymaids on the Young estate back home, and all had dairymaids' habits of early rising and hard work. They had been out and milked the cows and goats, and now as Bess stirred the pottage and Molly cut thick slices of yesterday's barley bread, Daisy mixed a new batch.

The menfolk, too, were already out and busy, but they soon came clattering through the door in search of the morning meal. The household sat down together at a long table to share pottage, bread, and ale.

"What this bread needs is fresh butter, or some nice cheese," Daisy said when the meal was done and the men had gone again, "and I mean to make butter as soon as we've done cleaning up here. I'd like to get started soon on making cheese, too."

"I'd be glad for some plum preserves," Kathryn said. "Do plums grow round here?"

"I've not heard of plums, but Matt told me in a few weeks, by the end of August, there'll be berries of all kinds," Daisy said. "We'll take a few days when they come into season and pick as many pails as we can, then make some preserves. I do miss the taste of anything sweet."

"You get enough sweetness from Matt, you don't need no preserves," her sister Bess teased, pouring out a bucket of water to scrub the bowls.

"As if you're not getting enough from Tom Taylor!" Daisy replied. "Beg pardon, Mistress Guy," she added quickly.

The girls were about Kathryn's own age—Daisy, the eldest, was a year older than she was, at twenty-one, while the twins were two years younger—but they deferred to Kathryn and often hushed or tutted at one another for foolish talk in front of her. Since they made a point of showing respect, Kathryn thought she ought to emphasize her own position as mistress.

"Enough light talk, now," she said, pressing her mouth into what she hoped looked like a stern line. "We all have work to be about." She would save her own light talk for the rare moments when she and Nancy were alone.

"I hope both those girls will get themselves properly married off, now, when that minister comes," she said to Nancy, once Bess, Molly, and Daisy had gone about their chores. "The governor expects the married women to preserve the virtue of the maids, but I can't be responsible for them and their young men every hour of the day."

"How glad you must be that I give you no worries on that account," Nancy said with a grin.

"Not for lack of trying on George Whittington's part."

"That great lummox! Never mind Cupids Cove; we'd have to be living at the end of the earth before I'd look twice at the likes of him." Nancy attacked the wooden floor briskly with the twig broom as she spoke. "The arrogance of some of these fellows—only to think that because we're out here, any woman would be glad to have them."

"More choice for you maidens than for the men—there are far more of them to choose from. And more coming soon, if Willoughby's men from Renews come to winter here," Kathryn said.

"Do they not mean to winter down there, then?"

"They hope to, but there has been so much trouble with pirates down along that shore that the masters fear it may not be safe to remain there." Kathryn removed the iron pot filled with bread dough from the hearth and turned the dough out on the table to knead. "If the rest of the apprentices are as ill-favoured as the ones who came over on the boat with us, they won't add much to the choice for you spinsters." A few of Sir Percival Willoughby's apprentices had come over with the women to Cupids Cove, but most, including his agent, had gone to the Renews site on another ship. The ones who had come to Cupids Cove had proved almost as much of a distraction to the colony as the arrival of the women had. The new men were apt to complain, and lacked the hard-working attitude of those who had already survived two years together in the colony. They had been put to work alongside the summer fishermen, catching and curing cod during these warm months, while the more established colonists worked at clearing land and building houses and boats. The daily work of tending the gardens and caring for the live-stock, along with tasks like weaving, brewing, and cheesemaking, had largely been taken over by the women.

It was the height of summer now, and on most days the cove was a beautiful place. It was beautiful this morning as Kathryn and Nancy stepped out into the fresh, bright morning and headed to the garden. The sun was clear and sparkling in a sky bluer than any English sky, Kathryn thought—though perhaps it was only that you could see so much more of the sky here than you could in a town like Bristol. The sun reflected off the water, casting back images of a thousand diamonds. It was generally warm enough to work with sleeves rolled up, and nobody thought of throwing on a cloak until evening.

This present run of good weather had lasted nearly a fortnight; before that there had been cold rain and fog every few days, but Kathryn hoped that now it was August, the foggy chill was behind them. If they could enjoy such fair weather through until harvest time, the gardens might do well despite the thin soil, and they would eat well over the winter months.

She and Nancy worked alongside the other women in the gardens all morning, pulling the weeds that seemed so much tougher and hardier than their vegetables. A little before noon, Ned Perry stopped by the garden fence to announce, "A ship is coming into the harbour. Master Nicholas thinks it may be the governor returning."

John Guy had been absent from his colony several times since his arrival from England, voyaging up and down the coast, bringing supplies and men back and forth between Cupids Cove and the new colony at Renews. Everyone was eager for the governor's return, not least the couples hoping to be married, for the minister he had brought over from Bristol had gone to the new colony at Renews. "There'll be time for marrying in autumn," Elizabeth Guy had told the young women. That there might be time for tumbling before anyone got around to saying vows did not seem to have occurred to her.

Everyone in the settlement—more than a hundred people now, with the addition of the summer fishermen who were staying in the cove—left off their chores and gathered at the wharf to see the approaching ship. "I don't say that's the governor's ship," one man opined. "That don't look like her. 'Tis an English ship, though."

"Not pirates, I hope." Thus far, despite all the tales of Easton's clashes with the French further up the coast, Cupids Cove had not been troubled by pirates, but the thought of the marauding ships flying the black flag was never far from any of the settlers' minds.

The ship proved to be neither Governor Guy nor a pirate ship, but once its men had rowed into the harbour, they had news of both. They were from an English fishing vessel, and they brought word that Governor Guy, on his way to Renews, had been attacked by pirates, and that one man of the governor's party had been shot and killed. Nobody knew who it was; four of the original colonists and four new apprentices had been on the boat with John Guy.

"We heard your governor is going on to Renews, but he's pulling all his men out of there, bringing everyone back here. 'Tis not safe down there on the south coast, no more than it is in Trinity Bay or out by Harbour Grace," the captain of the fishing vessel said. "We were boarded and robbed a fortnight ago. All the fish we'd cured, and all our supplies, taken at gunpoint. Seems 'tis mostly men they're seeking, though, to man their vessels, and those that won't willingly turn pirate are pressed into service. We fought them off, but our captain asked the governor if we might stay here with you the rest of the summer. Cupids Cove seems to be the one place that's able to defend itself against pirates."

The captain made this speech to Philip and Nicholas Guy, down on the wharf. Only those standing nearby—like Kathryn, who claimed a spot near her husband—could hear everything he said. All around them, the shore rippled with the noise of people turning to their neighbours, repeating what they had heard and passing it along. Kathryn wondered how the story would be twisted, how many of John Guy's men would turn out to have been killed by pirates, by the time the whispers reached those on the furthest reaches of the crowd.

"I am going to stand watch tonight, sweeting," Nicholas Guy told Kathryn over supper in their house. "We've divided the men from each house into watches. Some of us will be out on Spectacle Head, and the rest manning our guns here in the cove. Sam Butler and his lads will come on watch at midnight."

"Is it really needful to have men stand guard all night long?"

"We truly do not know what these pirates are capable of. We thought we had made peace with them, but if they have attacked our governor, then we know we cannot rely on any bond they make."

"What will you do if you see them approaching?"

"Those of us out on the Spectacles will fire a musket to warn those on watch here in the cove. They'll rouse the rest of the men so we will be prepared to fight." He stood up from the bench where they sat together by the hearth and looked down at her. "Are you worried? Do not fret, my little wife. 'Tis only for caution's sake—they may never come here."

He had begun calling her that, his *little wife*, only since she arrived in Cupids Cove. Back in Bristol, they had still been too new to each other for pet names. When she came off the boat and into his arms here in the New World, almost his first words had been, "Poor little wife—to suffer the loss of our child, and I so far away from you." She still felt as if Nicholas Guy were a stranger, but he was a kindly stranger, who called her *sweeting* and *little wife* and told her not to fret. And he was a fine-looking man, and seemed brave and fearless when he talked about standing guard and being ready for pirates.

After dusk fell, and her husband and the other fellows had gone to stand watch, she sat by the hearth fire with Nancy and Daisy. Bess and Molly were abed after a day's hard work, but Kathryn was wakeful and wanted to talk. Nancy thought the whole threat of pirates was made greater than it needed to be, but Daisy said, "Matt thinks the stone wall ought to be higher—twice the height it is now."

"'Tis not Matt Griggs's place to be making judgements of that sort. If the masters think we need more guards, they'll set guards, and if they want higher walls, they'll tell the men to build them," Kathryn said.

A noise stirred the door, and the three women startled, but it was only Ned, who had come back to the house for pipe tobacco and a flask of aquavit. "All quiet at the harbour," he reported.

"Of course 'tis all quiet. There's no need for all of ye to be down there all night anyway," said Nancy.

"What if all ye men are down watching the harbour, and we gets attacked by savages in the woods?" Daisy said.

"We've nothing to fear from the natives," Ned said, but Kathryn disagreed.

"My husband says the natives attacked James Fort, down in Virginia, after they had been trading with the colonists and all. If it could happen there, why not here?"

"I'm going to bed, Mistress," said Daisy. "With luck, I'll fall asleep and forget to worry about either pirates or savages."

Ned still lounged in the doorway after Daisy had slipped away to the bed she shared with her sisters. He seemed in no hurry to get back to his post.

"Could you have imagined, back in my father's house in Bristol, worrying about attacks from pirates or wild men of the forest?" Kathryn wondered aloud. "In truth, it does make me wonder if this land is fit for Christian souls to live in."

"Hush now," Nancy said. "I know I was the one who never wanted to come here, but here we are, and there's no good talking of what might have been. We must take the New World as we find it—pirates and natives and all."

"I don't think we've much to fear from the natives, truly," Ned said. "Englishmen have been fishing here for years and had little to do with them. 'Tis the Christian men like Peter Easton who burn and kill and steal from other Christians. Perhaps the natives in Virginia are a more warlike bunch, but I'd say when we meet the ones round here, we'll find them gentle as beasts of the field."

"Beasts will attack if they see a threat," said Kathryn.

"Mistress, please, let up with the talk of savages and pirates and wild beasts, will you?" came Daisy's voice from the bed. "Our Bess has been lying here listening to us talk, and if you says anymore about it she won't be able to sleep at all, not a wink."

Ned went back to his watch then, and Kathryn and Nancy each to their beds. Kathryn woke after midnight, when she heard men's voices and footsteps at the door. The men coming off their watch, bidding each other good night, taking to their beds. The door closed a final time, and she heard her husband's steps cross the floor to their bedchamber. He drew the bed curtains aside and sat down beside her.

"Is all well?" she asked softly.

He pulled off his boots with a little grunt. "Well indeed," he said. "As peaceful as ever."

"I felt safe, knowing you were out guarding us." She wasn't sure she actually had felt safe, but it was what he would want to hear. And she knew he wanted her to turn towards him, awake and willing. He was eager for her body, as what man would not be after two years in this desolate place? He was eager, too, to get her with child again, to have a healthy heir to replace the lost baby.

The thought of going through that agony again made her cold with terror. But there was no escape for it, so despite her fear she offered herself to her husband whenever he came asking. He was a handsome man, she reminded herself, still fairly young and quite well-made. And he treated her with kindness. She knew of men who beat their wives, or who treated them with cold disdain. Things could be much worse.

Silly tales in romances—how Kathryn had loved those! She missed the players who came to Bristol in the summer, when she had swooned at the thought of someday finding a Troilus or a Paris. In plays and romances, beautiful women fell in love with men who would fight wars and defy gods for them, and in the same stories men were cursed by witches or enchanted by fairies. Such tales were far removed from the world she had grown up in, the sensible grey streets of Bristol. Great passion, like great adventure, was not for folk like herself or Nicholas Guy.

Only as she fell asleep later, in his arms, did the thought strike her that she was, now, living in a tale out of legend. They had left Bristol, crossed the ocean; they were the first English people to settle and tame a strange land. At their backs stood a wilderness filled with beasts and wild men, and before them an ocean sailed by deadly pirates. If ever a witch was to curse you or a fairy to charm you, it would happen here. They were living in a story.

The new day brought lowering grey skies and the threat of rain. It was cooler than it had been, the wind blowing in off the choppy seas, and Kathryn wrapped up in a cloak as she went about her chores. About midday, while she and Nancy were spinning wool along with several other women in the large dwelling-house, they heard a shout from the wharf. Just as it had the day before, a ship had been sighted. But instead of the interest and curiosity that news had aroused the day before, a ripple of fear spread through the working women.

Matthew Grigg stuck his head in at the door. "Master Philip says, get all the women and the children into the one house, and all the men down to the harbour!" he called.

"Should not everyone stay within the wall?" Elizabeth Guy cried. All the women—those who were spinning, and the ones who were preparing the evening meal at the long table—stopped their work. Though Matt had said "the children" there were, of course, only two: Mistress Guy's own, James and Harry, playing on the floor at her feet. She gathered them to her skirts now, distracted by her concern for them. Elizabeth Guy was the most well-born of the women in the colony, and older than many of them. But she was, at the moment, distracted by care for her children, while Mistress Colston and Mistress Catchmaid were in another dwelling-house. Kathryn stepped forward and faced the women.

"'Tis for the men to decide how best to defend us," she said. "We have our orders—close the shutters and put the bars on the door, once we get everyone gathered in here."

Nancy offered to run outside and give the alarm, to bring the women into the main house for safety. Kathryn held the door open as the women scurried in from all corners of the settlement—save only the mill and brewhouse, which were far away from the dwellings, down near the stream that ran into the saltwater pond. If any of the women were down there, they would have to look to their own safety.

As the other women came in, Kathryn watched the bay. There was a ship still quite far out, too far away to guess whose it was. When Nancy had ushered in the last two girls, Nell and Hetty, Kathryn gathered up her skirts and hopped up on a bench, clapping her hands for attention. Mistress Colston and Mistress Catchmaid were there now, as well as Elizabeth Guy, but none of them stepped forward to take command.

"We must see if we are all here!" she called, and the chattering stilled at the sound of her raised voice. "Everyone stay quiet and in one place, and the mistress of each household, count the women who live in your house to be sure everyone is present."

"All of us are here," Mistress Colston said, and, "All the maids from my house are here," said Elizabeth Guy. Her smaller son, Harry, was gurning and whining in her lap, having guessed from the women's tones that something was amiss. Kathryn kept to her perch on the bench, looking for Nancy, Bess, Molly, and Daisy. She could only see one of the twins, and as she was only just learning to tell them apart she did not like to say at once which was missing. But the one who was present must have been Bess, for she let out a little shriek and said, "Where's our Molly?"

"She were tending to the goats," said Daisy, "last I saw her." She slipped an arm around Bess's shoulders.

"I ran right past the goat pen and saw no sign of her," said Nancy.

"We ought to have took in the goats, and the rest of the livestock. If they're out in the pens, they'll be taken by the pirates!" shrilled Sal Butler.

"Well, if it turns out that ship is not a pirate ship, we have learned a lesson and we'll do better next time. If it is, then the livestock will have to take their chances. But we cannot leave a woman outside, if there's any way of getting her to safety," Kathryn said. She kept her perch on the bench and, in truth, somewhat relished the view, looking down on the others and giving them orders. "Bess, Daisy, is there any chance Moll might have gone down to the mill or the brewhouse?"

"She'd not have been down there alone," Bess said, ready to burst into tears. "We always went together."

"I'll go find her," Nancy said quickly. "I don't believe 'tis a pirate ship anyway, and if it is, they'll not be ashore yet." As she left, the other women gathered at the windows, peeking between the shutters as the ship drew nearer, put down its boats. There was no sign of action from the men onshore, no warning shots fired.

"I'm sure it flies an English flag. 'Tis a fishing vessel, just like the one that came yesterday."

"If it is Easton, and he has enough men to overpower ours, he'll burn this place to the ground."

"Hush that talk, now." Again Kathryn wondered at her own boldness, taking charge of these women, issuing orders.

Down the path towards the dwelling came Nancy, holding a red-faced Molly by the hand. "I was in the privy," Molly told them as she came through the door, "and I heard all the shouting, and I was that scared, I couldn't bring meself to come out. I thought I'd be as safe there in the privy as anywhere, and when Nancy came hammerin' at the door I thought 'twas a pirate, and I said my last prayers, and then she hauled the door open and dragged me out."

Ripples of nervous laughter spread through the room as Molly's sisters gathered her into their arms. That broke a little of the tension; Nancy's announcement broke more. "We saw Matt and Tom on the way. They said the men are certain now 'tis no pirate ship, though they want us all to stay barred in until they know for certain who is on board."

Who was on board turned out to be their own governor returning from his adventure. The word went out to release the women, and everyone poured down to join the men on the wharf and hear John Guy's story.

He had, indeed, been shot at by pirates in his attempt to reach the new settlement at Renews. The pirates had let them go when they knew it was Governor Guy, but he had gotten there to find the new settlement in disarray. Not only had Master Crout and the other men there not been able to build any permanent buildings, but they had spent the weeks since their arrival in constant fear of Easton and other pirates.

"They never attacked us, but they were marauding all up and down that part of the coast," the man called Henry Crout told everyone when he came ashore. "I had some dealings with them myself and was compelled to give them two of our pigs in return for a promise to leave us alone. Four of our men, including our surgeon, were so frighted by the thought the pirates might attack that they fled into the forest. We heard nothing more of them—we think they must have perished in the woods, or been taken by the natives."

"A heavy loss," John Guy said.

"Heavier than even the loss of the men; in his distraction Master Oliver fled with his chest, so all the medicines and surgeon's tools we had were gone. I packed up our men and what gear we had down there, and came here, for 'tis not fit to try to plant a colony when one is harried about on all sides by pirates."

"No, indeed," said Philip Guy. "We have been fortunate here thus far. How many men are still on the ship?" The rowboat had gone back out to the ship after depositing Master Guy, Master Crout, and two other Renews men on shore.

"We plan to land sixteen men here, along with those who were in the ship with me," Governor Guy said. It transpired that the report of a man killed by the pirates was exaggerated: John Teague had been wounded when the pirates shot at Guy's vessel, but he was recovering. "Along with Master Crout, the minister Reverend Leat, and the apprentices, is Master Thomas Willoughby, the son of Master Crout's employer."

Kathryn noticed the glance that John Guy and Henry Crout exchanged at this comment. Sir Percival Willoughby had invested a great deal in the colony. No doubt he would be little pleased at the news that some of his men had been lost already, the new settlement abandoned, and his son threatened by pirates.

"Along with our own men and Master Crout's," John Guy went on, "some of the fishermen who were stationed at Renews will finish out the season here with us, giving us more hands to work and to defend the settlement. The rest will go to St. John's, to see if that port has recovered from Easton's attacks. It is said he captured thirty English ships there, and holds six of their captains as his captives."

"Six English captains?" echoed Nicholas Guy in disbelief. "How much power does he command?"

The men went on talking of the pirate Easton, whose fleet of ships had been attacking English, French, and Portuguese vessels up and down the coast all through the spring and summer. The governor said

Easton was looking for a pardon from King James. It seemed to Kathryn that capturing English ships and their captains, and harrying English fishermen and colonists, was an odd way to go about winning the king's favour, but she knew little of the ways of pirates and was mostly relieved that Cupids Cove was spared an attack.

Kathryn found Nancy and linked arms with her, walking down towards the water. "You were very brave, Nan, going out there to find Molly."

"There was naught to fear," Nancy said with a shrug. "I told you 'twas no pirate ship. If anything, you were the braver—hopping up on that bench and giving orders! I had a like to laugh at all of them running around like a bunch of clucking hens, but you brought them all to heel mighty quick."

"I did, did I not?" Kathryn felt a little warm flush of pleasure. "It seems I like being in charge."

"You'd best have yourself a whole brood of children soon."

Kathryn hugged Nancy's arm a bit closer. "I've not told Master Nicholas yet, but the truth is I've missed my flowers for the second time now. If I fell pregnant as soon as we got here, I'd be close to two months along now—do you think it could be true?"

Nancy wrinkled her brow. "I missed my courses the first month after we landed, and you know I'm pure as the driven snow—I put it down to the voyage, and the change of food. But I had mine again only a week ago. Missing two months in a row is surely a sign, but if I were you I'd wait another month to be sure before you say anything to your master."

"Of course—I'd not want to raise his hopes only to have them dashed. But today, Nan, I feel as if I could bear a child here, and raise it, and all might be well. How passing strange—we are facing the first real danger we've faced since we came here, but yet I am sure I could face down Peter Easton myself. I'm not a bit afraid today!"

Nancy laughed. "Hold to that feeling. I'm sure we'll all need all the courage we can muster. Ah, there's the boat; those must be the Renews men."

The young men scrambled up the ladders from the boat to the wharf, greeting the Cupids Cove men who had waited on the wharf to see them in. Ned beckoned the girls over. "This is Master Nicholas Guy's wife," he said to one of the strangers, "and this, her maid Nancy. You'll soon know Nancy because if you cross her she'll not hesitate to scold you."

John Teague introduced the Renews men. "These fellows are Hatton, Cowper, and Barton—all apprentices of Sir Percival Willoughby who have spent the summer fishing at Renews. And this here is Master Thomas, Sir Percival's son."

The young man identified as the nobleman's son did not, at first glance, stand out among the others. All the men were young and all dressed in shabby, work-worn clothes. "You are welcome to Cupids Cove," Kathryn said. The apprentices touched their caps to her, and Willoughby's son, who had been talking to Jem Holworthy, turned to greet her.

She held back the little gasp when his eyes met hers; they were the most striking, ice-blue eyes she had ever seen, shining cold out of his weather-tanned young face. He was just a boy—younger than most of the others, about her own age. Tall and slender, his brown hair falling ragged and unkept almost to his shoulders, he bowed to her. "Mistress Guy," he said, and flickered a brief glance and nod at Nancy before looking back at Kathryn.

He put out his hand, and she placed hers in it. He brought it to his lips and brushed it with a kiss as he said, "I'm well pleased to see a lovely face here, Mistress Guy. The presence of a lady will brighten this harsh place indeed." His eyes held hers; she found it impossible to glance away even as she took her hand back, and she knew her cheeks were colouring at the compliment.

"I hope you will not find Cupids Cove so very harsh, Master Willoughby. We have done all we can to make a little England here on these shores."

Thomas Willoughby's full lips looked as if they were more accustomed to pouting than to smiling, but he gave her a smile then, one that brightened his sullen, handsome face as if a lamp had been lit inside it. Even the icy eyes danced flame at her.

"Come up to the dwelling-house now, and meet the rest of our company," she said, finally managing to tear her eyes from his face to include the rest of the Renews men in her invitation. The clouds parted as she led the men up towards the settlement, and the day, though still chill and windy, was lit with a shaft of sunshine that touched the buildings and livestock, the hills and trees. Kathryn found herself thinking, *'Tis good that the first time Master Willoughby sees this place, the sun is shining on it.*

Then she caught herself in another surprising thought: that perhaps romance, like adventure of all sorts, was, indeed, more common in the New World than in the old, and not simply a thing for plays and storybooks.

CHAPTER ELEVEN

A Proposal is Made

To have me, thou tellest me, on me thou'lt dote.
I tell thee, Who hath me, on me must do't,
I may be cozened; but sure if I can,
I'll have no doting, but a doing man.

CUPIDS COVE
OCTOBER 1612

THE FIRST WEDDING IN CUPIDS COVE—SURELY THE FIRST English wedding in all of the New Found Land—was held in October, when the busiest days of early autumn had ended. The fish were in, salted, and shipped to markets in Europe, along with some furs and timber sent back to England. Turnips, carrots, parsnips, and cabbage were harvested, and nothing more had been heard of pirates since the Renews men had arrived back in August. It felt as if the colony could draw a breath. The banns had been read, and now Reverend William Leat, the minister that Governor Guy had brought out from England to perform marriages, baptize infants, and convert the natives, could perform the first of his duties.

Three men and three maids were being wed in one ceremony—"Like something at the end of a comedy," Kathryn said to Nancy. It seemed likely there would be more marriages to follow in the weeks ahead; with christenings, one assumed, following more or less nine months afterward.

One of the couples, at least, had had the benefit of long acquaintance: Daisy More had agreed to marry Matt Grigg back in Bristol, and when he went off to seek his fortune in the New World, she had agreed that when it was possible, she would come over and join him. They had both waited faithfully for each other for two years—though in Matt's case, there was no particular virtue in that faithfulness, since there had been no other women to tempt him in all that time.

Nancy remembered how Daisy had chattered about her darling Matt on the voyage across. At the same time, a shipboard romance had blossomed between Daisy's sister Molly and a young labourer named Tom Taylor. They, too, were marrying today, as sure of themselves after two months together as Daisy and Matt were after two years apart. The third bride was the dark and quiet Elsie, Elizabeth Guy's serving girl. She was marrying Jem Holworthy, whose father, a Bristol merchant, surely would have wished him to make a better marriage. But the governor had given permission, perhaps out of a suspicion that unsuitable matches were better than merrybegot babes.

"Between the two of them, I hardly know how they'll collect enough words to say their vows," Nancy had said to Ned, for Holworthy was almost as taciturn as his bride.

"No doubt 'twill be the happiest marriage in the cove, with neither of them to gainsay the other," Ned said.

Back home in Bristol, these were the comments Nancy would have shared with Kathryn in bed at night, voices low and curtains pulled around them. But now that Kathryn was reunited with her husband, Nancy slept near the hearth with Daisy, Molly, and Bess. As two of the new-wedded couples were from their household, that arrangement would change after today; new beds had been built upstairs in Nicholas Guy's house for Daisy and Matt, Molly and Tom. Nancy and Bess would be left to share the bed downstairs by the fireside.

Wherever anyone slept at night, and whoever they slept beside, it was all hands to work throughout the days, side by side at the hundreds of tasks required of colonists. Nancy had worked hard back in Bristol, but she felt a weariness at the end of every day here that was entirely different. Pulling weeds from the harsh, thin soil, hauling buckets of water

from the pond, chopping firewood, spinning the wool they had sent out
from England: all these tasks, in addition to the mundane household
work of cooking and cleaning and sewing and brewing, left her bone-
tired at the end of the day.

But Sunday was the day of rest—at least, the day when chores were
kept as few as possible, when the whole company gathered in largest of
the dwelling-houses to hear Reverend Leat read the service and preach
a sermon. There was a communal meal on Sundays after the sermon;
today two cooks had made an extra effort with rabbit pies and a fish
stew to provide something of a feast for after the wedding.

"For better, for worse; for richer, for poorer; in sickness and in health;
to love and to cherish till death us depart," echoed each of the brides and
bridegrooms in turn, save that the women promised also to *obey*. Those
vows surely carried more weight here than they would have done back
in Bristol, for here the chances of sickness, of poverty, of death parting
the couples, were even greater than they would have been at home.
Nancy scanned their faces as each of three couples in turn said their
vows. Daisy raised her round little chin a fraction, as if reminding herself she had chosen this lot, and was vowing her loyalty as much to the
colony as to Matt Grigg. Elsie looked, frankly, terrified; her hands were
knotted together and trembling. Molly was the only one who smiled as
she said her "I will," a dimple appearing in her round cheek. She had a
dimple on her left cheek; Bess had one on her right, and Nancy could
only be sure of telling them apart when they both smiled.

The date for the threefold wedding had been carefully chosen: after
the garden was harvested and the fishing done, but before the *Indeavour*
departed on its first voyage of exploration along the coast. The voyage
had been delayed till autumn because of the danger of pirates, but John
Guy now deemed it safe to venture further along the coast. The governor
was going on the voyage himself, as was Nicholas Guy; Master Philip
would stay behind with Master Colston and Master Catchmaid, to govern the settlement. Sixteen other men were going, all with the intention
of trying to find the natives of the country and open trade with them.

"In two years, we've seen no trace of them," Ned told her over the
midday meal following the service. "The pirates and fishermen say the

natives frequent this part of the island but little, so if we want to find them, we must needs go to them."

"But why do we want to find them? Would it not be better if they leave us alone, and we leave them alone?"

"The masters say we'll have to truck with the natives if we're to succeed here. Besides the chance of trading with them for furs, they know far more about the land than we do. The governor talks of bringing a few of them back to England, so they may learn our tongue and our ways."

"What if they do not want to go? Would they have to be taken captive?"

Ned frowned. "I'm sure if we can teach them enough English to make ourselves understood, they would be glad to come live among civilized folk."

"Perhaps. Do you remember Master Gale telling us about the wild folk from the North that were brought into Bristol?" The man, woman, and child from the far northern reaches of the New World had been paraded on display by a Captain Frobisher, and Master Gale, like many Bristol folk, had gone to see them when he was a younger man. But it was said they did not live long after being captured and brought to England. "And what of those Africans that the Spanish take for slaves? Like as not, most of the folk in the world would rather be left alone than set sail on any of our ships."

"They might not think of it as we do. In truth, we don't know how they think at all. That is why we must meet them, learn their ways."

"If you be so eager to learn of the natives, why are you not going on the *Indeavour*?"

Ned shifted in his seat and devoted his attention to his pie again. "I'm more use here, working on the walls and buildings," he said. "Every man to his best efforts. I am...not much of a seaman."

"Meaning you get sick every time you go out on the water?"

"Perhaps. A bit." He looked up again then, and grinned. "Oh, very well. I was sick as a dog all the way across from England. If I can help to build the colony by keeping my feet on dry ground, I'll stick with that." He looked wistful for a moment. "I do wish I could see those wild men of the forest, though. I am curious about what's out there."

"That is the great difference between us, then," Nan said, tearing off a hunk of rye bread and dipping it into the rich gravy of the pie. "I am not curious in the least about what's out there. I only hope to survive it. What if they find out we are here and are angry at us, and come attack us in our beds one night?"

"Neither savage nor pirate will dare attack this settlement," Nicholas Guy said, overhearing their conversation. "We are as safe here as back in Bristol, Nancy; you need not fear. Indeed, we may be better off, for the drought continues in England, while we have every abundance here."

"We've no shortage of turnips, anyway," said Nancy. It seemed that vegetables like turnips and cabbage grew better than grains in the New Found Land's thin soil and cold climate. There was indeed abundance in this land: fish teeming in the waters, all kinds of wild creatures in the woods to hunt, and fruit that grew rich and heavy on the bushes in autumn—berries of all kinds. But there had been no success at growing any kind of grain in the last year, and they still depended on barrels of wheat, rye, and oats shipped out from England to make their flour.

Nicholas Guy, Ned, and all the other men who had spent two years here, were almost painfully eager to convince the women they had come to a good place—a country that was safe where food was plentiful. Nancy stole a glance at Kathryn, seated next to her husband, across from Nancy. When the *Indeavour* left on its voyage and Nicholas Guy went with it, Nancy hoped she and Kathryn could have their long talks again. She wondered if Kathryn took as rosy a view of colonial life in private as she did in public.

Later in the afternoon, with chores done and shadows outside growing long, everyone gathered again in the large dwelling-house. This time, the solemnity of prayers and sermon was replaced by music and dancing in honour of the wedding. John Crowder played his fiddle and the three new-wedded couples got up to dance. Then other couples joined the set as men pulled women to their feet. A good number of the men danced on their own, feet flying to the lively tune.

Kathryn was quickly swept away by her husband, and Nancy sat on the bench chatting with Bess until George Whittington, fancying himself God's gift to the women of the New World, danced by and held out a hand to Nancy. "Come, Nan, we've not got nearly enough girls out on the floor. None of your sauce, now—I demand a dance!"

"Demand it from Bess, she's got far less sauce to go around," Nancy said, cocking her head towards her companion.

"What about it, Bessie? Fancy a turn around the floor?"

Nancy knew for a fact that Bess was waiting for Frank Tipton to ask her to dance. All the same, she lifted her chin with the exact same gesture her sister Daisy had used while saying her vows. "I don't mind if I do, Whittington." She took his hand quickly, no doubt eager to be out dancing rather than pining away after missed opportunities.

Nancy was congratulating herself on her lucky escape when Ned swept past her. She had seen him earlier dancing with Jennet, but now he had Philip Guy's son James, a sturdy little lad of about eight years, by the hands, and was whirling him about in a kind of jig till the child was nearly helpless with laughter. When the tune changed, Ned handed the boy over to his mother and collapsed onto the bench beside Nancy. "Come on now, dance with me."

"Marry, I think you're better suited to playing the clown to amuse the children—you've a gift for that. And did you not just see me turn down a perfectly good offer?"

"That wasn't a perfectly good offer; that was George Whittington. He's a conceited coxcomb, whereas I—"

"Yes? You are what?"

"An old friend. You'd not deny an old friend, would you?"

"I would. I'd rather sit out and not dance at all."

"But you can't do that, Nancy. Look around—three men for every woman. You're going to have to dance sooner or later, and you may as well dance with someone you can trust not to tread on your toes." He took her hand and she let herself be drawn to her feet. "We've danced before, after all. Remember Twelfth Night feasts, and Midsummer nights, back home in Bristol, when all the household danced together?"

Nancy followed him into the line, where a set of couples was being formed up for the next tune. All the women were on their feet with partners now. As she and Ned joined the line, Nancy felt keenly the truth behind his words: every woman here was going to be claimed, sooner or later. There was John Teague with Liza, and George Lane leading Jennet; even the sturdy and taciturn Maggie was dancing with one of the new apprentices. All this pairing off was for the good of the colony. The masters might respect a maiden's right to choose her partner, but no one would have much time for a woman who chose none at all.

Well-a-day. Letting herself get dragged into a dance was one thing. The fiddler played, and Nancy followed the steps, turning about and about as she moved up the line, catching hands with one man and then another. There was Nicholas Guy, smiling at her; there was George Whittington with a smirk. Matt Grigg scarcely noticed her as their hands met and they flew round each other, his thoughts occupied with his new bride. She darted in and out of the line past the other women, then met Ned again at the top and let him claim her hand as they tripped back down between the line of dancers.

The dancing went on for an hour or more; she danced twice more with Ned, and a few times with other fellows. Kathryn danced with her husband, but also, Nancy noticed, at least twice with the nobleman's son, Thomas Willoughby. When she did get Kathryn alone again, Nancy planned to have a good long chat with her about that young fellow.

Then there was the evening meal and a ration of brandy for everyone along with some vile-tasting berry wine Sally Butler had brewed. As dusk fell, the party broke up. Those who lived in the main dwelling-house prepared for bed, while the rest made their way back to the other two houses. Nancy, who had stayed behind to help Nell and Maggie with cleaning up the mess from supper, stepped outside alone into the crisp cool of the evening.

Alone, she thought, trying out the taste and feel of the word. The walk from the main dwelling-house to the one where she lived was short, but how rare to have even a few minutes by herself. The dying light was shot through with gold and orange, and her shadow was long and black on the stony path. Around her, voices called good night as she walked past the garden and the goat pen. On the horizon over the dark line of forest, the sky had already begun to darken, and a single bright star appeared low over the trees. Nancy kept her eyes on her feet, as it was always necessary to do here, to avoid stumbling on rocks or tree roots. She did not notice the second shadow that joined hers till she heard Ned say, "I'm walking you home, if you had not noticed."

"As we live in the same house, I can hardly stop you."

"You're contrary tonight. Did the dance put you in a foul mood, or that berry wine?"

"What does it matter? The mood is here, and you'd do well to hasten along in silence before you get stung by it."

"I'll take my chances. I've borne the sting of your tongue before."

He caught up and took her arm. She shrugged it away from him. "Ned, I'm not good company tonight, and I need no protection."

"The very time you want to be alone is when you most need a companion."

"In truth?" She stopped on the path, looked him full in the face for the first time since he'd caught up to her. "Who told you that nonsense?"

"My mother used to say it to me when I was a child." He stopped walking, too, and they stood on the path, facing each other. Around them, the voices quieted as people went into the dwelling-houses and Cupids Cove settled itself for the night. Their house was furthest from the main dwelling, tucked just inside the palisade fence and close to the dark woods beyond. "I never thanked you, by the by, for going to see my parents. 'Twas kind of you."

She had gone to visit them the week before she left Bristol, telling them that she, too, was going out to the New World, and that she would carry messages to him. Ned's father had gone to the curate to get him to write a letter. His mother had told Nancy all the family news: which of his brothers and sisters had married, and to whom; how many babies they had had. She had repeated the names of these nieces and nephews Ned would never see, trusting Nancy to carry them across the ocean.

Thinking now of Ned's mother's face, longing for news of her far-away son, Nancy no longer had the spite to be angry at him. "I was glad to do it," she said simply. "If you get Master Guy, or Mistress Kathryn, to write a letter for you and send it on a Bristol ship, they'll be very glad to have news of you. Your mother misses you greatly."

"And I miss her."

"I miss *everything*," Nancy said. "And I never even had my own family, as you did. The dearest person I had in Bristol was Kathryn, and she is here with me—but I miss Aunt Tib, and Master and Mistress Gale, and the children. I miss the hall and the hearth, and St. Stephen's and the sound of church bells; all of it." Her voice caught a little on the last words, and she bit the inside of her cheek as hard as she could bear to keep from crying. She silently begged Ned not to tell her how beautiful Cupids Cove was, how she would soon fall in love with this New Found Land.

Instead, he took her hands in his. "'Tis not so bleak if you form a new bond to replace the old ones."

She snatched her hands back. "Ned, please, no."

"Nancy," he paused, and when she did not protest any further he took that for permission. "We have witnessed three weddings today. There will be more before winter. You know the truth of it, what I said when we were dancing. Every single man here wants a wife, and every woman will be claimed, sooner or later."

"And you think—what? That I might as well throw in my lot with you?" She tried to keep bitterness out of her tone, but she could see from the wrinkling of his brow that she had hurt him. *I warned you about the sting of my tongue*, she thought.

"Is that so unwelcome to you? Is there someone else you fancy?"

"No!" She turned away, picked up her skirt in one hand, and began striding up the path as quickly as she could, leaving him to scramble behind her. *No, there is someone else you fancy.* The memory of the night after Kathryn's betrothal, the desire for their mistress that she had seen in his eyes then, lingered clear in her mind, three years later and half a world away. She had watched him watching Kathryn since they had arrived in the colony. She was sure Ned still desired her. Nancy would never be more than a cast-off, second-hand garment for him, a poor substitute for the woman he could never have. His offer of marriage was an insult, from one she had always thought of as a friend.

The sun had fully set behind the trees now, and the sky was a rich blue shading almost to purple as one star after another appeared. Between now and moonrise it would be hard to find one's way around the crisscrossing paths.

"Then why run away before I can even ask?" Ned persisted.

She stopped, stilled her breathing, tried to calm her temper. "You said it yourself; we are old friends. Do not force me to say anything cruel to you."

She could barely see him in the fading light; she turned more towards the sound of his voice and the warmth of another human body nearby.

"What cause is there for cruelty? The colony needs families to people the land. For all your mocking at me, you and I get on well. At least, we always have till now."

"I won't marry you." She would have cut out her own tongue before telling him the true reason. Instead she said a different thing, that was also true. "I've no wish to marry at all."

"But you must."

"I've no wish to marry just because John Guy needs folk to breed like cattle, to people his new land." She turned away from Ned, leaving him once again to scramble behind her on the dark path. In the distance she heard voices, one female and one male. Laughter. A rushlight bobbed up the path. It must be Bess, coming back even later than Nancy, with someone walking her home. Someone who, unlike herself and Ned, had the sense to bring a light. "Must every woman here be married and breeding a baby before this year is out? If you think so little of me as that, I'd as lief be wed to a fool like George Whittington!"

"And here he comes, pat on his cue," Ned said, looking back on the path. They could see the outline now: a man with a girl on one arm and the rushlight held aloft in the other. Now there was a man's voice from the other direction; Nicholas Guy, coming from his house, looking for his serving maids.

"Nancy! Bess! Are you out there?"

Ned called back. "I'm here with Nancy, sir, and George is coming behind us with Bess. We're all safely home." Then he lowered his voice and put his face close to Nancy's ear. "You must understand—" he began.

She hushed him with a gesture. "I understand enough. Still friends, only. Let us not speak of this again. Agree?"

He hesitated a moment, long enough that George and Bess were almost upon them. Then, "Still friends," he whispered.

"What's this, then? Dallying in the moonlight?" George Whittington laughed as he came upon them.

"The moon's not up yet, you dolt, unless you can see something the rest of us can't," Ned said. "The master's waiting to bar the door, so let us make haste."

"I was promised a goodnight kiss," Whittington protested. "And Ned, if you'll not claim one from Nancy, I'll take hers too!"

"Now then, Whittington." Nicholas Guy had come down the path, also carrying a light. "We have had a bit of a holiday, and much merriment, but we'll have no loose talk. These young women are under my protection, and I hope soon to see them as well married as those who were wed today. Come in, all of you, and go to your beds."

CHAPTER TWELVE

The Indeavour is Launched

What aim you at in your Plantation?
Sought you the Honour of our Nation?
Or did you hope to raise your own renown?
Or else to add a Kingdom to a Crown?
Or Christ's true Doctrine for to propagate?
Or draw Savages to a blessed state?

CUPIDS COVE AND TRINITY BAY
OCTOBER-NOVEMBER 1612

NED TUMBLED INTO HIS BED NEXT TO WHITTINGTON AND hoped the other man was already asleep. But no such luck; he began to talk in his piercing whisper. "God's teeth, what a pleasure to have pretty maids around again! I had my eye on Molly, but now she's wed I don't mind Bess. One's the same as the other—and have you seen the bubbies on her?"

"Hush, man! The women are only down below."

"I care not if she hears me—I'll not be long dropping my anchor in that harbour. What of you and Nan? You were having a fine cozy moment before we barged in on you."

"Shut up and go to sleep."

"Oh-ho, not so cozy at all, then. 'Twas you told me yourself Nancy was a spitfire. If you know her of old, you should have known what you were in for."

Ned said nothing; Whittington laughed and settled himself to sleep. But Ned lay awake, playing over the evening in his mind, wondering how it could all have gone so spectacularly wrong. When he ate with her at dinner, when he pulled her into the dance and she spun round the floor with him, he'd thought for certain matters were going his way. Marriage would be a sensible choice for them both. And if his thoughts, when he took her hand and skipped through the steps of the dance with her, were not entirely sensible ones — well, he could be romantic for both of them. If he had to win her hand first and then her heart, that was not the worst way to go about the business of marriage.

Then she had flung his offer back in his face like she was flinging a pail of dishwater out the door. What a ham-fisted fool he'd been not to take more care! If he had not rushed into a proposal, she might have had time to realize that his feelings for her were true, and not merely a matter of convenience. "Damn me for a fool," he said aloud, then tensed, fearing Whittington had heard. But all around him were the sounds of men snoring.

In the morning he sought out John Guy. The governor was down at the wharf overseeing the loading of supplies onto the barque, and Ned had to wait a few minutes to catch his eye.

"What is it...Perry?" Two years into life in the colony, the governor often still had that moment of hesitation before calling Ned, or most of the other workingmen, by name.

"Is there room for another man on board the *Indeavour*, sir? I know 'tis short notice."

The governor frowned. "Last night, I would have said our crew was full, but just this morning Thomas Cowper woke complaining of his stomach, and I trust not he will be well enough to make the voyage. I can use another man, if you be willing."

"I am, sir."

"Good enough. I had thought to leave today, but it looks as if 'twill be to-morrow at least, so you will have time to pack up your gear."

And time to say good-bye to Nancy, Ned thought. He would be clever, this time. He'd not get tangled up in his words.

But she proved hard to catch alone. It was a busy day, the twenty men going on the voyage preparing to leave and everyone else preparing to get along without them. Nancy was working in the dwelling-house with Mistress Kathryn and the other maids. Nicholas Guy and several of the men in the household were going on the voyage, though the two new bridegrooms, Matt Grigg and Tom Taylor, were staying behind with their wives.

Mid-afternoon Fortune favoured him: he found Nancy with some of the other women a little distance from the settlement, picking the last of the red berries that grew on low bushes in the marshy ground. He waited till Nancy was bent at her work, a distance away from the others, then moved closer. "I wanted to say—"

"Lord, Ned, you startled me! Don't be sneaking up on me like that!"

She sounded exactly as usual, only peevish in that way she had, that somehow twisted his heart. "Forgive me," he said. "Not just for startling you. I am sorry if—"

"Don't start with your foolishness from last night. Say it was the brandy that loosened your tongue."

"But I—"

"You were right about one thing: we have been friends, and I'm not so blessed with friends that I can afford to turn one away. So let's have no more foolishness now, all right?"

"Look, I only wanted to tell you that I'm going on the *Indeavour* to-morrow."

"You? You'll be heaving your guts over the side before you're out of the harbour."

"Don't be harsh with me. I could drown, or be killed by the Indians. Then you'd be sorry."

"Well-a-day, then don't get yourself killed."

"All I wanted to tell you was—"

"You are determined to say this, despite every warning, aren't you?" She rocked back onto her heels and looked at him.

"Only that I meant what I said last night, but I went about it all the wrong way. I'd take it kindly if you'd not agree to marry anyone else until I come back. Is that too much to ask?"

Nancy brushed sweat from her forehead with her arm. "Do you have some fool notion that going off on the *Indeavour* will prove what a brave man you are, and then you'll come back and pose the question again? For I'll tell you now, you're already a brave enough man, and my answer will be no different if you go sail around the coast or even if you meet a dozen wild men in the forest."

"Nor even if one of them puts an arrow through me, and I survive my deadly wound only to come back and declare my love for you?" He had not meant to jest about it, but when she was in this mood it was impossible for him not to play along with her.

"Not if you were as full of arrows as a pincushion is of pins!" She laughed. "Less talk of love, please. I'll not wed anyone while you are away—nor after you come back, neither. Will that content you?"

"'Twill have to," Ned said, nipping a few berries from her pail and popping them into his mouth. He did his best to walk away with a light step, whistling, so that she wouldn't guess how her second refusal stung his pride.

The next morning she was there along with all the others, gathered on the wharf as the men boarded the *Indeavour* and the smaller shallop that was to accompany it. Ned was glad that, having thrown his lot in with the expedition, he'd happened to replace a man who was to sail on the barque, for the men in the shallop had much the harder voyage ahead of them. The larger ship could better ride out the waves, and at least there was a deck to sleep on. Ned said his goodbyes, wishing he could take Nancy into his arms as he'd done the day she arrived. How quickly he had let that embrace go by! Now she gave him only a friendly hand in farewell and bade him to be safe.

At least he was not likely to die of seasickness. The barque sailed close to the shores of Conception Bay, so that the swell of the waves troubled his stomach little, and he acquired his sea legs quickly. And shipboard life, despite its regular tasks, felt like something of a holiday after the busy season they had just put in on shore. The October weather continued clear and fine, though it was colder out here at sea. They spent several nights at Harbour Grace, where the fortifications Easton's pirates had built earlier in the summer were now abandoned.

Then they pushed on past Baccalieu Island and around the headland called The Grates, where they turned southwards, down into the big bay the fishermen knew as Trinity Bay.

Whenever they put ashore, Governor Guy sent parties of men into the woods to search for signs of native camps. Finally, more than a fortnight after they had first set sail from Cupids Cove, two men returned from the woods in high excitement. "There's a camp in there all right—further up the stream, three or four of their tilts!" Frank Tipton announced.

"Did any of them see you?"

"We didn't even see them, sir. The tilts looked all abandoned, like. But they were never built by no Englishmen—all like tents made of skins, they were. Come in and see them!"

Four men were left at the shore to stand guard while the rest, Ned included, traipsed into the woods to the clearing where the shelters stood by the shore of a lake. As Tipton had said, they looked like tents: cone-shaped structures of wooden poles covered with animal hides.

"'Tis not long ago they were here," Nicholas Guy said, prodding at the remains of a fire pit with a stick he carried. "No more than a fortnight, I'd say."

"And we are not the first Christians they have met up with," John Guy said. He gestured to one of the tents that stood a little apart from the rest, and lifted the material that covered the poles. It was not animal hide like the rest, but sail canvas. "They got this in trade from some fisherman, or took it off a wrecked vessel."

"They've traded in the past. Not many Englishmen have seen them, but the Basque whalers spoke of trading with the natives." Henry Crout put his head inside one of the tents and drew out a battered copper kettle, holding it up for the men to see. "They've surely had contact with civilized men, for they have neither the art nor the materials to fashion such things themselves."

"But where are they? If this is their dwelling—"

"Has it not the look of a hunting camp?" Ned suggested. "And this would be the season, for them as well as for us, to hunt the bigger animals before winter comes."

The men wandered through the camp over the next hour or so, noting everything they saw. Henry Crout was especially keen; he was keeping a journal of their observations, and would write this all down when he returned to the *Indeavour*. Ned wondered what any of them would do if a group of natives, armed with hunting spears or bows and arrows, quietly emerged from the woods. Four members of the party were armed with muskets. They could likely shoot the natives before a spear could be thrown or an arrow fitted—but what hope, then, of ever starting trade, much less making Christians of them?

No wild men appeared from the forest. Ned felt all his senses heightened as they headed back to the beach. Though they had always known there were men somewhere in these woods, the fact that till now they had seen no trace of them meant he had been moving about the woods as if they were uninhabited. Seeing the camp made it real: these woods, these shores, were home to another race of men, as real as themselves.

A few days later in another cove, the barque and the shallop lay at anchor in the evening. Ned and two other men followed a small stream from the beach to the shores of a larger inland pond, where they dipped their buckets to take up fresh water.

"If this was summer I'd strip down to bathe in that," Whittington said as they stood near the calm pond.

"You'd be froze to death in a matter of minutes. 'Tis damn cold, this!"

"Hush. Look." Ned followed Tipton's pointing finger. On the opposite shore, a small boat cut through the water—not towards them, but running parallel to them so they had a good look at it. It was smaller than a ship's boat, with only two men in it, paddling with oars, one on each side. The prow and stern of the small boat were curved up to a point, a good shape for moving swiftly through these calm waters.

Ned raised his arm and shouted "Hail!" One of the men in the boat turned towards them and spoke to the other, a clear note of warning in his voice. The second man turned and looked straight at Ned, Frank, and George. He was too far away for them to make out his features in any detail, but his eyes held their gaze a moment before turning away. Both men were strong and powerfully built, and as they bent to their paddles, the little boat picked up speed. Soon it disappeared around a bend in the shore.

"Those were natives," Tipton said.

"Had to be."

"They saw us."

"What did you think they were going to do? Come over here and bid us good-day?" Whittington scoffed. "Englishmen have been fishing here for a hundred years, and 'tis rare to hear of friendly meetings with the natives. 'Twill not be easy to get close."

Back on the shore, they told the other men what they'd seen. "You should have taken off your shirt, waved it on a stick like a white flag," suggested Henry Crout.

"Would they even know what that meant? Have they seen a white flag before?"

"Surely any man would recognize it as a sign of peace," Crout said.

"But are they even men as we are?" Nicholas Guy asked. "They are not civilized; why would we expect them to know the things all Christian men know? It would be like expecting the bear or the deer to know what your white flag meant."

They talked long into the night around the fire about the natives—how they might respond when they finally made contact, if they had souls like Christian men did, if they could be taken and used for slaves as had been done with the natives in the southern islands of the New World. "Imagine how much more we could do with this land if we had the labour!" Crout said, shaking his head at the thought.

"I have not heard that anyone's had much fortune getting the natives in this part of the world to work for them," John Guy said. "In Virginia the English have traded with them. They are the ones who know this land, after all, and Englishmen might not long survive here if we do not make friends with them."

"They *know* the land, yes, but they do not use it!" Crout shot back. "Look at this great island, all its resources—the seas teeming with fish, enough timber in the forests to build an armada of ships, iron and copper and likely even silver and gold beneath the earth. A few thousand savages camp out on it in tents of skins, hunting wild beasts and gathering berries. They build no cities, they have no metal goods except what they get from fishermen. Half the world is going to waste under their rule. When God gave man dominion over the earth, He meant for us to use it, not waste it!"

Other voices joined in the argument, but Ned let his mind drift away from the debate. This was an argument for men like Guy and Crout, masters and governors. *Thank God I'll never have to make such decisions*, Ned thought. Perhaps those two men they had seen in the boat had souls that could be saved and minds that could be reasoned with, as Christian men did, but it was hardly for Ned to judge such things. *If I see a native coming at me with a weapon, and I have a musket handy, I'll shoot to save my life. Other than that, 'tis not likely I'll have much to do with them.*

So instead of thinking about savages and slaves and how the New Found Land could be tamed with a handful of Englishmen, he thought about Cupids Cove, and about Nancy. He pictured her firm, straight back and her clear-eyed gaze, imagined her milking a goat or pulling weeds from the garden. How quickly, how readily she had learned all these new things, even as that sharp tongue of hers reminded everyone she was trained as a housemaid, not as a goatherd or a farmer.

When he saw her in Cupids Cove beside her mistress, it seemed strange that he had spent his youth fancying Kathryn. Yes, Kathryn Guy was still a beauty, but putting Nancy in Cupids Cove had been like polishing a jewel and putting it in a new setting. She shone brighter, somehow, in this hard place—not only the beauty of her face and figure, but her spirit as well.

With Nancy by his side, he could imagine having his own little plot of land, a few chickens with some pigs and goats, children growing up around them. A hard life, in some ways, but they would share it, and make each other laugh through the lean times. Strange to think that was his dream now, when he'd once thought he'd live out his life in Bristol laying stone for rich men's houses and great churches. He would never have a hand, now, in building a great manor house, but if Nancy would marry him, he'd be content to stay here. Let the masters decide about treating with the natives and taming the land—he would tame his own little piece of this new world, and be well content with that.

On the third of November, they left the bottom of Trinity Bay and sailed northwest into a long arm of the sea. Governor Guy was anxious to find whether there was a passage that would lead them to Placentia, the great bay on the other side of the island. Such a passage might prove a shorter and safer way to get to Renews where, despite the skirmishes with pirates, he had not given up hopes of founding his second colony.

"A passage to Placentia's all very well, but we want to get safe back to Cupids Cove before the ice comes," grumbled George Whittington as he and Ned swabbed the *Indeavour's* deck. "I doubt we'll ever find those natives if they don't want to be found."

"I'd be glad to be back in the cove before the first snowfall," Ned agreed. "Has anyone spoke to the governor, asked him when we can return?"

George snorted. "Talk to that one? Governor Guy wants to be the first man to find a sea passage to Placentia Bay, the first man to explore the interior of these woods, the first man to make contact with the savages. 'Tis all first, first, first with him, and the one thing he's willing to put last is the good of his men."

Ned, like the rest, remembered how quickly ice had filled the harbour last November. Their first New Found Land winter had been mild, but this year reminded him of last, with the sharp cold coming on quickly. If ice blocked their way out of the Trinity Bay, the governor would want them to trek overland to Cupids Cove, a hard walk even in the mildest of weather.

They went to Nicholas Guy, who was leading the men in the small shallop, and told him of their fears. "I'll speak to the governor," he said, "though I know he mislikes the thought of turning back before he's sighted the natives."

On the fifth of November John Guy told the men they would spend two more days exploring that part of the shore, sending parties inland to search for signs of the natives and making notes on the lay of the land and any possible passage to Placentia Bay. On the dawn of the third day, they would begin the return journey.

Ned, George, and Frank Tipton joined a party led by Governor Guy to climb a hill the governor called the Powder Horn, to see what they could see of the countryside. Whittington, still unhappy they were not already headed back to Cupids Cove, grumbled all the way up the wooded slope, though not loudly enough that the governor could hear him. "What will we see up there? What do you think? I'll guess—trees, trees, and more trees. A bog, perhaps. What the devil else would you see in this country?"

At the crest of the hill they could see the forest spread out below, and it was so exactly like what Whittington had predicted that Ned almost laughed aloud. Trees in every direction; the leaf-bearing trees were bare-branched now, but the evergreens were still thick and dark. Two ponds dotted the landscape silver, and there was a low, brushy area of the type that the settlers had once thought might make good pastureland or farmland but which they now knew to be a wet, marshy fen incapable of producing anything but mud and some bright, tart berries that flourished in late autumn.

Off in the distance to the west, though, they saw a broad expanse of silver. Another lake? If so, it was a large one. "By our Lady—'tis not the sea, is it?" Ned asked.

"It is—those are the shores of Placentia Bay," Governor Guy told the men. "Could we but find a waterway that connects that bay to this, 'twould be far easier to travel through this land. At least we know now the land is narrow between the two bays, and the trail that Master Crout found, that the natives cut through here, might be widened to a great road. What a saving in sailing time, if goods and men could be brought across this little stretch of land from Placentia Bay to Trinity Bay."

Their small group camped that night on the Powder Horn, as it was too late to make the trek back down before dusk fell. In the morning they rejoined the rest of their party near the shore. As the various groups described what they had seen on their forays, Henry Crout scribbled notes and sketches in his journal. It was as they were finishing the mid-day meal that Nicholas Guy sighted a fire burning on the beach, a mile or two away.

"It must be the natives—is it a cooking fire?" Whittington wondered aloud.

"'Tis no cookfire—see how tall and bright it is, out in the open like that? They know we are here—that is a signal fire," Master Crout guessed. "They are bidding us to come to them."

"To the boats, men," John Guy said at once, getting to his feet. "Master Crout, you and I and another three or four stout fellows will take the shallop and row down the shore to the spot. The rest of you, follow in the *Indeavour*." He scanned the faces of the men around him on the beach. "Crowder, Teague, Nicholas—you join us. A few more—ah, Perry, Tipton, Whittington, come along, too. You young lads can row. Quickly now—and quiet, for we do not want to startle them away."

Ned hopped into the shallop along with the governor and the others. He took one oar and George the one beside him; the other men, save for Master Crout and Governor Guy, also bent to the oars. As they rowed a steady, rhythmic pull through the water, the men talked in low, excited tones about the possibility of finally encountering some natives. Would they find a way to communicate? What could they offer in trade?

"Most of what we brought for truck—the beads and the metal goods—are aboard the barque," the governor said, looking back at the *Indeavour*. "What have we here that we can give them, to show our intention to trade?"

"A knife?" suggested Master Crout, pulling his from its sheath.

"Do we trust to give them weapons at first meeting?" Nicholas Guy wondered aloud.

"They go about clad in animal skins and furs, sir," George Whittington said. "Some fine woven cloth—linen napkins, even one of our shirts or a pair of gloves—would be a wonder to them, would it not?"

"I've a brass button that's come loose from my doublet," Tipton said.

"Among us all, I am sure we can find a few things they will find enticing," said the governor. "Each man see what he can spare, even if 'tis only a handkerchief."

Ned had no handkerchief, no loose buttons, and no way to replace his knife if he gave it away. He kept his mouth shut, hoping he would not be called on to take the shirt off his back and give to one of the natives.

Even as they drew near the fire on shore, he still thought they might be mistaken: they would get out of the boat and find a group of English fishermen. But he could see the small boats just off the shore now, and they looked to him nothing like any English vessel he had seen. And as two men got out of the boats and moved along the shore towards the shallop, he could deny the truth to himself no longer. No English fisherman would be clad only in a short robe of animal skin, with long hair braided down his back. Hatless, bare-legged in this cold, the hardy strangers—there were about as many of them as of the Englishmen—moved towards the shallop. Then, as they noticed the *Indeavour* approaching in the distance, they backed away, towards their own boats drawn up on the beach.

Master Crout, who had studied accounts of the natives, said the boats were called canoes: they were fashioned in the same manner as the ones Ned and the other men had seen on the lake a few days earlier. As the shallop neared the island, the natives quickly boarded those canoes and pushed them back out into the water. A few moments later, two of them got out onto the shore again. One held a stick above his head with an animal fur hanging from it—it looked like a white wolf skin. Ned remembered the men discussing whether the natives would recognize a white flag of truce. It seemed they did, if the white fur meant to them what it did to the Englishmen.

"Pull the boat into shore, and one of you men get out with our truce flag." Governor Guy's eyes roamed over the younger men in the boat. He clearly did not intend himself or Master Crout, nor his cousin Nicholas, to be the first man to parlay with the natives. In the moment's silence Ned hoped the governor would not choose him as the first to approach these men, who seemed to him so strange and wild.

"I'll go, sir," said George Whittington, and the governor nodded approval as George stepped out of the boat, his boots splashing in the shallow water. Master Crout handed him the truce flag. He walked a few steps down the pebbled beach towards the natives, holding the banner aloft. The men in the shallop watched; Ned held his breath.

Step by step, the men approached each other: Whittington with the white flag and the two natives with the pale wolfskin. When they drew near, both Whittington and the native man lowered their banners and spoke to each other. "Can anyone hear what they are saying?" Henry Crout asked.

"They'll not understand each other's words, whatever those words might be," said John Guy.

But they must have understood tone or gesture, for with both banners now lying on the beach, Whittington and the native man gripped each other's hands, smiled, nodded at each other. Ned was startled to hear a peal of laughter ring out into the still air, then both men turned back to their fellows in the boats and gestured them to come.

"I'll go, Sir," Frank Tipton volunteered, and Ned quickly said, "I will, also."

He and Tipton joined Whittington onshore; two more natives had come ashore as well. Like the English, the natives appeared to be all men: it must be a hunting party. Each of them wore a single garment like a tunic that fell from the shoulders to just above the knee; all were bare-armed and bare-legged. Their eyes and hair were dark, their skin a ruddy colour—Ned had heard tell they rubbed earth into their skin to redden it.

The strangers turned away from the Englishmen, though one of them kept a wary eye on them. They spoke among themselves for a few moments. It sounded like no language Ned had ever heard yet it was clear enough that they were doing what he and the other Englishmen had been doing: consulting with one another about how to proceed with this parlay.

Then one of the men stepped forward, bent his head and removed a necklace from around his own neck. It was made of seashells strung together on a piece of animal hide. He proffered it to Whittington, who bent his own head to receive it. In return, Whittington took a white linen kerchief from his pocket and handed it to the native, who looked at it closely and showed it to his fellows. They looked at it with some interest, though hardly with the awe and wonder Whittington had predicted they would show at the sight of linen cloth.

"We wish to trade," Whittington said slowly, and though they surely could not understand the words, he accompanied them with gestures. He held out his hands in a sweeping gesture as if to suggest the English had much to give. Then he shifted back and forth with both hands, opening and closing them as if to indicate giving and taking.

Tipton offered his brass button and got another shell necklace in return; the natives showed more interest in the button than in the hand-kerchief and passed it around among them. One took it between his teeth to test how hard it was. When one of the men approached Ned, he spread his empty hands to indicate he had nothing to trade. The man reached back and took a bird's feather that was woven into the long, glossy plait of his hair. Reaching forward, he gently tucked it into Ned's hair, behind his ear. Their faces were close for a moment as the exchange was made.

Ned imagined for a moment he was standing next to a being almost like the centaurs of myth—half man, but also half beast in his wildness. Then the man laughed, a sound so familiar and homely that Ned joined in. He smiled once more at Ned, nodded, then turned to look at another handkerchief that John Teague was offering in trade. The moment of strangeness passed: now it seemed to Ned that he stood only among men who were doing business with one another. Men with skin of different colours who spoke different tongues, but then he had seen that before on the Bristol docks, where all the world came to trade.

Now the other men, both English and native, climbed out of the boats, crossing the shore to each other. They passed back and forth objects in trade including, Ned was surprised to see, Henry Crout's knife, which was given in exchange for an arrow. The two groups of men drew closer to the fire, and although neither could understand the other, there was much talk as the trading continued.

One of the men offered Ned a strip of dried meat, which was deli-cious—it tasted like venison. More food was coming out, and drink too, and he thought someone must have rowed back to the *Indeavour* for food, because he saw John Crowder unpack a basket with bread, butter, and raisins. Nicholas Guy handed around jugs of beer.

Ned shared his beer with the man who had given him the feather; the fellow took a swig and made a face as if to spit it out but then struggled to swallow, as if realizing it would be rude to reject a gift. It must have been an odd taste to him. People everywhere made some kind of strong drink, as far as Ned knew, but in this land where grain was so scarce, the natives might not have tasted anything like beer or ale. Likely they made wine out of the autumn berries, as some of the women were doing back in Cupids Cove.

Everyone sat on the ground around the fire, sharing the food and drink, passing around the objects they had traded. Ned wondered if the trip back to the *Indeavour* had only been for food or if the governor had also called for some of the better trade goods, like the amber beads he had brought for the purpose. But aside from a couple of knives, he saw only cloth objects—the handkerchiefs, a pair of gloves, the white truce flag. George Whittington, flushed with triumph at having been the first to make contact, stripped off his shirt and gave it to one of the natives, and the man responded by giving him the animal pelt they had waved as a banner. George draped it around his shoulders like a cape and took a hearty swig from the bottle of aquavit that was making its way around the circle.

One of the strangers took the bottle George proffered, drank from it, and said something in his own language that made the other men near him laugh. The gesture, tone, and expressions on the men's faces were so clear it was almost as if Ned had heard them say in English, *Well, at least this is better than the other stuff they gave us.* When the other replied with a short comment and both men laughed, he imagined the reply had been something like *Do you suppose they drink that sour swill all the time?*

Again something shifted in Ned's mind; he saw them, for a moment, as two men who might sit in a tavern in England, making a jest about how bad the ale was. *They are like us,* he thought, and then looking again at their animal-skin garments, the bare red skin, the shining black hair, he amended the thought. *Like us, and not like us.*

He shivered. Then he heard an unexpected sound: the beat of a drum. An older man, seated near the fire, beat a rhythm on a small drum he held in his lap, his hands striking the taut animal hide. Was there some ceremony, some ancient rite about to happen? Was the drum a signal for an attack?

Instead of raising spears, several of the men began to clap in time to the drumbeat. The young man with the feathers in his plait looked directly at Ned and stood up, as did several of the others. Ned and his fellow Englishmen followed suit. Then the Indians began to dance.

It was such a surprise, Ned almost let out a whoop of laughter. The nearest dancer did not break his gaze, keeping his eyes locked on Ned's as if the dance was a challenge. And maybe it was; maybe it was. Very well then: this was a challenge Ned knew how to answer.

Picking up the rhythm of the drum and the clapping, he began a few steps of a jig. In his head he played a fiddle tune to match the rhythm, and his feet flew through the steps of the dance. A shout of laughter and approval went up from the natives. Ned shot a glance at George, a wordless plea that he not be the only Englishman to make a fool of himself.

George Whittington did one better than just joining in the dance; he began to sing. Not the same tune Ned had had in mind but another that fitted just as well with the simple rhythm of the dance: "We Be Three Poor Mariners." As George's feet, too, moved into the dance steps, and Ned and Frank danced and sang along, the older men of the English party clapped the rhythm and added their voices.

> Come let us dance the round,
> A round, a round
> And he that is a bully boy
> Come pledge me on this ground

Laughter and shouts of approval, now, from both the natives and the English, as the younger men of both groups came together. Ned and George, Tipton and Crowder, along with four or five natives, formed a circle and began to dance in a wheel, as if they were doing Sellinger's Round.

Now the wild men began a chant that went along with the drumming and clapping, a chant that wove eerily in and out through the words of "Three Poor Mariners." It was joyous, it was a celebration, but in the middle of the dance circle Ned knew there was a challenge being thrown out too. Not just a challenge to dance as fast or leap as high as the others, nor for one song to drown out the other. *Here is our dance, here are our songs, this is our world. Can you match us?*

Deep thoughts for a dance. Ned brushed them away as George started up another tune.

Once I loved a maiden fair
But she did deceive me;
She with Venus might compare
In my mind, believe me.

Ned heard the voice of Nicholas Guy, who had abandoned the sober older men and joined the dance too now.

She was young and among
Creatures of temptation,
Who will say but maidens may
Kiss for recreation.

Whoop! A shout, almost a shriek, went up from the men of the forest as more joined the dance and the circle widened. The drumming, the clapping, the chant, the song all went on and on as they circled and circled, white men and red, fixing their eyes on each other, copying each other's steps.

When the dance ended, the panting, breathless dancers stumbled to a stop, laughing. The circle broke and each dancer returned to the men of his own kind.

John Guy stepped towards the native hunters and began to speak. He used an abundance of gestures along with his speech, hoping to make himself understood. Tonight the English would sleep aboard their ship; to-morrow they would return with more goods to trade. The native men nodded what looked like agreement, and talked among themselves. They bid farewell to the little party of Englishmen, and as Ned and the others climbed aboard the shallop and pulled away from the beach he saw the hunters moving towards their canoes, deep in talk with one another.

On board the *Indeavour*, the shore party shared their tale, and the plan for the morrow, with the men who had remained on board. "'Twas passing strange," Governor Guy said, "how they danced and sang with us. I am glad they met us in peace, but I know not what they meant by it."

"'Tis how they greet strangers, perhaps," suggested Master Crout. "A show of welcome?"

"What if it were meant for a threat, instead?" the governor wondered. "Some spell they cast in their own rites, to make us go away and leave them alone?"

"Any Christians who have dealt with them before have found them most willing to trade for our goods," Master Crout pointed out. "Who would not want steel knives and iron pots, if they had none of their own?"

It made good sense, but Ned remembered the fleeting thought he had had while dancing: that there was a challenge of sorts being thrown out on that shoreline, something the Englishmen could not fully understand. There had been a kind of joy in that dance, while it lasted, but who could truly know what the men of the forest had intended by it?

Nicholas Guy took from around his neck the chain of seashells one of the Indians had given him. "Surely these things they gave us show they are willing to truck with us. We'll bring these back as gifts for the womenfolk—I'm sure my Kathryn will fancy this bauble."

Ned had nothing to bring back but the memory of the dance. He imagined himself with a necklace of shells on a strip of animal hide, saw himself presenting it to Nancy. Heard the clear ring of her laughter as she said, "Now, what am I to do with these, Ned Perry, you great daft ape?"

He had danced with her, only a few weeks ago at the wedding. Taken her hand and run through the steps of the country dances they all knew. It was the dance he had always meant to dance, and now he could see that Nancy was the one he had always been meant to dance it with. Familiar tunes and steps and a familiar partner, even here in this strange land.

The dance he had danced this evening was the one he could never have imagined. If someone had told young Ned Perry of Bristol that at twenty years old he would be standing by a campfire deep in the forests of the New World, dancing to a skin drum with the wild men of the New Found Land, he would have said, "Go on, you're mad."

Now, here he was. The dance of his life had turned, and like the person at the end of the line who lets go of the others' hands, he was flung off in this strange and new direction. *I have changed; the world has changed*, he thought as he fell into a sleep filled with strange songs and drumbeats.

But when a chilly grey morning dawned, there was a fine rime of frost on the *Indeavour*'s deck, and no party of friendly natives waiting on the beach. Ned and the others from yesterday's landing party rowed in to shore, but nothing remained of the last night's gathering save the burned out ring of the fire. No men; no weapons; no canoes pulled up on the beach. All that remained were several poles with animal furs fixed upon them.

"Hung up to dry?" Crowder wondered aloud.

"Or a message of some kind?" said Frank Tipton.

"'Tis most like they are left for trade," Henry Crout said. "I have heard tell of the natives doing it in other places, when they wish to trade but not to have dealings face-to-face with us. I believe we are meant to take them, and leave metal goods in trade."

"But I was certain we had won their trust!" John Guy burst out in frustration. "They showed such friendship to us last night!"

"Was it friendship?" Crout wondered aloud. "Belike that whole gathering last night was some manner of a trial, a test."

A test we did not pass, Ned thought. It troubled him to realize that the men who had seemed so friendly the night before must have conferred among themselves and decided not to trust the Englishmen further. Decided they were fit to trade with but not safe to have in their company. Last night he had imagined Governor Guy and the others taking easy mastery of this land, trading with peaceable natives, building a great colony here. Now he saw that things were not so simple: not all was as it seemed.

They continued their search a little way further into the forest, then they breakfasted on ale, ship's biscuit and a bit of cheese while the masters discussed whether to take the furs and if so, what to leave in trade. George Whittington squatted next to Ned, the wolf's skin still draped about his shoulders. "'Twill take more than fair words and dances to tame the savages," Whittington said, his grim tone sharply at odds with the smiling face he had shown the natives the night before. "Our best hope now is to persuade the governor to turn back to Cupids Cove before it grows any colder."

Ned shivered in the chilly morning wind that blew across that empty and silent beach. "In faith, I hope you are right," he said as he got to his feet. "I am well ready to be gone from this place."

CHAPTER THIRTEEN

A Dalliance is Begun

If with such men you would begin again,
Honour and profit you would quickly gain.
Believe him, who with grief hath seen your share,
'Twould do you good, were such men planted there.

CUPIDS COVE
NOVEMBER–DECEMBER 1612

O N THE SECOND SUNDAY IN NOVEMBER, THE MINISTER
being absent, Philip Guy read the morning service and then
a homily from the book. It was the one about adultery and
fornication—"And to avoid fornication, saith the Apostle, let every man
have his own wife, and every woman her own husband." When the
exhortation was done, Master Philip seemed loath to let his congregation go. He began adding his own words, which, Kathryn thought,
he was strictly speaking not supposed to do. But who was to stop him?

He spoke of how good it was to see the marriages that had been
solemnized in the cove the month before, how Christian marriage must
be the foundation of the colony. He moved from that to saying how
the wives whose husbands were gone exploring with Governor Guy
must sorely miss their husbands and long for their safe return. This was
certainly true: Kathryn felt like a knot was tied about her stomach, a
band of fear she could not loose. But Master Philip assured them the
Indeavour and the shallop must soon return. "Exploring all of Trinity

Bay could not take them more than a month," he said, dropping the preacher's cadence from his tone, "even supposing they met with the natives and were able to treat with them. They will return before ice comes into the harbour," he said, "so we shall surely see them back again before the first of December."

Bess, sitting on the bench next to Kathryn, leaned up and put her mouth close to Kathryn's ear. "All very well, Mistress, to say they might trade with the natives—but what if they found the natives, and those wild men slaughtered 'em? What then, hey?"

Nancy, on the other side of Bess, whispered "Hush," as Master Guy directed a stern glance at their bench. Kathryn composed her face and looked down at her hands folded against the faded green of her kersey gown, and Bess fell silent. But her words echoed in Kathryn's head, followed by a litany more powerful than anything Philip Guy might recite from the prayer book:

> *What if they were attacked by savages....*
> *Or captured by pirates...*
> *Or shipwrecked and drowned?*
> *What if they never return?*
>
> *What will become of the colony if John Guy is lost?*
> *What will become of me if Master Nicholas is lost?*
> *What will become of us, what will become of us all?*

Serving girls like Bess could voice such thoughts aloud. Kathryn thought it her duty, as wife of one of the colony's leading men, to soothe the maids' fears and tell them all would be well. Her own fears she expressed to no one but Nancy when they were out of hearing of anyone else.

When the service was over, Bess began fretting again, joined by Molly who worried even though her husband Tom was safe here in the colony. "We'll have none of that kind of talk, now," Kathryn said, doing her best to sound firm. "Governor Guy and Master Crout and all are skilled seamen and well able to take on the natives should they prove fierce. And we know the pirates are all gone south—no sign of any of Easton's ships has been seen in these waters for months."

"Aye, the pirates are all harrying the Spanish in the West Indies now—they've more sense than to winter in a place so cold as this," Matt Grigg said, arriving with Daisy on his arm and taking a seat at the table. Pork pies were on the menu for today, along with turnips, parsnips, and carrots from the fall harvest.

Kathryn looked around. The whole colony dined together in the main house on Sundays. Sitting around her were her own dear Nancy, along with Bess, Daisy and Matt, Tom and Molly. They had worked so hard to prepare for this winter: she and the maids had boiled and preserved the berries they had picked in late summer and sealed them in jars, harvested vegetables from the gardens, salted and smoked meat and fish, milled grain, and brewed ale, all against the long season when no ships would come from England. The picture she had long held in her mind: herself as the mistress of a fine house, pleasing her husband and managing her servants, had come to pass in the strangest way in this faraway land.

"A merry little sermon to keep all our spirits up, was it not?" came a mocking voice from behind her. Thomas Willoughby lifted his long legs over the bench and laid down his trencher on the table, taking the seat next to Kathryn. "'*Among the Locrensians the adulterers have both their eyes thrust out.*' Who are these unfortunate Locrensians, I wonder, and is half their population wandering about blind?"

Matt Grigg and Tom Taylor bobbed their heads respectfully as young Willloughby sat down. He was, in strict order of precedence, the highest-ranking man in Cupids Cove, for his father was a knight. Here in the colony he was supposed to be subject to his elders, and when Master Henry Crout, his father's agent, was in residence, Thomas was held in check to some degree. But with Crout gone off exploring, Thomas paid little heed to any instructions Philip Guy gave him. When he was ordered to harvest crops or cut firewood, he was as likely to be found playing a game of dice, or making idle talk with Nicholas Guy's wife.

Kathryn knew that other people saw Thomas flirt with her; if she hadn't noticed it of her own accord, Nancy told her flat out only a few days ago. "You cannot let him go on like that; everyone is talking of it. You can be sure Master Philip will speak of it to Master Nicholas when he returns."

Now Kathryn felt the slow blush that crept up her throat and into her cheeks as Thomas sat beside her. She dared not reply to his sally about the unhappy blind Locrensians, so he went on, prodding at his pie. "Is anyone else as sick of pork as I am?" he said now. "I'd sell my soul for a good chine of beef."

There was some laughter around the table, and Kathryn smiled as she said, "Hush now, no talk of selling souls." And Matt added, "Only wait till Christmastide — they'll slaughter one of the cows then."

"Christmas! Lord-a-mercy, I'd not even thought of Christmas in this place!" Thomas said. "A merry twelve nights we'll have here, no doubt."

Matt Grigg was the only one at the table who had been there for the past two Christmases. He was a pleasant young fellow who always tried to put the best face on things—the very opposite of Thomas Willoughby. Kathryn wondered at herself: how could she find Thomas so charming when he made no effort to charm? "'Twill be the merriest Christmas yet in the New World," Matt said, "for we've the women here with us now, and men will be able to kiss their wives and sweethearts, and we'll have some higher voices to sing parts in the carols, and someone to dance with besides one another."

Thomas rolled his eyes up into his head. "You lot are the most determined to find good cheer that ever I saw, I'll grant you that much."

Nancy leaned forward. "One must be so, to be a colonist. Anyone who expects ease and comfort is far better to stay back in England."

"And that is exactly where I would be, had my father not packed me off to the ends of the earth." Willoughby reminded them often enough that coming to the New World was no plan of his. Very different from Nancy, who had had such misgivings about coming, but who never spoke them aloud now.

"Perhaps your father will relent and take you back in the spring, Master Willoughby," Kathryn said now. "Until then, we must all make the best of it. Matt has lived through two winters in this colony and can tell us what to expect."

Matt Grigg laughed. "Plenty of cold—colder than an English winter, I'd say. It seeps in through the cracks in the walls and gets right under your skin, till you huddle by the fire wrapped in furs and blankets and think you'll never be warm."

"All the more reason you'll be glad to have the women here this winter," Thomas Willoughby said. "At least, you lucky fellows with wives and sweethearts—for a woman is warmer than any fire, is that not right, Mistress Guy?" He nudged Kathryn's shoulder and she shifted further along the bench.

"You must needs ask my husband about that, Master Willoughby, once he returns."

"Oh, I hope they are all back soon," Bess said. "I cannot bear to think of poor Frank—ah, and Master Nicholas and Ned and all the rest of them. God willing, they'll be safe home soon."

Her little outburst sobered the mood at the table again. Kathryn went on eating her dinner, though she felt Thomas's eyes on her.

"You must not say such things," she told him afterwards. He had managed to find her alone on her way to feed the chickens.

"What things, Mistress, must I not say?"

"You know quite well. 'Tis unseemly for you to make jests about another man's wife, or to show familiarity. I am a married woman, and soon to be a mother."

"And well I know it—I weep over it every night," he assured her with a grin that belied all talk of weeping. "As if being banished to this desolate place were not enough—to come here and meet the fairest lady in all creation at the very ends of it. And then to find she's another man's wife, and already bearing his brat! Was fate ever so unkind to anyone as it is to Thomas Willoughby?"

Kathryn tried not to laugh. "I'm sure there are thousands of poor wretches who would say fate has been far less kind to them. If you must be here, do something useful."

Willoughby took a handful of grain and tossed it off into the yard quite a distance from where any chickens were—though, being resourceful little creatures, they made their way over to it and began pecking. Kathryn took a few handfuls herself and coopied down low to spread it around for them.

"I was not raised to chores such as this," he said. "Nor to splitting and gutting fish and covering them with salt. I took it amiss when my father's apprentices tried to make me do it down in Renews. Master Crout took their part, and the whoresons tossed me in an ice-cold river to teach me better manners."

"Perhaps you need to be tossed in again. Then perhaps you would learn to leave off courting another man's wife."

"I would, if that man's wife were not such a flirt-gill." He looked sidelong at her out of those blue, blue eyes. Kathryn found herself without words and took her leave as quickly as she could.

Days passed. Neither the *Indeavour* nor the shallop sailed into the harbour of Cupids Cove. Nor did any other ship: the fishing vessels had all departed for the winter. The fishermen who had taken shelter in the cove after being attacked by Easton's pirates had returned to England. Philip Guy had also sent six of the new men from Renews packing, all apprentices who had been sent out by Sir Percival Willoughby and proved troublesome and discontented. "It hardly seems fair," Thomas Willoughby complained to Kathryn, "that the punishment for men who displease the masters is to send them home. Yet I, who displease everyone, am punished by being forced to stay the winter here."

"Because they know how much you long to return, and so will not grant it." Privately she wondered what crime or misdemeanour had sent the son of a nobleman to the New World as a chastisement. Gossip about the colony only said that young Willoughby was inclined to wild ways and disobedient to his father, and that Sir Percival had hoped a time in the colony would settle and sober him. It was apparent Thomas had not thought his exile from England would last through a whole year: he had not even brought suitable clothes for the winter. As the weather grew colder, Kathryn took a badly worn cloak of her husband's and began mending it, lining it with strips of wool from a similarly worn blanket.

"I should look like a fool in motley if I wore that," Thomas said when he came upon her sewing on it, and she confessed it was for him. He had come to her house with Tom and Matt, but quickly left their company to join Kathryn by the hearth.

"You'd not survive even a Bristol winter, much less a New Found Land one, in what you have with you. You mock this cloak now, but you'll be glad for it come Christmastide."

"And buried in it by Eastertide, no doubt," he said, sitting down beside her. The day's chores done and supper eaten, the women used the last hour of daylight for the endless mending and sewing. Thomas rubbed the fabric between his fingers; the original cloak, at least, was of good cloth, though the new lining made it rough as homespun. "Still, 'tis sweet you'd make it for me. Any woman who would turn over her husband's old cloak for another man must care for that man at least a little, must she not?"

"Hush, you patched fool! I take it on only because I need a task to busy my fingers and my mind, to stop me fretting over my husband."

From a stool by the other end of the hearth, Nancy shot her a warning glance. Nancy had not approved of the plan to make over the cloak.

"If you need to keep hands and mind busy, as you said, you would be better employed knitting more baby clothes, instead of mending a cloak for that one," Nancy chided when they were in bed that night, the curtains drawn for privacy. Since the *Indeavour* had gone, Nancy had returned to her accustomed spot at Kathryn's side. Daisy and Matt had a bed, as did Molly and Tom, leaving Bess in a bed to herself for the first time in her life. She complained of loneliness, but Nancy would not take pity; her place was with her mistress. The young men who had slept in the loft above were away with the master at sea, and the dwelling-house felt oddly empty with only seven people living in it.

"I've plenty of baby clothes packed from...from before." Kathryn felt tears rising to her eyes. "Every time I pick up my needle, if I try to sew a little smock, I can only think of...."

Nancy threw an arm around Kathryn, pulled her closer. "I know. But you must put it from you. Your mother lost babies and still bore four healthy children. So many women have a difficult birthing, lose a child, and go on to have more fine babes. And you will be one of them. I am sure of it."

"Are you?" Kathryn felt like she had been keeping back tears for—how long? She had tried so hard to be brave, as a settler's wife should be. But her husband had been gone a month, there was no word of the ship, and winter was closing in like a fist. "The first time was at home in Bristol, with my mother and a good midwife, in my own comfortable bed. Here—at the end of the world, no midwife, in a rough-timbered house where the wind howls through every crack — how can I hope to bear a child safely here when I could not at home?"

"Now, now, Kat, you know all that's for naught. A child will be born live and healthy if God wills it, whether the house be made of wood or stone. Your first babe was not fated to live: 'tis as simple as that. If this one is meant to live, it will be born healthy and hale in this very bed. Mistress Elizabeth will help you—she's borne two, and Sal Butler says she has helped at a good many birthing beds. And you know I will be here to hold your hand through it all."

"As you were before." Kathryn gripped Nancy's hand. It was all in God's will. But what if God were to punish her by taking the child away? Could flirting with Thomas be a sin severe enough to put her out of favour with God? There was a story somewhere in Scripture, wasn't there, of a baby dying because of its parents' sin? She was almost sure there was.

And so Kathryn privately vowed to stop it, this light talk with Thomas, the images of him that danced behind her eyelids when she tried to sleep. She had had dreams of such a romance, of such a man, when she was a girl, but she was a woman now. A wife, and a colonist. Her dreams must be of motherhood and making a home for her good, kindly husband. She would put aside thoughts of Thomas. She would stop herself from imagining what she and her husband did in bed at night, but with Thomas Willoughby beside her instead. That was lust, pure and simple, just what the sermon warned against. For the sake of her child, as well as her own soul, she must give it up.

Still, she would finish Thomas's cloak; there was no reason he should freeze this winter just because Kathryn was a light and faithless woman.

By the twenty-third of November, everyone in Cupids Cove looked grim, and the possibility that the boats had been lost at sea was in everyone's mind, though never spoken aloud. Early that morning, before everyone turned to the day's tasks, a shout went up from the men on watch.

Kathryn sat up in bed. "'Tis the *Indeavour*! It must be!" she said, shaking Nancy awake. The other members of the household, too, were waking, putting on boots and cloaks over nightclothes and stumbling out into the grey dawn.

It was indeed a boat, but it was neither the *Indeavour* nor their own shallop that had gone along with it. It was a small boat carrying five ragged figures. First to step ashore was Sam Butler, whose wife Sally broke out of the knot of women and ran to him.

The other men climbed up onto the wharf: Rowley, Vaughan, Crowder, Hatton. The crew of men who had set sail in the shallop. Were all the rest lost at sea?

"What? The *Indeavour* not back yet?" John Crowder said when he heard the news. "We all left Trinity Bay over a fortnight ago, after we met with the natives. But our shallop was wrecked on the rocks, and we walked overland from there to Carbonear, where we found this boat and rowed the rest of the way. We thought to see the *Indeavour* safely back in port long before us."

"We fear her lost," Philip Guy said, framing the words aloud for the first time. "But we thought you all lost too, so perhaps the governor and his crew will likewise be returned to us by God. We can only hope and pray."

The five men were brought into the large dwelling-house and given warm food, spirits, and a chance to change their clothes before telling their story in full. All the community gathered to hear it, to marvel that the natives had indeed been found and seemed friendly and open to trade. Such a hopeful encounter—only to be followed by the wreck of the shallop and the disappearance of the governor's barque.

Listening to the story, Kathryn did not even notice Thomas Willoughby slip onto the bench beside her. His mouth was close to her ear. "God willing, the barque and its men will come back to us, too," he said, the most reverent and respectful thing Kathryn had heard him say yet. "But if it does not, and Master Crout, the governor, and your own master are all lost, do you know what this will mean?"

She tried to ignore him, but his breath was warm on her face. When she turned to answer him, she could feel the heat of his skin, and his hair tickled her cheek. "Hush," she whispered. "'Twill mean a great loss for all this colony, and a great many broken hearts."

"Yes," he whispered, "and it means I will be out of the authority of my father's agent, and you of your husband. Neither of us will have a governor, no more than the colony itself will. What would any of us here do, with no one to rule us?"

Misrule and madness, Kathryn thought. Her belly fluttered at the thought: half fear; half excitement. Or was it her child quickening in the womb? She whispered into the curve of Thomas Willoughby's ear, "I pray we would do God's will, whether we have masters or no."

He stayed beside her, so close on the bench that she could feel the hard muscle of his thigh through the heavy wool of her skirt and petticoat. He was wearing the cloak she had mended for him, and when she shivered, he spread it out to cover both of them, so she was wrapped in her husband's old cloak, snuggled against Thomas Willoughby.

Two days later, the *Indeavour* limped into port. Blown off course by the November gales, she had sailed past the fishing station at St. John's, abandoned now for the winter. She had sailed south almost as far as the Renews station, before adjusting her heading and returning to Cupids Cove. All aboard her were safe and well and full of tales of their voyage.

The day the *Indeavour* made land, the first snow fell.

CHAPTER FOURTEEN

A Cold Hand is Laid Upon the Colony

Those that live here, how young, or old so-ever,
Were never vexed with Cough, nor Aguish Fever,
Nor ever was the Plague, nor small Pox here;
The Air is so salubrious, constant, clear:
Yet scurvy Death stalks here with thievish pace,
Knocks one down here, two in another place.

CUPIDS COVE
JANUARY–FEBRUARY 1613

WHEN SHE FORCED HERSELF TO CRAWL OUT FROM under the covers, the first thing Nancy saw was the snow on the floor. The men had done all they could to prepare the house for winter, with the result that being inside the house often felt like being sealed in a coffin, so closed and gloomy was it. But the storm that had raged through the last two days and nights was too fierce to be kept out of doors. Every crack between boards and through the window shutters had been ruthlessly searched out by the wind, which seemed almost a sentient force, determined to drive snow into each corner of the settlement. Last night's gale had left a skirl of snow half an inch deep over the floorboards, soaking into the mats, drifting over the beds where the sleepers snored under piles of furs and blankets that weighed heavily without ever being truly warm.

In the bed she had just left, Bess stirred but did not wake. Nancy pulled on her boots before she used the chamber pot. When she was done, she reached for the broom. None of the household lessons she'd been taught by Aunt Tibby or Mistress Gale had prepared her for the task of clearing a snow-covered floor. *Turn your hand to the task at hand,* she thought with a wry smile: what would Aunt Tibby, with her sensible maxims and superstitious charms, make of life in this place?

She swept the snow as if it were dust, intending to open the door and sweep it back outside where it belonged. But when she went to the door, bracing herself for the assault of icy wind, she found she could not push it open. Stupidly, she checked the bar again, as if she had not just lifted it out of place herself, before she realized the barrier was not their own lock but the snow outside.

She went instead to the fire and began to build it up. The woodbox was getting low, and the larger woodpile outside the house would have to be dug out to refill it. *How much work everything is in this thrice-damned country*, Nancy thought. Opening a door. Putting wood on the fire. Carrying and birthing a child.

She worried about Kathryn, now six months along. She tired so easily, and except for her belly, she was so thin that Nancy wondered could the babe be growing properly. During Christmastide Kathryn had made an effort to be merry, but in the fortnight since Twelfth Night, the life seemed to have been sapped out of her. She spent much of the day huddled under her mound of blankets, reluctant to stir from the warmth of the bed. Mistress Butler had trudged her way up the snow-covered path a few days ago to visit and clucked her tongue, saying the child would grow amiss if Kathryn did not get up and move about a bit every day. But it was hard to force her out into the cold. Hard, too, to forget the months of lethargy Kathryn had suffered after losing her first child. Was she slipping back into the grip of despair?

Somewhere, amidst the snuffled breathing and snoring of all the people still asleep in the dwelling-house, Nancy heard a dry, barking cough. She stirred oats into the water, wondering who had taken a chill or an ague now. They all took it in turns to be sick, coughing and shivering and sneezing. "You told me this place had mild, gentle winters," she had accused Ned.

"The last two winters were nothing like this," Ned had said, by way of apology.

If they had been, would we be here now? Could John Guy have survived a winter or two like this and still thought the New Found Land was a fit place to bring women and children out to? They talked a great deal, down in the main dwelling-house, about how much better off they were than the Virginia colonists. But from all Nancy had heard, Virginia at least was warm most of the time. Why could not John Guy have taken it into his head to plant a colony some place warm and dry?

Again, the hacking cough, over and over, followed by the shuffling sound of someone in skirts climbing down the ladder. Daisy, coming from the bed she and Matt shared in the upstairs loft.

"Watch the floor, have you got your boots on?" Nancy warned. "We got snow in here last night."

Daisy wrinkled her nose. "It stinks down here."

"The pisspots are frozen over and the door won't open. Must be snow up against it. When the lads are up and about, we'll see if we can push it open enough to clear a way out."

"I don't know if Matt will be getting out of bed this day. I'm some worried about him." Matt Grigg had taken to his bed two days ago, weak and with pain in his joints. "I'll bring him up some pottage. Is there anything to have with it?"

"I've stirred in a little pork fat, but I'd not like to use too much—if this storm doesn't pass off till later today, we may not get down to the storehouse for more." That was, Nancy thought, the simplest of their problems. The greater problem was how much of anything was left in the storehouse. Their stock of everything except salt fish was dwindling. The last of the beef—first the salt beef, then the tough leathery strips of dried beef—had been eaten. The hens had stopped laying. Several of the goats had died in the harsh weather. They were getting through the cheese and the grain at an alarming rate. Their grain stores, salt fish, and some vegetables from the garden still held out, but the choice of food was becoming monotonous.

Of all the colonists, Kathryn Guy and Jane Catchmaid got the first and best of whatever food was going, since they were with child. After that, Governor Guy gave all the men, including himself, even shares. The women got a little less food, since their work was not as physically demanding.

At least there were still plenty of oats for pottage. Nancy ladled up a bowl and handed it to Daisy. "Give that to your man, see will it give him enough strength to get up on his feet." She did not approve of people lying abed when they could be up working: it was why she was so worried about Kathryn just now. Everything could be borne, everything survived, if you put your mind to it. If you could not—if you lay down and gave up—well, that was too terrifying to think about.

Governor Guy was fond of telling them that during the colonists' first winter, one man had taken to bed with a sore leg, and never got out of that bed again. The moral of the story was that if only the afflicted fellow had been able to drag himself upright and limp along on his sore leg, he would have out-limped death. Ned said it was foolishness, that the man's wound had turned septic and killed him, only Governor Guy would not admit to it because he liked the lesson so much. But Nancy found herself in agreement with the governor. For as long as she had to be in this harsh land, she would never succumb, never lie abed nor encourage anyone else to do so.

By the time Daisy returned with the half-filled bowl of pottage that Matt had been unable to finish, the rest of the household were all up, even those who were dull eyed and listless with sickness. After they broke fast, the men who were strong enough set to work to get the door open and clear away the drifts of snow outside.

Kathryn, who said she had slept poorly with the babe kicking at her, knitted while Nancy and the other maids cleaned up and made bread. One thing they had plenty of was the yarn they had spun months ago, and Kathryn was attempting to knit garments that would keep a baby warm in this winter. "Though surely spring will be here by the time he's born, don't you think?" she asked.

None of the women could answer her. Her husband, coming in from the storm long enough to hear her question, sounded irritated as he said,

"The worst of winter will be past by Lady Day, but 'tis not uncommon to have snowstorms well past Easter. It will freeze, and then thaw, and then freeze again. The weather will be as God wills it."

He was able to report that the wind had died and the snow slackened. The men cleared a path down to the storehouse and brought back some rye flour, ale, salt fish, and cabbage, as well as the news that several people in the larger dwelling-house had fallen ill during the storm. "Some have chills and ague, but there's a good few that the governor believes have the sailor's curse—the scurvy."

"Like as not 'tis what ails my poor Matt, too," said Daisy. "He's weak as a kitten, and all his limbs are giving him pain, and his teeth are bleeding."

"If 'tis the scurvy we have in the house, will it harm the babe?" Kathryn asked, her hand cradling her belly.

"No way to tell," her husband said, sitting down on the bed beside her, "for women have rarely been exposed to it, much less women with child. 'Tis always been a plague that struck men on board ships, and the surgeon thinks 'tis something to do with the stomach, for 'tis oftentimes cured by eating fresh food or drinking the juice of oranges and lemons. Whether it can spread from one to another like plague is hard to tell."

"Oranges and lemons! As if we could get such things here," wailed Daisy.

"If it cannot be cured by turnips, we are all like to die of it," said Ned, taking a few of the dreary vegetables from a sack.

"Boiled turnip and cabbage, pease pudding, and salt fish for dinner," Bess announced, "and them as don't like it can keep quiet, you hear now?"

So despite the sick man in the house and the news of more sick in the other houses, they were able to wring a bit of laughter out of the stormy day, and after dinner the men set to building stools and tables while the women knitted and sewed; all the work that could be done indoors was saved for these days when it was not fit to go out. There was even a bit of music, for Frank Tipton took up Crowder's fiddle and played a few tunes while they worked, which earned him an admiring glance from Bess. *Another wedding there soon, if we all live long enough, and a better match for her than that fool Whittington*, Nancy thought. George Whittington no longer lived under their roof; after returning with the

Indeavour, he had moved to the main dwelling-house, where he divided his time between courting Nell Bly and currying favour with the governor and Master Philip. Though he had often been at odds with the masters, after voyaging into Trinity Bay and being the first man to treat with the Indians, George was basking in their good graces.

Nancy glanced at Kathryn to see if she, too, had noticed Bess making sheep's eyes at Frank. But Kathryn was sunk in thought over her knitting, paying no attention to the flirtations of maids, and Nancy felt the cold clutch of fear at her heart. *Not Kathryn; not the baby.* Whatever illness swept over the cove, they must be spared.

The storms abated and a few mild days melted the deepest snowdrifts, but more and more people fell ill. Colonists took to their beds and found themselves too weak to rise in the morning. Matt Grigg lingered in the bed he shared with Daisy, while Frank, Tom, and Molly all fell prey to the aching joints, the bleeding gums, the bone-weariness that kept them to their beds. Nicholas Guy fell ill as well, and took himself off to one of the beds in the upstairs chamber, lest he might pass the illness to his wife. Kathryn stayed abed too, but swore it was only the weariness of carrying a child, not any sickness or plague, that laid her low.

The other men of the house, John Teague and John Crowder, were among a party of men that Master Crout had sent off into the woods, led by Bartholomew Pearson, to hunt and trap animals for furs. Nancy was left to run the household with Bess, Daisy, and Ned—or, truly, with Bess and Ned, for Daisy spent every minute she could with either Matt or Molly. There were as many sick in the other houses, and most agreed it was the dreaded sailor's curse that had struck them. No one was agreed on how to cure it. There was nothing in the colony's stores that even resembled fresh fruit.

"Beet juice is good for laziness," Sal Butler said to Nancy one afternoon as they both sought supplies for their household larders in the storehouse. Sal was as solicitous of Mistress Catchmaid as Nancy was of Kathryn, as if it were a competition which woman could take the best care of her mistress and produce the healthiest newborn for the New Found Land. "I've had great success putting it up our Sam's nose when he laid abed, but we've not many beets in store."

Nancy had heard of this cure from Mistress Gale back home in Bristol, but never seen it tried. She imagined herself going about the sleeping chamber with beet juice and a spoon, trying to pour it up the noses of the sick. "It might rouse one whose only trouble was laziness, but I've never heard it would cure scurvy, even if we had enough beets to try it."

"What of the berries? Them tart red berries we made preserves out of—are they still growing? If 'tis fruit that drives out the sickness, those berries might do it." Sal directed her question at Master Crout, who was tallying up the remaining stock on the shelves with a frown on his high forehead. He and Master Pearson had done more exploring of the forest and fens around the cove than anyone.

"I wondered about the turnips," Nancy said. "Besides the ones we have in store, there are more left in the ground that we never harvested. What if we were to eat them raw instead of cooking them?"

"Ugh—raw turnip is too bitter," Sal said.

"Bitter, yes—but so is a lemon. Maybe there's some good in it that the cooking takes away—something that balances the humours. What think you, Master Crout? Red berries, or raw turnip?" Nancy had not even been sure the man was listening to their talk; he paid little attention to the women, though he sometimes deigned to speak to Elizabeth Guy or Alice Colston. The maids he seemed to view as only a little above the chickens and the goats. But at Nancy's question he looked over his shoulder.

"Our surgeon has little knowledge of this sickness, and nothing in his stores to treat it, so housewives' remedies may be all we can rely on. We will try what we can. When Pearson and his men come back from the trap lines, I will send them out to dig under the snow to see if any of the berries remain. As for the turnip, you both may try serving it raw to the sick in your own households and see what the results are."

"Indeed I won't then," Sal Butler muttered. "I'll not go forcing raw turnip down a sick man's throat—'tis as like to kill as cure him." She shot Nancy a look from under the brim of her cap as she bustled out of the storehouse, her basket full. Nancy, who did not care very much what Mistress Butler thought of her, went her own way a few minutes later. But that evening, she cut the uncooked turnip into thin strips and gave some to each of the sick men in her house. With their loose teeth and sore gums it was no easy task to chew it, and poor Matt Grigg could not manage it at all, though Daisy tried to feed him tiny bits. Master Nicholas, Frank, and Tom all ate some, and though there was no miraculous healing, Nancy continued to make it a part of the daily diet. The hunters' quest for red berries under the snow had turned up none, so no one was able to judge whether they might work as a cure.

But whether it was the turnips or a thawing of the weather, as February wore on some of the sick began to rise from their beds. Frank Tipton and Tom Taylor were up and walking around again, though Tom's wife Molly still kept to their bed. Matt Grigg was weaker than ever, but Master Nicholas felt strong enough to urge his wife to walk outside with him and take a little exercise on a mild day. Kathryn was large and ungainly with child now, and Nancy wrapped both her mistress and master well in cloaks before letting them out of doors.

From the other two houses, the news was bleak. While some of the sick grew stronger, two men died in the Catchmaids' house, as did two of the apprentices in the main dwelling-house. Philip Guy's children fell ill and were slow to recover. And though Mistress Catchmaid, who had been sick, began to rally, she miscarried her child.

"'Tis a dark day for all the colony," Reverend Leat said in his sermon at the funeral service for the four men who died within a few days of each other. "Not only have we lost four strong men, with many more growing weaker by the hour, but with Master Catchmaid's heavy loss of his unborn child, we have lost half our hope for the future. Indeed, in such bleak times it may seem as if God has turned His face away from us, though we have come all the way to this far land to bring His gospel to the natives of this country."

Nancy, seated on the bench with Bess on one side of her and Ned on the other, stole a glance at the faces round her. How many, she wondered, had really come here with the thought of converting the natives? Making a fortune, or seeking adventure, had brought most of them to these shores, despite the minister's pious words. It did not seem likely the endeavour had earned them any special favour from the Almighty.

Be that as it may, she prayed silently, *You have spared my mistress and her child. Only keep Your hand over them, keep the sickness from them, and I will look after all the rest in our household, the best I can.* Then she almost laughed aloud in the gloomy solemnity of the meeting at the thought of Nancy Ellis blithely assuring the Sovereign of the Universe that she had matters well in hand.

The prayers were said, the dead men buried in shallow graves in the near-frozen ground. With the service done, Nancy set to work with Bess's help to prepare a meal that would strengthen those who were recovering.

"I do despair of our Moll," Bess said. "She grows weaker by the hour. I can't bear to think of her lying under that cold earth. We have never been apart, not for a single day in our lives." A sob trembled at the edge of her voice, and Nancy thought at once how selfish she herself was, to beg God for Kathryn's life and no one else's. Every sick person here was dear to someone, every death a blow to some beloved heart. Then Daisy crept down to join them by the hearth, weeping for both her sister and her husband. Bess put her arms around Daisy and both sisters cried, and Nancy was left to cook dinner by herself.

Matt Grigg died before dawn the next morning, the fifth man to fall victim to the disease, and the first of Nicholas Guy's household. Daisy wailed and sobbed until Master Nicholas begged Nancy to take her somewhere where her cries would not disturb Kathryn. Bess was left to wash her brother-in-law's body, and to tend to her dying sister Molly. Ned and Frank went to dig yet another grave.

Nancy walked the weeping Daisy past the small burying ground where the men were preparing her husband's grave. Rather than pass through the rest of the settlement, she led her up the path to the fresh-water pond where they drew their water, taking two buckets with her for good measure. The day was cold and the ground frozen, covered with the lightest skiff of snow. Spring seemed an eternity away.

"I can't bear it," Daisy said through her sobs. "So long I waited—two years, back in Bristol, all the time praying my Matt was still alive, that we'd be together again someday. And then that long voyage over here, only to be together a few months and him taken from me! And I am not even carrying his child, not a thing left to prove he was ever alive!"

There were no words for her comfort and Nancy did not try to offer any. When they got to the pond, she set the buckets down on the ground and put an arm around the weeping girl's shoulder; Daisy turned to her, burying her face in Nancy's cloak so that Nancy had no choice but to pull her into an embrace.

After a little time Molly's husband Tom, himself only just recovering his strength, came up the path in search of Daisy, saying that Moll had wakened and asked to have both her sisters by her side. Nancy thought this would bring on a fresh burst of tears from Daisy, but instead Daisy drew herself up, pulled her cloak tighter around herself, and took Tom's arm. "We must be very brave now, Tom, for her," she said, hardly sounding like the same girl who had cried such stormy tears a few moments before.

Nancy was left alone by the pond. She took up the buckets and picked her way out across the shore ice to the hole Ned had chopped yesterday, which was only just caught over. Breaking the thin ice, she filled both buckets, the icy water biting at her bare hands. Then she began the slow walk back with her burden, trying not to slop too much on the ground.

She heard someone crashing up through the brush along the path towards her and hoped it was Ned come up to help her carry the water. Hoped, too, that he did not come bearing news of Molly's death. This day was too heavy already.

"Ho there, 'tis the proud Mistress Nan! Need a hand with those pails?"

It was George Whittington, that preening peacock. He had been giving himself all kinds of airs since he went away on the *Indeavour* and came back with a wolf's skin and the honour of being the first man to talk to the natives. Nancy was glad he had been paying attentions to Nell Bly, for though he was no great prize for poor Nell, it gave herself and the other unmarried maids a rest from his attentions. Still, she was not fool enough to turn away help. She handed him one of the buckets.

"Nary a word of thanks?" he said, reaching for the other.

"I can take this one well enough. Thank you."

"Very short thanks, indeed."

"Poor Matt Grigg is barely dead, and the men still digging his grave. This is no day for light talk or merriment." She was glad he had the other bucket; it occupied at least one of his hands and slowed him down enough that she could step lightly ahead of him on the path.

"But when we are surrounded by the dead and dying, should we not taste the joys of life while we can?" he offered, and when she did not turn back to him with an answer, he added, "Why are you such a curst jade, Nan? Why so proud?"

Now she did glance back over her shoulder at him. "Have you ever stopped to think that I am not curst and proud, but only that I do not like you? I know 'tis a hard thought to take in, that a woman might not be charmed by you, but you should consider it."

"You are a right shrew, you know that?"

"Then why waste your time trying to charm me?"

She knew the bold words were a mistake even before she felt his hard grip on her shoulder, pulling her to a stop, turning her to face him. She tried to wrench out of his grasp.

"I've no interest in wooing such a harpy as you have turned out to be. I only want to know why you disdain me so—and not only me, but all men. Poor Ned follows round after you like a little dog after a bone, and you'll not give him the time of day. Do you think you'll find a better husband among the savages, proud Nan? Or do you fancy yourself too good for any man on God's earth?"

His fingers were like iron, and she knew she would see bruises if it were ever warm enough for her to peel off her shift and examine her arm. "You know well that I'd take an Indian for a husband long before I'd ever consider you. I don't know why you make it your business to torment me."

He dropped the bucket, then, spilling water all over the ground, and with a wrench to her arm he tore hers from her hand as well. She struggled in vain as he towed her off the path into the trees. Their dark branches were laden with snow.

"Torment you, is it? I've a better woman than you already, and she'll be in my bed as soon as this plague passes and the preacher says the words. But I'm tired of waiting for my bride, and a slut who thinks herself too good for all of us will do while I wait. Tell you what, you grant me one kiss and I'll trouble you no more."

Nancy twisted to wrench her arm from his grip. "Here's my offer—you leave me go, no kisses, never speak to me again, or I'll tell my master. Then he'll tell the governor that you force your favours on virtuous maidens. The governor won't—"

His mouth was on hers, hard and brutal as a slap. He pushed her back against the bare trunk of a tree, and a little fall of snow from the branches dumped down on both their heads. It did not cool Whittington: while one hand still gripped her upper arm and his mouth crushed hers, his other hand fumbled at her breast and squeezed hard. She wriggled and tried to twist away from him, and he thrust his tongue into her mouth. Nancy felt herself gagging; she could not breathe.

When he pulled away, she shouted in his face. "You filthy knave! Don't think you will get away with such behaviour!"

This time he stopped her mouth, not with his own, thank God, but with his hand over her face. She tried to get enough purchase on his flesh to bite down, hard, but he was skilled at holding a captive—almost as if he had done this before.

One hand over her mouth, the weight of his muscular body pressing against hers, he moved his hand almost lazily from her breast, down to her skirts. Holding her in place against the tree trunk, he reached through apron and petticoat, groping around between her legs. As if he could even feel her privy parts through all that woolen fabric, Nancy thought—but of course touching wasn't the point. Proving to her that he could touch, could take as he pleased—that was the point.

"Say one word to Master Nicholas Guy, or to the governor," Whittington whispered, his mouth next to her ear, "and I'll ruin you, my lass. I'm the governor's golden boy now, and I mean to rise high in this colony. If you tell tales, I'll tell some of my own. Perhaps I'll tell Nicholas Guy I'm not the only one stealing kisses. Thomas Willoughby stole them too, from your mistress. She's no curst shrew like you—she gives willingly, so I'm told. A most cheerful slut, more than willing to cuckold her husband. I've got young Willoughby's own word for it, but I swear I won't tattle on her, if you don't tell tales on me." His fingers pinched, hard through the heavy russet of her petticoat. Now the hand moved back to her breast, pinched and twisted again. "Have we a bargain, Nancy?"

She had been cold as long as she could remember, for months now, but that was an outside cold that worked itself from the skin inwards. Now she felt cold as if ice were in her veins, as if her heart stopped. "I make no bargains with the likes of you," she said. "But I'll give you no excuse to spread lies and slanders about my mistress, either. She would never stoop to such a thing."

But even as she said the words, she thought of Kathryn laughing with Thomas Willoughby, locking her eyes with his. *'Tis a foolish dalliance, and he a foolish boy*, Nancy had told her then. Surely it had gone no further?

"They are no lies, believe you me." Whittington laughed at her and pushed his mouth up against hers again. She had never been kissed by a man before, and it was a horrible sensation: his teeth and his lips and his stale breath all up against her own mouth. But none of that mattered, all that mattered was that the kiss distracted him enough to loosen his grip a little. With her arms free, she pushed against his chest as hard as she could; hard enough to make him stumble back a step.

"Nancy!" That was Ned now, coming up the path at last, and Whittington stepped away from her, almost lazily, releasing her from his grip and turning back to the path.

"There comes poor Ned, your devoted puppy—go throw him a bone, or at least a kind word," he sneered. "And do not forget our bargain, fair Nancy."

She followed him onto the path just before Ned appeared. How was she meant to explain that she was coming back from the pond with George Whittington and two empty water buckets? But when she saw him, she knew Ned had no thought for explanations or water buckets.

"Come quick to the house," he said.

"'Tis not poor Molly?"

"Just breathed her last, and Mistress Kathryn is most distressed—two deaths in the house in one day. Both Daisy and Bess are distracted with grief, and poor Tom, too. We need you to come and put all to rights."

He put out his hand. She took it, and followed him back to the house.

CHAPTER FIFTEEN

An Occasion of Hope

You say that you would live in Newfound-land,
Did not this one thing your conceit withstand;
You fear the Winter's cold, sharp, piercing air.
They love it best, that have once wintered there.

CUPIDS COVE
MARCH 1613

I N THE END, WHEN THE GROUND THAWED, THERE WERE NINE new graves dug in the little plot of land between the settlement and the woods. Eight men dead, and one woman. Nearly one-sixth of the settlement. Half the colonists had fallen ill, and some who recovered were slow to regain their strength. Master Crout gave great credit to raw turnip as a cure for the disease, though he did not mention that Nancy had been the first to suggest it. The men who had not fallen ill made forays into the woods on the trails they had cut last summer and autumn, hoping to hunt or trap animals to supplement their stores of food.

One morning in late March, not long past the turning of the new year, Kathryn sat by the hearth knitting and stirring the pottage. She shifted on her stool in a fruitless effort to find a comfortable position now that her belly had swollen to enormous size. The weariness that had bound her to the bed for weeks had rolled away, leaving her with a restless energy that felt almost as if her skin were itching from the inside. She longed to be done with carrying the baby inside her, to feel that her body was her own and free to move about again, but before that must come the childbearing itself, a prospect that filled her with terror. She tried to busy herself with what tasks she could still manage to do, to keep her mind from dwelling on it.

She was alone in the house. Her husband, impatient with how long it was taking him to grow strong after his sickness, was out chopping wood; she heard the comforting ring of his axe. Nancy, Bess, and Daisy had gone out to tend to the livestock. Ned, Tom Taylor, and the other men were out checking the snares they had laid in the woods for rabbits or other small prey. It seemed their efforts were successful, for Ned and Tom soon came back into the house with a brace of hares.

"Those will be a welcome change," Kathryn said, hauling herself to her feet with effort.

"Don't trouble yourself, Mistress. I've skinned them already; now I'll clean and dress them," said Tom, taking the small bodies and pulling out his knife as he moved to the table.

"Have something to eat," Kathryn said, gesturing towards the pottage that simmered in its pot, suspended over the fire. "The girls made barley bread, though there's not enough lard, so 'tis a bit tough and dry. But it is better than ship's biscuit. Is there any sign of a thaw at all out there?"

"Today is warmer than yesterday," Tom said.

"You can hear the snow melting off the trees when you're in the woods," Ned added. "But 'tis best not to put too much stock in that. This place is the very devil for making you think winter's over and spring's at hand, and then hitting you in the face with another blizzard the very next day. Sure, you cannot count on spring till it's halfway through summer. Like enough we'll get a few warm days in July or August." He darted a grin at Tom, then quickly arranged his face into a more sober expression. They were all cautious now, after the sickness, of any levity, though Ned's good humour was hard to repress. Poor Tom had not smiled since his Molly was laid in the ground. He gave only a grim nod as he busied himself cutting up the rabbits.

The others came back soon after. Daisy, as sad and solemn as Tom, moved at once to help him with his task, but Nancy and Bess were all caught up with a small bundle Nancy carried wrapped in her shawl. One of the nanny goats had died while birthing a kid early that morning—the latest of the goats to perish; they seemed to have had a plague of their own just as the settlers had had, though in their case it was likely to be the lack of good grass for fodder. The girls had brought the kid goat to the house in an effort to keep it alive near the fire.

Nancy sat on the bench beside Kathryn, cuddling the little creature. "See, I'm getting a bit of practice for when I need to play nursemaid to your young one."

"I hope my child will be a fair piece prettier than that. Truly, Nan, would it not be kinder to let it die? The poor thing cannot survive." The kid goat looked little different from the poor skinned rabbits Tom was now putting on the spit to cook.

"It can indeed. The other nanny goat has milk, and though she won't take this kid, I got a little milk from her—look, see how she suckles?" Nancy had dipped the shawl in the little bowl of goat's milk, and was taking great pleasure in watching the kid suck at it. Ned knelt beside them, his head and Nancy's close together, laughing softly at the little goat.

Well, let them laugh, Kathryn thought. The household, the colony, needed laughter. With the loss of Matt and Molly and so many others, and the loss of Mistress Catchmaid's unborn child, Kathryn felt as if all eyes were on her growing belly, waiting for a newborn to give them a shred of hope for the future. It was too heavy a weight to bear; what if something went wrong again? Let Nancy have her moment of pleasure in the little kid goat before it, too, died.

Kathryn took what pleasure she could in simple things: the gamey smell of meat cooking; Nancy's and Ned's smiles; the sight of her husband coming through the door with an axe over his shoulder. And one more small pleasure, though a private one: the news from the main dwelling-house that Thomas Willoughby, who had fallen ill, was out of danger and up walking about again. She had not seen him in weeks; communal meals and even worship services had been curtailed since the scurvy had struck down so many. When Frank Tipton came in for dinner and told them the news of how all the sick were faring in the other dwelling-houses, he mentioned Willoughby in the tally of those who were recovering. Kathryn felt Nancy's eyes on her, and studied to keep her face cool and uninterested.

Kathryn slept poorly that night. Thomas Willoughby's face rose up in her dream: he reached out a hand towards her, and she took it. Then the dream twisted: she was in bed in her father's house in Bristol, Nancy by her side, losing her first baby in a torrent of pain and blood. Then she was fully awake: the pain was real, and the bed beneath her wet. Her belly clenched like a fist, and she gritted her teeth to keep from screaming.

Between waves of pain she shook her husband, told him it was her time.

"What?" He flustered awake, turning to look at her. "I will fetch Mistress Butler. Do you—is there aught you need now?"

"Only wake Nan before you go—she will know what to do."

In seconds Nancy was at her side. The door opened and a gust of chilly wind blew in, then it slammed closed again as Master Nicholas went out into the dark morning to find the woman who might act as midwife. Bess and Daisy, roused by the fuss, went to build up the fire. Upstairs, the men slept in their beds, untroubled by the drama unfolding in the master's bedchamber.

Now the pains were faster, harder. No time in between to catch a breath. Voices in the background, women's voices, high and fluttering. Someone put a cup to her lips. She tried to drink the bitter brew, no doubt full of healing herbs, but she gagged and spluttered it over her nightdress. "Stop giving her that,'twill choke her!" she heard, and another voice said, "What do you know of it? I have seen many a woman through the birth pains with this brew."

Pain invaded her whole body, made her vision blur. She shut her eyes. Hands gripped her hands. Nancy? Yes, it must be Nan. Who else would hold her through all this?

"Say a prayer for me, Nan," she begged through gritted teeth. "One of Tibby's old prayers, if you know any."

Nancy's face was close to her ear. "I wish I knew all her charms," she said—Nancy who put no stock in charms and magic. "I only know the one *Mary the Virgin brought forth Christ...*" Kathryn gripped Nancy's hand tight as her friend whispered the old, half-remembered prayer charm, a reminder of home. *"Lazarus come forth, Lazarus come forth."*

"Push! Push! Bear down, now, bear down. This babe is quick coming!" A woman's voice: not Nancy. Very close to her ear, someone repeating the word *push* over and over. And she felt it, like an urge inside her, her whole body clenching to drive out the new life inside, force it into the world whether it was ready or not. Push! She pushed, feeling as if she was engulfed in flames.

The women's voices clamoured, layering over each other till she could not tell who was saying what. They all shouted orders and instructions, but the only imperative she could obey was that of her own body, that outward and forward surge. She wanted to hold back from the pain, but she could only rush forward into it, though her whole body would split in two.

And it was done. A thin, high wail replaced the cacophony of women's voices.

"Ah, he's a bonny lad," someone said.

"Listen to him! A good healthy cry," said another.

Kathryn wanted to open her eyes, to see what they were talking about, but she was suddenly so exhausted. The pain was ebbing now, though there was one more quick spasm as someone leaned close and placed something warm on her chest. "Look at your fine baby," Nan said. "See what a grand little lad you've had."

Kathryn blinked, looked down. The baby was small and red, still wet and slimy with the birthing fluids. She thought of the little kid goat, the skinned rabbits. Then he blinked too, and dark eyes looked up into hers. Another person—the baby that had been just a thought, a hope, a dream all these long months was suddenly a human soul who could look up at her, meet her eyes.

"Good-day," she said, not sure how to greet her child. "Good-day, little one." She looked from the baby to Nancy. "Where is my husband? Does he know of the child yet?"

"We shooed all the men down to the big house. Bess has gone to carry the news. I'm sure Master Nicholas will be up here as quick as he can to see for himself."

He was, indeed, there within the half hour, allowing time for Nancy to help her tidy herself a little while Daisy cleaned the baby and swaddled him. He was back in Kathryn's arms, rooting for his mother's nipple, when his father entered the house.

Nicholas Guy touched his wife's cheek before looking down at his infant son. "You look well. I am glad you have come through without too great suffering."

He gathered the baby in his arms, then, and looked long and solemnly at the little bundle while Kathryn looked at him. He was a good man, her husband. He had protected and provided for her in this harsh land, and she was glad to give him a son and heir. God willing, she would bear him more in the future.

Life was no minstrel's ballad, Kathryn reminded herself. She was not a maid in a romance, but a colonist's wife and now a mother. She took the baby back from her husband's arms as he said, "I wish to call him Jonathan. My grandfather's name, and a tribute to my cousin John as well."

"'Tis fitting," Kathryn agreed. Every time he had raised the question of a name before the birth, she had told him it was ill luck to talk about it. She had been so afraid she would never bear a living child. Even now, of course, a baby was a fragile thing. Especially in this harsh land, at the far end of winter. She held her warm, living child in her arms, and wondered if she could dare to hope he would survive.

CHAPTER SIXTEEN

A New Beginning is Celebrated

When they had wisely, worthily begun,
For a few errors that athwart did run,
(As every action first is full of errors)
They fell off flat, retired at the first terrors.

CUPIDS COVE
MAY 1613

THE BABY SURVIVED: INDEED, HE THRIVED, SUCKLING eagerly at his mother's teat and growing larger and lustier every day. When he was six weeks old, the Sunday for Kathryn's churching arrived. Reverend Leat had come to the house to christen Jonathan shortly after he was born, but this Sunday the babe would be brought out and shown to the community, while Kathryn herself would be declared cleansed from the stain of childbirth. And, as a small point of interest amid that holy ceremony, she would see Thomas Willoughby again.

She had had many visitors and small gifts during the weeks since the baby's birth, but young Willoughby had neither come to visit nor sent any message. Indeed, it would have been most unsuitable for him to do so. Those autumn weeks when she had teased and bantered with him while her husband was away on the *Indeavour*—before the sickness, before her child had been born—felt like part of a different life. When she walked outside on that first Sunday morning in May, tasted the outdoor air, Kathryn felt no connection to that other Kathryn Guy who had walked these paths last summer and autumn. She was a mother now, as well as a wife: she had a new role to play. And the colony itself must be different after this terrible winter. Surely one difference would be this: she would no longer feel anything when she looked into Thomas Willoughby's eyes.

A fresh, cold wind blew in off the water. True, the calendar said May, but no hint of spring warmth tinged that wind; green buds were tight-furled on the bare tree branches. The sky overhead was a blanket of grey cloud, broken here and there by weak beams of sun that tried to pierce the clouds. It was cold enough still that everyone's breath clouded on the air when they spoke.

But the mood was spring-like, as people gathered round Kathryn in the hall of the main dwelling-house, peering and cooing over the baby. Elizabeth Guy's little boys, well recovered now from the sickness, ran about the dwelling-house with hearty whoops and hollers, and had to be shushed to silence by their mother, who led them over to see their small cousin. James, the elder boy, looked at the baby once before turning his attention to a spinning top Ned had made for him, but little Harry stared a long time, as if finding it hard to believe there was now a resident of Cupids Cove even smaller than himself.

A few of the other women, like Kathryn herself, wore gowns that looked as if they belonged in an English church on a May morning, instead of the heavy dark woolens they had shivered in through the winter. Without blossoms or warm weather, they had still the promise of spring: the harbour ice had thawed; ships were arriving from England; the ground would soon be ready for planting. The baby that Kathryn carried in her arms, new life after so much hardship, was a symbol of that promise: like Philip and Elizabeth's little boys, he was a reminder that they were building something here that was meant to last, that there would be generations of English children in this land to continue what the colonists had begun.

"Forasmuch as it hath pleased Almighty God of His goodness to give you safe deliverance," the minister intoned as Kathryn knelt before him, "and hath preserved you in the great danger of childbirth, ye shall therefore give hearty thanks to God, and pray."

Hearty thanks, indeed. After the service, the benches were moved and tables laid for a communal dinner. After her long confinement, Kathryn was hungry for other faces, other voices, even as she could not help noticing the empty spaces, the faces that were gone from their circle. As they ate, the menfolk talked about the arrival of the fishing fleet, plans for summer exploration, and what news would come from the colony's investors in England. Governor John Guy had returned to Bristol a few weeks earlier, leaving Master Philip as acting governor— he had business to settle with the colony's investors. Kathryn heard Thomas Willoughby's elegant drawl above the voices of the other men, declaring that his father would certainly have to consider whether his investment in the New Found Land was worthwhile, given how harsh the winter had been and how many men had been lost. Over the heads of the company assembled, his blue eyes caught hers for a moment. With an effort, she looked away.

While the men spoke of the colony's hopes for summer, the women examined Kathryn's baby, offering advice about caring for an infant and suggestions of herbs that would keep her milk flowing well. They talked, too, of what crops could be planted now and what they might hope to reap next harvest. Amid their chatter, Jane Catchmaid sat quiet and pale. Her eyes followed little Harry and James Guy as they ran about the room, then came back to rest on Kathryn and the baby. *Poor woman*, Kathryn thought, *to lose a child and have to sit here while everyone celebrates mine.* Still, Jane spoke kindly to Kathryn, congratulating her.

Mistress Catchmaid's staunch supporter Sal Butler, who had served as midwife, was less generous. "You are most fortunate, Mistress Guy," she said as she bent down to peer at baby Jonathan, sleeping in a basket on the floor. "Still, 'tis often true that poor women such as we have an easier time birthing than ladies like my mistress, is it not?" Kathryn might be married to the governor's cousin, but Sal Butler was not about to let her forget that she was only a stonemason's daughter. And when Kathryn smiled and nodded, Mistress Butler added, "You'd have had an easier time still, had you been allowed to drink my ginger posset with spruce bark boiled into it. 'Tis a great help in birthing, that brew, but your girl would have none of it, and dashed the cup from your lips."

"If you'd as much experience birthing babies as you claim, you'd have known she was in no fit state to drink anything at the time, and not tried to force it on her," Nancy shot back.

Kathryn gave Nancy a stern glance. "'Twas a difficult time, as birthing always is, and there are bound to be disagreements. All that matters is I have a hale little boy out of it." She saw that her words had stung Mistress Catchmaid yet again and wished she had spoken with more care.

"By the time he's big enough to eat solid food, we'll have more than ship's biscuit to feed him—I know my two have grown tired of that, these last weeks," Elizabeth Guy put in, turning all their thoughts back to the ever-present topic of food.

"I knows 'twas some nice to knead out that first loaf of bread when we first got grain in after all winter," Daisy said. She smiled for a moment, then her round face grew sober again: she had not spoken of being happy about anything since her husband and sister had died.

"Perhaps the next ship will have cheese," Nancy suggested quickly. They had gone through their own stores of cheese over the winter and had no means to make more since all the cows and most of the goats had died for want of fodder.

"Raise up that little kid-goat of yours and we'll be getting milk from her before long," Daisy said, and most of the women laughed. Nancy had taken a good deal of teasing for nursing the baby goat to health and toting it around like a pet; she had even sat beside Kathryn, feeding the kid from a bowl of milk as Kathryn fed the babe at her breast.

"Yes, cheese...and plum preserves," said Bess in a dreamy tone, as a girl might talk about wearing diamonds or living in a palace.

"You will all have bread and preserves and cheese enough, once more supplies come from Bristol," said Master Philip Guy, passing by to hear their talk. "This is all a great experiment, you know—to learn by experience what it takes to survive here, so that every year we can support ourselves more and depend less upon ships from England."

"But one must ask if the experiment is even a sensible one," Mistress Catchmaid said. "I know I had not expected so harsh a winter, or I would have had second thoughts about coming out."

"Summer will be a kinder season," Philip Guy assured her. "We have committed to make this a success, and we must stay the course."

He passed on from the knot of women, taking his wife Elizabeth and the boys with him. Mistress Catchmaid said to the women around her, "Must we stay the course at the risk of so many lives? Think of the tales from the Virginia colony, of all the lives lost there! Will we bide here till we begin eating each other?"

With Elizabeth Guy gone, Kathryn was the only other woman of rank at the table, and thus the only one who could chide. "That kind of talk will put no heart in us, Mistress Catchmaid. After the hard winter we have come through, we need courage and good faith."

"Oh, and 'tis easy to speak of courage, when you are not the one who has lost a babe!" Sal Butler leaped to her mistress's defense. It might have turned into a quarrel indeed, had Jonathan not woken at that very moment and set up a howl. Nancy picked him from the basket and handed him to Kathryn, and the other women took the interruption as a chance to leave the table and go off to do those tasks that needed doing, even on a Sunday.

Back in her own household later that evening, Kathryn thought of the women's talk again. Around her table were gathered her husband and Nancy, Bess and Daisy, Ned and Tom, and three of the other men who shared the upstairs loft: Frank Tipton, John Teague, and John Crowder. To that small group she recounted Mistress Catchmaid's words, adding, "'Tis only natural she should be discontented, but it seemed as if others share her misgivings. Is there talk of folk wanting to leave the colony and go back to England?"

"That there is—I've heard it from many of the fellows," Ned Perry said.

"Now that the governor is gone back," Nicholas Guy said, "William Colston will follow—they says 'tis to raise more funds for the colony, but Mistress Colston and her sister will go back as well once their master goes, and they may not return. As for the single men, many of Willoughby's apprentices are not suited to this life—and, though 'tis a shame to say it, Willoughby's own son is no better. That puffed-up young coxcomb needs to be on the next ship to England, only his father won't have him back."

Across the table, Nancy lifted her eyes to meet Kathryn's. For the second time that day, Kathryn looked away from a gaze that cut too close her feelings for Thomas Willoughby. At the thought of him going back to England, she felt a queer mixture of relief and disappointment.

In their bed that night, curtains drawn, she turned to Nicholas. "If so many are going back to England, what of us? Will we go?"

There was a little silence; for a moment she listened to his steady breathing and wondered if he was already asleep. Then he said, "I have made no fortune here. If we go back to England now, I will not have the means to buy into the merchants' guild. I would have to go back to being a shoemaker." Though he had been a fisherman, a farmer, a hunter, and a boatbuilder since coming to the New World—and had repaired a fair few boots as well—she could tell how deeply he disliked the idea of returning to Bristol to take up his old trade.

"And if we stay?"

He propped himself up on an elbow: she could not see his face but could feel him looking down at her. "There is a fortune to be made here, but not in Cupids Cove."

"What...what can you mean?" She thought of the dark, tree-covered hills, the empty coves and bays, the fishing stations and the pirates' fort, the native camp the men had visited. What kind of life could an English family have in this land, outside of the settlement?

"This cove is too small, too crowded, and any man who hopes to make his fortune will need to clear land of his own. There is trouble, too, with the company back in England. The governor is afeared that the investors will withdraw their support, for we have been here three years, and instead of making them rich, we are still costing them money. I fear the whole venture may fall prey to petty squabbles and mismanagement."

Then surely, she thought, *we would go back to Bristol.* Back to being a shoemaker's wife, trying to wrest control of a tiny household from her sister-in-law's grip.

Her husband went on. "I've not spoken of this yet—I did not want to trouble you with it, so soon after bearing our son. But Kathryn, this land has changed me—changed my ambitions. I once thought nothing could be finer than returning to Bristol with gold in my pocket, to be a merchant of that city. You know 'twas always my plan. But after three years here—I look at this land, at the sea around it, at all the opportunities it offers, and I have thought...what say you, to making this our home? To building our own plantation here, being master and mistress of our own estate?"

"You mean—we would own our own land, live on it, and work it?"

"Yes. I have spoken to John, before he went away. While he would like to imagine that everyone will stay in Cupid's Cove and work for the good of the settlement, the governor sees that there must be room here for some men to strike out on their own. I want to be the first to do so. My work here has earned me the right to my own grant of land, and with a few men I could clear a plot of land up the shore, between Harbour Grace and Carbonear."

"You have given this a good deal of thought."

"I have. But I have not—I would not make any commitment to it, without consulting you."

She remembered the night in Bristol when Nicholas had announced he was going to the New World, and explained to her that men did not consult their wives about such things. Their year together in the colony had changed that, she saw. Perhaps theirs was becoming a true partnership, after all. "I hardly know what to say," she said. But she found she liked the thought of their own plantation. They could build a grand house and give it a lovely name, like an English manor.

Kathryn thought, for the first time in a long time, of the portrait of the woman in the blue dress she had once admired on the wall of a great house back home. Someday, perhaps, there would be an artist in the New Found Land, and he could paint her portrait to hang on the wall of their fine home. Not wearing silk, perhaps—but not in homespun, either.

"'Twould be hard work, no point in denying that," her husband went on. "We would build a house—for you and me and the baby, and such servants as are willing to come with us—and there we could farm our own land and raise our own stock. Catch and cure our own fish to sell back in England. We can be landowners here, as we could never be back in England."

The next day, while baby slept and the women washed out the clothes and bed linens, Kathryn told Nancy about her husband's new plan. Nancy nodded, scrubbing one of the baby's little shifts briskly along the washboard. "If you and the master were to go off and clear your own land, you'd need servants and labourers. When Bess and Frank marry, I'd say they'd be willing to follow. Daisy will go where Bess does, and you know I'll not leave your side."

"I know you've never wished to stay in this country."

"What choice have I, if you stay?" Nancy wrung out the baby's clothes, put them in a basket, took a petticoat from the pile of soiled linens. "There's naught for me back in Bristol."

"You might yet marry. Either some man who is staying here in the colony, or someone who goes back home."

"You know I've no wish for that."

"George Whittington spoke to my husband about you, some time ago."

A look that could only be fear passed over Nancy's face. "What—what did he say?"

"Only that he would make an offer for your hand in marriage—what else would he say?"

Nancy hesitated a moment before saying, "'Tis a strange offer to make, since Nell Bly believes he has pledged to wed her. What did Master Nicholas tell him?"

"That I would speak to you about it, as I am doing, but that the choice was yours. I suppose there has been no formal betrothal between George and Nell yet."

"Well, you know what my choice is," Nancy said. Her strong, work-worn hands knotted into the fabric of the petticoat as she scrubbed hard. "Even if I were to think of marriage, I'd not think twice about George Whittington."

A Bristol ship sailed into the harbour two days later. There had been sack ships already, and the colonists had been able to trade for a few items, but this was the vessel they had been awaiting, coming with supplies and letters from their own Newfoundland Company. All the settlers gathered by the water as the ship put down boats and sailors rowed into shore. Kathryn imagined what they might have on board:

barrels of grain and salt, for certain. Sugar. Peas and beans. Wheels of cheese, perhaps. By tonight there would be a change, at last, from the monotony of their rations.

Aboard the ship was not only food aplenty, but other necessities—cloth, rope, nails, window glass. Almost as welcome were letters and news from England. For Kathryn there was a letter from her father, with the news that her younger brothers and sister were all well. It contained greetings from the servants and apprentices, not only for her but for Nancy and Ned. Many of the other colonists, at least those whose families could read and write, received similar messages.

But not all the news was happy. As the settlers and sailors gathered for a meal together in the big house, the first meal in months where there was an abundance of flavours and plenty for everyone to eat, Kathryn noticed the absence of Philip Guy. "My cousin has had many letters from the merchants of the company," her husband told her. "He has closeted himself away to read them, but I think he is not well pleased with what he has read so far. Likely he'll summon some of us men tonight to discuss his plans."

"Is the company losing faith in this venture? Will they abandon us altogether?"

Master Nicholas frowned. "'Tis certainly what the governor feared before he went back—that having found no mines of gold or iron or copper here, but only the codfish that we knew was in the waters all along, they start to question whether this land is worth settling. And I do not think that, when they hear how we passed the winter, their concerns will be eased. The loss of life here has not been great compared to those lost in Virginia, but eight dead out of such a small colony may make the investors think this land is not worth the trouble of over-wintering."

"Nine," Kathryn corrected, tallying the dead on her fingers.

Her husband, too, counted. "We lost eight men, I am sure of it. So said all the reports we are sending back."

"Eight men, and Molly." A girl, especially a servant girl, hardly counted in the tally, she supposed. And Mistress Catchmaid's dead baby would not be counted either, having never even been baptized.

As he had expected, Nicholas was summoned after dinner to a meeting with the other high-ranking men of the colony—Philip Guy, in his role as acting governor, William Colston and William Catchmaid, and Sir Percival's agent Henry Crout. Distinctly not invited to the meeting was Sir Percival's son Thomas. When she went down to the brewhouse to fetch a jug of ale, with the baby nestled in a sling against her chest, Kathryn was startled to see Thomas Willoughby step into the room. They had not spoken alone in many months, and now he had followed her here to the most isolated building in the settlement.

"I had letters from my father," he said to her without preamble. "He will not allow me to come home."

Kathryn tried to quell the little quiver of excitement she felt. It was best, best for everyone and certainly for herself, if Thomas Willoughby were to return to England. "He says you must remain here for the summer?"

"For the summer?" Thomas laughed a short, harsh laugh. "Till I rot and die, more like. He says my duty is to make a life for myself here. He sends me a trunk of clothes and some trifles to cheer my exile, and informs Master Crout that by no means must I be allowed to take passage on any ship for England."

"Next winter will be better," she told him. "We have learned so much about how to survive here."

"Those are not the lessons I wish to learn. This is not the life I was born to." He lifted those eyes to her, their brilliant blue clouded like the sea on a stormy day. "There is only one thing might ever make this land bearable to me, and that one thing is denied me." As if to be sure there was no chance she might mistake his meaning, he took her hand and held it to his lips for the barest second, before he turned and left the brewhouse.

CHAPTER SEVENTEEN

A Second Meeting is Thwarted

Yours is a holy just Plantation
And not a justling supplantation.

CONCEPTION BAY
AND TRINITY BAY
MAY 1613

THE SPRING WEDDINGS LACKED THE FESTIVE AIR THAT HAD marked the weddings in the autumn. As Tom Taylor and Daisy Grigg stood before the minister to say their vows, it was impossible for anyone in the little congregation to forget that six months earlier they had each been vowed to another partner at this same altar. As for Daisy's sister Bess, her belly was already swelling with Frank Tipton's child. That wedding had to take place as soon as possible, and no one was very surprised when Tom and Daisy, who had comforted each other over the deaths of Matt and Molly, had announced that they planned to marry as well. But the shadow of loss was too recent for any true celebration.

Ned was keenly aware as he sat watching the two couples plight their troth that Nancy Ellis was now the only unmarried woman remaining in the colony. All the servant girls who had come out last summer had been married off—twice, in poor Daisy's case. Just the week before, Nell Bly had pledged herself to George Whittington: Whittington gave himself such airs now that he would not share a wedding with the servants from Nicholas Guy's household, but must have his own. Apart from

Nancy, the only women who had not found husbands in the colony were Mistress Colston's sister and her maid, who had both returned to England with the Colstons. There were still a good few unmarried men; Ned wondered if Governor Guy planned to return with another shipment of would-be wives.

As for himself, Ned had no interest in girls who might be travelling across the ocean. True, Nancy had flatly refused him the one time he asked, but she had refused others since then. He still had a chance.

Everyone shared a common dinner after the service, but there was no dance nor any other pretense of a wedding celebration. Only a Sunday afternoon, with chores still to be done, though fewer than on the other six days. No work on the walls or on buildings or boats, no fishing even now the season had begun, but the animals must still be fed, food cooked, and the houses kept clean. When he had done feeding the pigs, Ned walked up the path to the pond and found Nancy coming down with two buckets of water.

"Can I take one down for you?"

"No, I'm better with the two. They balance me out."

"I feel a fool walking along empty-handed," he said.

"'Twon't kill you to feel like a fool, else you would have died of it long since. If you want to make yourself useful, bring in some wood."

He gathered up an armload from the woodpile, and she lingered to walk back with him. Once inside, Ned threw the wood into the woodbox and bent to build up the fire again as Nancy poured water into a pot to heat over the flames. They were alone in the house, for once; everyone else was still down at the big house or going about their chores. Living on top of each other as they all did here, it was rare for any two people to steal a moment alone: Ned sometimes wondered how Frank and Bess had managed to snatch enough time together for him to put a child in her belly.

He kept prattling on to fill the silence. "'Twasn't the merriest of weddings, was it?" No, if he talked of weddings he might find himself offering marriage again. "Though 'tis good to have something to celebrate, with so many people gone back to England. I am glad some of our folk mean to settle and make a go of it here."

"There'll be more gone before summer's over. Here, don't sit idle—bring over those turnips, help me peel and chop them." He brought over the vegetables and began paring one with his knife as Nancy continued talking. "They say all Sir Percival's apprentices will be gone by summer's end, and Master Crout with them."

"They've never been content here, any more than Thomas Willoughby has."

The name of the young nobleman left an uncomfortable little space. Ned was sure Nancy knew of the gossip that said Thomas Willoughby was too familiar with Nicholas Guy's wife. He knew better than to speak of it; Nancy would give him the sharp edge of her tongue if he lent even a breath of credence to such tales. Instead he said, "Our own household will be down in numbers, I 'low—Crowder and Teague have gone to Master Philip Guy and told him they'll be gone at the end of summer too, unless they can each have a piece of land for their own. More of the Bristol men mean to break with the company and strike out on their own, just as our Master Nicholas does."

"What of you?"

"I intend to stay here in the New Found Land and to make a life of it." He looked at the turnip, not at her face, as his hands copied her movements, slicing the tough fibre. "Whether in Cupids Cove or somewhere else along the shore, I know not. I do believe there'll be Englishmen wintering all along this coast in twenty years, and I 'low I'll be one of them." *If I have a woman to marry and bear my children*, he did not add aloud.

"And the master is much of your mind," Nancy said, sliding the peels into a pan to throw on the fire. "Tom and Frank and the girls plan to go with him—will you?"

Ned nodded. "I will, if he asks me. But before I join him in clearing land up there, I mean to go on Master Crout's voyage into Trinity Bay, to see can we find the natives again, and trade with them. 'Twas a good beginning last autumn, but then they stole away from us in the night, leaving only furs laid out for trade, and we've had no sight of them since."

There was a noise at the door as the master and mistress came in, the baby setting up a lusty little wail as they entered the room. Master

Nicholas caught Ned's last words and replied to them as Mistress Kathryn soothed her infant.

"I would go on that journey myself," Nicholas Guy said, "were I not determined to clear my own land up the shore before the fish strike in. Last year's encounter with the natives held promise, but 'twas clear they are still shy of meeting with us. This land's riches will never be ours if we cannot truck with them and make friends of them."

Ned remembered that strange, enchanted night by the fire last November. How hopeful everything had seemed then. It had seemed possible that they could make peace with the people of the land and trade with them, and with their aid build a thriving English colony that would rival James Fort to the south. Sickness and hunger and discontent had taken a toll since then. Ned thought that if they saw the native Indians again, he might feel once more that bold hope. When Henry Crout had said he purposed to take a small group of men in a shallop back to Trinity Bay, Ned had been one of the first to say he would come along.

When their party set sail a short time later, they retraced their path of last autumn, up past Harbour Grace and around Baccalieu Island, then south again. They saw plenty of English fishing vessels, but no pirate ships, though with the coming of spring Philip Guy had warned the men at Cupids Cove to be vigilant. Word was that Peter Easton had moved on to warmer waters and richer prizes, but other pirates would follow in his wake.

Travelling down the same coast they had sailed along in November, they saw signs that the natives had camped there. On an island at the entrance to a bay, where a canoe was pulled onto the beach, Crout ordered his men to put ashore. "If one of their boats be here, they cannot be far," he insisted.

The six men of the party walked a little ways into the woods that fringed the beach. There was a trail here, for certain, and it led back to a clearing, much like the one they had visited on their previous journey. "They are here," said John Crowder.

"No, 'tis empty," said Bartholomew Pearson.

Ned said nothing, but was inclined to agree with Pearson, who was the most skilled hunter and tracker in the colony. There was a dwelling-house ahead of them, the same kind they had seen before, made of skins placed over a wooden frame. But there was no sound of voices. A small cooking fire stood before the shelter. There was cooked meat on a spit over it, and the stones were still warm, but no one was nearby.

"They left in haste," said Crout.

"Then they must be near." Pearson moved towards the edge of the clearing. "Let us search the forest."

"That will only fright them further. They might attack."

The natives, Ned thought, were elusive, as they had been even after that strange night of meeting and feasting together. Slipping back into the trees as silently as if they were a part of the landscape, evading contact with the English. He followed Crout into the empty shelter and saw the natives' belongings there—sleeping pallets of furs laid on the floor, clothing piled beside them or hung on the poles.

"This is no hunting party," Crowder said. "Look." He held up a pair of shoes made of animal hide. They were tiny, barely fitting two of Crowder's fingers in one shoe.

"A child. And belike these are women's garments," Crout said, looking at a tunic he had picked up, "for they seem to be smaller than what the men would wear."

"'Tis a family's home, then," said Ned, the first time he had spoken. It struck him almost as strange as it had when they had danced and sang and shared a meal with them: *they are men like us, with wives, children, homes.*

But these natives had not lingered to parley. Crout kept their party waiting on the beach for a time, though he stayed Pearson from going deep into the woods after them. "We ought to stay all night, or through to-morrow," Pearson argued. "They must come back before nightfall, if it is a family. Even a savage could not keep his woman and child on the run in the woods without food or rest. And all their belongings are here."

"I think you are right; they will return," Master Crout said. "Yet if they knew we were coming, and have retreated, what advantage would we gain by staying till they return? They will not be glad to see us."

"Whether they are glad or not makes no odds," Pearson grumbled. He sat on a rock on the beach, balancing the musket on his knees. "You talk as though they are Christian men."

"What would you have us do? We cannot force them to trade with us."

"What you ought to have done when you came out here last year—take a few captive."

Master Crout seemed shocked by this suggestion. Ned was shocked, too, though he was not about to interfere in an argument between his betters. He knew native people had been brought back to England, but they never lived long. Who would want to, after being stared at like beasts in a cage? *They are not beasts*, he thought, reflecting again upon the little child's shoes, upon the men's laughter on that night they had danced together. *But mayhap, like beasts, they have learned to fear us.*

Crout was the leader of the party, and he prevailed. They left the cove that night without seeing the natives, leaving some food next to the fire to show they had been there and meant no harm. The shallop continued on along the coast, stopping at other sites, including the place where they had met with the Indians the year before. Here and there were tantalizing signs that the natives had been there—empty shelters, evidence of cookfires—but they never came as close to seeing the wild men themselves as they had on the day when they stood by the still-warm fire with meat cooking over it.

Finally, as they began to sail back towards home, they approached that same spot again. This time, a fire burned on a nearby beach. "They must certainly be near, and perhaps are signaling to us," Master Crout said. "We will put ashore, and see can we find them this time."

"I'd find them, did you let me track them properly," Pearson said, but was quelled with a glance from Crout.

By the time the shallop reached shore, the fire was burned to ash, wisps of smoke rising from it. "They must have run for the woods as soon as they saw us," Crowder said.

"They have left something, this time." Ned pointed at a row of birch poles stuck into the earth at the edge of the strand. Animal skins were draped over the poles, as they had been on that morning last fall when the men of the *Indeavour* woke to find the native hunters gone from the beach.

By now the other men were out of the boat, and all moved towards the poles to inspect the display. "Good quality pelts," Crout said. "Fox, beaver, otter. Left to trade, as they did before, no doubt."

"Look yonder! There they are!" Pearson cried. He pointed; they could all see men moving through the trees a little distance inshore. Master Crout hoisted the truce flag and called out, but the natives came no closer, and Crout stayed Master Pearson from going into the woods after them. Instead, he decreed that they would take down the pelts and leave what trade goods they had with them at the base of the poles.

"'Tis most unfortunate, after the pleasant meeting we had with them last year, that they will not trust us to trade face to face, but we must show them we mean good will," Master Crout said as they set to work.

"It might not be the same lot at all." Crowder pulled down one of the poles to cut loose the fox fur tied to its top. "Or perchance since last year they have met with fishermen who treated them ill, and now they want no truck with our kind."

Although the shallop was laden with good-quality furs, Ned felt a curious sense of loss when they put back to sea a few hours later. He shared Master Crout's regret that last year's meeting had not led to the start of friendly trade. He wanted to know more of these red men, of how they lived, perchance even learn to speak a little of their strange tongue. Now, as they sailed past the empty coves of Trinity Bay, he felt that hope receding, just as the red men themselves were receding, melting back into the forest.

This land is not ours, he thought—a traitorous thought, but one that would not stop rising up as they made for Cupids Cove through the sparkling sunlight of a day that finally felt like summer. The soil would not yield to their crops; the winters felled them with sickness; the natives would not treat with them. Even Englishman turned his sword against Englishman, once the black pirate flag was raised. Ned felt his usual good cheer harder to maintain on that voyage home than it had been at any time in the past, even in winter at the height of the sickness.

After they passed Carbonear, Henry Crout suggested putting in at Nicholas Guy's plantation site, where Master Guy and a few other men were working at clearing the land. That cheered Ned a little: a good laugh with Tom Taylor and John Teague would lift the gloom from his spirits, and he could lend a hand to the work. It was the long hours in the boat with nothing to do that led him to brood, he concluded.

"Are we all for spending a night here, lads?" Master Crout asked as they pulled the shallop ashore in the little cove where a clearing held the frame of what would someday be Nicholas Guy's house.

"Master Crout, if it please you, sir, I'd be glad to stay here longer, and have you go on back to Cupids Cove without me," Ned said. "I promised Master Guy before we left that I would help him here when our expedition is done. I'm his man, sir, and I mean to work for him here."

Crout eyed Ned more closely. "So it goes," he said. "Each man clearing his own land; each loyal to his own master. Well, I cannot change that, and I am not governor of this colony. If you've given your word to Nicholas Guy already, stay here and work for him. God's teeth, 'tis no odds to me."

CHAPTER EIGHTEEN

A Storm Approaches

If Madmen, Drunkards, Children, or a Fool,
Wrong sober, discreet men with tongue or tool,
We say, Such things are to be borne withall.
We say so too, if Women fight, or brawl.

CUPIDS COVE
JUNE 1613

MASTER JONATHAN GUY WAS A HUNGRY, ANGRY LITTLE creature, who needed to be fed and have his clouts changed constantly, and in between those times seemed to cry for no reason at all. Perhaps all babies were like that, Nancy thought. She had had little to do with them until now. She was not a good nursemaid, but she had been thrust into the role whether she liked it or no, as with so many other roles she played in the household. Nursemaid, cook, scullery maid, gardener, goatherd. She was even doing the work of a manservant now: Ned and John Crowder had gone off in the shallop, while Master Nicholas had taken Tom Taylor and John Teague with him to clear his new piece of land. Frank was the only man left in their house to care for Mistress Kathryn, Nancy, Bess, Daisy, and the baby.

"I'm off to chop wood for the fire." Nancy gladly handed Kathryn the squalling infant, pulled a cloak on, and went outside. The calendar had turned over to June, but it was a wet, gray, foggy June month so far, with little hint of summer's warmth save for the scattered day of sun. Since the last frosts, the settlers had hoed and planted cabbage, turnip, carrots, and parsnips, but the cold spring kept the plants from flourishing. Before he left for England, Governor Guy had declared they would plant no corn this season. Each of the past three summers, the settlers had tried different varieties of grains, but none had flourished. A waste of good seed, the governor had finally declared. Best to concentrate on growing the few things that grew well in this country, on raising livestock for milk and meat, on killing wild game and salting away the abundant codfish for winter.

Truth be told, as little as she liked playing nursemaid, Nancy enjoyed some of the additional tasks she had taken on with the men away. Splitting firewood, in particular, gave her great satisfaction. Back in Bristol they had bought firewood, and the apprentices had taken turns to split it up into smaller pieces for the fire. Now Ned had taught her to split logs, and she thought that when he returned she could challenge him to a splitting contest, for she had the rhythm of it finally, and the strength in her arms. Whenever she felt peevish, as she often did, it was a great relief to take her anger out on the axe head and the wood.

She was going to it with a will, cleaving clean junks of birch and enjoying the ring of the axe in the still air, when she looked up to see George Whittington leaning on the rail fence, smoking a pipe. "Sure you're as good as any man with that axe," Whittington called.

"Am I now? And if you were as good as any man, you'd be down below working."

"I'm only catching a few minutes' rest, feasting my eyes on your beauty."

"Go on with you, Whittington. You've a wife at last; high time you left other women alone."

"Oh, my Nelly's a fine wife, indeed—pretty and sweet, and of a more biddable nature than some I could mention. She does as I tell her." He vaulted to sit on the top rail of the fence. "You'll be sorry one day that you turned me down—I'm going to be a great man in this colony." He was well settled in to lecture her now, but fortunately between the wind and the sound of her axe she couldn't much hear him. "'Tis the one good thing about this godforsaken place," he yammered on, "how a man can rise. I'll be master of my own plantation and captain of my own ship someday. Yes, a man can rise—and a woman can, too, if she got the good sense to hitch herself to the right man."

Nancy paused; her arms were throbbing and she needed a moment's rest. "Aye, all kinds of things rise to the top in this land," she said. "Only this morning I boiled the kettle and saw how all the hot air rose up. And you'd not believe what rises to the top of the chamber pot when I heave it out in the morning."

Whittington laughed. "You'll have a sharp tongue in your head till the day someone cuts it out of you, Nan Ellis," he said. "I said you'd regret refusing me—watch and see if that does not come true." He leapt lightly off the fence rail, but landed hard. "Damn your eyes, look what you made me do!" he cried with a howl of pain.

Nancy laughed. "Yes now—and did I make you come up here, or sit on the fence, or jump off it? What have you done, turned your ankle? Serves you right for pestering me at my work."

Whittington hobbled away, much less sanguine than he'd been when he arrived, and Nancy went back to her woodcutting with a lighter heart. Still, she had not forgotten the threat Whittington had made months ago. She was sure he had not forgotten either.

She kept an eye to her mistress and Thomas Willoughby every time the two of them were in the same room. Surely, with her husband's heir born now, Kathryn would not be such a fool as to risk a dalliance with that sullen young lordling. But Master Nicholas was away again. At nights, now, Nancy shared Kathryn's bed, and with the curtains pulled about them she could raise the topic of Thomas Willoughby in private, warn her mistress of Willoughby's boasts and George Whittington's threats. But she had not done so. Out of fear, perhaps, that she might learn a truth she did not want to know.

She had to go down to the storehouse that afternoon to replenish their supply of flour and hoped she would not encounter Whittington again. Walking down the rocky paths that connected the colony's buildings felt far different this summer than it had when she had arrived almost a year ago. Every turn and stone in the path was familiar to her now, familiar as only a landscape could be when she had seen nothing else for eleven months. But the settlement itself had changed. Last summer Cupids Cove had been bustling: the old colonists and the new ones, and a goodly number of summer fishermen as well. Well over a hundred souls in all; it had felt like a village, though one composed mainly of men.

Now the place felt hollow as an empty bowl. So many people had returned to England, including the governor himself. Those who had died of the sickness in winter left empty beds behind, and now that Master Crout had taken a boatload of men on another expedition, there were fewer than fifty souls left in Cupids Cove.

She passed some of them on her walk: Maggie and Liza feeding chickens, with help from little James Guy; Jennet helping two of the lads tote a bundle of barley down to the mill. In the big house she found Elizabeth Guy, Jane Catchmaid, and Sal Butler making tallow candles. "Have you come to lend a hand, Nan?" Mistress Guy greeted her as she came in. "Every house is running low on candles, and when this is done we have soap to make as well."

"I came to fetch flour, and I need to bring it up to the house so Bess can begin the pies. But if I can spare an hour afterwards, I'll come back down to help."

As she passed into the storehouse, she heard Sal Butler's sharp tones. "'Tis no good asking that one for help, she serves her own mistress and no one else. Some folks here cannot see that all must work for the good of everyone."

"That will not be true for long, if everyone goes off on their own plot of land and looks only to their own needs," Mistress Guy replied. Which confirmed, as Nancy had suspected, that there was a division between Philip and Nicholas Guy, that the former was not best pleased with his cousin's plan to leave Cupids Cove. "This place cannot thrive if everyone looks only to their own ends."

Her flour sack filled, she had now to pass back through the main room, where the three women were still talking about the selfishness of folk who would not work for the good of all. Nancy lifted her chin a little as she passed through, and meant to say nothing at all, but when Mistress Catchmaid said, "So, Nan, will you be able to spare us an hour for candlemaking?" Nancy could not bite back a reply.

"I think it best if Daisy, Bess, and I help Mistress Kathryn to make our own candles. 'Twill be less labour for the rest of you. Every man for himself, is that not how the tune goes?"

She had the pleasure, as she had had with Whittington earlier, of getting in a smart jab, and she closed the door behind herself so they had no time to reply. But her own words, and those of the women, gnawed at her as she walked through the quiet grassy paths of the cove under the lowering grey sky. Those gossiping housewives were right: the reason the colony had thrived last summer was that all were working together for the common good. Now that hearty spirit had gone out of the cove. Something different was growing in its place: she did not know what to call it, but she heard it in Sal Butler's sniping tongue, in George Whittington's empty boasts, even in her own tart replies. Something loomed over them like these rain clouds did, dark and heavy.

As she reached the door of their dwelling-house, the first drops of rain fell.

CHAPTER NINETEEN

A Temptation is Presented

When you do see an idle, lewd, young man,
You say he's fit for our Plantation.
Knowing your self to be rich, sober, wise,
You set your own worth at an higher price.

CUPIDS COVE

JUNE 1613

KATHRYN WAS NURSING THE BABY WHEN NANCY CAME through the door hefting a bag of flour. Kathryn shifted him from one breast to the other, and after a moment's fumbling, he latched on and sucked strongly. There were moments when feeding him, thus, made Kathryn feel powerful. She loved thinking of herself as a mother, like an old painting of the Virgin Mary and Jesus, giving life to her son from her own body.

Other times, it simply hurt, and her nipples were sore. This was one of the latter times.

At the table, Daisy and Bess were boning and gutting two wild ducks that Frank had brought down that morning. "Ah, that's grand, I can get on to making the pie crust now," Bess said as Nancy dumped the flour into their barrel.

"You can get at that; I'll finish those birds," Nancy said. "Oh, and I beg pardon, but I've sentenced us to making our own candles and soap, all because I could not hold my tongue and was saucy to Sally Butler."

Daisy and Bess groaned: making soap and candles were both oner-
ous tasks, made lighter if all the women worked together. "'Tis hard to
blame you though, that one got some mouth on her," Daisy said.

"I fear I'm as bad as she is," Nancy admitted. "I doubt not I'd make
fewer enemies if I held my peace. But it seems Mistress Elizabeth Guy
does not think much of our master's plan to take us away to a plantation
of his own, which likely means Master Philip likes it not."

The baby squirmed away, the nipple slipping from his mouth, and
Kathryn put him over her shoulder, patting his back till she heard a tiny
belch. "'Tis true, there was dissension between them over it, but 'tis not
as if Master Philip rules my husband."

"He is governor in his brother's place."

"He is, but Master Nicholas is no indentured servant. He has given
three years to this colony, more than he originally agreed to, and the
governor agreed to him clearing his own land. Master Philip cannot
overrule that, though he fears every man of substance will abandon
Cupids Cove. But he cannot force folk to stay."

"Well, I for one will be glad to be out of here," said Nancy, "there's
too many gossiping tongues in this settlement."

"But off in the wilderness, all by ourselves?" Bess darted an apolo-
getic look towards Kathryn. "Forgive me, Mistress—I know the master
means well, but I can't help but fear at the thought of going off by ourselves in the forest with the animals and the savages and all."

"We shall be as safe on our own land as we are here in Cupids Cove,"
Kathryn said, trying to sound sure. The baby had settled now, and
Kathryn tucked him into the cradle and crossed to the table where the
three maids were all at work. "My husband will be back before long
and will tell us his plans for the new plantation. Until then, we all stick
close and hush any foolish talk."

She felt very wise and grown-up uttering those words, though a
moment later she looked around and it all seemed incredible—that she
was the mistress of this house, her babe lying in the cradle, these three
young women relying on her to lead and guide them. She felt like a little
girl dressing in a woman's clothes, betimes.

It was early afternoon when the pies were done and all four women turned to their own tasks. Nancy went out again—she had been roaming out of doors a great deal these days, despite the poor weather, as if she felt caged inside the house. This time she took her little pet goat, Petal, still too small and frail to be put in the pen with the other goats; the kid trotted at Nancy's heels as she went off to feed the livestock. Bess and Daisy turned to mending clothes, and Kathryn thought she might go down to the main house and offer to help with the candles and soap, to smooth over whatever trouble had been caused by the disagreement between Nancy and Mistress Butler.

"Keep an eye to the young master while he sleeps," she told Bess and Daisy, as the baby still snored in his cradle.

In the big house she found the women had dispersed; the candle-making was done, and Jane Catchmaid told her they had put off the soapmaking for another day, for that was better done out of doors. "And to-morrow may be warmer," Mistress Catchmaid said.

"Surely we'll have some spring weather soon."

"In England we'd be going about with no cloaks on by this time."

Kathryn did not linger long talking to her: Mistress Catchmaid was gentle and sweet natured, but there was a hunger in her eyes whenever she looked at Kathryn, even when the baby was not there. The fact that one babe had been lost and the other born hale and hearty stood between them. "Sal went down to the mill to get more flour, and I believe some of the maids are down at the brewhouse," Mistress Catchmaid said. Kathryn went that way, past the yard where the men who remained in the settlement were working on building a fishing boat and a new storage barn. George Whittington stood in their midst leaning on a stick and complaining loudly about something: likely he had injured his fool self in some way. Kathryn told herself she was not looking to see if Thomas Willoughby was there, but she glimpsed him in the circle of men, and their eyes met for a moment before she continued on her way.

The brewhouse made her think of him: she remembered the moment they had shared there, when he said what ought never to have been put into words. Was that what drew her down there? Surely not—she would offer to help with the brewing, if any help was needed.

The brewhouse was empty and still, save for the bubble of the copper keeler on the fire. The other maids had gone. The wort needed to boil for several hours before the yeast could be added, and someone would come every little while to check it and stir the mixture. The women would be about other tasks now. There were always other tasks to do; Kathryn could think of a dozen she could be doing, including returning to care for her child. Yet she lingered in the empty brewhouse, until she heard a footstep outside—one that was not the light step of any of the maids.

He came through the door, late-afternoon light spilling in around him. The sun had broken through the clouds at last. He was sweating, his curling hair tousled and damp from his labour, and he did not smile.

"I've hardly seen you these last weeks," he said.

"You know why that is."

"Yes, you are much taken up with your husband's brat, nursing him like a farmer's wife." He crossed the floor and stood close enough to touch her.

"What, do you think I ought to have hired a wet nurse? We are all farmers and farmers' wives out here, no matter what our station might be back in England."

He shook his head. "I know what I am. Time will come when I am back in England and have my rights again, and I will never pick up hammer nor hoe nor fishing line till the day I die. But for now ..." He reached out and touched her face with one finger, a light pulling motion as if drawing her towards him, though neither of them moved besides that single touch.

"For now, what? We all have our roles to play. And I am a wife and mother, as well you know." She had tried so hard to play that role, to paint pretty pictures in her mind of herself as a good mother, a good colonist, a true housewife. Yet this other picture kept showing through from behind, this other role she might play. Heroine of a romance, as doomed as poor Juliet or Thisbe.

"Wife to a husband who has gone off and left you. Again."

"That is the way of men. If you had a wife, you'd leave her too."

"If I had a wife like you, dark lady, I'd not let her out of my sight for fear another man would take what was mine."

"Flatterer." She meant to tell him to stop, that he ought not to speak so. She meant to leave the brewhouse before the maids came back. Instead she let him draw her face towards his. Her breath came hard and fast. She had lain with her husband night after night, conceived two children in his bed, and nothing Nicholas Guy had ever said or done had made her feel as Thomas Willoughby's one finger on her cheek made her feel.

He stepped away for a moment, but only to bar the door. "No!" she said. "They will come back—the maids—what if we are here, and the door barred?"

He glanced at the covered copper pot. A spark snapped in the low fire underneath it. "They have not long gone—'twill be some time before they return to see to it. What I have in mind will take but little time."

"You are a fool."

"Then I am your fool."

His hands were on her now, at her waist, drawing her close, and while her mind still chattered away about all the reasons it was wrong, her body wanted his. This body, so lately torn by childbirth, with milk still leaking from its breasts, this body that was no longer that of a maiden but of a wife—it wanted to be touched, and kissed, and entered by this arrogant, beautiful youth.

"I have wanted this ever since I stepped off that damned ship last summer and saw you for the first time," he said. Her breasts were bared as he pulled away her waistcoat and the petticoat beneath it. He laughed when he saw the milk running from her breasts, and licked it with his tongue like a kitten. Then he put his mouth on hers.

Pleasure thundered through her body like the hard pulse of water on the rocks outside. She wanted Tom Willoughby's hands all over her, wanted him inside her—

Outside, the high chatter of women's voices. Kathryn pulled away, rearranged her clothing over her bosom. "They are coming—the maids coming back to see to the ale," she said. "I must not be alone here with you—what will we say?"

He shrugged. "Say what you will. Who cares what the likes of them think?" Arranging his own disheveled garments, he looked like a young lord of the manor who had been about to tumble a farmer's wife. He looked, then, like what he was.

The voices went on past; the girls were going on to the mill, likely to check the brewhouse on their return. Thomas left alone, stealing one more kiss before he went. Then Kathryn, a few minutes later, lifted the lid on the keeler and stirred the wort with a bit of broom straw. The flush on her face would surely be from the rising heat of the fire. She left and went the other way from Thomas, down to the mill to tell the maids that she had checked on the ale, and all was well.

In bed with Nancy that night, the baby settled between them, Kathryn longed to confide in her oldest and only friend. But it was Nancy who spoke first.

"I looked for you today, after I saw you on the path. Where did you go?"

"Down to the brewhouse, to help with the ale making."

"Ah." Silence, for a few moments. The others all slept in the upstairs room now, so the room outside their curtained bed felt empty.

"What means that—ah? You know if there's aught you wish to say, Nan, you can't keep it secret from me." *Though I can keep secrets from you, it seems.*

"Nothing, only—be careful. You did not see Master Willoughby, did you—nor meet with him alone?"

"Stop harping on this matter! You warned me before, and I told you I am no such fool." Kathryn tried to make her voice sound now just as it had sounded when they spoke of Willoughby before: like the voice of an innocent woman. She could still feel every place his hands had touched her.

"Even if you be no fool, he might be a braggart. I think—I believe he has said things. To other men."

"What? When did you hear this?"

"It was months ago," Nancy said, and Kathryn let out the breath she had been holding. "Something Whittington said, is all."

"George Whittington? But you know him for a fool and a liar."

"Yes, but that is not to say Thomas Willoughby might not be a fool and a liar as well."

But I am neither, Kathryn wanted to say, only it was not true. She was both, and there would be a price to pay. "My husband knows nothing of this slander," she said. "If 'twas months ago, and anyone meant him to hear of it, he would have heard by now."

"And if he does hear?"

"I will tell him it is all lies, that I have never been untrue to him."

Nancy laughed. "As every woman accused of being faithless has said since time began. And no doubt every man believes her."

After Nancy fell asleep, Kathryn lay awake beside her sleeping maid and her sleeping child. Why would Nancy bring this up again, after so long? Could she have seen something, or did she only suspect? Her eyes and her mind were as sharp as her tongue. *But none of them*, Kathryn thought, *as keen as her loyalty to me.* And then she remembered she had just lied to Nancy, a bold-faced lie she could not untell.

A lie to her friend; a betrayal of her husband; a mortal sin averted only by the maids coming near to the brewhouse. But none of those were on her mind when she finally slipped into sleep. Only Thomas Willoughby, his lips and hands and the hard young body covered with its fine sheen of sweat, that moved seamlessly from her memory into her dreams.

CHAPTER TWENTY

An Accusation Is Made

These are strong Arms to buckle with the Devil,
Fasting, Faith, Prayer, bearing, forbearing evil:
If with these weapons God do us assist,
Satan will ne'er stand to it, nor resist.

CUPIDS COVE

JUNE 1613

IT RAINED ALL THAT NIGHT. RAIN LEAKED IN AROUND THE windows and through tiny cracks in the roof and walls. In the morning, Nancy got up and mopped the floor while Bess built up the fire. The young master whimpered, a thin reedy cry, and within the bed curtains Nancy heard Kathryn rousing to feed him. It was Sunday morning, and after breaking the fast they would go down to the main dwelling-house for the morning service.

The residents of Cupids Cove huddled on benches around the fire, their damp clothes still drying in the chilly morning air. When the women had first come to Cupids Cove last summer, all the colonists sat together cheek-by-jowl for Sunday services. But over the course of the winter they had sorted themselves by class as they might do in a parish church back in England: masters and mistresses at the front, with servants and labouring men together on the back benches. Nancy remembered speaking of such things with Kathryn long before they had come to the New World, and all had come true as Kathryn had said.

The divisions between master and man, mistress and maid, continued as sharp as ever on this side of the ocean.

So it was that on the centre benches Kathryn sat with her baby on her lap and her husband's place empty beside her; in front of them sat Philip and Elizabeth Guy and their little boys, and behind them William and Jane Catchmaid. Nancy sat towards the back with Daisy, Bess, and Frank; the other servants and apprentices also clustered onto the back benches. Sam and Sal Butler, George and Nell Whittington, and a few others whose status was less clear, occupied a middle area in between.

At the end of one of the front benches sat Thomas Willoughby alone, handsome and disdainful. Nancy watched to see if his eyes sought out her mistress's. She did not entirely trust Kathryn's protestations of innocence: while Kathryn would surely not be such a fool as to betray her husband, she might not be above carrying on a dalliance through soft words and sweet looks. As for young Willoughby himself, Nancy trusted him not one whit.

Reverend Leat rose and began the service. He prayed for the safe return of the men who had sailed up the coast with Master Crout, that they might meet the natives, and treat peacefully with them, and soon return home. He prayed also for the safety of "others" who were away from the cove, but did not mention Nicholas Guy by name. Philip Guy read the Gospel and led them in a psalm tune, and the minister read the rest of the morning service and then launched into his sermon. He tended to lengthy sermons, so much so that Nancy wondered if he might incline towards Puritanism. She shifted on the bench, wishing it were a more comfortable seat.

She was drowsy and already could not remember what the text had been, but the minister had veered off into one of those terrible bloody Old Testament stories, this one about the Israelite man who had stolen something that was meant to be destroyed, and lots had to be cast till the guilty party was discovered and then stoned to death. "For where there is sin in the camp," he droned, "there can be no blessing. And indeed, can the Lord bless our camp here, our colony in this New World, if we cherish sin in our camp? If we do not name it and drive it out from our midst, then we shall see what we are seeing: disease, dissention, discouragement, and death."

Murmurs from the worshippers on the benches. Nancy, pulled from her reverie, focused on the minister's words. Likely he was only going to give a general exhortation on the subject of sin, but there was something in his tone that hinted at the particular. *Sin in the camp.*

Then she saw the fair head of George Whittington, from where he sat on the bench next to his meek little bride, turn right around and look at her. His big, flat, smug face locked on hers so that there could be no mistaking; his broad mouth quirked in an unpleasant smile.

Sin in the camp.
If you tell tales, I'll tell some of my own.
I said you'd someday regret refusing me.
Sin in the camp.
Sin in the camp.

Whittington turned back to the preacher, just as Reverend Leat said, "If there is sin in the camp, we must name it, we must condemn it, we must cleanse it from our midst. It weighs heavy on my heart today, that I have heard tell of a woman in our midst who has committed the gravest of sins, who has offended against the Lord our God and against this whole community. Brethren and sisters, we must not let this pass."

Nancy was alert enough now, staring at the backs of all those in front of her, staring at Kathryn. George Whittington had made good on his threat: he had carried the slanderous tale of Kathryn and Thomas Willoughby to the minister. And no doubt to Philip Guy, too, for Reverend Leat was too much of a mouse to make such an accusation without Guy's approval. *I hope you are as innocent as you swear you are, dear heart,* Nancy thought at Kathryn's back.

"Yet we will harbour no accusations without a proper hearing to determine the truth," the reverend said. "I call upon the man who brings this accusation to stand and tell us what he knows. George Whittington?"

Whittington stood up. Nancy took some pleasure in the fact that he favoured his foot as he rose. But she had never imagined he would do this in public; the worst she had thought was that Whittington might put a private word in Nicholas Guy's ear. Was this her fault? If she had given in to Whittington's embraces, could she have saved Kathryn this public shame?

"It gives me no joy to say this," Whittington said, looking like it gave him great joy indeed. "'Tis a shameful thing to have in our midst, but there is a woman in this congregation who has sold herself to the Devil, and uses her powers to the ruin of our whole colony. If Cupids Cove has not prospered, this last year, 'tis because of one woman who has taken up the darkest of arts. Though it pains me to say it, Nancy Ellis is…a witch."

The room was silent as a grave. Nancy felt breathless, as though someone's heavy boot had stepped on her chest and driven all the air from her lungs. She had been braced for Kathryn's name, for words like *adulteress, harlot, whore*. But to hear her own name, and the word *witch*…. It was as if Whittington had spoken in Spanish or in French: she knew the words had meaning but could make no sense of them.

And every person in the congregation was staring, no longer at him, but at her.

Kathryn's voice broke the silence. "What? This is madness!" she cried, but the minister raised his hand.

"It is indeed a grave accusation," he said. "And as such it must be heard. Silence, Mistress Guy. Whittington, tell us your evidence against Nancy Ellis."

Whittington limped to the front of the room, took Reverend Leat's place at the pulpit. What would he say? *Nancy Ellis refused to marry me, or even to lie with me, and therefore she must be a witch?*

Never did a man look more out of place than George Whittington in a pulpit. He settled his big meaty hands on either side of the desk and cleared his throat. "Masters, I came before you in private," he said, addressing himself to Philip Guy and the minister, "when I happened to find out what wickedness this girl, this Nancy, was doing. I made her acquaintance, all of us being thrown into each other's company so much as we are here, working side by side, and she made, sirs, she made some most improper suggestions. She tempted me, as only an evil woman can tempt a man. This was before I was married to my Nell, but still, sirs, I knew it weren't right. I told her, if you wants that kind of carrying on, we ought to get married proper in front of the minister. But she said no, no marrying for her, she would take lovers but she wouldn't have a husband, because she—er, she were already promised. To the Devil. She'd made a vow to the Devil, she had, and he'd given her a power to charm any man she pleased."

The silence was shattered now: all around on the benches were gasps and whispers as Whittington went on. "She has used the Devil's power to sow troubles in our midst, and to curse our colony with disease. She has her familiar—you all have seen it, this kid-goat she carries about with her—and a goat, as we all well know, is a symbol of the Devil himself."

Nancy clapped a hand over her mouth, for she was seized by a sudden wild desire to laugh aloud. *Her familiar?* Poor little Petal that she had rescued and fed and nursed, was a demon in goat's form?

Whittington was still talking. "She has placed curses on them that have crossed her—just yesterday, I had words with her, and she cursed me so that I near to broke my ankle, and you see before you how I am lamed. And 'tis not my word alone, for there are others can speak to the truth of these words."

"Who is that?" the minister prompted. "Who has anything more to say about these accusations?"

Sal Butler got to her feet. "Masters, forgive me, I know 'tis not a woman's place to speak in meeting. But when young Master Whittington spoke to me of this matter, I had to unburden myself, and he said I must speak before you all, to tell what I know."

She, too, was enjoying this: even in the midst of her terror Nancy could see the wicked glint of enjoyment in Sal's eyes—much like the pleasure in Whittington's eyes when Sal gave him the undeserved title of *Master*. Sal Butler liked being the centre of attention: what woman would not, when men so rarely listened to what they had to say?

"Masters, ye knows, we all knows, how hard the times were here last winter, when so many fell sick. And 'twas no natural sickness, but I believed all along 'twas brought about by some curse. And my lady, good Mistress Catchmaid, was with child, and so was the wife of Nicholas Guy. When the sickness struck, my mistress's child was taken from her before it ever even drew breath, while Mistress Guy bore a hale and hearty child."

Jonathan Guy, as if knowing he was being spoken of, stirred in his mother's arms and let out a little whimper, and again all the heads of the congregation turned, as if they were drawn on so many strings, towards the baby and his mother. Kathryn was still sputtering, choking back words she was not permitted to speak.

"Masters, this wicked wench Nancy placed a curse on my mistress, so she should lose her child, and so Mistress Guy would be the only one to bear a healthy child. When I attended her mistress's lying in, Nancy was never far from her side, and she was muttering incantations and papistical prayers, casting a charm to see the child born safe. And — and even before that, as I lay in my bed one night last winter, sleeping sound, I woke and saw Nancy Ellis in my room, though the doors were barred and there was no way for her to get in, and she laughed and said the Devil had come to her and told her only one child might live, my mistress's or her mistress's child. And then she pricked me with a pin, and vanished from my sight, and when I woke in the morning, sure, that was the day Mistress Catchmaid lost her child."

"A fine story!" Kathryn burst out. Nancy was surprised to hear Thomas Willoughby speak up from the far bench as well. "Why did you say nothing of this at the time?"

Sal Butler hesitated only a moment, then said, "She threatened me, when she came to me in her spirit form—she said if I told anyone, the curse would fall not only on my mistress but on me as well." She looked about to finish, but then, as if the thought had just struck her, added, "And she were riding upon a goat, when she came to me in that form. Riding upon a goat, indeed."

Shouts and clamour now rose from all the benches. Amid the noise Nancy could hear the word "Witch!" as well as the word "Nonsense!" and a good deal more, including an ear-piercing howl from little Harry Guy who was surely excited by all the adults shouting in church. His mother quickly silenced him as George Whittington stepped back to the pulpit.

"'Tis passing strange, indeed," Whittington said, "that we lost so many good souls this winter, but no plague fell upon Nicholas Guy's house—they were all spared."

"How dare you say so, Whittington, you great daft fool!" Now it was, of all people, the gentle Frank Tipton who rose to his feet. "I live in Nicholas Guy's household, along with Nancy and all of us here." He gestured along their bench. "My own wife's sister Molly died in the plague, and so did our Daisy's husband, Matt Grigg." And, adding her voice to his, Daisy cried, "How dare you say we lost no one?"

"Oh, and 'tis mighty convenient, is it not," Sal Butler shot back, "that it was those two poor souls who died, Matt and Molly?" She pointed her finger at Daisy. "You got Nancy to put a curse on your poor husband and your sister too, for everyone could see you and Tom Taylor was sweet on each other and wanted those two out of the way. Sure they were hardly cold in their graves before you two was going at it!"

Daisy howled as if she had been slapped, and Bess gathered her sister into her arms. Kathryn got to her feet and shouted above the din, "I demand to speak! I demand to defend my maid!" Just as she did so, the baby in her arms began to howl in earnest, a great blood-curdling shriek that drowned out all the arguments and protests. That set his young cousin Harry off again, with another volley of hoots and howls. And amid all the chaos sat Nancy, like a rock in a whirling stream.

I must say something. I must defend myself, she thought, but then *What can I say? And who would listen?* She had known that George Whittington desired and despised her, that Sal Butler resented and disliked her. But she had never imagined either of them capable of this.

Amid the chaos, Philip Guy strode to the pulpit. Everyone except the crying baby stilled, and the three people standing at the front of the room—Sal Butler, George Whittington, and the minister—stepped away as Guy took his position.

"I heard this accusation for the first time last night," Philip Guy said. "Seeing it brought forward today, I know not what madness has taken hold of this congregation—whether 'tis that of witchcraft, or only the spirit of petty spite that brings false accusations against neighbours. I will say it sounds more like the latter than the former. We have long months of short rations, bad weather, and close quarters, not to mention the loss of eight good men. Tempers are short, and in such times folk may turn on one another." A murmur rose, and he put up his hand to still it. "But this is a grave accusation to bring into a Christian congregation, and such an accusation can never be taken lightly. We must withdraw, and consider this matter. Then we shall hold a proper trial to determine the guilt or innocence of Nancy Ellis, who stands accused of the vile crime of witchcraft."

"You know 'tis false!" Kathryn cried, trying to shush the infant in her arms.

Her husband's cousin turned a stern face to her. "None of us knows that. We only know that she is accused, and that we must have a proper hearing. If your husband were at home, I would release Nancy into your custody, but with no master in the household, I cannot lay that burden upon you. Therefore I will keep Nancy close guarded until such time as we can hear the charges properly, and weigh them. And may God have mercy on each and every one of us."

He walked from the pulpit down between the benches, through the room that had grown suddenly silent again, until he reached the bench where Nancy sat. He gestured for her to stand, and when she did, he put a hand heavy as iron upon her shoulder.

There was no gaol in the colony; there had been no need of one. There were no private rooms at all, but that hard hand steered Nancy away from the warmth and light of the fire, towards the door of the dwelling-house. She knew with a sickening fall of her stomach where he meant to take her: there was a little outbuilding just outside the main dwelling-house that they used to store tools and barrels and other oddments. It had a heavy door that could be barred from the outside, and she knew Philip Guy meant to lock her away in there, in that cold, windowless place, until they could rig up some sham of a trial.

As he pushed her through the door, his grip tight on her shoulder, she heard a voice she had rarely heard before: that quiet and biddable girl Nell Bly, who was now Nell Whittington. In her soft voice, Nell quoted from Scripture the last words Nancy heard before she was forced into her prison, and the door bolted behind her:

"Thou shalt not suffer a witch to live."

CHAPTER TWENTY-ONE

A Bargain is Struck

Whilst conscious men of smallest sins have ruth,
Bold sinners count great Sins, but tricks of youth.

CUPIDS COVE
JUNE 1613

"SAY WHAT YOU PLEASE, MASTER GUY, I AM YOUR COUSIN'S wife," Kathryn said, knotting her hands together to prevent them trembling. She had never found Philip Guy a fearsome character before. But now, sitting by the hearth fire in the main dwelling-house flanked by the minister on one side and William Catchmaid on the other, he looked stern and unapproachable. George Whittington had come to these men with his ridiculous accusation against Nancy, and they had taken him seriously. Kathryn realized the trembling in her hands was not fear alone, but also rage.

"I know you are, Mistress, and I would not bring shame upon my kinsman's household without good cause," said Philip Guy. His eyes shifted to Reverend Leat, who leaned forward with his hands on his knees.

"These charges against your maid are serious ones. The king himself has written a book against witches, and a great many have been found guilty in England. I heard tell of near a dozen witches hanged in Lancashire last summer alone. His Majesty is bent on stamping out witchcraft, and if we allow it to take root in this colony, we damn ourselves and doom our enterprise."

"I know all this, Masters, but even the king himself knows there are such things as false accusations. People accuse one another out of spite. There has been bad feeling between Sal Butler and my maid Nancy for months now, and as for Whittington—well, he sought Nancy's favour, and she spurned him. Now he seeks his revenge."

Nancy had been locked in the makeshift gaol of the storeroom for hours, since before dinnertime. Master Guy, Master Catchmaid, and Reverend Leat had been closeted away, too, listening to the tales of her accusers, and they had left two men to guard the door. Those men had not let Kathryn see or speak to Nancy. Now she had left the baby in Bess and Daisy's care, and come to plead Nan's cause.

She felt entirely alone, with no protector. The only man in her household at the moment was Frank, a common labourer with no status or standing in the colony. Her husband was leagues up the coast. His cousin Philip, filling the governor's role, looked to be trying hard to be impartial. The minister was bound by his profession to stamp out even the suggestion of witchcraft, and as for William Catchmaid, he could hardly be expected to take Nancy's part. Sal Butler, her second accuser, lived in the Catchmaids' house and had cared for Mistress Catchmaid in her confinement, and she had accused Nancy of placing a curse on the Catchmaids' unborn child.

There was only one man in the colony of good birth who might be kindly disposed towards Kathryn, and she did not know if Thomas Willoughby could, or would, help her now.

"What I do know of witch trials is that cases must be properly heard, with evidence for and against," she said carefully.

"There is no witchfinder among us, of course," Reverend Leat said, "but I have read books on the subject, including His Majesty's book, and I have read many accounts of witch trials. I think I am capable of discerning if your maid is a witch or no."

"But...you will give her a chance to speak, and those of us who know her? For I'm sure I can make it clear to you that this is all folly, and that Nancy is no more a witch than I am a—a—" for a moment she faltered, not able to think of something outlandish enough, "than I am a duchess," she finished.

"We will examine the girl, of course, and you may make a statement in her defense—if you are certain you wish to defend her," Philip Guy said.

They hoped she would denounce Nancy, Kathryn realized. If she refused to do so, suspicion might cling to her as well. *How little they know of me*, she thought. For now, she begged two boons: that she be allowed to visit Nancy and bring her some food, and also that they postpone the trial till Master Nicholas came home.

Philip Guy would not agree to the second: who knew, he said, how long it might be before her husband returned? "We must take time to think this through, and the girl will not be tried in haste. While we review the matter and plan our course, if your husband returns, then 'twill be all the better, for we will have the benefit of his testimony. But should he tarry at this plantation site of his for weeks or months—well, we cannot wait so long. The matter must be dealt with, for 'twill lead to division among the people."

That gave Kathryn the hope that there would be at least some delay, some time to hatch a plan. And Master Philip did allow her to take some bread and cheese to Nancy.

The small outbuilding was guarded by two apprentices from the Catchmaid house, men she did not know well. Master Catchmaid brought her to them and told them to let her in, "but she is to stay no more than a quarter of an hour."

"May I light this candle, to bring in a little light?" Kathryn asked, taking a tallow candle from the pocket of her kirtle.

"Nay, no need of that."

What does he think—that Nan and I will burn this storeroom down, to set her free? But Kathryn meekly gave up the candle and let the guard open the door for her to step through.

There was a rustle in the corner and Nancy sprang towards the door. She stopped short, blinking in the light, and then the men outside slammed the door and it was dark again.

"Oh—'tis you. Are they letting me go?"

"No—not yet. I brought you something to eat."

"What good is that? Kat, they must let me go, you must tell them to drop this foolishness!" Nancy's voice was fevered and frantic. As

Kathryn's eyes adjusted to the dim light that seeped through the cracks around the door, she saw her friend's face was wild enough to match her voice, her hair was loose and bedraggled around it. Nancy, always the calm one, the strong one. Her strong hands gripped Kathryn's wrists hard enough to hurt.

"You must eat—you know not how long they'll keep you before your trial."

"Trial! What, will I have to stand and swear I am not a witch? Are they truly taking this—this spite of Whittington's, seriously?"

"'Tis not only Whittington—he has Sally Butler on his side, too, and you know the Catchmaids trust her."

"That sour-faced besom! She hates me, but she'd not have done this alone—Whittington put her up to it. He threatened me, told me I'd be sorry if I turned him down." Between words her breath caught as if she were fighting back sobs.

"Yes. But—his threat was not against you. He told you he would spread a tale about me and—Thomas Willoughby." Kathryn's voice shook as she whispered the name. When the preacher had begun speaking of sin in the camp, when Whittington had stood up to give testimony, she had thought she was about to be branded as the adulteress she very nearly was.

"He is more evil than I thought," Nancy said. "I had not thought even a mind as twisted as his could conceive of calling me a witch."

She let go of Kathryn's wrists and sank to the floor, her back against a barrel. Kathryn opened the basket and handed her a piece of bread. Nancy tore at it, despite rejecting it a few moments earlier. Kathryn settled onto the floor beside her and handed over the cheese.

Each bite seemed to calm Nancy a little. She was less frantic now, more measured. As she ate, Kathryn put a hand on her knee. "I swear, I will find us a way out of this."

"There is no *us* in this matter. You must not tangle yourself up in my misfortune."

"It is us. It is always us—in this and every matter. You crossed the ocean for me—what would I not do for you?" Her hand gripped Nancy's knee more tightly. "And in truth, if he has made one false claim, he might as well make the other. Neither of us is safe from him."

Adultery and witchcraft—the two worst things a woman could be accused of. She and Nancy stood in danger of both. And Nancy did not know—must never know—that while one accusation was a lie, the other, now, was not. Not truly. Kathryn had not completed her sin the other day in the brewhouse, but only chance, not virtue, had saved her.

When she left Nancy in her makeshift prison, dusk was falling. Everyone hurried to the dwelling-houses for their evening meals, walking in little knots as they gossiped. A witch among them! Even now they would be lining up, taking sides for or against Nancy. She chilled a little, thinking of how she had stood before those three leaders of the colony, with no man to defend her. She thought, too, of Nancy locked in that dark small storeroom, of the terror in her voice. Nancy could not be left there, to face whatever fate these men might decide on.

Her babe would be restless now, Daisy or Bess no doubt walking the floor with him. Kathryn's breasts were tender with milk; she must get back and feed him. In a moment.

She met Willoughby on the path heading down towards the dwelling-house she had just left. Mercifully, he was alone.

"I must talk to you, Thomas. Tonight."

"With great pleasure. When and where?"

She had thought it through. No good going to the brewhouse or anywhere else they might be found. Strange though it seemed, the safest place in the colony was her husband's bedchamber. When Bess, Frank, and Daisy were all settled to sleep upstairs, she could unbar the door and let Thomas Willoughby in, and the only danger would be discovery by the members of her own household. Bess and Daisy were frantic with worry over Nancy, and if Kathryn told them she was meeting in private with Willoughby to concoct a plan to save Nancy—true enough, in its way—they would believe her. And Frank, if he did not entirely believe, would not deny it.

"Only be sure no one sees you come to our house," she charged Willoughby. "Come before the moon is up."

He glanced at the cloudy sky. "There'll be no moon to see tonight."

"All the better, then."

He came when the house was still and quiet, and everyone, even the baby, was asleep. He swore no one had seen him, and she led him by the hand through the main hall and took him into her chamber, up into the bed with the curtains drawn, "but only so that we might speak with none to hear us," she charged. The enclosed space felt small and full of his presence.

"You know what happened this morning in church. I need your help."

"Your maid was accused as a witch, is all I know."

She knelt at one end of the bed, trying to keep as much space between them as she could, in this dark curtained world. "She was falsely accused by two people who bear her ill will. And we have no man to speak for us. William Catchmaid, Reverend Leat, and Philip Guy all seem ready to believe the tale. Governor Guy and Master Crout are not here."

"And your husband is gone."

"Yes."

"So what would you have me do?"

"Stand up for us. Tell them that Nancy is an honest Christian girl, and no witch."

"I barely know the lass."

"You know me. And I tell you this accusation is madness."

He reached forward, took both her hands in his. There was no comfort in his touch. "What if I do tell them that? Philip Guy has no respect for me, and the others less. They see me as a brash, willful youth who was sent here for his punishment and will not be shaped into a good colonist."

"That matters not. You are Sir Percival Willoughby's son, the only true gentleman here. They are merchants and tradesmen. No matter what you have done or why you are here, you carry authority in your name. Your father is a knight. If you tell them you believe my testimony, you lend me the weight of your word."

He drew her towards him, pulling gently on her hands, closing the space between them. "What if I say 'tis no affair of mine?"

"You can ruin me with a word," Kathryn said. She paused, drew a breath, decided to tell him the rest. "The same man, Whittington, who slandered Nancy, told her he would also slander me. That he would publish it abroad that I had betrayed my husband, with you. 'Twas a lie when he told her that, but now we have made it true. If it comes out, you will be shamed, but I will be utterly destroyed."

"Will it not be worse for you, then, if I speak in your maid's defense? Guy and the others will think I speak for you because I am your paramour." He took one hand from hers, but only to trace a line down her cheek with his fingertip. All the desire she had felt two days ago in the brewhouse flooded back, sharpened by her terror, the risk she was taking, the danger Nancy already faced. *God help me, but despite it all I want to finish what we began.*

"You will tell the truth about Nancy, and lie, if you must, about me," she said. "We will cut the legs out from under Whittington's threat, if he breathes a word of it. You will go to the minister and the masters and swear this lie has come to your ears and you will not hear such slander against a good and true wife." Closer, closer now, his face nearly touching hers, his breath on her eyelids. "You will tell them I am a good Christian woman and so is my maid, and swear on your honour as a gentleman that all George Whittington's words are lies."

I am a good Christian woman. All the pictures she had tried to paint, all the roles she had tried to play, shattered in pieces about her. Nicholas Guy's true wife, Jonathan Guy's loving mother, one of the leading women of Cupids Cove, mistress of her household—none of that was any good to her now. But this other role was open to play—the brave heroine who would risk reputation and all for her friend. And playing that part, she could also be the woman she had longed to be since she first set eyes on Willoughby—the reckless wanton who trembled beneath her lover's touch. *I will be ruined*, she thought. But oh, what a lovely ruin.

Willoughby said nothing. His lips grazed her forehead, a gentle, slow movement that made her tremble more. There had been no time for this in the brewhouse. They had hours of the night. Finally, his lips against her ear, he whispered, "And in return? What boon do I gain— besides the chance to stand up to the masters of this colony, and wield the power of my name?"

She had not even thought of this, that he might welcome the chance to use his authority, to show himself more than the nobleman's wastrel son. "If that be not lure enough for you," she said, her words barely more than breath, "then here, in my husband's bed, I give you your reward—for 'tis my reward, too. What you swear before the masters will be a lie. I will be yours—for tonight, at least."

His fingers plucked at the laces of her kirtle. "For tonight. And perhaps another night or two, if we can steal them, before your master returns. A rich reward indeed, Mistress Guy."

"But you must swear to do it." She placed her hand flat on his chest as if to push him away, though she gave no pressure to it. She thought of Nancy, like a captive creature in that darkened room. She could not allow herself this pleasure unless she knew it would buy Nancy's freedom.

He caught the hand, took it to his mouth. "Swear true to you that I will swear false to them?"

"False about my virtue, but true about Nancy. Only you can save us both."

She heard a footstep above her, and they both froze. One of the servants upstairs, getting up to use the chamber pot, no doubt. Her hand was still at his lips, and she put a finger over them for silence, but he took that finger and suckled it, and she pressed her lips together to keep back a moan.

I am sacrificing my virtue to save Nancy, she told herself. The truest of lies.

The footsteps upstairs fell silent. She pulled him into her arms, back onto the mattress of her husband's bed.

CHAPTER TWENTY-TWO

A Hasty Decision is Made

Search close, thou may'st some Felony find here:
From all Fool-hardy Treason these are clear.

CUPIDS COVE

JUNE–JULY 1613

FOUR PACES BY THREE. FOUR BY THREE, OVER AND OVER again, from the barrels to the rack where rakes and hoes were stored. Nancy had begun pacing as a way to keep her legs from cramping and her mind from running mad on the first night of her captivity. This was, she thought, the third night. Or the second? Apart from a brief daily visit when Kathryn brought her food, she had seen or spoken to no one.

I am a sensible woman. I have been falsely accused. I will await my vindication, and I will not...I will not...I will not go mad. She said it over and over to herself, a litany, when perhaps she would better have been praying. She did pray, too, but the thing that kept her closest to sanity was repeating those lines over to herself as she paced. *I am falsely accused. I will not go mad.*

Sunday: the accusation. Monday, then Tuesday, and now—was it Tuesday night? Nancy thought perhaps she had lost a day. Each hour she expected the door to open and Reverend Leat or Philip Guy to call her forth to a witch trial.

She thought of tales she had heard, of witches dunked in rivers to see could they sink or swim. One way, the woman was doomed; the other, she was damned. They tortured witches with hot pokers and irons. Kept them in chains in their own filth. Nancy had been given a bucket to piss in, and there were no chains. Yet.

There had never been a witch trial in Bristol in her lifetime; all she had heard were tales from far away.

But now I am far away, she thought.

She tried not to think of being hanged, or drowned, or even burned—had she not heard tales of witches being burned? She was not a creature of fancies and dreams like Kathryn; she was practical Nancy Ellis, who turned her hand to the task at hand, and did not fret about what might be.

But the matter at hand was life and death. And try as she might, alone in this dark, cramped space with no work to busy her hands, she could not but think on death.

What is a witch? A witch was a woman who sold her soul to the Devil. Could anyone do that, in truth?

Some said a witch was no more than a cunning woman who used her powers for evil instead of good. *But I have no such powers.*

Nancy thought of the herb-lore she had learned from Mistress Gale; there was no magic in that, only knowledge. She thought of Aunt Tibby's charms. *But those are nothing more than old prayers, and I hardly know them, or even believe that they work.*

A witch is a woman who…a witch is a woman….

Her mind scurried like a frantic creature tethered to a stake, thinking it was running free but only going round and round.

A witch is a woman who is accused of being a witch.

At last her mind, exhausted, curled up inside her body and slept. When she woke, stiff and chilled on a pile of empty sacks, she thought of it as morning. Gray light crept under the door. Morning, or evening? Small wonder she was losing track of the days.

She had dreamed she was out of this room, out of Cupids Cove altogether, in some green open place where there were no accusers and no enemies. Ned was there, laughing at some foolishness, and when she woke she missed him fiercely. She thought of him often. If she had married him when he asked her, she might have been spared this. Safety was, perhaps, a good enough reason for a woman to marry. There were other good reasons—laughter, kindness, even love. But she had passed beyond all that now. Ned could not save her, even if he were here.

He was so much in her mind that when the door opened, she half-expected him to be there. But it was not him, nor was it Kathryn with a basket of food. Philip Guy opened the door wide and strode into the building.

She tensed, gathered her petticoat in her fists, darted towards the door. Master Guy caught her, iron hands gripping her upper arms. "Now, now, none of that," he chided. "If you try to run, you will be kept in this same strait keeping, aye, and chained if need be."

She wanted to scream, to spit in his face, but she gathered her wits as she had just gathered up her skirts. Bundled them together into something that could put on a calm face and say, "I beg pardon, Master Guy. I have been so frightened, alone in here, I know not what came over me." Forced herself to look up into his face. He must see that she was a poor, pitiable young maid, and certainly no witch. And in truth, it took little craft to appear frightened and wretched.

It worked; his face softened. "Your good lady has convinced me that we are doing you harm by holding you thus. Your mistress swears on her own good faith that you can be trusted, if we keep you under a kindlier guard until your trial."

"You will release me to the care of my mistress?"

Philip Guy shook his head. "No, for the master is not there to watch you. You will come to my house, but we will keep you in a chamber where you have light, and a bed to sleep in, and no door to bar you in, if you give your word not to flee. My wife has agreed to keep watch over you."

So they did not trust Kathryn to guard her. Why release her at all, even to a limited degree? Perhaps, Nancy thought, the masters were afraid she would curse them if they left her in the little storeroom.

She was brought out of that dark building, four paces by three, and allowed to have light, and to move about, and sleep in something resembling comfort and warmth. She was given regular meals in a small chamber by herself—a closet where herbs hung drying in bunches.

This room had a bed in it, and a curtain instead of a door barring it off. She was not allowed to visit or talk with anyone other than Elizabeth Guy, who gave her a large basket of mending to do and made as little conversation as possible. Mistress Guy's littlest boy, Harry, poked his face around the curtain once or twice as if he would come in and talk to her, but he was quickly hustled away.

Sunday came around again, and Mistress Guy told Nancy she must stay alone in the chamber and could not attend the service. She heard everyone gathering out in the main room, heard the hymns and the prayers. She tensed for the sermon, lest the word "witch" rise above the drone of the minister's voice.

She was more comfortable in Philip Guy's house than she had been in the storeroom, and the comfort made her feel safer. But she was not safer, not really. They had given her food and light and a bed, but not her freedom. At any moment, they could still name her a witch and she would be swinging from a hangman's noose.

Beneath the hum of voices in the outer room, Nancy said her own prayers. She recited, as she always had, the prayers she had been taught growing up in the Gale household. People were put to death for having too many opinions about religion, and Nancy had always contented herself with very few. God was in Heaven; church was on Sunday; she would worship in whatever form was dictated by the king. She did not say Aunt Tibby's old charm-prayers; she repeated what everyone else said from the prayer book, and that would keep her safe.

Here in Cupids Cove religion had seemed a simple matter, for there was only one church and one minister, and no Catholics or Puritans among the handful of colonists—none, at least, who dared claim those names. Nancy's own creed was to work hard and trust that God would save her immortal soul; otherwise, she gave little thought to such matters.

Now she stood accused of selling her soul to the Devil, a character to whom she had given even less thought than God. So she recited her childhood prayers and added her own petition: *Almighty God, look with pity upon your servant, and get me out of this bloody mess.*

Something had happened out in the main room. Nancy heard raised voices, a commotion, benches shoved back. Then, footsteps coming towards the chamber where she waited. Her fists clenched in her lap; she held her breath.

But this time, when the curtain pushed aside, it truly was Ned Perry. He crossed the tiny room in a single step, pulled her to her feet. "God's teeth, Nancy, are you safe? What madness is this?"

Right behind Ned a half-dozen other people crowded into the doorway, Elizabeth Guy at their head. "Lay hands off her, Ned. No one is permitted to see or speak with her."

Ned did not lay hands off her; he kept Nancy's hands in his as he turned quickly, a retort forming on his lips. It was Master Nicholas Guy who stilled him with a hand on the younger man's shoulder. "Peace, lad. We will comb through this coil quick enough now." He turned to Nancy and said, "Do not fear—I will set this right."

She pulled her hands from Ned's, gave him a little push. "Go. I've no wish to make trouble for you, or anyone. Let the masters sort it out." Kathryn was there too, now, edging past Ned to say, "All will be well, Nancy—you will see."

Then everyone was herded out of the room, and Elizabeth Guy stood in the doorway, looking uncertain of her authority for the first time since she had become Nancy's gaoler. "Your master has returned, all unexpected—so it seems you have a champion. But you will still remain here till you have a trial."

In the event, Nancy remained there only until after dinner. Reverend Leat came to fetch her. "Master Nicholas Guy, Master Crout, and Master Willoughby have all insisted your trial be held at once," he told her. He did not look pleased, but with the return of Master Nicholas as well as Master Crout and the men who had gone with him in the shallop, the balance of power in the colony had shifted.

And it had shifted in her favour, for reasons Nancy could not fully understand. She had hoped that if Master Nicholas returned in time he would support her, for Kathryn's sake. She did not think Henry Crout even knew her name, and as for Thomas Willoughby, it was strange indeed for him to take on any role of authority in the colony, though his father's name certainly gave him the right to do so. The men sat arrayed at the front of the room: Philip Guy, Master Catchmaid, and

Reverend Leat on one bench, with Nicholas Guy, Henry Crout, and Thomas Willoughby on the other, looking for all the world as if they were on two opposing sides. Nancy sat in a chair between them, facing the rows of benches on which the rest of the colony sat. Kathryn and the rest of their household sat on the front bench, joined now by Ned and the others who had returned. Nancy would not let her eyes meet either Kathryn's or Ned's; they were too filled with hope.

The minister played the role of witchfinder; he repeated last Sunday's accusation and ordered George Whittington and Sal Butler to repeat their charges. The week had wrought some change in Mistress Butler: she spoke with less fire, though she still insisted Nancy had cursed Mistress Catchmaid's unborn child. When asked about Nancy's spectral appearance in her house at night, she hesitated a moment before repeating, "I am sure I saw her there."

"Could it not have been a dream?" Henry Crout asked, speaking for the first time. "Have you never had a dream so vivid you thought a person was standing before you, when all the time you were fast asleep?"

Sal Butler raised her chin a fraction. "No, sir, I am a good Christian woman and I have no dreams of witches tormenting me. If I saw her, she was there, by means fair or foul." But she sounded uncertain, and everyone had a moment to reflect upon vivid dreams.

Whittington, however, was as firm in his denunciation as he had been a week ago. "She put a hex on me," he said staunchly. "I know her for a wicked woman and a witch."

Nicholas Guy stood to question him. "You say she made improper advances to you, but my wife claims the opposite—that Nancy told her it was you who made the advances, and this wicked accusation is your revenge on her for rejecting you."

"No indeed, sir. I am true to my wife, and I am a man of good faith. Even before I was wed, I was not one to go about forcing my attentions on unwilling maids."

That was a misstep on Whittington's part, for there was a flurry of whispers and even some nervous laughter from the women on the benches. Everyone knew he had hounded all the single maids from the time they had arrived in the cove. But Nancy sat still and uneasy. If

Whittington were backed into a corner he might yet lash out by accusing Kathryn of adultery. At the moment, Nicholas Guy and Thomas Willoughby looked to be allies, but one word from Whittington could sever that tie and throw Kathryn into an even more dangerous position than Nancy herself was in.

The questioning continued. Jane Catchmaid would not support Sal Butler's assertion that Nancy had cursed her child; she affirmed only that her infant had died in the womb, but she refused to speculate why this might be. The claim that no one in Nicholas Guy's house had died during the winter sickness was easily disproved, and Nicholas Guy himself questioned why, if Nancy had such powers, she had not used them to save Molly More or Matt Grigg.

Kathryn testified that she had known Nancy all her life as a good and virtuous maid, which Nicholas Guy affirmed. Philip Guy briefly asked the other members of Nicholas Guy's household if they knew aught against Nancy or had any reason to believe her a witch, but all assured the masters she was innocent. "Nancy is good Christian girl, and true, and I cannot credit that anyone would believe a word out of George Whittington's lying mouth!" Ned burst out, rising from his place on the bench to speak out of turn, but Frank pulled him back down to sit and Nicholas Guy gestured him to silence.

Finally, Reverend Leat turned to Nancy. "It is time for the young woman herself to answer these charges. Stand before this assembly and tell us who you are."

You all know me, Nancy thought, but she bit her tongue, vowing not to say a word that might sound impertinent or light. She had men, now, who were on her side, and with careful and sober replies she might pick her way through this mire.

"My name is Nancy Ellis, servant to Mistress Kathryn Guy. I was born in Bristol and I am in the twenty-first year of my age."

"And what do you say to these accusations made against you?"

"They are false. I am no witch. I am a good Christian woman, sir."

Now the minister was the one pacing, back and forth in front of her as he fired questions. She had always thought of Reverend Leat as an ineffectual man, well-meaning but hardly bold. This was his one great moment: if he could catch and punish a witch, he might make a name for himself.

His questions came like little pellets of hail. Was she true to the Church of England? Yes. Was she a secret Papist? No. Did she pray to the Virgin Mary or the saints? No. Was she a Puritan? No. Did she believe the king had authority over the church and the sacraments? Yes, so far as a serving maid could understand such matters. "I pray as my masters tell me to pray, sir," she replied, keeping her eyes on the ground. "I try to do my work well and to be obedient."

"Did you assist at the birth of your mistress's child?"

"I did, sir."

"Did you recite pagan charms to bless the birthing bed?"

"No, sir. My mistress asked me to pray for her, and I did, but I worked no magic, for I know none."

"Was Mistress Butler there, and did you quarrel with her?"

"I believe we disputed, sir, in the matter of a posset to be given to the mother. It may be that I spoke out of turn. Mistress Butler has assisted at more births than I have, and no doubt she knows better."

"What of her claim, that you cursed Mistress Catchmaid, so that her child would be stillborn?"

"Even if I knew how to place a curse, sir, I would not do such a thing to an innocent child."

Question after question. The mundane: "Did you make potions and medicines for those sick with the scurvy?" next to the outlandish: "Does Satan visit you in the form of a kid goat?" She kept her replies as simple as possible. *Let your yea be yea and your nay be nay.*

"Did you curse George Whittington, to lame his foot?"

"No, sir. I saw him jump down off a fence rail, and I believe he twisted his ankle." Another small ripple of laughter spread through the gathered congregation. She would not dare to smile.

"Did you consort with George Whittington in any improper manner?"

Nancy lifted her eyes at last, looked squarely at the minister. "The only improper consort I had with George Whittington was when he tried to force his attentions on me, and I am sure I am far from the only woman in this colony who could say the same. Does refusing him make me a witch, sir? I would say it makes me a good Christian maid."

Plenty of talking, now, from the benches. The minister turned to the other men arrayed on the benches. "Is there anyone else who wishes to question the accused woman?"

Henry Crout stood up, but gestured to her with a wave. "Sit down, Nancy. I have no questions for you: this case seems to me as plain as it can be. A spiteful man and a bitter woman have made charges that no one can prove, against a girl who has offended no one. Her master and mistress have spoken for her, and her own testimony makes it clear she is no more a witch than I am. Master Guy," he went on, addressing Philip Guy, "you may be acting as governor in your brother's absence, but this whole bungled case shows clearly you have not the wisdom nor the judgement to rule a colony. This accusation should have been dismissed as the petty village gossip it is, rather than subjecting your cousin's maid to imprisonment and terror simply because her master was away and could not defend her."

Now Philip Guy was on his feet. "You dare to question my authority, Master Crout?"

"I dare indeed. I am in this colony as Sir Percival Willoughby's representative, and I dare to say my master will sink no more money into a colony whose governor would listen to such malicious troublemakers!"

It was the reverend who shot back: "We have a charter from King James! Do you suggest the king would be pleased for us to ignore the threat of witchcraft, an attack by Satan on the very foundations of Christian civilization in this land?"

"Oh, very fine words." That was a new voice that had not yet been heard: the high-born Nottinghamshire accent of Thomas Willoughby. He stood up lazily: all the masters were now on their feet, and there was no attempt to quell the babble of conversation on the benches. Nancy sat still, her hands clasped tight in her lap.

"Indeed, Reverend, you would be failing your duty to ignore a witch—if there were a real witch here," young Willoughby went on. "But this is mere folly, and we all know it. There's not a shred of evidence the girl's a witch, only the idle tongues of folk who ought to know their places and be about their work. That is all she has done—keep to her proper place and do her work. All this coil has been caused because you have allowed troublemakers to rise above themselves." His long-lashed eyes flickered about the room, resting with disdain on George Whittington, who was red-faced but silent.

"When I return to England at the end of the summer, I shall have many things to tell my father about how this colony is being managed." Willoughby's glance flickered ever so briefly to Henry Crout, who did not contradict the surprising claim that Thomas Willoughby was at long last returning home. Willoughby waved his hand in Nancy's general direction. "In the meantime, let this girl go. You make fools of yourselves with this proceeding."

There was a brief silence before Henry Crout added, "My young master speaks aright. I add my voice to his to say that this matter must be dropped and the maid set free."

If the masters were to vote amongst themselves, it might go three against three, Nancy thought. William Catchmaid had been very silent, given that one of the crimes she was accused of was the murder his unborn child. *He never believed it,* she thought, looking at his pale, downcast face, *nor did his wife.* It was, indeed, all Sal Butler's spite egged on by George Whittington's malice. Even if she were freed, how could she go on living here, working alongside these people every day?

There was no vote. As it had done on the Sunday before, the assembly broke into little pockets of people talking, exclaiming, arguing, until Henry Crout silenced them. "We have had enough of gossip. Masters, do you agree with me that this matter is to be dismissed as idle mischief making, and the girl to go free?"

Philip Guy looked at Catchmaid, who nodded. "I agree," Guy said, "that the case against her is weak. Yet it was our duty to examine such a severe accusation. Reverend Leat, are you settled in your mind that she is innocent?"

The minister, who had still been pacing the room, sat down. "I have wrestled with this in prayer," he said. "The Lord told me that if one more witness came forth to confirm that accusations against this woman, we must take the testimony of three witnesses and condemn her as a witch. But we have heard testimony, and it seems there is no third accuser."

There was a terrifying moment of silence in which Nancy tried to think who else she might ever have offended, who might hate her enough to seal her doom. Or was this the moment Whittington would hurl his second accusation and brand Kathryn an adulteress?

But nobody spoke, and the minister said, "I agree with Master Crout's judgement, and Master Guy's, that there is no basis to condemn her as a witch. Therefore, let her go. She is innocent."

Innocent. No dunking in the cold pond water then, no hot pokers, no rope around her neck. Nancy felt as if she could slide to the floor. Both Kathryn and Ned took her arms, leading her back to the bench. "Come, let us go back to the house," Kathryn said, but Kathryn's husband's voice cut across the clamour.

"Wait. There is one more thing that must be said here."

Everyone settled; Nancy collapsed onto the bench between Ned and Kathryn. Nicholas Guy strode to the centre of the room, his hands clasped behind him, and addressed his comments to his cousin Philip. "You all know I have been absent for a month, clearing the forest on my land up the shore. My intention was to spend this summer and autumn building a house and outbuildings there, and move my family and servants to that site next spring. Instead, my work was interrupted by a messenger who came overland from the colony to tell me that my wife was in great distress over this business with her maid, and had need of me. As this message came while Master Crout's men were breaking their journey at my site, we all returned home together to find this shameful mockery in progress."

Philip Guy opened his mouth to speak, but Master Nicholas gave him no opportunity. "I must tell you now, Cousin, that I cannot leave my wife, child, and servants in a place where such an injustice can be done to an innocent girl. Though the shelter I have built on my new plantation is rude as yet, 'tis better than leaving them here. By the end of this fortnight, I plan to take my household from this place and remove to Mosquito Cove."

"This is hardly the time—" began Philip Guy.

"We spoke of this," Nicholas Guy reminded him. "The governor gave me his permission."

"Yes—at some future time. But right now, when we have lost so many people, we need all to stay here, to work together for the common good! The colony cannot thrive if men go off into the wilderness to clear their own land, catch and cure their own fish, make themselves little princes on their own patch of ground!"

Now Henry Crout stepped forward. "'Tis a dream to think we can all survive in this place! Instead of trying to scrape a living from the land, we should turn our attention to the bounty of the sea. Your brother has gone back to England and I will be surprised if we ever see him return. My master's apprentices, and his own son, have declared their intention to return to England, and I mean to do the same. If Nicholas Guy or any man wishes to try to make a success of it as a planter in this country, God go with him. 'Tis folly to force men to stay in Cupids Cove—this place cannot sustain a large population. If this New Found Land is to be peopled, we must spread out, found new plantations, and turn to the sea—exactly as Nicholas Guy intends to do. More men should do the same!"

Then the whole room went mad, men—it was all the men, the women sat as if stunned by this sudden turn of events—on their feet, shouting and arguing. Nancy turned to Kathryn, who was trying to soothe the baby. It was in her mind to ask if Kathryn knew who could have sent a message to Master Nicholas on her behalf, for surely Kathryn must have had a hand in that, but the answer would have to wait. Half an hour ago she had been on trial for her life and now, within breaths of her acquittal, the whole affair seemed forgotten, swallowed up in this greater quarrel among men.

"I should take you back to the house," Kathryn said, "and my young master here, too. Whatever comes of this, you need rest and food and your own bed, after all that has happened."

"I'll go back to the house, and gladly, but I don't say there'll be much time for rest." Nancy stood up, though her legs trembled under her. "I'd wager as soon as Sunday's gone, we'll need to begin packing our goods."

CHAPTER TWENTY-THREE

A New Journey is Begun

Great Alexander wept, and made sad moan,
Because there was but one World to be won.
It joys my heart, when such wise men as you,
Conquer new Worlds which that Youth never knew.

CARBONEAR AND
MOSQUITO COVE
JULY 1613

O N THAT DAY—A DAY THAT WOULD SCATTER ALL THEIR lives in different directions like a handful of stones tossed into the sea—Kathryn Guy was, for once, the first to awake.

Her small son cried in the bed beside her, rooting for the breast as he whimpered both himself and his mother awake. Kathryn settled herself on the pillow and took out her breast to nurse him. On the other side of the mattress, Nancy opened her eyes. Kathryn saw in her dear friend's face the same confusion she had felt herself a moment ago: opening her eyes in a strange bed, trying to remember where she was and how she had come there.

They were no longer in Cupids Cove. They had sailed, only a few days ago, up the coast, to the stretch of land where Nicholas Guy was clearing his ground and building his house in a cove the fishermen called Mosquito. After showing her the site and leaving Ned, Frank, and Tom

Taylor there to continue the work, Master Nicholas had sailed the borrowed shallop a little further up the coast, to the house of a planter called Gilbert Pike, who lived with his wife, infant son, and two servants on a plantation of his own.

"I'd no idea there was another Englishman living nearby when I chose the site," Nicholas had told Kathryn on the short voyage, "but the Pikes have kept apart from us at Cupids Cove. I suspect it is because they have been trading with the pirates. I judge this Pike to be a pirate himself, perhaps one who sailed with Easton, who has decided to give up life at sea and settle here on this coast. Like as not he still has ties to the trade. He has two manservants, but no woman on the place save his wife, and he says she is anxious for some female company. So 'tis in my mind to leave you, Nancy, Bess, and Daisy with her for a time, until we have built a better shelter for you."

And here they were, the four women from Cupids Cove, in the household of three men who were most certainly pirates, and a haughty Irishwoman with an infant about the same age as Jonathan. Despite Mistress Pike's husband having said she missed female company, Kathryn did not find the woman overly welcoming. But she was housing and feeding them, which was generous.

Kathryn saw the memory of all this flicker across Nancy's face in the moments between sleep and waking. "Do you know what I was thinking of?" she said to Nancy as she settled the baby, trying to get him into a more comfortable position.

"Were you thinking that Mistress Pike is going to challenge you to a duel over which of your babies was born first? She mislikes the idea that someone else might lay claim to bearing the first English child in this land."

"Hush!" Kathryn said, stifling a giggle. Oh, but it felt good to laugh with Nancy again. How good to be free, to begin again!

"I was thinking how long it is since we came to this land," she said. "A year, is't not?"

"More than a year. It was June when we came."

They were both silent a moment, thinking of that journey across the ocean last summer. "What fine hopes we had," Nancy said at last.

"'Twas mostly I who had the fine hopes," Kathryn admitted. "You only came out of loyalty—and look what trouble I landed you in! If things had gone another way—"

"Hush—no talk of that now. We are both safe, and all that is behind us."

"Yes." Safe, in so many ways. Nancy safe from the awful charge of witchcraft, and Kathryn safe from the fear that someone would charge her with adultery. Not to mention, safe from the temptation to commit that sin again.

Give Thomas Willoughby credit: he had kept his word. He had stood up for Nancy to the masters and insisted they wait for Nicholas to return before trying her. He had sent a man with a message for Nicholas to return at once. He had sworn to defend Kathryn against the entirely true charge of adultery if Whittington raised it, though that had proved unnecessary.

All that, Thomas had done in return for seven nights in Kathryn's bed. While she had worn herself almost sick with worry over Nancy's fate during those awful days, she had paid her debt to Thomas Willoughby at night. And she had found greater pleasure in those seven nights than in all the nights of her marriage bed.

Then Nicholas Guy had returned, and Willoughby had joined him, and persuaded Crout to join him too, in putting the whole mockery of a witch trial to rest. Thomas had not troubled her again once her husband was back in the colony. She had caught him alone only for a moment, to thank him, but he shrugged off her thanks. "You owe me nothing," he said. "All debts are paid." He had given her only a hint of a smile with the words, nothing more.

She saw a change in him. It came from his having stood up among the masters of the colony at Nancy's trial, from having spoken with authority, from his own declaration that he would return home and the way Crout had accepted that decision. Thomas Willoughby was something more, it seemed, than the troublesome son banished by a righteous father. He was going home a man instead of a boy, and Kathryn did not know what part, if any, she had played in that change. Perhaps none at all. It was flattering herself, to think so. What mattered was that he was leaving the New Found Land, and the affair was over. Done. It had flared into life, one bright flame that must be enough to warm her for a lifetime.

She had left Thomas behind, along with Cupids Cove and its tangled web of troubles. The canvas was clean, the stage swept bare for a new play. She had had her turn at playing the heroine of romance; from henceforth she would be the good wife. She would think no more of a lord's son with ice-blue eyes and hands that could waken her body to delights she'd not guessed at.

"'Tis a new beginning," she said aloud now. "My husband will build a grand new house for us, far grander than—" she dropped her voice, "grander than the Pikes have here, and we will make our own fortune right here on this coast. The first year was only to test us: this is our true venture, beginning now."

Her small son, sated with milk, squirmed away from the nipple and braced his little feet against her stomach, pushing himself back with a mighty cry. Another answered it: on the far side of the sleeping loft, the young Master Pike was awakened. Nancy took baby Jonathan from Kathryn's arms. "This one needs his clouts changed," she said. "Let me do it, and you try to sleep a little more, before we begin this grand new venture of ours."

NED AND FRANK ROWED THE TWO-MAN PUNT UP TO GILBERT Pike's wharf late in the morning. Taking the punt and their own labour from the plantation had cost them a morning's fishing and an afternoon's work on the house and barn, but Nicholas Guy had decreed that if his wife and her maids were to remain at the Pike house, he ought to send some of his own food stores to the Pikes, to repay them for their kindness.

After an hour in the Pikes' house, Ned was not sure "kindness" was the right word. They arrived in time for the midday meal and sat down at table with Master Pike and his wife, their two menservants, and Kathryn Guy. Nancy, Daisy, and Bess were put to work serving the meal, then had to take their own food at the hearth instead of sitting to the table with the others. Mistress Pike's longing for female company seemed to be mostly a longing for female servants.

Sheila Pike was a striking-looking woman with mass of shining dark hair piled atop her head. By way of introducing herself and her husband to Ned and Frank, she told the story of how the ship on which she travelled from Ireland to her convent school in France had been attacked by the Dutch and she taken captive, and how the Dutch ship had in turn been captured by Peter Easton. "My father is a king in Ireland," she managed to say at least three times during her story, which ended with her marrying one of her captors and settling down on the shores of the New Found Land with him.

Frank's eyes widened with a touch of awe at Mistress Pike's revelation of her parentage. But Ned had heard this tale before from Nicholas Guy, who had also told him that rather than having one king over all as the English had, the Irish had dozens of petty chieftains who all called themselves kings. Perhaps Mistress Pike was the daughter of such a chief, but if so, would not the entire point of capturing such a prize be the riches that could be earned by ransoming her back to her father? The part of the story where she married the pirate and settled down on the other side of the world with him made no sense, but that was the one part that was indubitably true, for here they all were around her table.

After the meal, Pike took Ned and Frank outside to show them around his property, commenting on the outbuildings he had built and how each had survived the winter. "Ye'll know some of this as it is, having been three winters here," he observed, "but 'tis a different matter, one man and his wife and servants on their own plantation, different altogether from a colony. I don't mind saying there was times last winter I thought we were mad for building here instead of down in Virginia where 'tis warmer, but I was determined to tame a land Englishmen have never tamed, and by God, we're doing it. And ye will do the same, for your Master Guy is a canny fellow."

Ned was leaning over the wall of Pike's pig-run, wondering if the plump animals rooting in the straw were the same pigs the pirates had taken as bribes from the Renews colony, when Nancy came up behind him. Leaning in close to speak softly, she said, "Find a way to get me out of here, back to Master Guy's plantation. Tell Mistress Pike some of us womenfolk are needed to help with the work back there."

He felt a quick rush of pleasure, that she wanted to return rather than staying here. "Frank won't have Bess come back yet," he said. "He wants her here for her confinement, thinking she and the babe will be safer."

"She thinks so as well. Mistress Kathryn will stay with her, to care for her own babe and look to Bess. But you can get me and Daisy out, anyway, by saying we're needed to work."

"Indeed I can, and with pleasure," Ned said. "The punt won't hold four of us, so we'd have to make more than one trip."

"There is a footpath along the coast, is there not? Mistress Pike spoke of it."

"There is, but 'tis rough, and not cleared all the way."

"You know I'm strong. Frank could row Daisy back in the punt, and you and I go overland."

So it was that less than two hours later, Ned found himself hiking ahead of Nancy, breaking aside branches for her on the rough-hewn woods trail that followed the coast from Gilbert Pike's plantation down to Nicholas Guy's. As long as they kept in sight of the sea, it would be hard to get lost, however rough the path.

Master Guy had told him it was a couple of hours' walk, but Ned added an extra hour to allow for his own uncertainty of the way and Nancy's womanly frailty—though, in truth, with her skirts kilted up above her ankles and a sturdy pair of boots on, she was keeping pace well and he had not needed to slow down at all. She even had breath to complain about Mistress Pike.

"I have my doubts she really is the princess she claims to be, but 'tis true enough she acts as though she's used to having a dozen servants to wait on her. I'm glad enough to serve my own mistress, but I've no wish to be My Lady Pike's skivvy."

"I don't blame you. It makes all the difference in the world, working for someone who—ah! Watch your footing there!" Ned pulled his boot free of a sucking pool of mud that had been disguised by innocent-looking grass. "'Tis like a swamp all along here—we'll have to pick our footing carefully." When the marshy ground turned to a stream bed, he reached a hand back to help Nancy cross it on stones. He devoutly hoped neither of them would lose their footing; with wet, soaked clothing this walk would take them till nightfall.

"Thank you—you've rescued me yet again," she said when they both scrambled back onto dry ground. "I should be more gracious." After a pause she added, "Gratitude comes hard to me."

"And so it means all the more, when you do say thank you." Still marching ahead of her, not looking back, he added, "When I truly wanted to rescue you, I had no power to do it. Thank God that Master Nicholas had the authority to take your part. I don't know what foolishness I would have tried if those dolts back in Cupids Cove had condemned you."

He paused for a moment to catch his breath; they had just climbed up a little slope from the stream, and the pine trees parted to reveal a stunning sweep of sea and sky under the late-afternoon sun. Nancy stopped beside him.

"I know I sound an ungrateful minx," she said. "Not long ago I was locked in a storeroom in fear of my life, and now I dare complain about scrubbing Mistress Pike's floor for her. I ought to be as grateful every moment as I was when that trial was over and I knew my life was spared."

"I remember on the crossing from England, how afeared I was and how I thought a dozen times I was like to die of seasickness. When my boots touched ground, I swore I'd give thanks to God every minute I had solid earth under me—but I forget, too, from time to time. Not that 'tis the same thing," he added, fearing he might have belittled the ordeal she had endured.

But Nancy only laughed—a joyous sound that echoed off the rocks and made him want to laugh himself. "True enough, we mortals will always find something to complain over."

"And in way, 'tis all of a piece," Ned added. "Not that scrubbing for Mistress Pike is to be compared to standing trial for your life—but I think that you hate to feel your life is in the hands of another, that you are not free."

She looked up at him, her eyes locking his in a serious gaze. "But I have never been free. Nor have you—we were born to serve, and always will."

"True enough. But I think the choice of who to serve matters much to you, as it does to me."

"You know me well."

Ned took a deep breath. "I would be glad to know you better. If I asked you the same question I asked last year, would you have a different answer for me?" His heart knocked against his ribs and his breath came hard. He had not meant to ask her again, not just now—he told himself he would wait for the right moment. But it was she who had suggested walking back to the plantation with him. She had given him the moment.

He looked for that expression on her face—that amused contempt she had shown him when he had first asked for her hand in marriage. But so much had happened since then. They were neither of them the same people they had been a year ago.

No mockery: there was another look on her face entirely, one he had long dreamed of seeing. Her eyes met his with such hope, such joy in them—and then she turned away, looking out to sea. "My answer has not changed."

He felt it like a blow to the chest. "Still no? After...everything?"

"This, too, sounds like ingratitude, does it not? After what I have come through, I should be glad to have a husband to shelter me. Glad that you will take pity on me, marry me for the sake of friendship and convenience." Her words were bitter as the tart little red berries that grew in this land, and she kept her face to the sea.

"Friendship? Convenience? Is that what you think I offer you?"

"What else should it be?" Finally, now she turned to meet his face, lifted her chin a fraction. "You forget that I know where your heart truly lies."

"My heart?" He put his hand across his chest, a gesture like a player might make, but how else to show her what he felt? "My heart, Nancy—it is all yours, entirely. This is no mere matter of convenience for me, you must know that. I have lost my heart to you long ago."

"But—you fancied yourself in love with—with my mistress. Don't deny it. Do not ask me to be your wife only because you cannot have her."

He reached for her then, and thought she would pull away, but she stood still and suffered him to put his hands on her arms, to draw her closer. "Has that thought been troubling you, all this time? That I was still tied to a boy's fancy?" It was hard, now, even to remember the lad he had been, the apprentice starry-eyed over the master's daughter. "That is long gone. I have thought of nothing but you, waking and sleeping, since you set foot in Cupids Cove. Friendly and convenient as it might be, I would not ask you to marry me for anything less than love."

Her face softened, as if she fought not to cry. He realized she must have held this thought so long—that he was in love with Kathryn, that she was only the poor substitute. If only he could go back in time and cut out those moments in Bristol when he had confessed that fancy to her, slice them from the fabric of his life! "Nancy," he said again, her name a delight on his lips. "I was a boy then. I dare say I am a man now—would you deny me that?"

Now, at last, she laughed again. It was the faintest sound, like the ripple of water in the stream below them, quickly stilled. "I would not deny it. You are a man."

"And you are the only woman I desire. We can make a life for ourselves here. I said before — we make the choice of who to serve. And we make the choice, too, of whose bed we will lie in at the day's end. There is no other bed for me but yours. Will you say yes, this time?"

Her answer was in her eyes and on her face, but still her lips hesitated over the words. Then, instead of speaking, those lips moved towards his, and he gladly opened his own mouth to her kiss. He thought of how he'd devoured that first loaf of warm bread out of the oven after the long hunger of winter. He wanted Nancy like that now: her lips; her body; her vow.

EARLY THE NEXT MORNING THEY CAME, HAND IN HAND, THROUGH the pines and the birch trees onto the cleared ground of Nicholas Guy's land. Nancy listened as Ned told their master the tale they had agreed upon: that they had lost the trail and decided it was safer to make camp for the night. Master Nicholas nodded solemnly. "We thought as much, when Frank and Daisy returned with the news that you were walking back. I would have come out looking for you if you were not back by now, but as it is, all is well. You saw no one in the forest, man or beast?"

"None at all, sir," Ned said. "We were quite safe. And though 'twas a matter of necessity, you need have no fear for Nancy's virtue, for she has pledged to wed me as soon ever as we can sail down to Cupids Cove and persuade the minister to marry us."

No fear for my virtue, Nancy thought, for she had given it up willingly—the first time with a little trepidation, the second time joyously and with laughter, on a rough woolen cloak laid atop the moss and under the stars. The roots and rocks underneath Ned's cloak had poked into her back and made sleeping uncomfortable, but there had been very little sleeping, after all. The night had been warm, and it had been easy to shed clothes, to bare skin, to touch and taste and begin a discovery they would have a lifetime to continue. Ned's touch had erased the memory of George Whittington's harsh and brutish hands: where Whittington had sought only to take from her, Ned wanted to give, and she was glad to give pleasure to him as well.

The only thing that troubled her on this golden morning was why she had waited so long to say yes to Ned Perry, when she could have known this simple, uncomplicated happiness months ago.

But perhaps it would not have been the same, she thought, back in Cupids Cove. With a quick kiss and a handclasp they parted to their day's work, already both thinking of the night ahead. Back in the settlement, surrounded by people and wagging tongues and suspicion, she could not have found this same joy in their union, she was sure. All her memories of the cove were tainted, now—she did not want Reverend Leat, who had so recently believed she might be a witch, to perform her marriage ceremony, save that there was no other Christian clergyman along this whole coast. She felt no need of prayers or vows save the ones she and Ned said together. But she knew Kathryn would take pleasure in standing as witness at their marriage, and she looked forward to telling Kathryn of this—though not all of it.

The men were hard at work finishing the walls and roof of the dwelling-house, while Daisy and Nancy fed the goats and chickens and then turned the salt fish on the flake. They cooked the noon meal over an open fire, and Daisy talked of how the hearth in the house would soon be done and the house almost ready to move into. "Master says 'twill be just like our house back in Cupids Cove, with sleeping chambers up above, and all our own beds with proper hangings like himself and the mistress have—one for me and Tom, and one for Bess and Frank and the baby. And now I suppose there'll be one for you and Ned too."

"Yes, we're all paired off like partners at a dance," Nancy laughed. How the thought had troubled her once, that everyone must pick a partner, and now she could think only of the delights she and Ned would enjoy behind the curtains of that bed. Someday, perhaps, they would have babies and a little cottage of their own, here near the main house. This would be her life: this plot of land with its view of the shining sea, Ned for her husband, good folk like Daisy and Tom, Bess and Frank to work alongside of, and Kathryn always nearby. It was a thousand miles from any life she had ever expected to live, but she could not now imagine wanting any other.

They gathered and ate together, and then Ned and Frank went off into the forest with Master Nicholas to cut more wood. Tom stayed to work on the house while Nancy and Daisy weeded the small garden plot. The few carrots and turnips the men had planted when they came up at the end of May to clear the ground would not yield a great harvest this year, but it was a step towards living off their own land, and Nancy went to it with a will despite how tired she was—she'd not, after all, slept much the night before, though she did not confess that to Daisy while they pulled the tough, deep-rooted weeds from the thin soil.

"There's a ship out there," Daisy said, standing up to stretch and pointing out to the water.

"Is it the *Indeavour*?"

"No, 'tis too big. One of the fishing ships, mayhap."

Nancy stood up, too, working the knots out of her back as she did so. The ship was indeed a good-sized carrack of the type that had brought them from England, much larger than the *Indeavour*. It was also closer to shore than the vessels of the fishing fleet usually came: they would have no reason to put in at Nicholas Guy's plantation. After a moment, she realized it had dropped anchor and already put out a boat. Men in the boat—four of them, she thought—rowed towards the beach.

"Daisy, run and get Tom." It might be a fishing ship. It was still too far away to see the colour of the flag.

Daisy was already running towards the sawpit where her husband was shouldering a long board to carry back to the house. "Tom! Tom! Pirates! There's pirates, God help us!" And Nancy, who had just been thinking what a good, sensible soul Daisy was, stood rooted to her spot watching the boat row in.

The boat was nearly at the beach now. She thought how empty-headed and silly Daisy was, to raise the alarm when they didn't yet know that these were pirates. She might be running like a chicken with her head cut off, from some friendly English sailors coming to—what? What would fishermen be doing here on a clear, fine day when they ought to be hauling their lines or making fish on shore?

Chicken with her head cut off. The chickens. The goats. Nancy looked towards the pen where the chickens scratched about, unconcerned. The goats ranged freely, grazing. The smallest of them was her little pet from Cupids Cove, Petal. Three goats, half a dozen chickens, a few sacks of grain and some other food stores — all that Nicholas Guy had claimed as his due and taken from Cupids Cove with him. No great wealth here to plunder.

Now there were men in the water, two of them hauling the boat onto the strand. "Nancy!" She heard Tom's voice coming from a long ways away, or so it seemed. "Get back here, get under cover with Daisy." But Nancy stood like in a dream where she could not move. What shelter was there to hide in? The unfinished house, the pen for the animals. The men were sleeping under sailcloth on the floor of the house; two of its walls were open to the elements and could provide no safety.

Nancy stepped backwards into a little stand of pine trees, never taking her eyes from the four intruders. She had heard of the deeds of pirates ever since coming to the New Found Land, but had seen none save for Gilbert Pike and his two servants. Pike was supposed to have given up the bloody business, but who else, outside of Cupids Cove, even knew that Nicholas Guy was planting here?

These men looked no rougher or more cruel than Pike—perhaps no rougher than any other sailors. The one in the lead was climbing up the strand. Tom strode out to meet him.

"Who is master here?" the newcomer challenged.

If only Master Nicholas were here, she thought. If Ned—no. Not Ned. She could not bear to see Ned face down four pirates. She could see Tom trying to hold himself steady. Nancy took a few more steps back, quietly, towards the false shelter of a stand of trees. Daisy must be crouched behind one of the finished walls of the house, or perhaps hiding behind a pile of logs in the sawpit. *I should have taken cover with her*. Too late now.

"This is Nicholas Guy's plantation," Tom said. "He came here with Governor John Guy, who has a charter from King James to settle this land." His voice quavered on the king's name, and the pirate laughed.

"King James, is it? King James gives away a good many things, so I've heard. And would you be Nicholas Guy, little man?"

"You—you know I am not. Nicholas Guy is cousin to Governor Guy. My name is Tom Taylor, his servant."

The pirate now stood in front of Tom, his three men backing him up. Nancy looked out at the ship, resting at anchor. How many more men were aboard her? How many guns? The four men standing in front of Tom all wore swords, and two carried muskets as well. The only gun on the plantation site was Master Nicholas's musket. Where was it now? In the woods with the master, or somewhere about the place?

Nancy imagined stepping forward, confronting the men. *I am a witch, or was nearly hung for one, anyway*. If she truly were a witch she might know a charm to protect her home, the people she loved; a curse to strike down pirates.

"Well, Tom Taylor, can you whistle and fetch your master for me? For 'tis him I have business with. Our captain claims all this shore, and he'll have no planters building houses along here."

"I—my master holds this land from the king...."

Now the pirate was close enough to touch Tom, though he did not. One hand rested lightly on the hilt of his sword. "I've told you, laddie, I don't care a fig for what the king thinks he can grant. The king is not ruler here, nor is John Guy, not on this part of the coast. This is our land. Did you learn nothing last summer from Captain Easton?"

Our land. Whose land, Nancy wondered. She thought again of Gilbert and Sheila Pike, of their supposed hospitality. Of Kathryn and the baby and Bess, still under the pirate's roof.

"I've no more time to prattle with serving boys. Is your master here, or is it only yourself and the two women on the place?"

"I—there's no women—"

The pirate glanced towards the trees that did not hide Nancy. "There's one over there in the trees, and another went hollering back towards the sawpit as we came ashore. We'll spare the both of them, and you as well, if you all surrender to us before your master returns. I've no taste for bloodshed; I'd much sooner take an able-bodied sailor and two fine wenches, along with your animals and stores. When your master gets back, he'll know that he's to leave these shores and scurry back down to Cupids Cove. As for yourself, you'll do better with us than you would trying to scratch a crop out of this soil. You and your women won't be ill-treated."

"You'll never take me alive—nor my wife, neither!" Tom shouted, his voice breaking as he began to stumble backwards. Nancy saw his goal: he had left an axe plunged into a tree stump not far away. Did he mean to wield an axe against four armed pirates? One of the men in the back raised his musket and kept it trained on Tom as the leader gestured to him to hold his shot.

"Your wife, is it?" The pirate laughed. "That skinny one over there by the trees?" Tom said nothing and the pirate laughed. "No? Must be the other one then. I hope she's a bit plumper, and more bonny— that's more to my liking. That's right, laddie, go grab your hatchet. I'll let you think you died in a fair fight. Defending your wife and an innocent maiden, is that it? Is that the death you choose instead of a fine life at sea?"

The whole thing was like a play, so quiet and staged, only the pirate's voice ringing out. And then Daisy burst from her hiding place, tore from the sawpit to the tree stump, and grabbed the hatchet. She wrestled it from the stump and swung it above her head, shrieking like a seagull. *Oh no no no no no no.*

Nancy realized she was saying it aloud, keening and moaning *no no no* at Daisy, who was screaming and couldn't hear her anyway. Daisy, who had lost her sister and her husband and had tried to start anew with her sister's husband. Who had crossed an ocean to scrabble at the rocky soil and wrest a living from the land, and who would not give up one inch of her life without a fight. Daisy Taylor brandished her hatchet and ran full-tilt, screaming, between her husband and the pirates.

Nancy stood frozen. Everything was frozen, and then everything happened all at once. The gunshot rang through the air and Daisy dropped to the ground, the hatchet falling useless, blood blooming through the front of her kirtle. Screaming, screaming—but it wasn't Daisy screaming now, it was Tom and it was Nancy.

Tom ran to his wife's side, picking up the axe where it had fallen beside her. He ran towards the pirates, as Daisy had done. Nancy ran the other way, towards the woods. What could she do for Daisy and Tom now? She screamed, "Ned! Frank! Master Guy!" as she stumbled towards the line of trees.

Shouts and more running feet behind her. She wanted Ned and Master Nicholas to burst out of the forest to save her and also she wanted them to be so far away they could not hear, could not come till it was too late, because the pirates would shoot them like they had shot Daisy—

She stumbled over a root, tripped in her kirtle. Damn these skirts; they were not made for this country, she'd told Ned only yesterday. Yesterday. Someone was behind, close behind. She braced for a gunshot, for cold steel, but instead as she tried to get up, she was pushed down again, pinned to the ground. The man's knife was drawn but he held it almost as an afterthought; his weight was more than enough to pin her to the ground with his knee, leaving him with a hand free to put over her mouth. She tried to bite his hand but he pressed harder.

"Now lass, don't be a fool, come quietly. Come along, there's worse fates than life aboard ship." He twisted, lifted her, and somehow she was on her feet, locked in his grip, unable to pull away or break free. "This will go a deal easier if I don't have to hold a knife to your throat," he said, but she kept struggling and shouting. Now she shouted, "Tom! Tom!" There was Tom on the ground, not far from Daisy. His head moved, turned towards her, his lips forming words his voice could not carry. Blood all over his shirt. One pirate led the goats down to the boat, while two more carried the sacks of flour that were supposed to have been their supplies for the next several months.

When they tried to put her in the boat, she fought harder, and it took two of them to load her in like one of the flour sacks. A pirate held her there, hand over her mouth and a small knife against her throat. "That leaves only three of us to load up the goods," the leader said with disgust. "This damned woman's going to be more trouble than she's worth. Better to kill her and have done with it."

The other pirate, the one holding Nancy, made a noise, a sort of grunt, but he did not seem to take the comment about killing her as an order. If she could bite his hand, struggle to get out into the water, would he kill her? It might be worth it. If she could not survive to escape, to get back to Ned and to Kathryn, then it would be better to be dead than to be captive aboard a pirate ship. Regardless of Sheila Pike's tales, Nancy had no romantic ideas about pirates. She knew what kind of men they were and why they might want to keep a girl alive to take on board. She was no Irish chieftain's daughter; they would not hold her for ransom.

The boat was full now, with her, and the sacks of flour, and the goats. One of the men began to row it back out to the ship. Petal, her little kid-goat, bleated piteously. The two men left on shore were rolling barrels down to the beach, collecting the chickens in crates. When Ned and Frank and Master Guy came back, they would find everything gone, and Daisy and Tom dead. And no one would be left to tell what had happened to Nancy.

They were nearly back to the ship. They would load her on board like cargo. The man holding her had loosed his grip on her mouth and taken the knife from her throat, though he still held her about the waist to keep her from jumping overboard. She was crying aloud, wailing open-mouthed like baby Jonathan did when he wanted the teat, but there was no one to hear.

He went up the ladder first and hauled her up behind him, the other man shoving her backside. She tried to kick his hands away, but the man above her was hauling her under the armpits, and before she could get in a good kick, she was dumped on the deck. For a moment she only lay there as the two pirates went on with the task of unloading the goods they had stolen. She heard Petal bleat again and again. Another man knelt nearby with a drawn knife.

"Well now, what prize have we here?"

"Is she worth a ransom?"

"Nah, just a serving wench by the looks of her."

"Ah, well, she can serve me!"

Then a voice cutting sharp with command across the others, "Leave her be till the captain sees her. But watch she don't try to jump."

She would try to jump, if the pirate would move that knife and take his knee off her shoulder. She could not swim, of course; she would sink like a stone. Knowing that, why not make the attempt and die quickly, a pirate's dagger to her neck? A quicker death than Tom would have, with that wound in his belly. Did she lie still on the deck in hopes that a miracle might still save her, that Ned would somehow appear on the beach and fight off an entire ship of pirates with the help of Frank and Master Guy? *He would if he could*, she thought, one last pleasant thought to hold to.

But it was a fancy only. A fancy, like the idea of surviving, finding her way to safety. Better the ocean's dark depths, or failing that, the knife.

More shouts. A whoop and a cheer from the men on deck. "'Tis been that dry this past week, she's going up like tinder!" cried one.

Fire.

She struggled, then, to rise, but the pirate pressed his knee into her shoulder. "I only want to see. Let me see!" she said. The first words she had spoken, here on this ship, to these men. The first words of her new life, which might be a very short and ugly one.

"Aye, lass, you can see. See what happens to those who build where they've no right to build, who think the king's writ matters in this land." He moved his knee, hauled her up to the rail where she crouched, his arm pinning her from behind, mindful of his orders not to let her throw herself into the sea.

The boat was rowing back towards the ship again. The pirates, a crate of chickens, some barrels and sacks of food. The boat was laden to the gunwales. On shore, tongues of flame licked at the grass. Smoke spiralled up above the treetops. The fire would spread, beyond the cleared land to the sawpit, then leap to the trees. Perhaps Ned, Frank, and Master Guy would never make it back to the site; perhaps they, too would be burned up. If they did come back to Master Guy's ruined and ravaged piece of land, Tom's and Daisy's bodies would be charred in the ruins. Doubtless they would think Nancy, too, had died in the fire.

She thought she heard voices on shore. Perhaps they were coming back now, this very moment, in time to put out the fire, to see Daisy and Tom, give them at least a decent burial. But not in time to stop the ship that was even now pulling up its boat and anchor. Not in time to rescue Nancy. She looked at the swirling spirals of smoke, at the flames rushing across the grass, and saw no human figure moving there. It was too far away to tell; too far away to hear anything.

Nancy licked her dry lips, tasted her own blood there. She had prayed for rescue when she was tried as a witch, and rescue had come. But what would prayer avail her now? There was no one to come to her rescue.

She would have to save herself.

Afterword

THIS NOVEL, LIKE ANY WORK OF HISTORICAL FICTION, IS A BLEND of what we know from the historical record and what I've imagined to fill in the gaps. Its inspiration began with a single, striking fact that captured my attention back in 2010 during the Cupids 400 celebrations: midway through the process of writing this book, I discovered that even that fact may not be totally accurate. Such is the process of making fiction out of history.

In 1612, John Guy returned to his colony at Cupids, Newfoundland, where he had settled thirty-nine men two years earlier. One frequently quoted source says that on this return voyage from England, Guy brought with him ten heifers, two bulls, sixty goats, and sixteen women.

That's it. No names: nothing to indicate who these sixteen women were. Sixteen women without names or history, planted on what was, to English people, the edge of the known world. As a novelist whose work has centred largely on unearthing the untold stories of women, I was of course fascinated.

We know exactly one fact about one of these women: she was the wife of a settler called Nicholas Guy, and she must have gotten pregnant very shortly after her arrival in Newfoundland in the summer of 1612, for on March 27, 1613, settler Henry Crout records that the wife of Nicholas Guy gave birth to a son. We do not know her name (there are records in a Bristol church of a Nicholas and Anne Guy being married, but their age makes it by no means certain this is the same couple who went to the New World; we also do not know what relation, if any, Nicholas Guy was to Governor John Guy).

About the rest of these women, nothing is known—whether they were the wives of men already settled there or, as happened in some other colonies including Jamestown, Virginia a few years later, young women brought out with the intent to marry them off to single men in the colony.

In fact, we don't even know that there were sixteen of them. That account, in which their number is tabulated along with the livestock, comes from an eighteenth century source in the Bristol Records Office. In his *A History of Newfoundland*, published in 1895, Prowse says that six women spent the winter of 1612-1613 in Cupids but, despite his claim that he got this information from *Purchas His Pilgrims* (1625), Purchas actually makes no mention of this. The figure may just have been speculation on Prowse's part.

By the time I discovered this discrepancy I was quite invested in those original sixteen women, many of whom already had names, faces and personalities in my mind, so for the purpose of my story I have stuck with the number sixteen. There may have been fewer: what is striking to me is that none of the men who recorded the events at Cupids while they were there felt it necessary to keep an accurate record of the number of women in the colony, much less to record their names or tell us anything about their backgrounds.

There is ample room for imagination in this story, because so much is unknown and there is space to weave a lot of fiction in between the accounts left behind by John Guy, Henry Crout, and others. While for the most part I have tried to keep my inventions firmly rooted in the soil of Cupids and the things we know happened there, I have made minor changes to details such as the dates of death for the men we know died during the first winter, and the dates on which various people came to or left Cupids, when the plot of my story required those changes.

There are, however, a few areas I have taken more significant poetic license to imagine events that, while they conceivably *could* have happened, almost certainly did not.

The first of these is Nancy's trial for witchcraft. There is no record of any woman ever being tried as a witch in colonial Newfoundland (although, to be fair, there's no record from Cupids of a woman doing *anything* other than arriving and, in one case, giving birth). The early 1600s, the reign of known witch hater King James I of England, was a period rife with these accusations. In the process of researching this book I learned about the Pendle witches of Lancashire, who were hanged in the summer of 1612, just as my sixteen women were arriving at Cupids. While no evidence of any witch-hunting in Newfoundland remains, it seemed well within the scope of possibility to imagine frayed tempers and personal resentments within the small settlement turning in such a direction.

My second major invention is the pirate attack on Nicholas Guy's property in the summer of 1613, the event which closes the novel and lays the foundation for its sequel. We know that Nicholas Guy eventually left Cupids and settled elsewhere along the coast of Conception Bay, though this likely did not happen as early as 1613. Many of the original settlers followed this same path: records show that by 1617 the Bristol men had left Cupids and established a second colony at Harbour Grace. By 1625 there were also English colonies at Carbonear, Ferryland, St. John's, and Renews.

Pirates were a clear and present danger for these early English settlers. Peter Easton has gained an outsized reputation as a folk hero (or folk villain) in Newfoundland, although he was probably only active in the waters around Newfoundland during the summer of 1612 (but it was certainly a busy summer, and included threats to John Guy's planned second colony at Renews). A pirate attack in the summer of 1613 in which an English plantation house is burned, two servants attacked, and a third taken captive, is entirely the product of my imagination—though, I hope, closely enough tied to the real history of pirates in Newfoundland waters that it does not strain credibility too much.

Speaking of outsized folk heroes who strain credibility, a word about the couple my characters encounter at the end of the novel—Sheila and Gilbert Pike. Many Newfoundlanders know the poetic legend of Irish princess Sheila NaGeira, her capture by pirates and eventual settlement on these shores. With my apologies to the town of Carbonear, I have to accept that scholars have concluded there is not a shred of contemporary evidence that Princess Sheila ever existed. In fact, references to her in oral tradition do not even seem to go back very far—although, of course, some weight must be given to those who claim that a tradition has been handed down in their family for 400 years, even though nobody thought to write it down before the early 20th century.

So why include this probably fictional character (and her equally mythical pirate husband) in my novel? Simply because Sheila NaGeira has taken on such a mythic life in Newfoundland that it was hard to exclude her. Like the witch trial and the pirate attack, it *could* have happened, even if we know almost for certain that it didn't. Sheila insists on a larger role in the sequel to this novel, so, historical or not, I will be exploring her character further.

For any writer who is the descendent of English settlers to write about early English colonization in this land is to grapple with the fact that my ancestors came to a land they had no right to, and blatantly stole it from the people who lived there. Attitudes among English colonizers in this period towards the native population of North America varied wildly, from those who saw the natives as sovereign people with whom treaties and alliances must be made, to those who saw them as little better than animals. Some wanted to convert the natives to Christianity, some to trade with them, some to enslave them. Very few Europeans seem to have seriously considered the possibility of just going away and leaving the native people to their own land, but this, of course, was true all over the world, not just in Newfoundland.

I have tried, in this novel, to replicate the attitudes of John Guy's colonists towards the native population of Newfoundland in a way that accurately reflects what they would have thought and said at the time (this includes their widespread use of the term "savage") while also challenging these views. The story of English relations with the native people of Newfoundland, the Beothuk, is especially poignant because it started, from the English perspective, with such promise. The account of Beothuk and settlers singing and dancing together on the beach at what Guy and his men called Truce Sound (today called

Bull Arm) in Trinity Bay is described by both Henry Crout and John Guy in separate journal entries. It ended just over two centuries later in the most tragic way imaginable, with the extinction of the Beothuk as a distinct nation upon the death of Shanawdithit in 1829. The tale of contact between settlers and the native population, and the ways in which my fictional characters confront their own assumptions about First Nations people, will be a recurring theme throughout this trilogy.

Finally, a few technical points:

In the early documents, John Guy's settlement in Conception Bay is variously called Cupers Cove, Coopers Cove, Cuperts Cove, Cupits Cove and Cupids Cove. That the original colony and present day Cupids are one and the same has been known since the late 19th century. While there was some confusion earlier in the nineteenth century, the rediscovery by Newfoundland historians of two key documents in the 1880s put the debate to rest: one was a letter written from the colony by John Guy on May 16, 1611; the other Sir William Alexander's *An Encouragement to Colonies*, published in London in 1624. In the latter Alexander states that, "The first houses for habitation were built in Cupids Coue within the Bay of Conception where people did dwell for sundry yeeres together, and some, well satisified both for pleasure and profit, are dwelling there still." The earliest unpublished document that refers to the colony by its current name is a letter written from the colony by Bartholomew Pearson on April 2, 1613. Bartholomew, who had arrived in Renews with Henry Crout in the summer of 1612 and then moved on to the Cupids colony, wrote to Sir Percival Willoughby that, "I brought all the fowl which you sent over unto Renews, which was our first landing place, and from thence to cupids kove."

I have referred to the colony as "Cupids Cove" throughout the novel for the sake of consistency. I recommend to anyone able to do so a visit to the Cupids site. If you're lucky, you may even encounter archaeologist William Gilbert, the man who knows more about Cupids than anyone living. If you're unable to visit in person, please visit virtually at www.baccalieudigs.ca.

All the male characters at Cupids Cove in the novel are based (sometimes quite loosely) on men who actually settled there between

1610-1613. We know a lot about those colonists who wrote letters and journals and whose writings have survived, but almost nothing other than a name, an occupation, or the cause of death for many others. I have invented freely to fill in the gaps. For example, I gave George Whittington humbler origins than he likely had in real life, the better to illustrate how an ambitious man might rise in the colony. I also provided a more detailed story for the first man to die in Cupids, Thomas Percy, whom John Guy records as having died "of thought of having slaine a man in Rochester." Percy's suicide is my own interpretation of that cryptic cause of death. The women characters, as well as almost everyone in the Bristol chapters, are entirely products of my imagination.

To simplify things for the modern reader, I have used modern style dating, so that Chapter Fourteen, for example, is dated "January – February 1613" even though English people at that time would have referred to those months as January and February of 1612—their New Year began in March.

The quotes from Robert Hayman's *Quodlibets* used in the epigraph and chapter headings are from the first work of English poetry written in Newfoundland—in fact, the first in all of what he would have called the New World. Hayman was not, by any stretch of the imagination, a great poet. He wasn't even a very good poet. But he had strong feelings about a lot of things, including Newfoundland, where he served as governor of the Bristol's Hope colony at Harbour Grace for about ten years, arriving there about four years after this novel ends. It's worth noting that despite his heartfelt tribute to the beauty of Newfoundland's winters (excerpted at the beginning of Chapter 15), Hayman spent only one winter in Newfoundland, and thereafter came over to govern in the summer months only. Nice work if you can get it.

For those who would like to know more about the historical background of the Cupids colony, I recommend the work of the late Gillian Cell, and the biography of John Guy written by the late Alan Williams. The best source for anything about Cupids today is the aforementioned William Gilbert, archaeologist and historian, who was endlessly patient in answering my questions and in reading through this manuscript to catch my mistakes and anachronisms. The errors that doubtless remain are entirely my own.

Among the many other people who helped with various aspects of the historicity and accuracy of the story, special thanks are due to Dru Brooke-Taylor, Michelle Porter, and Chris Dreidzic for answering some of my many questions. On a personal level, I remain, as always, grateful to my family—my husband Jason, my kids Emma and Chris, and my dad, Don Morgan, who always reads my early drafts—as well as to a wonderful network of friends. Special thanks to Jennifer Morgan, Christine Hennebury, Tina Chaulk, Lori Savory and Natalie Hallett (my Strident Women), as well as to Michelle Butler Hallett and Angela Antle, all of whom gave helpful feedback on an earlier draft of the novel.

I am grateful to the Newfoundland and Labrador Arts Council for a Professional Project Grant that helped support my research and writing on this project, as well as to my employers at The Murphy Centre for allowing me time away from my day job to focus on writing, and to the staff at various local coffee shops who made that writing time so enjoyable with their great service. Thanks to the excellent team at Breakwater Books and my editor Marnie Parsons for all they've done to make this book a reality—and a special thanks to a publisher who believes in me enough to commit to three books, so you all get to find out what happens after the last page of this one.

TRUDY MORGAN-COLE IS A WRITER AND TEACHER IN ST. John's, Newfoundland. Her historical novels include *By the Rivers of Brooklyn*, *That Forgetful Shore*, *A Sudden Sun*, and *Most Anything You Please*. At her day job, she teaches English and social studies to adult learners. She is married and is the mom of two young adults. Trudy's passion is uncovering and re-imagining the untold stories of women in history.